The Last Spring
in Paris

Also by Hans Herlin

HANS HERLIN

The Last Spring
in Paris

Translated by
J. Maxwell Brownjohn

DOUBLEDAY & COMPANY, INC.
GARDEN CITY, NEW YORK
1985

ISBN: 0-385-18936-2
Library of Congress Card Catalog Number: 83–27458
English Translation Copyright © 1985 Doubleday & Company, Inc., and
Andre Deutsch Ltd.
Originally published in German as *Der letzte Frühling in Paris*
Copyright © 1983 by Marion von Schroeder Verlag GmbH, Düsseldorf
and Interlit Jost AG, Zollikofen
Printed in the United States of America
First Edition in the United States

Library of Congress Cataloging in Publication Data

Herlin, Hans, 1925–
    The last spring in Paris.

    Translation of: Der letzte Frühling in Paris.
    I. Title.
PT2668.E748L413   1983   833′.914

Doing without witnesses what one would be capable of doing in front of everyone: that is true valor.

La Rochefoucauld

PART ONE

Paris

SHE LEFT THE SUBWAY at George V. Her long brown hair fluttered in the updraft from the swing doors as she climbed the steps to the street. It was the same color as her eyes, but a little darker.

She paused at the top of the steps. After the warmth of the Métro, she shivered in her light coat. Short and tightly belted, the coat made her slim legs look even longer. Her silk stockings were only an illusion —a dusting of powder.

Multicolored sun umbrellas blossomed outside the crowded cafés on the Champs Élysées. Conversation and laughter filled the air, mingled with music from a restaurant on the corner.

Spring had arrived, at least in the minds of the German soldiers who thronged the sidewalks. Whether or not they sensed that this would be their last spring in Paris, they were determined to enjoy it. Paris, after all, was still theirs to enjoy.

Perhaps it was this thought that made the girl pause and shiver. For a moment she seemed tempted to turn and dive back into the subway's warm and protective embrace. Then she walked on.

It was the click of her high heels, more than anything else, that attracted attention. Heads swiveled as she passed. How could shoes constructed of a few scraps of wood and imitation leather produce such a titillating sound? How could any woman walk on heels so absurdly, provocatively high? None of the watching Germans would have dared to take such frivolous confections home to his wife or girlfriend. *Oh, là là*, these Frenchwomen certainly had style!

She turned left along Avenue George V. Twilight was draining the color from the opulent buildings that flanked it. Like the brown of her hair, the black of their slate roofs deepened in the fading light.

Some German officers were standing outside the main entrance of the Hôtel George V, wasp-waisted in their pistol belts and flared breeches. She was glad that Berger never wore a gun, in spite of regulations. A burst of laughter drifted across the street. The hard, cold shafts of light projected by the hotel's lofty windows were being extinguished, one by one, as the blackout curtains were drawn.

She disappeared down a side street. Leading off it was an even narrower street, deserted except for some German soldiers standing in line outside one of the shuttered gray houses. She paused again, as she had at the top of the subway steps, but not for as long.

The sign above the entrance—"Trente-et-un"—was the number of the house and the name of the establishment. The line of waiting figures straggled along the sidewalk for twenty yards or more. The door opened and four German officers emerged, none too steady on their feet. With them came the smell she remembered so well: a blend of stale tobacco smoke, sickly sweet face powder, and mildew.

Léon, pallid as ever and far too pigeon-chested for his Ruritanian general's uniform with its festoons of yellow braid, held the door for her. He gave her an almost sheepish grin that looked incongruous on a face as sly as his.

"You know your way. Nothing's changed. Same cheap champagne, same lousy floor show."

The musty smell grew stronger as she descended the stairs. It came from the red felt drapes that camouflaged the damp-stained walls. The crowded cellar was long and cavernous. Tables and chairs stood jam-packed together, all the way to the stage at the far end. The gloom was only slightly relieved by wall lamps with dusky red shades.

She threaded her way over to the bar, hugging her shoulder bag. On the stage, dimly visible through a haze of tobacco smoke, three girls were engaged in a striptease routine. Their efforts seemed to be largely unappreciated.

A woman in a fluffy pink pullover was serving drinks at the counter. She wore too much mascara and had a lopsided, coarse-looking mouth. "He's expecting you," she said coldly, "upstairs."

"Thanks, I'll wait for him down here."

The woman shrugged and opened a small door at the back of the bar. "Monsieur Dargaud," she called up the steep flight of stairs beyond it.

He appeared a moment later, cradling a cat in one arm—a seal point Siamese. There was a bland smile on his face, but his eyes were alert. Julien Dargaud was an observant man.

"*Bonsoir,* Jannou." He continued to hold the cat in the crook of his arm, ruffling its fur.

"So you found her?" she said.

"Is it really so long since we saw each other? Yes, somebody knew how fond of her I was—fond enough to buy her back at any price."

"You called the studio."

"Why don't we talk upstairs?"

"I can't stay." She felt exhausted, as though the decision to see him, the long subway ride from Billancourt and the walk from the station, had sapped her strength.

Dargaud turned away and gently deposited the cat on the stairs. Then he came back to the counter and leaned across. He took her by the elbows and brushed her cheeks with his, first one, then the other, barely touching her. There was nothing possessive about the gesture.

"Your hair's longer, it suits you. Why not take your coat off?"

She removed her coat and draped it over the counter. She was wearing a black pleated skirt and a black silk blouse. One side of the open neck was adorned with a little appliquéd rose. She wore no jewelry, not even earrings.

"Have a drink?"

"Léon still doesn't think much of your champagne."

"It isn't as bad as he makes out. What are you working on?"

"A Jeancoles picture," she said, wondering what he really wanted. Whenever she recalled that Dargaud had been her first lover, it surprised her to think how much older he was—all of twenty years.

"Another of his period melodramas?"

She nodded and sat down on a barstool. The body warmth of the man who'd just vacated it seeped through her thin skirt. It made her feel uncomfortable. The strippers onstage, naked now except for a pair of panties, were swinging their legs in time to a German marching song. All three were trying hard, fighting for attention with their legs and their smiles. Their routine had a professional touch and their legs swung in perfect unison, but the audience remained unimpressed. When they dropped their panties just before the stage lights went out, only a smattering of applause could be heard above the general hubbub.

Jannou picked up the glass of champagne Dargaud poured for her.

Not having eaten since lunchtime, she felt it take effect at once. A glow pervaded her body.

"How about a snack? I've got some caviar from Petrossian's—the real thing."

She shook her head. "When they let me out of prison, Berger said he wanted to give me a treat. He took me to the Tour d'Argent. I was famished, but I couldn't get a mouthful down. It sickened me to see all those people gorging themselves."

"The caviar there is substandard."

She clung to the recollection. "They were Germans, nearly all of them, and the way they ate—the diabolical *relish* . . . At the time, I thought he'd only taken me there to humiliate me."

Dargaud looked at her intently, striving to read her expression. "Has something changed—between you and Berger, I mean?"

"Yes and no."

She cupped a hand over her glass when he tried to refill it. "Pumping Berger was your idea," she said. "I've never had much success, have I? Berger isn't the kind of man who discusses his work."

"This is really important, though. An Abwehr agent in Lisbon, name of Schneevogel—"

She cut him short. "No, Julien. I can't, not anymore."

Dargaud had hesitated a long time before using her as a source, even though she'd volunteered—even though there were so many points in her favor. Jannou had worked for Roman Kacew and the British network in Paris. She'd given nothing away when arrested and interrogated. She'd even withstood torture at the hands of the SD in their Avenue Foch headquarters. Most important of all, she was close to Berger. Dargaud had notified London and requested instructions, but without result. He'd drawn no response, not even a hands-off.

"A lot of things have changed," he said at length.

"Two years are a long time."

She turned to look at the stage. Arrayed in front of a desert backdrop were three dark-skinned girls, their bare black bodies glistening with oil, and three men dressed as British colonial troops in khaki shirts and knee-length shorts. Each man held a swagger stick, and each was standing over one of the girls, who were bent double with their buttocks neatly defined by gold G-strings that bit into the cleft between them. To a roll of drums, the uniformed Britons began to wield their canes, though not too hard for comfort.

Such was "Perfide Albion," one of the *tableaux vivants* for which the

Trente-et-un was renowned—one of the attractions that kept prospective customers standing in line outside.

Still watching the spectacle, Jannou had a sudden awareness of how stiflingly hot it was. A bead of sweat gathered in the hollow of her throat and trickled down between her breasts. She could feel the heat all over her body now, like a spreading stain. She turned back to Dargaud.

"How will you explain all this when the time comes?"

"Collaboration with the enemy, you mean?" He smiled and gestured at the crowded tables. "Bare flesh—who's going to hold that against me?"

"I live with a German," she said, "a captain in military intelligence. How am I going to explain that?"

"That's why it's so crazy to go soft on the Boche—any Boche—at this stage. Everyone else is backing off fast."

"So I've noticed."

"You owe Berger nothing. He saved the lives of your group, but only because it paid him to." Dargaud looked at her with eyes that had suddenly hardened. "How many of our people has Berger arrested? How many are in jail right now? Doesn't he ever brag about it?"

"He isn't like that," she said stiffly.

"How many has he persuaded to betray their country? And the ones that refused to play ball—what became of them? Did he prevent what happened to you at the Avenue Foch?"

She felt an itch in her toes, nothing more. They didn't hurt, just itched like mad.

"He knew nothing about that," she said.

"You think he'd have done anything, even if he had? He'd have looked the other way and nursed his conscience, pleading that he couldn't intervene. I detest these well-meaning Germans and their tender consciences!"

She slid off the stool. Pain shot through her toes when her feet touched the ground—real pain this time.

"I'll survive," she said, but the words lacked conviction.

Dargaud lifted the flap and came out from behind the counter. He helped her on with her coat. "I've a friend in the Resistance, Jannou. He was arrested, but he managed to escape. They recaptured him, tortured him, sent him to a camp in the East. He escaped again."

"Well?"

"People in his camp were executed daily—shot at random, or so it seemed. Then my friend noticed that the SS officer who selected them had an aversion to men who wore glasses: they were always earmarked for the firing squad. My friend had poor eyesight. Without his glasses he could only see a blur, but he slipped them into his pocket whenever the SS man appeared. He swears it saved his life. See what I mean? There's no logic to survival." He smiled with narrowed eyes. "None at all."

The band struck up again. Jannou could sense that the mood of the audience had changed. They were silent but restive.

"Think it over," Dargaud added.

"*Ausziehen!* Strip!" The impatient voice came from one of the tables just behind her. She froze, then turned to look at the stage. Other voices took up the cry like a multiple echo. "Strip! Strip!"

The girl was young and long-legged. She stood there stiffly, uncertainly, forlornly.

"Go on, strip!"

That was the first voice again, harsh and peremptory.

Dargaud took her arm and escorted her to the foot of the stairs.

"Make a note of the name," he said. "Schneevogel, an Abwehr agent based in Lisbon—a colleague of Berger's. Try to find out what's happened to him. It's important."

The sky was so clear that a dim red glow still lingered above the rooftops. Jannou returned the way she'd come. The streets were emptier than before, and the few people who passed her hugged the shadows like fugitives from justice.

Wooden barriers had been dragged across the entrance of the Hôtel George V, which was guarded by German sentries. Any cafés still open on the Champs Élysées were in process of closing for the night. Deserted and ghostly, the huge avenue looked even longer and wider than it did by day. The Arc de Triomphe was just a big black U upended against the sky.

With a clatter of hoofs, a horse-drawn cab came clip-clopping down from the Place de l'Étoile. The soldiers in it waved and wolf-whistled as they passed. For a moment Jannou thought they were going to stop, but the scrawny horse maintained a slow, arthritic trot as though it would collapse if the cabby reined it in.

Down below in the Métro station, all was light and life and voices. A German soldier sat enthroned on a shoeshine stand while a Frenchman knelt in front of him, polishing his black leather boots.

The German was fiftyish, with bucolic features and a drooping mustache. He looked like a conscripted farmer—the kind of man who was used to wearing mud-encrusted clodhoppers—but army life had made him more fastidious. He pointed imperiously at his boots.

"You Frogs are behind the times. Never heard of shoe polish?"

He sounded more jocular than annoyed. Jannou, who knew enough German to grasp his meaning, would have laughed if it hadn't been for the man submissively bending over his jackboots. He reminded her of the other Frenchman, the one who had knelt before her in the SD's Avenue Foch headquarters, clasping her foot in one hand, applying the pincers to her toenails . . .

She turned away. The platform was crowded, and a tide of humanity bore her along when the train pulled into the station. Just before the doors closed, someone yanked the bag off her shoulder. Jannou saw a boy, no older than ten, sprinting off down the platform. She thought how disappointed he would be. She'd spent the last of her cash an hour ago, on the new pair of shoes she was wearing.

2

Paris

BERGER WAS STANDING at the window of his third-floor office in the Hôtel Lutétia. He had switched off the light and raised the blackout shade. The window was open, and the accumulated cigarette smoke of the last few hours drifted past him into the dusk.

Sèvres Babylone, the Métro station across the way, was a busy junction. A train must just have come in, because Berger could see people streaming out of the subway entrance. He was surprised to note how hurriedly they scuttled off down the darkened streets. The rush usually came later, just before curfew time.

A German naval cadet had been killed during an exchange of shots outside the station. General Oberg, who commanded the Paris SS, had decreed that ten prisoners from various jails should be selected for execution and shot in reprisal. He had also imposed a fourteen-day curfew extension to 9 P.M., but Berger wasn't sure if the two weeks were up yet.

Near the spot where the cadet had died, a wreath was propped against the station's iron railings. Two uniformed sailors stood guard over it. The vigil would be maintained all night by sentries who relieved each other at two-hour intervals.

Berger shook his head as if someone in the empty office had asked his opinion. As he saw it, posting sentries was a stupid and pointless demonstration. All they advertised to the Parisians hurrying past them was the vulnerability of the occupying power, not its strength.

The last of the incoming passengers trickled out of the station entrance and went their separate ways. Some walked swiftly in the direction of the Bon Marché. The corner turrets of the big department store were adorned with flags; not swastikas but long, thin pennants announcing that the "Grand Summer Fashion Weeks" had begun. Hoisted at the beginning of May, regardless of the fact that this would be the fifth summer of the war, they fluttered bravely in the evening breeze.

A solitary figure crossed the street below, heading for the Lutétia. The woman's raincoat was tightly belted, and her legs were long and slender. She looked like Jannou, but he couldn't be sure.

Berger's world was flat and two-dimensional. He'd lost the sight of his left eye at the age of eleven, blinded by a stone from a schoolmate's slingshot. He couldn't remember how physical objects had looked before, nor did pain play any part in his recollection of the incident. What he did still recall was the humiliation he'd experienced for so many years—the sense of being at yet another disadvantage in life. To Berger, who would be forty in two months' time, the blind eye didn't matter anymore. Like his other handicaps, it had even proved to be a long-term advantage. Its immobility enhanced his looks and lent him a faintly saturnine air. His face seemed to hint at a knowledge of secrets denied to ordinary mortals.

Berger carefully lowered the shade and drew the curtains before switching his desk lamp on again. He was in uniform—not an invariable custom with Abwehr officers. Two of the stars on his shoulder straps were shinier than the rest and looked new. He dialed an internal number, lighting another cigarette as he did so.

"Can the colonel spare me a minute?" For a man of his appearance, Berger's voice was surprisingly gentle.

"It is essential?"

"I need his signature."

The door to the outer office opened and a small, energetic-looking woman bustled in. "Berlin," she hissed. "It's Wiemann." She put a clean ashtray on the desk and gestured at it sternly.

"Thanks," Berger mouthed, tapping his cigarette on the rim. "Fine," he said aloud. "Tell the colonel I'll be with him in fifteen minutes."

The outside phone started ringing, but he took his time. His "Most Urgent" telex message to headquarters had gone off six hours ago. Berlin's long silence was an answer in itself. He picked up the receiver.

"Berger."

"Wiemann here. What's new in Paris? How are—"

"What did you find out?" After a six-hour wait, Berger couldn't be bothered with conversational refinements.

"I've got some news that'll please you: 'Joseph' has earned himself a medal—isn't that great? It just came through from Zossen, from Colonel von Roenne himself. They're giving your man in London the Iron Cross—Second Class, to begin with."

"What about my telex, Wiemann?"

"Don't you realize how rare it is for an agent to get an Iron Cross? I can't recall a similar—"

"What about Schneevogel?"

Silence fell. Wiemann seemed to be conferring with a third party. Berger had a vivid mental image of Wiemann's shabby little office, which lay at the far end of a maze of corridors, its sole luxury a view of the Landwehr Canal.

"Did you turn up anything that might give us a lead?"

Wiemann had finished conferring. "Go easy, that's our advice. It's a hot potato."

"Is that all you've got to say?"

"You Paris people live in an ivory tower. Doesn't anything filter through to you? The SD are busy swallowing us whole."

"They've been trying for years."

"Except that this time it's all signed and sealed, apparently. Military Intelligence and the Security Service are to be amalgamated under the command of Reichsführer Himmler."

Berger wearily rubbed his eyes. "And Schneevogel? Can't you tell me anything at all?"

"He was being brought here for interrogation. To Prinz Albrecht Strasse."

"Via Paris?"

"Paris was handling it, I gather."

"Reckzeh?"

"You should know. That's all I could find out—that and the fact that there's been a foul-up somewhere along the line."

"Why should Berlin have wanted to question him?"

"No idea. What's it to you, anyway?"

"When the SD shanghai an Abwehr officer," Berger said dryly, "it affects us all, wouldn't you say? Is Canaris in Berlin?"

There was another momentary pause. "No."

"Know where he can be reached in an emergency?"

"Burg Lauenstein."

Lauenstein Castle, in the wilds of Thuringia, housed one of the Abwehr's most important facilities: the laboratories and workshops that turned out forged papers, microcameras, invisible inks, and other tools of the secret agent's trade.

"What's the Admiral doing at Lauenstein?"

"The *ex*-Admiral, that's what the SD call him nowadays. There's renewed talk of putting him on trial."

Berger held the receiver away from him, as though fearful that his breathing alone might betray the alarm he felt.

"Listen," he said, "Canaris visited Spain last year, first week of August, for a conference at Santander. Schneevogel made the arrangements."

"A conference with whom?"

"If there's any record of the meeting, destroy it." Berger drew a deep breath. "Those chestnut trees outside your window, are they in flower already?"

"Not yet. This is Berlin, not Paris." Wiemann's voice took on a note of urgency. "What about the Allied invasion? Anything new?"

That was the question everyone asked sooner or later—the ominous, inevitable adjunct to every conversation. Berger, engrossed in his own thoughts, didn't reply. *Ex*-Admiral . . . Was Wiemann exaggerating? If he'd heard the story once, he'd heard it a dozen times. Canaris had been written off again and again.

"Everyone at this end has been predicting a landing for weeks," Wiemann was saying. "What are the British and Americans waiting for? What's the word in Paris? What does Rommel say?"

"Your guess is as good as mine." Berger yearned to hang up. "Remember what I said about those papers. Destroy the lot—don't put it off. Thanks for calling me back. Oh yes, and thanks for the good news."

"You'll be getting written confirmation by courier."

"Fine, thanks again."

The ice was getting thin, he reflected. He was strangely unperturbed by the thought, which held a certain fascination for him. His mind went back to a summer day in 1942 and the windmill in the Bois de Boulogne. Horses were out training on the Longchamp racetrack. The Admiral, whose choice of rendezvous it was, had turned up in civilian clothes. His dark felt hat and double-breasted suit looked at odds with the hot midday sun.

"Lieutenant Berger?" That was how the conversation had begun. "Let's take a turn round the mill . . ."

Berger didn't harbor any very strong beliefs. Ambition, yes. Vanity? That, too, but what really made him tick was a quality unusual and dangerous in one of his profession: he was a sentimental man with romantic inclinations. Hence his memory of the conversation beside the windmill, and hence his pride: Canaris, the all-powerful secret service chief, conferring with a humble lieutenant and giving his cherished plan a hearing.

He wrenched himself back to the present. There remained the problem of Schneevogel, the Abwehr's Lisbon representative. He pressed the buzzer, and the typewriter next door stopped clattering.

Hermine Köster reappeared, looking tired but indomitable. Hermine was forty-eight and had never married—never had a man either, Berger suspected. She'd been his secretary ever since he came to France, first at Brest and then, for the past three years, in Paris.

He proffered the last cigarette in his silver case and gave her a light. She puffed at it distastefully, inexpertly, just to please him. In her eyes he could do no wrong. Her sole reason for smoking, in all probability, was to make him feel less guilty about his own consumption of cigarettes. She even forgave him for living with a French girl and had doubtless devised some elaborate justification for it.

"They've awarded Joseph the Iron Cross Second Class."

Her face clouded over for a moment—she came from Poznań and had no love for the Poles—but brightened again in a flash. "Congratulations."

He smiled, reassured by her dogged and unchanging devotion. Her very presence in Paris was a token of loyalty. Hermine had jibbed at first, flatly refusing to accompany him there on the grounds that Paris was a vice-ridden city where no staunch and self-respecting Catholic should ever set foot. She now lived not far from the Lutétia in one of the French capital's most clerical quarters, surrounded by churches, Catholic schools, convents, and shops filled with religious knickknacks. The German soldiers she passed on her way to work were heavily outnumbered by priests and nuns.

Berger refilled his cigarette case, ten cigarettes a side, and glanced at his watch, which he habitually removed and kept on the desk in front of him.

"Send Schmidt to me. I don't want to see you here this weekend.

They say the weather's set fair, so get some sun. Go on home now. Good night."

"Good night."

He waited, musing. Was Schneevogel in Paris? Was he already being interrogated? What did the SD hope to get out of him? What did they suspect him of? What had Reckzeh, who headed the Paris SD, found out?

He didn't hear the unobtrusive tap at his door and became aware of Schmidt's presence only when he entered the office. The sergeant was a man accustomed to being ignored, as his physique and manner conveyed. He was Berger's age but looked older, with weary, colorless eyes. Even in his uniform, which was a size too big, he made a thoroughly unmilitary impression.

"Captain?"

"Sit down." Berger had discovered Schmidt in the Lutétia's gloomy, airless cellars, where the Abwehr kept its records. He sometimes wondered if he had done Schmidt a favor by disinterring him and making him his assistant. "Any news?"

"I checked the frontier posts. A vehicle crossed the Spanish-French border at Hendaye around eleven-thirty this morning. A Citroën van with diplomatic license plates."

"How many passengers?"

"Three. They all had Spanish diplomatic passports."

"Well?"

"The van was carrying a zinc coffin."

Berger frowned. "It doesn't make sense. They can't get anything out of a dead man. We'd better get onto the Corsicans."

"You want me to go and see them?"

Berger noted the change in Schmidt's expression, the veiled annoyance. He loathed having to leave his desk and the filing cabinets he tended with such loving care.

"Just tell them the name. I'll take care of the rest."

Berger tidied his desk when Schmidt had gone. The cash voucher was ready for Colonel von Steinberg's signature. He picked it up, collected his cap and coat from the hatstand, and lit another cigarette before leaving the office by the outer door.

A dimly lit passage stretched ahead of him, running the full length of the building. Steeped in artificial twilight, even by day, the Lutétia's corridors always gave him claustrophobia. The air in them was stale and motionless.

He walked to the elevator and pressed the button. The folding grille was half open when he flinched at the thought of entering such a cramped little cage and pulled it shut again. He made his way to the stairs and climbed the flight that led to Steinberg's fourth-floor office.

Men going on night duty passed him with files under their arms. They saluted and he saluted back, but none of them paused to chat as they used to in the old days. All seemed anxious to closet themselves in their offices as soon as possible. Uneasiness was rife at the Abwehr's Paris headquarters. The excitement and euphoria of former times had given way to mounting apprehension.

Berger coughed and stubbed out his cigarette in an ashtray on the wall. He promised himself, for the umpteenth time, that he'd give up smoking tomorrow.

3

London

ROMAN KACEW left the Underground at Notting Hill Gate, preferring to walk the rest of the way. He didn't mind walking. Long perambulations through London had become his staple pastime.

He felt rather foolish, carrying the birdcage. People stopped and stared. A few went so far as to accost him and inquire what was under the cloth. Budgerigars, canaries?

Beneath his raincoat, Kacew was wearing a Harris Tweed jacket, a blue striped shirt, a woolen tie in a darker shade of blue, baggy flannel slacks, and brown brogues—Gahagan's style—but even in this getup he didn't look English. He had, as Gahagan put it, a "Tartar's face": dark eyes, dark hair, broad cheekbones, and a complexion that retained its tan without benefit of sun.

He reached Bayswater station. The evening was damp and misty, but the rain had stopped. Clouds scudded low overhead, propelled by a stiff west wind. He headed for Paddington without bothering to check the street signs. Because flying had been his trade for so long, Kacew had a sense of direction as acute as any musician's sense of pitch.

The handle of the cage was biting into his fingers, so he switched hands. The birds made no sound. This was their second or third move in the six months since he'd had them. Apart from wanting to be rid of the cage, Kacew was in no hurry.

His new lodgings, chosen for him by Gahagan, would be little different from his last ones in Putney or their predecessors in Lewisham, Clapham, and other parts of London—a succession of places he'd already forgotten. He must have moved house and changed his alias at least a dozen times since embarking on his intricate life as a double agent.

He was "Joseph" to Berger and the Abwehr, "Cato" to Gahagan and the British Secret Service. Beyond that he didn't exist, however many other names he assumed for everyday use. Sometimes, and lately with increasing frequency, Kacew tried to imagine what would happen when the war was over. Would he still be told what name to use and where to live?

He peered at the darkening sky. The clouds had lifted since his poker game at the Rathbone Hotel. The other players, a bunch of Free Polish fliers, had been unexpectedly recalled to base because the weather was improving.

He quickened his pace, checking the street names now. The address Gahagan had given him turned out to be in a terrace of identical houses. Each had an entrance approached by a flight of stone steps, and all looked dark and forbidding. No. 17 was no different from the rest. The flame from his lighter disclosed a visiting card thumbtacked to the doorjamb below the bell. The name Pinikieski meant nothing to him.

He'd been given a key, but the door swung open before he could use it. A dim figure, gaunt and slightly stooping, beckoned impatiently.

"I've been here an hour." Gahagan's voice sounded harsh and irritable.

"You didn't say a time."

"Come in, come in."

Kacew followed him into the hallway. His bags had been dumped on the tiled floor at the foot of the stairs, with their strip of worn Axminster and chocolate-brown banisters. The whole house reeked of floor polish and carbolic, as if it had been thoroughly disinfected after a long and fatal illness. The only light came from a half-open door on the left. Gahagan stood outlined against it, his lean face in shadow.

"Anything wrong?" Kacew asked. It was unusual to see his controller out of hours.

Gahagan didn't reply. He led the way into the room on the left. The pockets of his tweed jacket bulged, and Kacew noticed that a section of the lining had come adrift and was sagging below the hem. Didn't he have anyone who would sew it up for him? Kacew briefly pondered the question. Gahagan knew almost all there was to know about him, but he, Kacew, knew next to nothing about Gahagan. Jeremy Gahagan . . . Was it his real name? It might even be an alias.

A chintz-covered three-piece suite stood clustered around the unlit gas fire, as garish as the matching curtains.

"Make yourself at home."

Kacew was still holding the cage. The birds hadn't stirred under their green baize cloth. In one corner of the living room, on a fluted mahogany stand, stood a potted plant. Kacew removed it and put the cage there instead.

"Fancy lumbering yourself with those birds," said Gahagan. "Only a Pole would get such a crazy idea." The two deeply incised furrows on either side of his nose were a by-product of the ulcers that made his life a misery. He was forty-three, nine years older than Kacew, and his close-cropped hair was already turning gray.

Kacew sat down on the sofa. He made an all-encompassing gesture. "Have I got the whole place to myself?"

Gahagan pointed to a brown paper parcel on the coffee table between them. "A housewarming present."

"I don't feel like drinking on my own." Kacew had never seen Gahagan drink anything but milky tea.

"It's genuine Polish vodka." Gahagan unwrapped the two bottles and stood them side by side.

"Pinikieski, the name on the door—is that me?"

"Yes, I'll give you your new documentation before I go."

"One day you'll run out of names for me."

"I doubt it." Gahagan grimaced like a man in pain. "Whenever I need a name I pick one from the Polish military cemetery at Newark. There are more than enough to last you the rest of the war."

It was an uncharacteristic little admission. Kacew eyed him intently. "What's happened?"

Gahagan picked up one of the vodka bottles and studied the label with every sign of interest. He even traced the lettering with his forefinger and silently mouthed the name to himself before putting the bottle down again.

"When you got to Lisbon after escaping from Paris," he said at length, "you contacted the Abwehr representative there, Schneevogel."

"Well?"

"What was your impression of him?"

"I told your people all I knew when they debriefed me."

"You took to him?"

"He'd been a flier before he joined the Abwehr. That gave us something in common."

"A loyal German?"

"Paris trusted him. That's to say, Berger did."

"No one suspected him of working for us?"

Kacew looked surprised. "Was he?"

"Schneevogel has been abducted. Our information from Lisbon is still pretty vague, but it seems he was down at the docks, checking some cargo, when three men in civilian clothes overpowered him and hustled him into a car."

"Any idea who they were?"

"Only a hunch."

"Well?"

"The SD—Himmler's boys."

"Why?"

"Schneevogel was your contact man for payments from Berger."

"Is that why you moved me from Putney?"

"It pays to be careful."

"Was he really working for you?"

Gahagan gave an almost imperceptible smile. It wasn't pronounced enough to disguise the pain on his face. Evidently, his ulcers were acting up today. "We'll see how Paris reacts."

Footsteps sounded in the hallway. Someone had come in—someone with a key to the house. There was a knock on the living room door, and a girl in a trench coat and head scarf came in.

"Good evening, Colonel."

"Evening, Alison." Gahagan didn't turn round, just glanced at his watch.

The girl went over to the fireplace, bent down, and inserted a shilling in the meter. She struck a match, and tongues of blue flame began to lick the fireclay ribs. Straightening up, she deposited a pile of spare coins on the mantelpiece.

"Shall I make some tea?"

"Good idea," said Gahagan.

She left the room. Above the sound of a kettle being filled, Kacew could hear the muffled voice of a BBC radio announcer. He glanced inquiringly at Gahagan.

"Her name's Alison Mills," Gahagan said. "She's a lieutenant in the FANY—First Aid Nursing Yeomanry to you. Works for the Firm."

"Will she be staying here?"

"Even in the back streets of Paddington, people would wonder why a solitary Polish flight lieutenant should have a whole house to himself." Gahagan took an attaché case from the floor beside him and put it on his lap.

"One moment," said Kacew. "The life I lead—it's so dull, so routine. An hour a night in front of a transmitter, that's all. Isn't there anything else I can do?"

"Maybe after the invasion." Gahagan opened the attaché case and produced an envelope. He shook out an identity card, a ration book, and other papers.

"One mission, Jeremy—one little field assignment, that's all I ask. I can't go on like this."

The girl returned, carrying a tray. She put the teapot and milk jug on the table, together with cups and saucers for two. She wore no makeup of any kind, Kacew noticed. She had blue eyes, auburn hair, and the clear complexion of a country-bred English girl. Her nose was slightly freckled.

At the door she turned. "No air raid warnings so far."

Kacew waited until she had gone. "I mean it, Jeremy. I can't go on living like this."

Gahagan shook his head. "Getting our troops back to France, that's all that matters. We've got to go back, and go the way we came. Goddamn it, you know my feelings on the subject."

Kacew had a sudden vision of Dunkirk in June 1940. His unit, all Polish volunteers, lay pinned down in the dunes near the harbor, awaiting embarkation. By day the ruined town and docks were battered by mortar fire and dive-bombed by Stukas. Darkness offered the only hope, because that was when rescue ships could run close inshore.

What made the memory so vivid was that Kacew felt much as he'd felt then: hemmed in and at the mercy of forces beyond his control. He could still recall the shock of those two successive defeats, first in Poland and then in France, where he'd fled in December 1939.

It was on board the overladen cutter that finally picked them up and threaded its way between scores of sunken craft, heading for the open sea, that he first saw the British officer leaning over the stern. He was unhurt, but his face was agonized—twisted with pain.

Many hours later, when Dover loomed out of the mist and everyone crowded forward to look, the officer still had no eyes for the English coast. He continued to stare in the direction of France, and Kacew heard his voice for the first time, hoarse and troubled: "One day we'll go back. We'll never win this war unless we do . . ."

Two months later, Kacew reported to the Victoria Hotel in Northumberland Avenue, where he met the man again. He had a name this time—Jeremy Gahagan—and was now a captain in the infant SOE, or Special Operations Executive, whose principal function was to train secret agents and sneak them across the Channel.

After four months' training, Kacew was parachuted into France. Within weeks, he'd installed himself and his radio in a seedy Paris hotel on Rue de Mazagran and was transmitting his first signals to London . . .

The exhilaration of the memories Gahagan had revived was only momentary. They left him feeling flat and disenchanted.

"I've heard of an assignment," he said. "They need a couple of officer volunteers to reconnoiter the minefields off Calais. Just one assignment like that, and I'd feel better. This present setup is killing me by inches."

"You're far too valuable to us here. More valuable than you ever were in the field."

"You think I've lost my nerve?"

"I didn't say that."

"Then give me a chance."

"I already did. We expected to find your name on a death list after they arrested you in Paris. Instead, you made a spectacular escape from France with the Abwehr's connivance—in return for a promise to spy for the Germans over here. Quite a tale! Not everyone in the Firm was in favor of reemploying you."

"Sometimes," Kacew said, "I'm suspicious of my own story. Hasn't Berger ever caught on?"

"Our lies are like needles in a haystack of genuine information. Don't ask me what the haystack costs us." Another twinge of pain crossed Gahagan's face. "Let's drop the subject, it's a waste of time." He pushed the papers across the table. "You're Flight Lieutenant Pinikieski, a liaison officer to the Royal Air Force. You've got a desk at the Polish headquarters in the Hotel Rubens, but most of your time will be devoted to tours of inspection. From the Germans' angle, that'll give you a chance to gather information unobtrusively."

There were no more sounds from the kitchen. Footsteps could now be heard in one of the rooms upstairs. Kacew listened to Gahagan with only half an ear. It was the same old story: everything had been devised and arranged without him. All he had to do was carry out instructions.

"You'll start in the Eastern Counties, in Lincolnshire . . ."

The radio came on overhead.

". . . at a Bomber Command base: Elsham Wolds. What is it?"

The name jolted Kacew like an electric shock, but he couldn't afford to dwell on what it meant to him. He had to say something, explain himself.

"Nothing. I'll be glad to get out of London, that's all."

"It'll only be a flying visit. We can't leave Berger too long without a transmission."

Karski, thought Kacew—yet another severed link with the past which Gahagan had forced him to bury. When he'd last heard, Karski's squadron was based at Elsham Wolds. Would he still be there? He might even be dead, except that the newspapers would have reported the loss of such a well-known and highly decorated flier.

"It mustn't look too easy," Gahagan went on. "I don't want Berger underestimating the risks his agent runs."

"Like falling under a London bus?" Kacew said bitterly.

Gahagan's smile didn't conceal the weariness in his eyes, with their dark, unhealthy shadows. "We've already hanged three German agents this year."

"You hang them?" Kacew's surprise was genuine.

"We British have some pretty antiquated ideas."

The radio was still on upstairs—a comedy program, to judge by the sporadic roars of laughter. Kacew sipped his tea. Although he'd never grown used to the English habit of drinking it with milk, the displacement activity was welcome. He listened to the rest of Gahagan's instructions and answered mechanically when called on to reply.

His thoughts revolved around Karski, Schneevogel, and Pinikieski, the dead stranger whose name he'd borrowed, but especially Karski. It seemed a lifetime since he'd set foot on an airfield or flown a plane.

He was leaving London tomorrow morning. He was going to visit a bomber base, feast his senses on the sights and sounds he loved. He might even see Karski again. The prospect filled him with almost unbearable excitement.

4

Paris

BERGER DIDN'T KNOW why the Abwehr had requisitioned the Hôtel Lutétia as its headquarters when the Germans occupied Paris. Wiemann hadn't been so wide of the mark when he called it an ivory tower. The Lutétia was a rather ostentatious building in the grand hotel manner. Perhaps it had been chosen because it was the only hotel on the Rive Gauche, the left bank of the Seine, big enough to accommodate the entire administrative setup.

But why the Rive Gauche? Every other individual or headquarters of importance was located on the Rive Droite: Commander in Chief, France, in the Hôtel Majestic; the Military Governor of Paris in the Place de l'Opéra; the multifarious organs of the SS, Gestapo, and SD in and around Avenue Foch.

The Rive Droite was chic, glamorous, and expensive; the Rive Gauche artistic. That, after all, might have been why the Abwehr's leading lights had settled on the Lutétia. They'd always regarded themselves as a race apart, an exclusive club with cultural and aesthetic pretensions.

On the other hand, thought Berger, as he paused outside the door of Colonel von Steinberg's anteroom, the Lutétia might simply have been chosen because it was a stone's throw from the Cherche-Midi, one of the biggest jails in Paris. Very handy, in view of all the prisoners held there for interrogation.

Steinberg's offices were the hotel's former "royal suite," a trio of fourth-floor rooms overlooking Boulevard Raspail. Berger knocked and entered the anteroom. Mikosch, the colonel's driver, was lolling at the senior secretary's desk studying a racing paper.

Outside the double doors leading to the inner sanctum stood a row of valises. At that moment an elderly corporal emerged, laboring under the weight of two more. Berger could imagine what they contained. France was still rich in loot, especially for those with connections and the power to exploit them. He couldn't resist a dig.

"It'll be standing room only, with all that baggage."

Mikosch looked up from his racing paper with a grin. "No problem, Captain, we're taking the big Mercedes." He had a knowing face with crafty little eyes and outsize ears. "Like a tip for Longchamp tomorrow?"

"Where's the colonel off to?"

"Why not ask him yourself?" The driver licked his pencil and underlined the name of a horse.

Through the doors, which were ajar, Berger could see Steinberg standing at his big Louis Quatorze desk, telephoning. He was wearing civilian clothes, a double-breasted suit in pale gray flannel and a white shirt with a bow tie.

Many section heads followed Steinberg's sartorial lead. Gray flannel suits had been in vogue with the Abwehr's Paris personnel for at least a year, together with silk shirts and bow ties or foulards. "No need to advertise our military associations," was the colonel's maxim. "We aren't a horde of uncouth Teutons."

Steinberg was still on the phone, not saying much himself, just listening. Berger walked in unannounced. The colonel's two obese dachshunds made a beeline for him, wagging their tails and weaving around his legs.

Steinberg looked startled, then infuriated, when Berger came up to the desk and deposited the voucher on it. "Just your signature," Berger murmured.

The colonel glared at him. "Yes, yes," he said into the phone, "I quite understand. If it comes to it, we'll cooperate . . . One hundred percent, naturally. Thank you, yes . . . I should have left by now . . . Of course, General, I'll attend to it before I go. Many thanks."

He slammed the receiver down, strode over to the doors, and banged them shut. Then he strode back, fuming.

"What the devil do you mean by barging in like this?"

"Sorry," said Berger, "I know you're pressed for time. I need your signature, that's all."

Steinberg inserted a finger behind his bow tie, a blue polka dot, and eased it away from his Adam's apple. "I'm signing nothing more to-night—nothing!"

Berger replaced the cap on his fountain pen, outwardly unruffled, and picked up the voucher.

"Too much soft living, that's the trouble with you people," Steinberg rasped. "A little action might do you good."

That was the ultimate deterrent—excommunication from the flesh-pots of France—but it only served to reinforce Berger's contempt for the man behind the desk. Steinberg, with his wining and dining and black-marketeering, had milked his Paris job for all it was worth. Hermine Köster puritanically insisted that, if the Abwehr's stock in France had sunk, this was due more to the effects of Parisian decadence than to any encroachments by the SS and SD. She could well be right, thought Berger. Men like Steinberg were to blame for the falloff in efficiency and the fact that so many key posts were held by well-con-nected incompetents.

Berger had fought might and main to become a member of this elite organization. Nothing had predestined him for it—no *"von"* in front of his name, no private income, no family connections. Men of his back-ground were seldom admitted to a club as exclusive as the Abwehr, so he'd elbowed his way into its ranks by dint of sheer hard work. Even now that the Steinbergs needed him, however, they contrived to make him feel dependent on their grace and favor.

"What did you want me to sign, anyway?"

"A cash voucher for Joseph." Berger had a welcome ability to drain his voice of emotion.

"Why can't the paymaster sign it? Let me see." Steinberg glanced at the slip of paper and went purple again. "A thousand pounds sterling? You're crazy!"

"It's drawn on the secret fund, that's why I need your signature."

"Once, just once, I'd like us to employ an agent who works for honor and glory's sake." Steinberg sat down at his desk and pulled the voucher toward him. "What in God's name does Joseph do with all the money we pay him?"

Berger felt himself back on safe ground. He wasn't even tempted to sugar the pill by mentioning Joseph's Iron Cross. The colonel, he re-called, had declined to endorse Joseph's earliest reports. He persisted in his refusal until Army General Staff Headquarters at Zossen evinced a sudden interest in them. As soon as he learned that they were ending up on the desk of Colonel *Baron* Alexis *von* Roenne, collator of all incoming intelligence reports and a man with personal access to the Führer, everything changed: thenceforward, no signal from Joseph was to leave the premises without Steinberg's initials on it.

"Things have reached a critical stage, Berger—not that I think the Allies will really attempt a full-scale landing. Even if they do, they won't last more than a few hours. Rommel will pin them down on the beaches and knock hell out of them."

There it was again, the everpresent thought: the likelihood of an Allied invasion, of impending doom—of *finis Germaniae*, as Canaris would have phrased it. The prospect held no terrors for Berger. It would spell the end of his power and privileges, but it would also put paid to his doubts, his pangs of conscience.

"A thousand pounds! Tell Joseph he'd better start earning his keep, Berger. What about the invasion? When and where do they intend to land? Above all, *where?* That's what he's to concentrate on: where are they planning to come ashore?" Steinberg signed the voucher and waved it in the air to dry the ink. "How do you propose to transmit the money now that Schneevogel"—he hesitated—"now that Schneevogel's out of commission?"

"We have a man at the Mexican Embassy in London. Did you read my preliminary report on the incident in Lisbon?"

"Yes, and I find your conclusions rather farfetched. There's no firm evidence of SD involvement." Steinberg handed back the voucher and pointed to the phone. "That call just now—that was Oberg. He made no mention of it."

"You could always call back and ask, Colonel."

One of the dachshunds nudged Steinberg's leg. He bent down and fondled it absently. "There's no point in crossing swords with the SS."

"What about the Commander in Chief? His legal section could make inquiries—it's their province."

"A legal section is the last thing likely to impress a man like General Oberg."

Steinberg's white-jacketed orderly appeared. "Your uniform, Colonel."

"What uniform?"

"You ordered it for the journey."

"Ah yes, thank you. And take these dogs off my hands." Steinberg waited till the orderly had retired to the inner room with the dachshunds in tow. "What could they have against Schneevogel, Berger? I mean, even the SD need something to go on."

"He arranged the Santander conference."

Steinberg rose and walked over to the window. "Make peace with the Western Allies, fight on against Russia," he said in a low voice, "—that's the Admiral's pet idea. An illusion, Berger, a dangerous illusion. Unauthorized contacts with the enemy: the SS have been trying to pin that charge on him for ages. They'll bring him to trial if they find any evidence to support it."

Berger recalled what Wiemann had told him over the phone. "There's talk in Berlin of a merger, a negotiated settlement."

"Why do you think I was talking to Oberg, for fun? I don't preach cooperation without a very good reason. By the way, Oberg complained that you refused to send copies of Joseph's reports to Standartenführer Reckzeh."

"The SD asked for them, yes," Berger said guardedly.

"Well?"

"It was only a request. I turned it down."

"You *what?*" Steinberg gave his bow tie another tug. "I thought you had more sense than to tangle with Reckzeh." Wearily, he resumed his seat. "It's true," he said, "there's a merger in the offing. We're to be amalgamated with the SD."

"What does the Admiral say to that?"

Steinberg spread his hands in a gesture of resignation. "No idea. I'm told he's at Burg Lauenstein. Under house arrest, according to some people—I honestly don't know. We'll just have to soldier on here as best we can. It would be a useful gesture if you gave Reckzeh those copies—copies of all Joseph's signals. In return, I undertake to have a word with the Majestic about Schneevogel. Well, I think that's all."

"Thank you, Colonel. Have a pleasant trip."

"Pleasant? I detest all-night drives, but there's nothing for it now that the Luftwaffe can't guarantee our safety on the roads by day." Steinberg hesitated. "Can you spare a moment?"

Berger, already on his way to the door, turned in surprise.

"I'd appreciate your advice. It's about my son. You remember my son? He's the reason for this trip. You remember him?" There was a sudden note of entreaty in the colonel's voice.

It was a couple of years since Steinberg had invited Berger to the villa he then occupied, and his recollections of the visit were hazy. He recalled a plump blonde in a tiara and a gown that bared her milky shoulders—the colonel's wife, much given to flaunting her Viennese French: *"J'aime beaucoup Paris, j'aime beaucoup la langue française."*

The son was a pallid youth of around sixteen, with lank fair hair. He'd worn dark glasses all evening.

"Yes," said Berger, feeling no more sympathetically inclined now than he had then. "I remember him."

"Well, he's in trouble again. He made an imprudent remark about the Führer—the Führer, mark you! How could the boy have been so foolish? Hence this trip. I'm trying to save his neck."

Berger was at a loss for words.

"Fortunately," Steinberg went on, "there weren't many officers in the mess at the time, and his company commander happens to be a distant relation. Think we could get him transferred?"

"Your son? To the Abwehr?"

"If you only knew what a constant source of anxiety he's been to us, Berger. 'The Führer should be put up against a wall and shot . . .' I ask you!" Steinberg lapsed into horrified silence. "Can you imagine what this could do to me—the repercussions it might have on me personally?"

"If you did request his transfer, are you sure he'd go along with it?"

"Why shouldn't he, if it offers him a chance of saving his neck?" Steinberg fell silent again, as though the force of Berger's reservation had sunk in. "I'll call you from Trier as soon as I've spoken with him."

"I could have a word with Personnel in the meantime."

"No, not yet. This is just between ourselves, eh?" The colonel, struggling to regain his composure, mustered a faint smile. "You're lucky, Berger—no wife, no children. That's an asset at a time like this." He glanced furtively at each door in turn. "If the worst happens, what do you plan to do?"

Now you're talking like your son, Berger wanted to say, but he resisted the temptation.

"Would Spain be a safe bet?"

Berger was racked with the dry, chronic cough induced by two packs of cigarettes a day. It spared him the need to answer.

"Very well, I won't detain you any longer."

Berger shook the outstretched hand. Still at a loss for words, he repeated, "Have a pleasant trip, Colonel."

His first act in the outer office was to light a cigarette. It tasted harsh and acrid. The valises had disappeared. Mikosch, who was still engrossed in his racing paper, looked up.

"Sure you don't want a tip for Longchamp?"

"I never go to the races."

"You're passing up a lot of easy money, Captain."

"If you say so."

Berger had long wondered where the colonel's sergeant driver got the cash to throw away on horses. Ever since he'd found out, he'd been doubly wary of him.

"The switchboard rang." Mikosch grinned broadly, suggestively. "There's someone waiting for you downstairs in the lobby."

"Thanks." Berger retrieved his cap and coat from the hook where he'd hung them.

Mikosch didn't move for a while after Berger had gone. Then he got up and cautiously opened the doors to Steinberg's office. He peered inside, closed them again, and returned to the desk. Picking up the phone, he dialed a number.

"Koch?" he said. "Mikosch here. The colonel's leaving Paris."

The voice at the other end asked a question. "One day, maybe two," he replied. "Trier. He hasn't told me anything definite."

Again the voice asked a question.

"No, I haven't had a chance yet. Yes, I know it's urgent, but it isn't as easy as you think. I'll take care of it, just give me a bit more time. By the way, you can do me a favor. Stick something on a horse for me at Longchamp this Sunday."

The dachshunds began yapping in Steinberg's office.

"It's called Der Führer."

All that came back down the line was a startled *"What!"*

The doors opened and Steinberg appeared, in uniform now, followed by his dogs. Mikosch put the phone down and snapped to attention, simultaneously pocketing his paper. The horse whose name he'd underlined was running in the third race. It really was called Der Führer.

5

Paris

THE HOUSE ON AVENUE FOCH might have been designed for giants. Everything about it was outsize, from the tall windows and colonnaded portico to the big black railings enclosing the grounds. Its prewar owner, a midget of a man, had been a wealthy cosmetics manufacturer noted for his lavish parties. Many Parisians used to amuse themselves by watching his guests roll up for soirees in their glossy limousines. Now they avoided the house and the entire neighborhood like the plague. The big white mansion at No. 82–84, Avenue Foch, was the headquarters of Himmler's Security Service: the SD.

SS men patrolled the grounds with dogs, and two sentries stood guard outside the wrought iron gates. One of them kept a pair of binoculars trained on the avenue. He stiffened every time a car approached from the Bois de Boulogne end. Koch, Reckzeh's adjutant, had issued a general alert: his boss was on the way.

A black Mercedes convertible swung into view on the central carriageway. The face of the man at the wheel was clearly recognizable in the sentry's night glasses.

"Hell, there he is! Koch must have called him away from some shindig or other."

The second sentry turned. "Look out," he shouted into the forecourt, "he's coming!"

Two SS men doubled to the gates, hobnailed boots clattering, and opened them wide. The Mercedes veered left into the side road, which was separated from the main thoroughfare by a strip of grass lined with trees. The avenue itself was deserted. Only at the far end, where the shadowy bulk of the Arc de Triomphe presided over the Étoile, could a few masked headlights be glimpsed in the darkness.

The sentries saluted as the car swept through the gateway. Koch, flaxen-haired and baby-faced in a way that made him look younger than his twenty-four years, was waiting at the entrance to the inner courtyard. He whipped the driver's door open almost before the Mercedes came to a halt.

"*Heil Hitler*, Standartenführer!"

"*Merde!* A fine old mess you've made of things." If the man who got out of the car hadn't spoken German, his appearance might have conjured up memories of the mansion's prewar soirees. Reckzeh was wearing a soft white tuxedo with a black silk handkerchief tucked casually into the breast pocket. Nestling against his silk shirt, also black, was a tie as white as his jacket. On the surface, Reckzeh represented the antithesis of Himmler's Nordic racial ideal. He was a Mediterranean type with an olive complexion and jet-black hair. His thin, dark Clark Gable mustache made him look more like an apache than a colonel in the SS.

He stared past Koch at two vehicles parked in the spacious courtyard. "Has Ulitzky examined the body?"

"He's drafting his report right now."

Reckzeh set off, lithe as a cat. Koch, booted and in uniform, followed stiffly. Ornamental green trelliswork, half obscured by creeper, covered the walls overlooking the courtyard. The Citroën van was thickly coated with dust. Reckzeh opened the rear doors. Inside lay a zinc coffin with the lid removed. It was empty.

"Where are Focke and the other two?"

"Under arrest, as you instructed."

Koch left it at that. Long experience told him that it would be inopportune to say more.

"Bungling idiots!" said Reckzeh. "False papers, diplomatic passports, no frontier checks—it should have been child's play. Where's the body?"

"Wouldn't you like a word with Dr. Ulitzky first?"

"I asked you a question, Koch. Dig the shit out of your ears and listen."

"It's in the basement, Standartenführer."

Koch could never get used to the contradictions in Reckzeh. His bawdy language he reserved for intimates and subordinates. The public Reckzeh was very different: courteous, urbane, refined of speech and manner. He was *Dr.* Erich Reckzeh, even though the doctorate was only an honorary degree conferred by Prague University.

They entered the mansion's entrance hall, which was lit by a gold-bronze Louis Quinze chandelier extending the height of two stories. A curving staircase led to the upper floors. The marble flagstones underfoot were laid in geometrical patterns.

A man rose from one of the high-backed brocade chairs flanking the walls—a barrel-chested little man with spindly legs. He was holding an instrument case in one hand and a sheet of paper in the other.

Reckzeh walked over to him. "Sorry about this, Otto. Hope I didn't spoil a good party."

Ulitzky put his bag down and shook hands. His eyes were hugely magnified by thick-lensed glasses. "We're in the same boat, I see."

Reckzeh smiled. "You were holding a séance?"

"As it happens, yes."

"What say the dead?"

Ulitzky didn't pursue the subject. He removed his glasses and rubbed his eyes. "I've made out a preliminary report," he said.

Reckzeh took the sheet of paper and ran his eye over it. "Mind coming with me?" He walked on ahead. "Would you take me along to one of your séances sometime?"

"Of course, if it would interest you."

Ulitzky found Reckzeh an enigma, as usual. At twenty-eight, only half the doctor's age, he held the rank of colonel but carried more clout than an army commander. Many of these influential young SS officers had sprung from total obscurity and were at pains to conceal the fact; Reckzeh seemed to relish advertising his humble origins, perhaps because they underlined the irony of his exalted status: here in the Avenue Foch, he was master of all he surveyed.

Another contradiction: Reckzeh's notorious cruelty to the French and his pride in being an ex-legionnaire. A framed *certificat de bonne conduite* hung on his office wall, and the rosette that even now adorned the buttonhole of his white tuxedo—as of all his uniforms—was that of the Croix de Valeur, which he'd won at the battle of Djebel Baddou, while serving in Morocco with the Foreign Legion.

They had descended a flight of steps and were down belowground in the mansion's labyrinthine cellars. The walls were of bare, unrendered stone, and the chill, still air reminded Ulitzky of his dissecting room.

Koch's boots made the flagstones ring; Reckzeh, in his low-heeled patent leather pumps, was inaudible. Koch, Ulitzky noticed, swung his hips in an effeminate way; Reckzeh's affair with a male French film star was the talk of the town, but no one would have guessed it from his erect and soldierly bearing.

They entered a room like a square stone box. The body, dressed in a lightweight linen suit and laid out on a wheeled stretcher, looked unnaturally small. The dead man's feet were bare. His white canvas shoes reposed beneath a small table on which lay the articles found in his possession: a wallet, a wristwatch, a pack of cigarettes, a lighter, some small change, and a passport in the name of Christian Schneevogel, insurance agent.

Reckzeh went to the head of the stretcher. Even in the glare of the naked bulb suspended from the ceiling, the bloodless face preserved a little of its tan.

"Plenty of sun in Lisbon," said Reckzeh. Neither loud nor subdued, the remark was directed at no one in particular. He moved to the table and flicked through Schneevogel's passport, examining the visa stamps, then glanced at the body again. "All I wanted was a little chat with him."

Koch, standing in the background, cleared his throat. Reckzeh swung round.

"Take those men to the wine cellar."

"Dr. Ulitzky can confirm that . . ."

Koch broke off, though Reckzeh hadn't interrupted him. It was a gesture that had caught his eye. Reckzeh took the silk handkerchief from his breast pocket, refolded it, and put it back. Still mesmerized by the handkerchief, Koch swallowed hard and clicked his heels. "Certainly, Standartenführer."

"If you want my opinion, Erich," Ulitzky said, when they were alone, "it was an accident. They shot him full of Gardenal to knock him out. I don't suppose it was the first time they'd used it."

"In that case, what went wrong?"

Ulitzky removed his glasses again. "Gardenal's a common enough narcotic. The trouble is, some subjects are allergic to the stuff. If you're hypersensitive, even a moderate dose can be lethal."

"How could they have overlooked that possibility?"

"Come now, Erich, the man himself may not have known."

"So *was* he allergic to it? Precisely what did he die of?"

"To answer that, I'd have to do a thorough autopsy."

"Then do one. Right away, preferably."

"What about his next of kin?"

Reckzeh pocketed the report. His eyes were very bright. "You have my consent."

"Normally I'd need—"

"Please, Otto! Let's not complicate matters, they're difficult enough already."

"Very well, I'll send an ambulance."

"Thanks—and forgive me again for interrupting your séance."

"You're welcome to attend one, anytime."

Reckzeh turned as he led the way out into the passage. "Know anything about this Russian clairvoyante who's set up shop at the Ritz Hotel—this Madame Gurdyev? Is she good?"

"I only know she's booked up for months ahead."

"Some pretty illustrious people have consulted her, I'm told. Our ambassador, the Military Governor, sundry generals—even Rommel himself. They're all extremely interested in their immediate future."

"Aren't you?"

Before Reckzeh could reply, concealed loudspeakers flooded the basement with soft, languorous music. A woman's voice began to croon a sentimental French ballad. Ulitzky, who could guess what it portended, broke out in a sweat. "Don't be too hard on them, Erich," he said. "I'm willing to bet it was an accident—an unfortunate coincidence."

Reckzeh merely smiled. "Can you find your own way out?"

The wine cellar, another bare, rectangular chamber, had mottled stone walls and a musty smell left over from the wine that had once been stored there.

The three men—Focke, Herwig, and Patzig—allowed Koch to shepherd them inside without a word. All were veteran agents with long experience in the field, and none had protested when he announced on their return that Reckzeh's orders were to detain them until further notice. They were tired after their long drive and disheartened by the failure of their mission. Now, for the first time, the spirit of self-preservation stirred.

"Hey, Koch, what's the form?" The speaker was Patzig, the eldest of the three, a sandy-haired man with a foxy face. "What happens now?"

Even in here, music was seeping from a loudspeaker mounted above the door. "*J'attendrai*," sang the treacly voice, "*le jour et la nuit j'attendrai toujours ton retour . . .*"

"What's he planning to do with us?" Patzig's tone was suddenly shrill and apprehensive.

Koch's initial sympathy for the trio vanished. The fear they exuded transformed the emotion into its diametrical opposite. "You're in big trouble," he snapped, unaware that Reckzeh had appeared in the doorway and was listening.

"Strip, the three of you." Reckzeh came in and closed the door behind him. "Face the wall." He didn't raise his voice, which matched the monotony of the music from the loudspeaker. "Move, if you know what's good for you."

The men glanced at each other and began to undress, their movements stiff and awkward. Nudity made them look still more defenseless.

"Hands on the wall and spread your legs."

They obeyed. The aura of fear given off by their naked bodies, their twitching shoulder blades and tightly clenched buttocks, was almost palpable. Their labored breathing mingled with the music.

"J'attendrai, car l'oiseau qui s'enfuit vient chercher l'oubli dans son nid . . ."

Reckzeh stepped over the clothes on the floor, fastidiously spurning them with the toe of one gleaming shoe. "Your gun," he said to Koch, holding out his hand.

Koch shook his head, but simultaneously groped for the holster on his hip and opened the flap.

"I thought I'd made myself clear." Reckzeh surveyed the three naked backs. "Your orders were to bring him back alive, and you turned up with a corpse. If there's one thing I hate, it's slipshod work."

Koch put the Walther in Reckzeh's outstretched hand, powerless to protest. He held his breath as Reckzeh extended his arm and placed the muzzle against the neck of the man on the left, just where the hairline began.

The man on the left was Patzig, but it was Focke, the youngest of the three, who gingerly, inch by inch, turned his head and stared at the gun. The blood drained from his face and he gave a sort of groan. His shoulders sagged, his palms slid down the wall.

Darting forward, Koch seized Focke under the arms and heaved him erect. It was fear that galvanized him, not another fit of compassion. He knew, only too well, that human frailty sickened Reckzeh and rendered him capable of any act, however irrational.

Reckzeh moved over and stood behind Focke. "If you prefer," he said indifferently, "I can start with you." He removed the magazine and slipped it into the pocket of his tuxedo.

Koch stared at the bulge in the soft white material. His fear persisted even now. He felt his own neck muscles go taut when Reckzeh cocked the pistol and applied it to the base of Focke's skull. This time he squeezed the trigger. Light-footed, he stepped behind the other two in turn. He cocked the gun twice more, and twice more his finger tightened on the trigger. Three times the drowsy music was punctuated by the metallic click of the bolt slamming home.

Reckzeh took two paces to the rear and handed Koch the pistol, then the magazine. Very slowly, crossing their hands over their genitals in an instinctive, protective gesture, the three men turned around. The expression on their faces betrayed a lingering disbelief that their ordeal was over: their execution had been only symbolic.

Koch followed Reckzeh out of the cellar. Reckzeh didn't speak until they were back upstairs in the brightly lit entrance hall. Then he said, "They can go—for now. Tell them to get some sleep and report to my office at ten o'clock sharp."

Koch made every effort to hide his relief. "Certainly, Standartenführer."

"Ulitzky's sending a meat wagon for the body." Reckzeh paused at the foot of the stairs, one hand on the newel post, the other kneading his brow as if he had a headache. "Try to locate General Oberg for me. Have him put through to my office."

"Mikosch called. Colonel von Steinberg's off to Trier. Mikosch doesn't know why, but he'll call again as soon as he finds out."

"What about that personal possession of Berger's he was supposed to get hold of?"

"Still no luck, I'm afraid."

"It's important to me, Koch."

"Yes, Standartenführer." Koch stood watching as Reckzeh climbed the stairs. His patent leather pumps made almost no sound.

6

London

FROM WHERE HE WAS STANDING in Portman Square, Kacew could see searchlights probing the sky with smoky white fingers. Bells clanged urgently in the distance as ambulances and fire engines sped about their business.

The No. 53 bus had dumped its passengers when the air raid warning sounded. Everyone else had dashed to the nearest subway station while Kacew continued his journey on foot.

The searchlight beams meshed and separated, weaving intricate patterns against a dark backcloth. All at once, with feverish urgency, they converged on a single sector.

Kacew saw the trapped plane, but only in his imagination. All he could discern with the naked eye was the illuminated underside of a cloud. He couldn't even tell for sure whether it was a cloud or the smoke from burning buildings, yet he could visualize the pilot in his cockpit, dazzled by the luminous fingers that held him captive, and share the impotence he must be feeling at this moment.

To the northeast, the sky glowed red. Hackney again? Kacew himself had been bombed out there. He recalled the night vividly—the muffled thud of bombs exploding all around, the crash of collapsing masonry, a street hemmed in by flames. A warden had run up and seized his arm, trying to hustle him into a shelter. He'd smiled and shown his special pass, so the man gave up, doubtless dismissing him as a crazy foreigner. How, after all, could Kacew have explained the fascination danger held for him?

He tore his eyes away from the spectacle overhead and set off across Portman Square. As always when he approached Braille House, he was struck by its resemblance to the Hôtel Lutétia in Paris. Presumably named after its architect, it was a four-storied building constructed of the same pale sandstone and had a similar array of fleurons and wrought iron balcony grilles. Radio masts on the roof, jutting into the sky like spears, completed the likeness.

Instead of using the main entrance, an imposing excrescence protected by blast walls of sandbags, he turned down a side street. The sign on the inconspicuous door said "Tradesmen." He thumbed the button and the door swung open.

The interior was bleak, colorless, odorless. He walked up to the glass cubbyhole and slid his pass across the counter.

"Good evening, Howard."

"Evening." The man's face was utterly impassive. He had lost his left arm. The stump twitched a little as he rubber-stamped a slip of paper and pushed it back, together with Kacew's pass.

"Get that signed and hand it in when you leave."

That was all he'd ever said, night after night for over a year. Kacew's exchange of greetings with the guard outside the elevator was just as devoid of warmth.

"Good evening, Colvin."

"Evening."

They always contrived to keep their distance, these cold and frosty Britishers. Kacew felt a resurgence of anger at the prospect of seeing Gahagan again.

He left the elevator in the basement. Before him stretched a long expanse of gleaming linoleum. Naked bulbs glowed above the doors flanking the corridor, some green, some red. Turning a corner, Kacew paused outside the door marked "XX Personnel Only."

The room was a sterile place with pale gray walls and merciless lighting that drained every face of color. Gahagan and a radio technician were seated at a pair of desks. Slowly and silently, a red sweep hand circled the big round clock on the wall.

Gahagan glanced up from some typewritten sheets. The furrows on either side of his nose looked deeper than ever. "How are things up top?" he asked. "Is it a bad one?"

"Hackney," said Kacew. He stopped short as if even that were one word too many. It was impossible, in these clinical surroundings, to imagine that people were actually dying as he spoke, or that the room had any connection, however remote, with the war.

"What's eating you?"

"I could use some of your vodka."

"Still feeling low?"

"I feel lousy—and redundant."

"Stop harping, can't you?" Gahagan got up from the desk. He knew the disease that was afflicting Kacew; he'd observed the symptoms in himself for long enough. They still troubled him occasionally, and he was nearly ten years older. There was only one remedy—active service —and no possibility of using it. He recalled how Sir Graham had taken him aside after the last conference.

"How's Cato these days?"

"Restless, edgy. He keeps pestering me for a field assignment. Pretty thankless, his present role."

"Watch him like a hawk, Jeremy. Poles have plenty of virtues but no sense of proportion. Keep him on a tight rein."

"I can't keep it any tighter."

Gahagan banished the recollection. "We've got work to do," he said. He picked up the sheaf of typescript and led the way into an adjoining room. Laid out on a circular table in the center were paper, scissors, glue, and a tray of colored pencils. There was a safe in one corner and a photographic blowup on the wall, a section of the French coast taken from the sea. Chalk-white cliffs fringed the shore.

They seated themselves at the table. Gahagan pushed the typewritten sheets across. "Better get a move on, you're later than usual."

"Is there really no chance of a different assignment, Jeremy?"

"I already told you."

"After the invasion?"

Gahagan didn't reply at once. He stared at the blowup.

"I can't make any promises."

"But you'll ask?"

"Yes."

"And they'll say no?"

"Probably."

Kacew pulled the first of the sheets toward him and started reading. He shook his head, took a pencil, and crossed out a word. "Sounds suspect."

"What does?"

"This bit here: 'Your query of May 3. Confirm transfer of crack 6th Airborne Division . . .' Maybe it is a 'crack' formation, but I wouldn't bother to ram the point home. Berger knows me too well."

"Then cut it out," Gahagan said testily.

Kacew gave a wry smile. "I'm *his* agent, remember?" He toiled away at the typewritten draft, altering a word here, shortening a sentence there. The process was so routine, it left his thoughts free to roam. "What ever made him think I'd work for him?"

"Who?"

"Berger."

"Give it a rest, for God's sake."

"But what made him so certain, Jeremy? A Polish officer, agreeing to work for the Germans . . . What made him bank on talking me into it?"

"It took a year—and a death sentence. He hung onto the girl too, don't forget. She was his security."

Kacew looked up. His dark face had turned pale. "Is she still with him?" It was a question he'd never asked before.

"I don't know."

"You mean you wouldn't tell me if you did. Did you ever forward my message to her?"

"You honestly thought I would?"

"No."

"You know the rule: a man who changes sides has no past." Gahagan got up and walked over to the safe. He took out a buff manila envelope and put it on the table. "Better start enciphering."

Kacew hesitated. "The Germans never located our Paris transmitter in spite of their new D/F equipment. It was Berger who tracked us down single-handed, the easy way: he found a member of our group who was willing to betray us."

"If it's any consolation to you, all our agents find Paris a hot spot to work in, particularly since Berger took over the counterespionage section."

"He was so damned patient, Jeremy. He waited until he could catch the whole group together. We were celebrating our first anniversary."

"Drop the subject. What's the point?"

"He asked me to work for them right away, that very first night. Imagine what it was like, Jeremy: German MPs surrounding the apartment and sealing off our escape routes; two men with submachine guns bursting into the room; the room itself, champagne on the table, all of us sitting there, couriers and radio operators included, the transmitter in the room next door, the code book. And then, Berger's grand entrance . . ."

Gahagan was feeling more and more uncomfortable. He wished

Kacew would stop. Berger was a kind of obsession with him, especially here in this room.

"Berger had just made first lieutenant," Kacew went on. "He was so pleased with himself, so smug. My God, I thought, what a cocky bastard! And then he smiled at me and suggested we have a word in private."

"You told us all this when you were debriefed."

"Not this part, Jeremy, it would have sounded too farfetched. We went into the kitchen together and Berger offered me a cigarette. He had a silver cigarette case, I remember. I refused. He must have known I'd reject any approach he made, but he wasn't discouraged. 'We've enough evidence to charge your entire group with espionage,' he said, 'and you know what that would mean. However, I've decided to make you an offer: work for us instead—for the Abwehr.' He wanted to keep our transmitter in operation. In return, he undertook to see that we were treated like prisoners of war, not spies. In other words, he promised to keep us alive—he, Berger, a humble lieutenant! What made him think I'd take him seriously? 'Think it over,' he told me. 'You can have the time it takes me to finish this cigarette.' I just stared at him, but he didn't lose his temper. He finished his cigarette, still smiling, and stubbed it out in the sink. Then he said, 'If you change your mind, my name's Berger. You can contact me anytime.' Now do you see why I didn't take him seriously at first?"

A telephone started ringing in the room next door. The duty technician answered it. "Mr. Gahagan," he called, "it's for you."

Gahagan rose and left the room. A moment later he stuck his head round the door. "I'll be back by transmission time."

Kacew opened the buff envelope and took out the code book and Abwehr key. The key was a slim volume coming apart at the spine from long use, an English edition of Joseph Conrad's *Heart of Darkness*. That had been Berger's idea. Kacew's Abwehr code name, Joseph, was of similar origin. Had Berger chosen it as an appeal to Polish national pride?

Kacew leafed through the book until he turned up the page to be used on Friday, May 12. None of the messages sent to Paris was composed by him. Aside from the fact that he enciphered and transmitted them, his contribution to them was minimal.

Although Gahagan had never taken him into his confidence, it was inevitable that Kacew should, as time went by, have discerned a pattern in the messages, if only because of the queries and instructions Berger radioed back from Paris. There was no mistaking the growing urgency of his requests that Joseph should concentrate on one particular line of inquiry. Not even Gahagan's stubborn silence could conceal that pointers to an invasion were Berger's overriding interest.

Kacew didn't know how much of what he transmitted was true or false, but it was noticeable, especially of late, that more and more of his messages referred to an invasion force assembled in Southeast England. They reported that this army, deployed in the counties of Surrey, Sussex, and Kent, beside the narrowest part of the Channel and opposite the Pas-de-Calais, was being continuously reinforced with men and equipment.

To make the Germans believe that this was where the attack would be launched? If so, where would the landing really take place? These were points on which Kacew usually forbade himself to speculate, and he did so tonight.

Gahagan still hadn't returned when Kacew finished enciphering the text. He replaced the code book and key in their envelope. The technician came in and unlocked the door of the radio room, then switched on the set to warm it up.

"Five minutes to go," he announced.

Kacew picked up the text and followed him in. The radio room was even more sterile, even more remote from the outside world, than the other rooms. He seated himself at the transmitter, flexing his fingers like a concert pianist.

He had no precise idea of where the Abwehr's set was located—in what building or part of Paris. He was just as ignorant of the identity of the other operator, who would now be sitting likewise over his set. He only knew the stranger's "handwriting," just as the stranger knew his. It was as unique and unmistakable as a fingerprint. That, he thought bitterly, was the sole source of his importance to Gahagan.

He heard footsteps behind him, then Gahagan's voice: "One minute to go."

Kacew's hand poised itself over the Morse key. The voice behind his back began to check off the seconds. At 2400 hours London time, an hour ahead of the clocks in Paris, he sent his call sign.

Joseph—Joseph—Joseph . . .

He waited tensely. When there was no response, he repeated the call sign. His fingers felt stiff, almost paralyzed. Holy Mother of God, he thought, I need a drink.

He changed frequency, switched to receive, and waited again. Moments later Paris replied loud and clear, tuned to perfection: his signal had been received.

Kacew switched back to transmit. He could think of nothing but the vodka he'd left to chill in the ice compartment of the refrigerator at Paddington. The frost-filmed bottles took shape in his mind's eye, vivid as a hallucination. Then they vanished, and the vacuum in his head was filled with the monotonous cheeping produced by his fingers on the Morse key.

7

Paris

THE VILLA WAS IN MONTMARTRE, in a quiet side street not far from the Sacré-Coeur. Nothing could be seen above the high wall surrounding the property except the roof and the trees in the garden. The garden itself was a wilderness. The gravel paths and flower beds were invisible, overgrown with waist-high grass and littered with rotting leaves from last winter and the winters before that.

Punctually at seven every morning, a man in a track suit and sneakers emerged from the gate and set off down the street at a loping run, to return an hour later, his flushed face streaming with sweat. The same routine was repeated at five in the afternoon. Every night, with equal regularity, a gray Simca sedan pulled up outside the gate. Another man, older than the first, got out and let himself in with a key of his own. He seldom spent longer than half an hour on the premises before driving off again.

The Simca had appeared tonight, true to form, and Berger and the radio operator were closeted in the attic, a room with sloping walls and a single dormer window, carefully blacked out.

"Signal's weak tonight," the operator muttered.

Berger, peering over his shoulder, watched him jot down four-letter groups on a pad. The first few lines had been scrawled in haste, but the characters were growing neater and more legible.

So far, Berger had managed to restrain himself. Now he stepped back, fished out his old silver case, and lit a cigarette. He was wearing an inconspicuous gray suit.

The attic had once been used for storing hairpieces, hats, and feather boas. The boxes were still there, whole shelves of them, and the mingled scents of perfume and powder hung in the air.

Faint though they were, the bursts of Morse escaping from the headphones seemed to fill the room. Suddenly, they ceased. Gehrts, tracksuited as usual, tapped out an acknowledgment and tore the sheet off the pad. He half turned and handed it to Berger. "He's coming through stronger now," he said. There was something soft and pampered about the radio operator's face. His fair hair, tousled by the headset, was thin for a man of only twenty-nine.

Berger sat down at the table. The cloth-covered copy of Joseph Conrad's *Heart of Darkness*, one of a pair he'd found on a bookstall beside the Seine, was lying open at the relevant page, but he didn't set to work right away. Smoking as he listened idly to the chatter of Morse behind him, he thought of the first night—the first signal he and Gehrts had received in this room from Roman Kacew, alias Joseph.

It seemed only yesterday, all that waiting. They had maintained a listening watch for weeks and months after Schneevogel reported from Lisbon that Joseph was on his way to London by air. It was the same thing night after night: Gehrts hunched over the silent set, checking his frequency, staring expectantly at the dull gray box that refused to come to life. Six whole months they waited, wondering if the plan had misfired, hoping that the wary British would yield to temptation.

Gehrts had probably been motivated by a straightforward fear that his special status—an easy life, pleasant surroundings, civilian freedom and independence—might be revoked. Continued failure to establish contact with Joseph would mean reassignment to the Lutétia and routine duties in the monitoring room.

And he, Berger, still a lieutenant in those days—why had he sat there with bated breath, forehead and armpits sticky with perspiration. Summer had come, and the attic was almost as much of a furnace at night as in the daytime.

He had simultaneously yearned for the moment and dreaded it. Ambition required his plan to work; prudence warned him that if it did—if the radio started pecking out a signal from Joseph in London—he would have passed the point of no return.

"Let's be quite clear about this, Berger: once the operation's under way, there can be no going back."

He seemed to hear the voice once more, quiet and uninsistent, utterly undramatic, as if Canaris were speaking of a practical joke, not high treason . . .

The attic was becoming oppressive, making him breathless, preying on his nerves as all confined spaces did—or was it his recollection of the meeting that had started it all? This was the second time he'd recalled it within a few hours.

Berger could endure the room no longer. He rose and went over to Gehrts. "You finish off," he said, laying a hand on his shoulder. "Decode the text yourself." Gehrts was unable to hear him because of the headset, but he knew what to do.

Berger breathed easier once the door closed behind him. He made his way downstairs to the drawing room. The décor, unaltered since the villa's former owners fled from Paris, resembled a set from a Folies Bergère review. The Art Deco furniture and jukebox were two inches deep in white, shag-pile carpet. White predominated in the music room next door, which was lit by a Tiffany lamp on the Pleyel concert grand, also white. In the pool of light stood a framed photograph of three young women, all with identical platinum blond hair and identical smiles. The Molly Sisters, a trio of much acclaimed and highly paid American review stars based in Paris, were so reluctant to quit France that they'd had to clear out overnight when America entered the war. Their villa had then stood empty until the Abwehr requisitioned it for radio communication with Joseph. The main reason was geographical. Montmartre being the highest part of Paris, the site was an aid to reception.

Records lay strewn across the floor of the music room. So did the dumbbells Gehrts used for his workouts. Glucose tablets spilled from a bowl on the massive phonograph, which had been left on. Irritated by the general chaos, Berger walked over and turned it off before going to the telephone. He hesitated for a moment, then lifted the receiver and dialed a number.

"Jean Daniel here," he said. It was one of the aliases he used from time to time. "Has Emanuele come in yet?"

He heard voices in the background, punctuated by the click of billiard balls. Then came the elder Spirito's voice, deep and husky, with a strong Corsican accent.

"It's better you shouldn't call here."

"Did you discover anything?"

"We don't owe you any more favors."

"I could be useful to you sometime."

"We haven't been there for over a week."

The SD relied mainly on Frenchmen for torturing prisoners under interrogation. Whether this was common practice or one of Reckzeh's idiosyncrasies, Berger didn't know, but the Spiritos' services were regularly employed at his Avenue Foch headquarters. The brothers were alert to any fluctuations in the balance of power among the German authorities, and it was clear from the Corsican's tone that the Abwehr's stock had slumped.

"What's on your mind, Emanuele?"

"Could we talk about passports sometime?"

"Maybe, it depends."

"Very well. The name means nothing to me. I've never heard it mentioned or seen it on a list. No one by the name of Schneevogel has been taken to Avenue Foch or interrogated there."

"I'm pretty sure he's in Paris."

"A Citroën van turned up there yesterday evening. Later on, an ambulance collected a corpse. The guard I spoke to didn't know the man's name."

"He wasn't interrogated?"

"Reckzeh showed up too. Koch warned the sentries that he was in a bad temper. Does that tell you anything?"

"Perhaps."

"Don't waste time trying to call me here again."

"You're leaving Paris?"

"I'll be in touch about the passports."

The line went dead. Questions were milling around in Berger's head. A corpse? Schneevogel dead? If so, had he talked first? What had Reckzeh hoped to achieve by abducting him? Steinberg had said that even the SD needed something to go on—a suspicion of some kind. But what was the basis of their suspicion? What had given rise to it?

"This conversation never took place . . ."

Inexorably, Berger returned yet again to June 1942 and his meeting with the Admiral. In his office a few hours ago the recollection had imparted a sense of security. Now he wondered if their plan did not, after all, contain some fatal flaw.

"Lieutenant Berger?"

It was his first time alone with Canaris, not during one of the Admiral's official visits to the Lutétia, but really alone.

"Tell me about yourself, Lieutenant."

The voice was soft, the handshake diffident and aloof. Canaris seemed unaffected by the heat in spite of his double-breasted suit. The hair beneath his dark felt hat was silver.

How much could Berger really recall after two years? How had he responded to the question, and what had he said about himself? He only knew how obsessed he'd been with the thought of submitting his plan.

"You say he's agreed, this Captain Kacew? A Pole, you say?"

"A Polish officer, formerly a captain in the Polish Air Force. Fought with the Polish volunteers in France. Trained as an agent in England and parachuted into France. Gathered intelligence and radioed it to London until arrested."

Berger had come straight from Fresnes Prison and his latest interview with Kacew, a discussion of the finer points.

"And he's prepared to work for us in England? Remarkable."

"He took a long time to make up his mind."

"You mentioned something about a prearranged escape."

"It could take place two weeks from now, on July 14. That's Bastille Day, so all our units will be preoccupied with the possibility of demonstrations. I propose to collect Kacew from Fresnes by car and drive him to the Lutétia for further questioning. We'll have an accident on the way—a collision with a truck. Kacew's in poor physical shape. He'll be handcuffed, too, but he knows his life is at stake. There'll be a safe house a couple of blocks away. He can hide there."

Berger had continued to expound the details of his beloved plan, awed by the Admiral's presence but eager to gain his consent.

"He'll lie low till nightfall. I'll get him out of the city after dark and sneak him down to Portugal by stages, via Spain. Once he's in Lisbon, Schneevogel can take charge of him."

"How do you propose to feed him into England?"

"Word of his successful escape will have reached the British by the time he surfaces in Lisbon. He won't have to make a move himself—they'll contact him themselves. He was their agent. It'll all seem quite natural."

Once again, Berger had no precise recollection of what came next, only of the suspense that gripped him, of the interminable silence that succeeded his words, of gravel crunching beneath their feet as they circled the windmill, of Longchamp racetrack and the horses training there, which seemed to claim the Admiral's undivided attention.

"A Polish officer," Canaris said at last, "—a former British agent? I don't see what there'd be to prevent him from telling them that we planned to use him as a double agent."

"This is his only chance of survival."

"Things would look different once he was at liberty."

"I'm also holding a hostage—a girl. She was his courier."

"That won't deter him, not if he's the kind of man you say. An agent is an agent first and last. In my experience, human ties don't count when a person has espionage in his blood. No, Berger, he'll turn himself over to the British and blow your plan sky-high. We'll have an agent in England, but he'll be worthless to us. His reports will be bogus, skillfully concocted but bogus."

Berger was already mourning the demise of his scheme, the collapse of his laboriously constructed edifice, when Canaris came to a halt. He removed his hat and patted the interior dry with a handkerchief. "We'll try it," he said. "Let him go. They'll welcome him with open arms."

"So you don't think it'll work?"

There was a strange smile on the Admiral's face, half shy, half furtive. "They may not be able to resist. Let's wait and see if they play. If they do, so will we."

Had Berger grasped the implication right away, or was he still too obsessed with the idea of scoring off men like Steinberg? The Admiral's next words put his intention beyond doubt.

"The question, of course, is this: Are you willing and able to see it through?"

He couldn't recall his reply, if any. He could only hear the echo of the Admiral's voice.

"This war, Berger—we should never have allowed ourselves to be dragged into this shameful war. All we can do now is end it as quickly as possible. Whenever there's a chance of doing something, making some contribution, we must seize it. That's why your plan appeals to me. To repeat, though: Are *you* prepared to see it through?"

It was a question Canaris must often have asked himself—pondered, weighed, and examined. Would he have voiced it at all if he hadn't thought Berger capable of treason in a worthy cause?

"Can you live with such a secret, Berger? You won't be able to cite our little talk in your defense. This conversation never took place. Once the operation's under way, there can be no going back. You can only follow it through. Are you equal to it?"

Two years, Berger reflected as he stood there in the unreal surroundings of the villa's music room—how did he feel after two long years? His career had prospered, bringing him certain privileges, but what else? Even his awareness of committing treason—high treason, though

Canaris represented it as an honorable, commendable course of action —was dwindling. Treason had become a mere habit, devoid of triumph and illusions.

Silence. That was the worst thing of all, perhaps, having to resist the urge to tell someone, confide in someone. That was the ever present temptation . . .

Gehrts came in, his hair still tousled and his face as flushed as if he'd been training. He looked more of an athlete standing up. It was easier to believe that he'd once run four hundred meters fast enough to win a bronze at the Berlin Olympics in 1936. That was why he'd been assigned to the Abwehr when war broke out, to conserve the precious legs that might yet win a gold for Germany. Gehrts was an Abwehr outsider like Berger himself, which may have been Berger's reason for selecting him. There would be no gold for Gehrts, not now.

"Here it is."

Gehrts handed Berger two typewritten sheets in clear. Berger skimmed through them, not really absorbing the sense, wondering again what had aroused Reckzeh's suspicions.

"You destroyed your notes?"

"Of course."

"Are the key and code book back in the safe?"

"I've never forgotten yet, have I?" Gehrts ran a hand through his sparse fair hair. "Two years in London—how does he stand the strain?"

For a moment Berger felt tempted to picture Kacew and his life in London—Roman Kacew, the agent he'd arrested in the Rue Vercingétorix apartment, the prisoner in Fresnes, the man he'd last seen just before he crossed the frontier into Portugal. *That* man still existed for him, with his swarthy face and bold eyes, but Kacew in London? Kacew in London was Joseph, and Joseph was just a cipher, a code, a nightly influx of dots and dashes.

"Anything else?" Berger asked. "How did he react to his Iron Cross?"

"He didn't. He simply asked us to expedite that last payment. Says he can't pay his subagents unless he gets it and threatens to close down until he does."

Whoever Joseph's London controller was, thought Berger, he knew his job. Joseph's work was never made to seem easy. His messages conveyed that he was operating under hazardous conditions, forever in fear of detection, subject to nervous tension and emotional strain. The irony of it, Berger reflected, was that Joseph had nothing to fear from the British; the only threat lay on this side of the Channel.

"About the money. Did you tell him to get in touch with Chavero at the Mexican Embassy?"

"Yes."

Berger handed the sheets back. "Pass this on to Berlin. When's the transmission scheduled?"

"Midnight plus thirty."

Berger walked on ahead, through the drawing room and into the hall. A bicycle was propped against the wall beneath a Folies Bergère poster of the Molly Sisters.

"You still train every day?"

Gehrts nodded. His round face, rather on the plump side now, turned even pinker. "Will you be coming tomorrow?"

"I may skip a day. I'll call you."

Berger switched off the hall light and stepped quickly out into the weed-infested garden. He didn't shake hands or say good night. Gehrts, too, represented a temptation to confide in someone, and it was wiser not to nourish such a feeling.

The steep, tortuous streets of Montmartre were deserted. He crossed the Seine by way of the unlit Pont Royal, following a route that took him past the Lutétia, with its armed sentries, and the sinister bulk of the Cherche-Midi Prison. Place St. Sulpice, which was just as deserted, made an even bigger and more theatrical impression than usual. Two French gendarmes and a German military patrol were standing outside the police station.

Reaching the Jardin du Luxembourg, Berger turned into Rue Guynemer and pulled up outside a *fin de siècle* house on a level with the puppet theater. It wasn't until he got out to open the gate—the sky was clear and cloudless, with a sprinkling of stars—that he saw the words daubed on the wall in red paint:

MORT AUX TRAÎTRES!

Berger had occupied an apartment in the house ever since his transfer to Paris. He passed for an ordinary tenant and never appeared there in uniform. The card outside his door read "Berger," as unremarkable a name in France as it was in Germany. He spoke the language without an accent and lived with a French girl. It would have been ironical had the threat been leveled at him, a German officer. Could it, he wondered, have been meant for Jannou?

He unlocked the gate, parked the Simca in the courtyard, and locked up again. The elevator was already on the ground floor. He walked over to it, then changed his mind and started to climb the stairs.

Jannou . . . Yet another person he could have confided in—in her more readily than anyone else. The urge to do so was a physical ache, a nagging pain in the lips.

8

London

SIRENS WERE SOUNDING THE ALL CLEAR by the time Kacew got back to his new quarters in Paddington. The same smell of wax polish and disinfectant greeted him when he opened the front door, mitigated now by a whiff of something else. Without stopping to take his coat off, he went straight to the kitchen.

He opened the refrigerator and removed a bottle of vodka from the ice compartment. Then, still without putting a light on, he groped his way to the living room. The chintz upholstery and the cloth over the birdcage were paler than the surrounding darkness. He sat down on the sofa. The bottle was so cold that it almost stuck to his fingers.

Paris would have decoded his signal by now. Did Berger supervise the process himself? Presumably. And the Iron Cross—had that been his idea too?

Kacew got up and turned the light on. He removed his coat, uncorked the bottle, and took a swig before fetching himself a glass from the fumed oak sideboard. The coins for the gas meter were still neatly stacked on the mantelpiece. He listened for signs of life upstairs, but the house was silent. No footsteps, no radio.

Alison Mills . . . She'd looked so trim in her discreet woolen dress with the discreet little brooch at the neck—so very English. Was that the other scent in the house, her cologne? Lieutenant Mills, he felt sure, was made of the same stuff as Gahagan. She wouldn't understand why he was sitting there, drinking vodka and thinking of a German intelligence officer in Paris.

He got up again and went over to the fireplace. Reaching for a coin, he knocked the whole pile over. Shillings cascaded onto the hearth. He retrieved one and put it in the slot, turned on the tap and struck a match. The gas ignited with a dull plop. The birds stirred under their cloth. He made a mental note to give them some fresh water.

He switched off the light and settled himself on the sofa. The glass reflected the glow of the gas fire as he filled it and drank. His death cell at Fresnes had been bathed in harsh white light, twenty-four hours a day. In his previous cell he'd spent 221 days in semidarkness.

Executions at Fresnes took place in the morning, at first light. Was there some special reason for this? Were the men of the firing squad fresher at daybreak—were they better marksmen? The priest had come to hear his confession. He was a redheaded German army chaplain so gigantic that the makeshift altar on the chair looked toylike in comparison.

"Is there anything else I can do for you?" he asked eventually.

Kacew's pride told him to say nothing, but his flesh rebelled, commanding him to speak. He nodded. "I'd like to see Lieutenant Berger."

Then he'd waited, appalled at his own weakness. For how long? A few hours, a day? Memory failed him at this point, but he knew they'd come to fetch him. His next picture was of the interrogation room and Berger with his back to him at the window, trying to open it.

"Do sit down." It hadn't sounded like an order, more like an apology for having forgotten that prisoners weren't permitted to sit down uninvited. Berger continued to struggle with the window, and Kacew thought it must be because of the foul stench given off by his prison uniform.

Berger finally gave up. He came over and sat down across the table from him. "I'm sorry we have to meet again under these circumstances." He put his cigarette case on the table with a lighter beside it, as though Kacew might be offended by a direct invitation to smoke.

"What's happened to the girl—to Jannou?"

Berger didn't reply at once. He showed no surprise. His expression conveyed that he was simply pondering the question and its implications. Realizing that he had blundered, Kacew went on, "Her function in the group was unimportant. She did little more than make coffee and run errands." He paused. "How much time do we have?"

"As much as you like. I'm a good listener." Berger lit a cigarette, still without offering one to Kacew.

"Where is she? Are you still holding her?"

"Yes, at the Cherche-Midi."

"Hasn't she been tried yet?"

Berger flicked the ash off his cigarette and gestured as if to say, "That's not the way we handle these things."

"How has she been treated?"

"If I answer that question, you may think I'm trying to pressure you."

"Tell me!"

"You're an experienced agent, Kacew. You've been trained to withstand interrogation—and worse. You must have known she wasn't prepared for such an eventuality. How old was she when you took her on —eighteen? How could you have employed her in a trade like ours?"

Kacew gritted his teeth. "Go on."

"Counterespionage isn't an Abwehr monopoly. We have some competitors here on our doorstep: the SD."

"But this is an Abwehr case."

Berger stubbed out his cigarette and lit another. "Unbeknown to us, she was"—he hesitated—"questioned by the SD. They're always trying to prove how out-of-date our methods are. They prefer to use their own."

"What did they do to her?"

"She may not wish to tell you. I certainly won't."

He didn't seem particularly impressive, this German, as long as he sat there and said nothing. When he spoke, a transformation occurred. Berger's voice was, without doubt, the most powerful weapon in his arsenal—his principal means of manipulating and influencing others.

"You mean I can see her?"

"It might be arranged."

"Does your original offer still stand?"

"Circumstances have changed. Your Paris transmitter is out of commission. You're no use to us here."

"Would you let the girl go?"

"Would you go back to England for the Abwehr, as our agent?"

Berger smiled for the first time, outwardly calm and composed, but Kacew could detect his sudden surge of excitement and sense the thoughts that were racing through his head. Beneath that serene exterior was a man whose whole career hinged on the outcome of a single operation.

Returning to reality and the present, to the living room of the house in Paddington, Kacew made a surprising discovery: Berger must have found the weeks and months of suspense quite as long as they'd seemed to him in his prison cell.

He thrust the empty bottle aside and tried to stand up, meaning to fetch the other bottle from the kitchen, but flopped back onto the sofa. Then he heard someone moving outside in the hall.

Alison Mills appeared in the doorway. She came toward him in a sudden blaze of light. Her eyes were very blue.

"Must you?" he groaned. "You're blinding me."

The overhead light went out. The next thing he noticed was the scent of her cologne as she knelt and began to pick up the scattered coins. She was wearing an ankle-length dressing gown of some blue material that clung to her body. It annoyed him that he should have noticed this and allowed it to disturb his train of thought.

"Do you come with the house?"

She straightened up, pale even in the glow from the gas fire, and steadied herself against the mantelpiece. With the perspicacity of the truly drunk, Kacew knew he'd scored a direct hit: he wasn't the first agent to have stayed here.

He stood up, successfully this time, and tottered off to the kitchen. She was still standing stiffly beside the fire when he came back with the other bottle, but the color had returned to her cheeks.

"You'll have an awful head tomorrow morning."

"How long have you been with the Firm?"

"Ages."

"Ever been across the Channel?"

"They sent me on a field training course, but I flunked it." She smiled. "Too impulsive, not calculating enough. Then Jeremy Gahagan offered me this job."

He tilted his head and drank, straight from the bottle. "There were girls in my Paris network."

"You really ought to put that bottle away."

"An agent's more secure with a woman around—less suspect. I lived with a French girl. I shouldn't have let her in on what I was doing, I know, but I couldn't keep her in the dark indefinitely."

"That was against the rules."

"She insisted on working for us. I warned her of the risks, but that was what attracted her, the possibility of death. She'd had an unhappy love affair—she'd even contemplated killing herself—so this seemed a better solution. If she lost her life, at least it would be *for* something—a 'worthwhile suicide.'"

"Is that what she called it?"

"She said some surprising things sometimes."

The gas fire was going out. The girl bent down and inserted another shilling in the slot.

"Her name was—is Jannou. With two *n*'s. She changed the spelling herself. Her mother was superstitious, apparently. She claimed it was bad luck to meddle with your given name . . ." Kacew lost the thread. He took another swig of vodka. "She stayed behind—that was part of the deal. She had to stay, to guarantee I wouldn't renege. I . . . I left the decision to her, but she was all in favor."

"Another form of worthwhile suicide?"

"She hated him. She didn't have to tell me, it was written all over her face. She was sitting at the table when they arrested us, and then Berger walked in . . . She didn't say a word. She didn't have to, the look she gave him said it all. I'm sure she . . . That can't have changed, not even after two years . . . She agreed because she hated him!"

"So you saw her again?"

"Yes, before I left Paris. He brought her to the apartment where I hid out till nightfall."

"Were you left alone with her?"

"She agreed—she understood why I'd gone along with the plan. Berger was our common enemy."

"Did you make love to her that last time?"

"What?" He stared at her till the vivid blue of her eyes made his head swim.

"I just wondered."

Kacew hauled himself to his feet. He walked unsteadily to the door, then turned. "The birds . . ." he said.

"I gave them some more food and water. What kind are they?"

"Canaries." He felt her arm around his shoulder, guiding him out into the hall and up the stairs.

"They're white. Can canaries be white?"

"That's what the dealer said they were."

It was all he could do to stand. His head was spinning and his legs had turned to jelly. He hated feeling so helpless. She opened the bedroom door and turned on the light without letting go of him.

She'd unpacked his things, he noticed. Laid out on an old-fashioned washstand were his razor, brush, shaving mug, and—for a man—surprisingly luxurious manicure set. At Fresnes, he'd kept his fingernails short by filing them on the concrete floor of his cell.

He sat down on the edge of the bed without knowing how he came to be there. She knelt and undid his laces, then helped him off with his jacket.

"You're an expert," he said.

"I'll get you an aspirin."

"I don't need one. They make me sick."

She lingered, looking down at him with both hands thrust awkwardly into the pockets of her dressing gown.

"You haven't been in touch with her since, I suppose?"

He grasped her meaning at once. "You know the rules and you know Gahagan. Anyone who changes sides has to kiss his past goodbye. Here, sit down beside me for a moment."

She did so without hesitation, as if she'd been expecting him to ask. He bunched the hair above her neck between his fingers and held it up to the light. "Nice color."

"Would you like me to stay with you?"

"I need someone to talk to, that's all."

"If you want to sleep with me, it's all right."

"Don't you have *any* illusions, damn it?" He let go of her hair.

"How many illusions do you expect a woman to have, after four years of war?"

"I'm too drunk," he mumbled, and sank back on the bed.

He either felt her undressing him or imagined it; whichever it was, he didn't resist. Darkness and silence closed in. Then he heard something. It wasn't in the room, or even in the house, and it sounded like a train on the move.

He propped himself on his elbows. She was still there, a dark figure silhouetted against the open window. The sound was real too: a train was pulling into Paddington Station.

Elsham Wolds, he thought with a sudden thrill of excitement. *Karski!*

He could see the airfield, the bombers lined up on the runway, the crews heading for their machines, laughing, arguing, horsing around, encumbered by the parachute packs that bobbed on their rumps at every step.

"Mustn't miss my train," he said thickly. Then he yielded to the gentle pressure of her hands on his shoulders and lay back again.

9

Paris

"Ausziehen! Go on, strip!"

"Hurry up, strip! Face the wall!"

Bewilderment overcame her. What did it mean, this sea of blinding light? Where was she? And the voice? How could a woman in a gray uniform have a man's voice and a man's face?

"Hands flat against the wall! Now bend down! Lower! Spread your legs! Wider!"

Her cell in the Cherche-Midi—yes. Hands were exploring her body, fingers probing her ears, her vagina, her anus.

"Nothing on her, the bitch!"

Then the scene changed. She was back in the Avenue Foch. From above, she could see the man's scalp showing through his sparse hair as he made a grab for her feet. She stared down at his balding head, his clawing hands, her feet with their painted toenails.

No, not again!

The instrument in his hands was new and shiny. One hand imprisoned her foot, the other held the pincers. Steel jaws closed on the end of the nail. Soft, sentimental music was coming from a loudspeaker:

"J'attendrai, le jour et la nuit j'attendrai toujours ton retour . . ."

She clenched her teeth and braced herself.

The cuticle at the base of the nail ruptured and the matrix filled with blood as the kneeling man proceeded, slowly but surely, to extract it. She stared at the blood oozing from the crescent-shaped rent. The music from the loudspeaker was drowned by a scream: hers.

The man gave the pincers a little shake and the nail fluttered to the floor. The jaws fastened on the next nail, but by that time she was awake, roused by the sound of her own cry.

She lay motionless, listening, then sat up in bed and switched on the light. The strapless nightgown left her shoulders bare, and she hugged them as she sat there with her knees drawn up, staring at her feet.

The nails had grown again, but unevenly. However much lacquer she applied, it couldn't conceal the fact that some were stunted and others reduced to mere sheaths of horny skin.

She heard a voice through the closed door, muffled and remote. Berger was talking to someone in German. Jannou's hostility toward him flared up, fueled by her nightmare.

She got out of bed. The raincoat was lying on a chair. For want of a bathrobe, she pulled it on over her nightgown. Berger was still on the phone. She could hear his voice through the living-room door, a deep and surprisingly melodious voice, even when he spoke German. She detested the language, with its rasping consonants and snarling vowels. To her it seemed a language composed entirely of imperatives—of commands. No one who spoke it had a right to sound as human or humane as Berger did.

Even when she first heard his voice in prison, in the Cherche-Midi's interrogation room, she'd realized at once how *dangerous* it was. The Germans fetched you from your cell starved of sympathy, hungry for any human emotion, and they knew it. They banked on it, hoping to dispel your vigilance and worm their way into your mind. They acted so friendly, sounded so innocuous, and then, when your guard was down, they struck. That was their technique, but you countered it with a technique of your own: you kept your mouth shut.

With Berger the position hadn't been as simple and straightforward. He never bullied, never threatened or lost patience. He made strategic withdrawals and left you to yourself. "Think it over," was his favorite expression.

Back in the darkness and solitude of your cell, your private hell, his voice lingered with you until, days or weeks later, all you could remember was how *good* you'd felt in his presence. Something inside you wanted—no, yearned—to hear his voice again . . .

Berger had finished phoning by the time she came in. He was leaning against the mantelpiece, sipping some coffee which he must have made himself. He was so preoccupied that he didn't notice her at once.

She stood there, drawing the belt of the raincoat tighter. He turned and looked at her inquiringly. She sometimes found it hard to distinguish the sightless eye from the good one. When he was tired, there seemed little difference between them.

"Like some coffee?" he asked.

"At this hour? What time is it, anyway?"

He put the cup down to look at his watch, but it wasn't on his wrist. "It must be after one. Anything wrong?"

"Nothing, just a dream. Don't you ever dream?"

"You came to the Lutétia. They told me you were waiting downstairs in the lobby, but you'd gone by the time I got there."

"I couldn't wait any longer."

"I tried this number."

"I know."

"Why didn't you answer?"

"Have you ever known me to use this phone?"

"What's the matter?"

She shook her head. "Nothing." Then she said, "It was one of those days. I laddered my last pair of stockings in the Métro this morning. Everything went wrong at the studio. Finally, this evening, a boy ran off with my bag."

"You've never come to the Lutétia before."

"All my papers were in the bag. I was scared of being stopped by a patrol. Is that good enough for you?" Her voice had hardened, as it always did when she suppressed her real feelings.

"Was it the slogan?"

"What slogan?"

"I phoned them. They're coming to remove it."

"What slogan?"

"It'll be gone by morning."

"You must think I'm a child. It takes more than a few splashes of paint to scare me."

"It's only one of the usual daubs."

"What is?"

" 'Mort aux traîtres.' "

Her belt was as tight as it would go, but she gave it another tug.

"They're all over the city," he said.

"That one was meant for me, though, wasn't it?"

"Why you?"

"A floozy who's thrown herself at the enemy."

"Please, Jannou."

"I'd like some coffee after all."

"I'll bring you a cup."

"Thanks, but not in here."

She hated these gloomy rooms, especially at night. The top-floor apartment had high stucco ceilings, ponderous mahogany furniture, somber wallpaper and curtains. Berger, who seemed indifferent to his surroundings, had rented the place furnished and left it just as it was. There were no personal touches, no photographs or pictures, and he received no mail there.

Without ever discussing the subject, they had evolved a way of coming and going at different times. If their paths crossed at all, it was in the kitchen, a sunless room overlooking an air well.

She sat down at the kitchen table. Berger poured her a cup of coffee and sat down facing her.

"All right," she said eventually, "truce."

"I didn't know we were at war."

"About the Lutétia," she said. "I had a sudden fit of panic in the lobby. I never thought it would happen, but with all those German uniforms around me . . . I just couldn't stand it anymore. I was furious with myself, but I couldn't."

"All your papers?"

She nodded.

"They'll have to be replaced. Leave it to me."

"Of course," she said acidly. "You've got my file."

"It'll be easier if I handle it."

"Thanks."

"What went wrong at the studio?"

"The negative your people promised us didn't turn up."

"Will you be working tomorrow?"

"No, we've had to interrupt our schedule."

"Perhaps we could go out for the day."

"Since when don't you work weekends?"

"There's some racing on. Longchamp tomorrow, Enghien Sunday."

"Are you keen on racing?"

He shrugged. "We could go for a drive in the country."

"I haven't been out of Paris for years."

"Well, would you like that?"

"My father took me for a ride in his new car once. He wound up dead, I survived by the skin of my teeth. That was my last drive in the country."

"It was only an idea."

For a moment it seemed that this conversation, too, would end like all the rest, stopped in its tracks by a recurrent feeling that they had something to tell each other but couldn't find the words. They felt safer wearing their masks, clinging to their customary roles.

Berger wouldn't help her break the ice, she knew. He became a different man off duty. In his official capacity he was always sure of himself; here she saw another Berger, awkward and uncertain, not knowing where to look or what to say. The residue of hatred from her dream had vanished, giving way to an emotion she couldn't identify. She only knew she wanted to talk.

She slid her hand across the table. "I'm always making good resolutions and breaking them." When he made no move to take her hand, she went on, "You didn't answer my question. Do you ever dream? Do you have nightmares sometimes?"

She saw him look down at her bare feet, with their painted, misshapen toenails.

"Not often." His voice was almost inaudible.

"When you do, what do you dream about?"

"Confined spaces. Being shut in."

"I thought so. You always stood at the window during those interrogations at the Cherche-Midi—it was all you could do to walk over to the table. We're four floors up here, but you never use the elevator. You don't like little movie theaters—you always sit at the end of the row, as near the exit as possible."

He glanced at her in surprise but said nothing. A tide of pain and pleasure flowed over her. She felt it in her legs, her thighs, her crotch: a desire to go to bed with Berger, right now, that very minute. It wasn't a romantic impulse, just a straightforward physical urge.

"Would you like to go to bed with me?"

He winced, but his discomfiture only accentuated her desire. "Why are you staring at me like that? Sex isn't a male monopoly, you know—women can take the initiative too. If you want me, why not be honest and say so?"

"Don't!" he snapped. "It doesn't suit you."

"You mean it doesn't fit your image of me."

His harsh, aggressive tone was something new in her experience. It angered her that he'd killed her original impulse.

"Never look back, press on regardless—that's what life has taught me," she said. "It's the only ideal I can afford, survival." She raised her feet and inspected the toes, with their ten vivid blotches of lacquer. "You couldn't graduate from a finer school."

"Jannou!"

But she got up and went back to the living room. He followed her. Although the windows were closed and the curtains drawn, they could hear a truck pulling up in the street below, right outside the house, then voices.

"I still hope it isn't true, sometimes," she said. "Roman Kacew, a Pole, a man who hated the Germans, working for you." Berger seemed about to say something. It wasn't the first time she'd sensed this hesitancy in him. She waited, but he preserved his usual silence.

"I never thought he'd really work for you. When you come back late, like tonight, does it mean you've been receiving a signal from him?"

"Yes."

"So you were right. I was wrong." She laughed, and surprisingly it sounded quite unforced. "It was easy at first—staying behind here seemed worthwhile. As long as I thought Roman had only pretended to accept your offer, I had my hatred and my sense of triumph to console me. Then, when his first signals arrived and you seemed so confident, I began to have doubts—it was hell. How did you talk him into it?"

"We made a deal."

"On your terms."

"Perhaps, but the fact remains that he's free. So are you."

"Am I?" She looked at Berger curiously, without hostility. "Free to go? Could I pack a bag and walk out, just like that?"

"Now would be an opportune time."

"So people keep telling me."

"It's in the air."

"You want me to go?"

"It would be logical and sensible, that's all I meant. If you're interested in survival, you shouldn't leave it too late."

"I'll think it over." At the door, she turned. "What about tomorrow?"

"You decide."

"Could we drive down to the sea? My father used to have a house at Trouville before the war—we always spent the summer vacation there. Is it too far?"

He shook his head.

[66]

"Could we stay the night?"

"If you'd like to."

"Yes, I think I would." She went out, still marveling at her desire for a man of whom she knew so little after two whole years.

10

Paris

RECKZEH, with his elbows propped on the roof of the Mercedes, was watching the three riders through the binoculars he always kept in the glove compartment. He found it as curiously pleasurable as ever, observing others without being observed himself.

It was early—just after 7 A.M.—and a thin film of mist floated above the racetrack, but it was the sort of mist that gave promise of a gloriously sunny day.

Oberg, an unmistakable figure with close-cropped hair, spurred his horse briskly over the hurdles and water jumps. The other two, a red-faced man and a dark-haired woman, cantered round them.

The Hippodrome d'Auteuil was the smaller of the Bois de Boulogne's two racetracks. Many of the houses nearby were occupied by senior members of the German hierarchy in Paris, so service officers and government officials could be seen out riding every morning in the park or on the racetrack itself.

The three riders turned off. Reckzeh saw them walking their horses side by side to the paddock. Oberg was deep in conversation with Gürtner, the Military Governor's chief legal adviser. Was it pure chance, Reckzeh wondered, that had taken them out riding together on this particular morning?

Horses and riders disappeared into the trees, heading for the stables and clubhouse.

Reckzeh lowered the binoculars. Not only was he in uniform; he had already visited his office to study Ulitzky's autopsy report and dictate his comments on it. Reckzeh was a man who never showed the effects of a night without sleep.

He got into the Mercedes and drove to the Pavillon Tyrolien, a local restaurant commandeered by the Germans and run by the Luftwaffe. The waiters were military personnel in white jackets—all of them, Reckzeh noticed, able-bodied young men.

Choosing a table inside, he sat down to wait with the file he'd prepared in front of him. The car drove up a few minutes later. The threesome must have changed at the clubhouse. Gürtner was wearing plus fours, the woman beside him a costume tailored in the same tweed, Oberg his white summer uniform.

The SS general, Reckzeh's boss, was forty-eight and going gray. A stocky man with an incipient paunch, he looked taller on horseback than he really was.

Gürtner was the first to approach the table. He stuck out a big, meaty hand. "I'm *très, très heureux* that you could meet us here. It's made my weekend."

Reckzeh glanced at Oberg. Although the general detested Germans who made a habit of interlarding their remarks with snippets of French, Reckzeh could detect no reaction on his broad face. Once upon a time, he thought, they'd have sorted out a mess like this among themselves, without involving civilians. He wasn't scared of men like Gürtner, even when they held ministerial rank. It simply exasperated him that he might have to account for his actions in Gürtner's presence.

"You know my wife?"

"We've met."

Gürtner smiled. "You aren't married, are you?" It was a statement rather than a question. He refocused the smile on his wife and added, "The Standartenführer has his own ways of enjoying *la vie parisienne.*"

Reckzeh controlled himself with an effort. A man in Gürtner's position couldn't fail to know of his homosexual relationships. Again he glanced at Oberg, and again there was no reaction. The general just stood there with a faint, almost sheepish smile on his lips.

They sat down. Gürtner summoned a waiter and ordered breakfast for three. He was precisely the type of old-style public servant whom Reckzeh loathed and mistrusted most of all—a representative of the pre-Hitler establishment and its obsolete moral attitudes. There were more of Gürtner's kind in Paris than anywhere else in German-occupied Europe.

"What about you, Standartenführer? May I order you something?"

"Coffee," said Reckzeh, "black." He stared after the waiter's departing figure. "All he needs is a pair of white gloves."

"They wear them here, but only for serving dinner." Gürtner chuckled. "That's the danger of working in this city, too much *haute cuisine*. Why do you think we beat the French hollow in '40? They were all *à table*, that's why!"

"Let's hope," Oberg said suddenly, "that we aren't at table ourselves when the Allies land." His voice was surprisingly soft—less of a voice than a hoarse whisper.

"Is there any news? I'm told they can't try it without a spell of really fine weather."

"Let's get down to business, shall we?" Oberg looked at Reckzeh. "The fact is, you've stirred up a hornet's nest."

"To put it mildly," Gürtner chimed in.

Reckzeh eyed them both in turn. "I know I'm here to answer questions, but may I ask one of my own? Why should the Majestic be interested in this affair?" The name of the hotel on Avenue Kléber was a collective term for the Military Governor and his staff, who were based there.

Gürtner threw up his hands. "Honestly, Standartenführer! You trample on every corn in sight and wonder why there's an outcry? Naïveté is the last thing I'd suspect you of."

"It was a run-of-the-mill SD operation."

"Snatching an Abwehr officer in broad daylight? You can't blame the Lutétia for screaming blue murder."

"Who at the Lutétia?"

"One question, you said. I take it for granted you've a perfectly reasonable explanation. All we want is a chance to interview Schneevogel ourselves and hear his version of what happened."

Reckzeh stared at Oberg, unable to believe that he hadn't told Gürtner the full facts, but the general continued to sit there as before, smiling faintly, looking detached.

"I'm afraid that won't be possible," said Reckzeh. "There was an accident." He paused. "A fatal accident."

"You're joking, of course." Gürtner gave a mirthless laugh. "I always knew you had a very special brand of humor."

"The drug that was used—someone slipped up. I thought you'd been informed."

"What!" Gürtner turned to Oberg. "What is all this?"

"Eh?" Oberg didn't appear to have been listening.

"It was a regrettable oversight," Reckzeh went on quickly. "We had no reason to shut the man up. On the contrary, we were bringing him here so he could talk."

"This is outrageous!"

But Gürtner's tone belied his words—it lacked conviction. Reckzeh relaxed a little. The man's indignation was just an act put on in response to outside pressure. He obviously disliked his present role and didn't know how far to carry it. In other words, he was scared.

Reckzeh, who had rehearsed a lengthy explanation, jettisoned it. All he said was, "I have here the result of the autopsy, together with transcripts of statements taken from all concerned." He pushed the folder across the table. "Schneevogel was being brought here to talk, I assure you. I can further assure you that what he had to say would have been of the greatest interest to you and your colleagues at the Majestic."

Gürtner shuffled uneasily in his chair. He glanced at his wife. It was clear that he didn't wish to go too far, but equally clear that he had no wish to look small in her presence.

"What was Schneevogel suspected of?"

"Financial irregularities."

"I see." Gürtner looked surprised and relieved.

"The sums were substantial. We wondered where he was getting them from, but it wasn't feasible to question him properly in Lisbon. I should add that we obtained Berlin's approval. Prinz Albrecht Strasse were all in favor."

"I know," said Gürtner, "I checked."

"Actually, we were only a staging post. Schneevogel's final destination was Berlin."

Silence descended on the table at these words, as though each man needed to ponder their meaning for himself. Oberg smiled at no one in particular. When he spoke, his voice was oddly expressionless. "Why not take the file with you, Gürtner? Study it over the weekend—discuss it with von Stülpnagel." His smile broadened. "Karl-Heinrich and I are old friends. He's always grateful when I take, er—unpleasantnesses off his hands."

Gürtner cleared his throat and picked up the folder. He looked at his wife and rose. She followed suit at once. "Excellent suggestion," he said. "If I do come up with any more queries, which is always possible—"

"Don't hesitate to call me," said Reckzeh, "anytime."

"Yes, well, thank you for sparing the time. And thanks for the ride, General. Have a good weekend. I'm sure the enemy won't begrudge it us."

Oberg's smile froze as soon as he and Reckzeh were alone. "Dear old Karl-Heinrich," he said bitterly, "tucking himself away in the Majestic and leaving us to do the dirty work!" He transferred his ire from von Stülpnagel to Reckzeh. "What was all that about financial irregularities? Embezzlement, you mean? It's the first I've heard of it."

"Corruption is something lawyers understand."

"So it seems. Still, your people really fouled things up."

"I was sure we'd get a confession out of him." Reckzeh was still digesting what Oberg had said about the Military Governor. He thought the same of the Abwehr, a privileged caste accustomed to looking down on the Security Service, whose function it was to do what Oberg called the dirty work. "Schneevogel would have supplied us with enough dynamite to blow the whole Lutétia gang to blazes. Even Canaris would have caught some of the blast."

"Forget it, Reckzeh. The Abwehr's digging its own grave, it doesn't need any help from us. Be patient. There are too many nooses dangling around the Admiral's head—he's bound to wind up with his neck in one of them. Anyone would think we hadn't got enough on our plate here already." Oberg was still sweating from his ride. "Let's go. I'm sick of this decadent dump."

Reckzeh paid the bill and followed Oberg out onto the terrace. The tables were crowded with officers and their wives or mistresses. They lowered their copies of the *Pariser Zeitung* and stared. A few of them nodded mutely, but all turned their heads as the two men passed by.

Listening to the chorus of whispers behind them, Reckzeh was amused. There were plenty of Germans in Paris, military and civilian, who thought they ran the city. Many played at being men of power, yet their power was as nothing compared to that of the man now striding past those crowded tables: SS General Oberg, almost a caricaturist's general, short-legged, short-winded, thickset, corpulent.

Reckzeh had parked his car on a bend in the avenue, which was lined with chestnut trees. Oberg's car, another Mercedes, was parked behind it with the windows up. His driver was standing around, smoking. So were his two armed outriders.

Oberg removed his cap and mopped his brow. He looked feverish. "All right, spit it out."

"I'll have to go back a bit."

"As far as it takes."

"Only to last summer. That's when Canaris attended a secret meeting in Spain, at Santander. He had the gall to get together with the heads of the British and American intelligence services. It was Schneevogel's job to make the arrangements."

"Canaris is an old fox."

"We think he submitted a plan to his opposite numbers: the Führer to be eliminated or handed over to the Allies, a cease-fire in the West, continuation of the war in the East. High treason, pure and simple."

"But unproven."

"Heydrich always thought Canaris harbored treasonable intentions, ever since the outbreak of war. Remember that proposal of his in '41? He wanted the Abwehr disbanded and incorporated in the SD."

"Reinhard Heydrich was a great man, a great loss to the Reich." Oberg's tribute sounded stilted and insincere. "You admired him, I know. Wasn't it he who got you out of the Foreign Legion and into the SD?"

Reckzeh nodded impatiently. "May I continue?"

"Of course."

"We kept an eye on Schneevogel, had him tailed and photographed. One batch of pictures showed him with a man—a Britisher, though we didn't get a line on him for some time. Everyone seemed to have a different name for him: Callaghan, Cadogan, Cardigan. He was eventually identified as a Colonel Gahagan—Jeremy Gahagan."

The sun had burned off the mist and was growing hotter. Oberg mopped his brow again and indicated a pool of shade on the other side of the avenue. They strolled over to it.

"From Lisbon," Reckzeh went on, "Schneevogel financed a handful of Abwehr agents operating in England. In fact, most of them had been arrested and turned by the British. This man Gahagan was their controller."

"And Schneevogel knew it all the time?"

"That was one of the things I wanted to ask him."

"All right, get to the point. What were you really after?"

"I managed to get a look at some of the agents' reports that came via Schneevogel. When I compared them with Joseph's—"

"Good God, how did you come by those? You've been bombarding me with complaints for a year because you don't get any copies."

"I get them all right, but I thought it wiser not to let the Lutétia know."

"So you compared them. What of it?"

"A connection emerged. Remember when Joseph first began transmitting? Doubts were voiced at first, even in the High Command. Was Joseph on the level? Let's wait, everyone said—let's see what he comes up with and check it out."

"I still don't get your point."

"It was the reports from Schneevogel's agents that gave the game away. Nothing of great importance—trivial stuff, mostly, but there was always some little detail that corroborated Joseph's latest information. Now do you see where the British went wrong?" Cool no longer, Reckzeh was speaking with genuine passion. "They gilded the lily! All that really counted with them was Joseph. *He* was the soloist. The others supplied an accompaniment, but the tune was all his, and our High Command have been dancing to it for months."

Oberg wagged his head. "I might have guessed. It's Berger you're gunning for—too damned envious of his success, that's what it is."

"If I'd persuaded Schneevogel to talk, everyone would have seen Joseph in a different light."

"You're forgetting Roenne and his evaluators at Foreign Armies West. They're no fools, Reckzeh. Joseph has proved, again and again, that his material can be trusted. What about the raid on Nuremberg? Thanks to his advance information, the Luftwaffe shot down fifty enemy bombers—Göring admits as much himself. You really think the British would sacrifice fifty bomber crews, just like that?"

"I wouldn't put it past them, not if—"

"Let me refresh your memory," Oberg cut in. "Why did you try and sell me on the idea of offering Berger promotion and a transfer to the SD? Why did you bring him to see me? Because the SD wanted to steal the credit for Joseph—because he was our finest source of intelligence on enemy soil. He still is."

Nothing could have stung Reckzeh more than the recollection of Berger and himself in Oberg's office at No. 72, Avenue Foch, a few doors down from SD Headquarters. The general's words still rang in his ears.

"Come in, Berger, have a seat. Congratulations on your coup. Still a lieutenant, I see. The Abwehr doesn't seem to appreciate all you've done for it."

"Things take time in our outfit, General."

"I'll come straight to the point. Why not join us?"

"The SD, you mean?"

"You're our kind of man, Berger. Say the word and I'll fix it inside a week. You and Reckzeh would make an unbeatable team."

That was the moment Reckzeh had been waiting for—his reason for broaching the idea to Oberg in the first place. He longed to see Berger squirming on the horns of a dilemma. No one, least of all a humble lieutenant, could afford to reject such an offer.

Berger had sat there with his head bowed as though giving the matter serious consideration. "I'm honored, naturally," he said at last, "but I can't accept. It's a question of—how shall I put it?—a question of approach. The SD are successful in their way; at the risk of sounding immodest, so am I in mine. If I changed my methods, I'm afraid I wouldn't rate any kind of job in your organization."

He's dished himself, thought Reckzeh, but he was wrong. Oberg not only took Berger's brushoff in his stride but may even have admired him for it, and Reckzeh smarted at the memory quite as much now as he had all those months ago.

"Be honest, Reckzeh," Oberg was saying, "you've got a blind spot where Berger's concerned."

"Two weeks before the Pole made his spectacular escape, while this scheme was still being hatched, Berger got together with Canaris."

"Well?"

"I happen to know they had a talk, just the two of them."

"Nothing odd about that. Berger couldn't have launched such an operation without authority from higher up, and Steinberg isn't the type to stick his neck out."

"Berger's a goddamned amateur! I don't trust him."

"Steady, Reckzeh, he's becoming an obsession with you. That business with the girl was bad enough. You snatched her and got nowhere —I had to cover for you. Now it's Schneevogel." Oberg frowned. "Enough's enough. Leave Berger alone. He may have his own way of doing things, but he gets results."

"The question is, are they desirable?"

"You see? Sheer professional jealousy! Why is he good at his job? No idea. Maybe it's got something to do with his name: Berger . . ." Oberg drawled the word mellifluously. "Now listen to this one: Reckzeh!" He rolled the initial letter with a sound like ripping canvas, then smiled, proud of his ingenuity. "Who's more likely to extract a confession from you, a man with a quiet voice and nice manners, or someone who brandishes a pair of pincers in your face?" Oberg's laugh was cold, cruel, and abrupt.

"Thanks for the tip, General."

"Forget it. The Abwehr's finished in Paris. Stop flogging a dead horse. We've enough live ones to contend with, God knows."

Oberg walked to his car. The driver whipped the door open; the outriders mounted their motorcycles.

"By the way, what's happening to the body?"

"It'll be handed over to his next of kin."

"Any explanation?"

"There's a war on."

"And the men who fouled it up?"

"I'm seeing them in my office at ten."

"They deserve a lesson."

"I've something in mind for them."

"Like what?"

"There's a consignment of prisoners leaving for Buchenwald next week. They'll escort them to the camp and stay on there as guards. I trust you approve."

"Gürtner was right for once—you've a special brand of humor." Oberg chuckled reminiscently. "I must say, I liked that little dig of his: 'You aren't married, are you?' " He tried to mimic Gürtner's voice. "But you *are* married, aren't you, Reckzeh?"

"Every SS officer has a duty to marry, the Reichsführer says so."

"How does your wife react to your affair with that young French Siegfried?"

"She knows nothing about it," Reckzeh retorted coolly.

"I'm too damned normal, worse luck. Some day you must tell me what it's like—with a man, I mean."

"Much the same as with a woman, General, but rather less complicated. Fewer strings."

"Is that so?" Oberg climbed into his Mercedes and wound the window down. "Know what tickles me? That French boyfriend of yours— he looks like a founder member of the Hitler Youth!" He emitted a raucous, vulgar laugh, very much louder than his speaking voice.

The Mercedes made a three-point turn and drove off toward the city. Sunlight glinted on its windows as it disappeared from view, one outrider ahead, the other bringing up the rear.

Reckzeh folded back the roof of his convertible with a face like stone. Then he got in and drove off, too, but not in the direction of the city. He still had a few more minutes to kill.

The Bois de Boulogne's two biggest lakes were already thronged with soldiers off duty. Some had spread blankets on the grassy banks, others were paddling around in rowboats. Background music came from a scattering of portable radios.

Surveying the peaceful scene, Reckzeh was reminded of another day in May three years before. He'd accompanied Heydrich from Berlin to Paris for an official function at the Ritz Hotel, where Oberg was to be installed in his present post as Senior SS and Police Commander.

Afterward, when they were alone together, Heydrich had suddenly said, "Maybe I ought to have taken the job myself, Erich. Nothing seems to be happening here. Paris and France are peaceful now, hundreds of miles from the nearest battlefield, but this is where the things that matter—the real issues—will be decided."

Reckzeh circled the Lac Inférieur and left the park by the Porte Dauphine. Turning into Avenue Foch, he drove along the side road until he came to the big white mansion. Heydrich's words still lingered with him.

11

Elsham Wolds, Lincolnshire

FROM THE WINDOW of the Nissen hut, Kacew could see bombers lined up on the runway. They were Liberators, and had obviously seen service. A Liberator's fuselage resembled a giant coffin, heavy and unwieldy. The cumbersome tail unit might have been designed to weigh the machine down, not guide it through the air, and the four engines, each powering a thin-bladed triple propeller, looked too puny to lift the hulking monster off the ground. To Kacew, however, those eight unlovely airplanes were the prettiest sight he'd seen in a long time.

Half an hour before, shortly after his arrival, he'd watched them being loaded with bombs and ammunition belts. Since then, nothing had happened. Busy at their desks, the clerical staff paid no attention to what went on outside. One of them was hammering away at an ancient Underwood whose keys kept on sticking. Nobody looked up when Kacew left his place at the window and strolled to the door.

There was a stiff breeze blowing outside. The sun slanted down, intermittently piercing banks of cloud driven inland from the North Sea. With them had come the gulls that were wheeling and swooping on something at the far end of the runway. The ground mist had almost completely dispersed.

Elsham Wolds was twenty miles or so from the coast. A lot of rain must have fallen in recent weeks—the turf under Kacew's feet looked lush and felt spongy. He wondered if the weather over the Channel and northern France was worse than here. Was that why the bombers' latest mission had been canceled or postponed?

His first thought that morning in London had also been of the weather. He'd hurried to the window as soon as the alarm clock went off, but it was still too dark to see.

Kacew felt lively and refreshed in spite of all the vodka he'd drunk the night before. There had been time enough for a quick workout at the open window before taking a bath and putting on his uniform.

Alison Mills was already having breakfast in the kitchen when he came downstairs. She was also in uniform, a khaki FANY uniform, the usual camouflage for female members of the Firm. Her hair was pinned up at the back, presumably because it looked more military under her cap.

"Coffee's ready," she said. "Good morning."

"Did Jeremy tell you I preferred coffee?" He joined her at the kitchen table. Uniform or no, she looked more than ever like a country girl.

"We aim to please."

"What's the weather like?"

"Still improving."

He sipped his coffee, trying to recall what he'd said last night. Snatches of their conversation had lodged in his memory, but some of it eluded him. "I hope I didn't behave too badly."

"You were a perfect gentleman."

"Did I talk a lot of nonsense?"

"It must be hard at times, living in a city with millions of people all around you and not being able to talk freely."

He stared at her. "Did I say that?"

"Of course not. I gathered it, that's all."

They'd left the house together. The sky was blue. A long line of Londoners stood waiting at the nearest bus stop, all looking cheerful and relaxed, perhaps because of the better weather. The headlines in their newspapers confirmed that Hackney had borne that brunt of last night's raid.

Alison had accompanied him to King's Cross Station and left him there. In the five minutes before his train left he'd called the Mexican Embassy and fixed a rendezvous with Chavero. He would pick up the cash that evening, at a prearranged time and place, but the prospect seemed infinitely remote to him now, as he made his way over to the mess hut.

Bombs were stacked in the open under camouflage nets. He walked past them, still heading for the Nissen hut which, like a monstrous corrugated iron radio, gave out muffled bursts of music and laughter.

He opened the door and went in. A wave of noise, heat, and tobacco smoke engulfed him. Despite the heat, the twenty or thirty occupants of the hut were all in flying suits. Some were playing cards or dice at tables, others reading in a cluster of shabby old armchairs at the far end, but most were watching a couple of navigators prancing around to the radio.

The carpet was torn in numerous places and stippled with cigarette burns. The only things that looked new were a pair of Polish flags nailed to the wall on either side of a photoportrait of General Sikorski. A piece of black crepe had been thumbtacked to the frame.

Kacew was still standing by the door, scanning each face in turn, when someone gripped his arm.

"Holy Mother of God, it's Roman!"

He found himself looking into a face as round as a baby's, though the eyes belonged to an old man.

"Frykowski!"

"What on earth are you doing here? What's that uniform you're wearing?"

Kacew gestured at the room. "Is Jan still around?"

"A pilot and his copilot bite the dust together. What do you think I am, a ghost?"

"Where is he?"

"Roman Kacew, the prodigal son—this calls for a celebration! I hope you've brought some vodka with you. Know what Elsham Wolds is? The wettest, driest dump in the whole of England. It's wet here all year round—snow, sleet, buckets of rain—but we never see a drop of decent Polish vodka. If you've volunteered for this place, you're out of your mind."

"Hello, Roman," said another voice.

The cigarette dangling from Karski's lips distorted his smile as well as his speech. He made no move to take it out of his mouth, did nothing that might have encouraged a spontaneous embrace. His was the kind of face that went with a monocle.

Kacew felt the eyes studying him, noting changes, asking the questions Karski would never ask because it wasn't his way. "Hello, Jan," he said eventually. "It's been a long time. Afraid I couldn't get in touch after Dunkirk. Something came up."

"I thought as much." Karski smoothed his dark hair, which was combed straight back. His hands looked almost too slender for the heavy signet ring he wore.

With backgrounds as different as theirs, it was a miracle they'd become friends at all. Karski—it was an assumed name—had been born into a rich and aristocratic Polish family; Kacew was the son of an impoverished village schoolmaster. Their friendship went back a long way, to the prewar days when they'd both been mail plane pilots.

"I miss flying," Kacew said, as though that said it all. He glanced at the window. "Is the weather holding you up?"

Karski removed the cigarette from his lips, and his smile became less wry. He didn't speak, but Kacew could read his thoughts. In their day, any weather had been flying weather.

Frykowski laughed. "Crumbs from the rich man's table, that's all we get."

"What would your target have been?" Kacew asked.

"Le Mans," said Karski, in his quiet, drawling voice. "They always give us the milk runs."

He had a red and white silk scarf around his neck. Kacew made out the ribbon of the DSO on the left breast of the uniform blouse he wore beneath his flying suit. It was reserved for those who had completed three hundred missions or more, but few Polish fliers had ever been awarded it.

"Preinvasion raids?"

Karski nodded. "We clobber anything we find—anything that moves."

"Freight trains are my favorite," Frykowski put in. "The locos go up like fireworks if you hit them."

Le Mans, thought Kacew. He was beginning to feel less like an interloper. When it came to flying, Karski and he were like a pair of compatible chemical elements.

"Is it tough, crossing the coast?" he asked.

"Not if you know where. Once you're inland, it's plain sailing. Either the Germans are holding their fighters in reserve, or they don't have any left."

The music came to an end. The two dancers stopped cavorting, laughter and conversation died away. There was a moment's suspense. Then more music filled the silence. A deep, gravelly voice sang the refrain in English:

> *"Small fry, my, my, put down that cigarette,*
> *You ain't a-grown up high and mighty yet . . ."*

Karski smiled and lit another Craven "A." He exhaled slowly, letting the smoke trickle from his nostrils. "You really miss flying, don't you?"

"Me?" Kacew grimaced. "Yes, I'm still suffering from withdrawal symptoms."

> *"Oh, small fry, dancing for a penny,*
> *Small fry, counting on how many . . ."*

Frykowski sang along with the vocalist and tap-danced in time to the music. "Our new national anthem," he said ruefully. "That's all we are to the British, small fry. I always thought they were our staunchest Allies, but just you try sneaking a bottle of vodka past the sentries!"

Still tap-dancing, he went on, "There's a Free French squadron based at Biggin Hill. Their wine comes in by sea from Algeria—duty free, no customs clearance, nothing. Everyone turns a blind eye because the poor old Frogs would die of homesickness without their beloved wine. Haven't the goddamned British ever heard of a homesick Pole? You shell out fifteen pounds for a half-liter bottle on the black market, and it's confiscated at the gate."

Kacew went to the window. He pointed to the bombers on the runway. "Yours?"

Karski nodded. "They're in an appalling state. I don't know if it's official policy to give us factory rejects, but they start giving trouble as soon as we sign for them."

Kacew continued to stare fixedly out of the window. "They look great to me."

"You should try flying one sometime."

Kacew's heart raced. He felt a fierce stab of pain in his left side, as though the cardiac muscles were strained to breaking point. "Anytime," he said. He laughed the self-lacerating laugh of someone in agony and trying not to show it.

"More withdrawal symptoms?" said Karski.

An insane, irrational idea flashed through Kacew's head. "Let me fly a mission with you," he said. It didn't sound as childish or nonsensical as he'd thought it would.

Frykowski stopped dancing. "For ten bottles of vodka—ten bottles of genuine Wyborowa—you can fly copilot instead of me." He laughed, then broke off abruptly when he saw the look on Kacew's face.

The pain in his chest was even fiercer. "What did you say? Ten bottles of Wyborowa for your place on this mission?"

Frykowski glanced helplessly at Karski, but Karski's face remained impassive. Frykowski said, "He's crazy."

Kacew took two coins from his pocket. He cupped them in his palm and held them out for Frykowski's inspection. "Two-up?" he said.

"Crazy!" Frykowski repeated, but the coins—a pair of florins—drew his gaze like a magnet.

"If I lose," Kacew said in a flat voice, "I owe you ten bottles of Wyborowa. If I win, I fly this mission."

Frykowski shook his head. "There may not be a mission today."

"In that case, you still win." Beneath the two-shilling pieces, Kacew's palm was greasy with sweat.

Again Frykowski glanced at Karski, willing him to intervene. Karski might not have been listening. His lips looked a little thinner, his deep-set eyes a little more somber, but that was all.

"Okay," Frykowski blurted out, "but let me toss."

Two-up was a traditional Polish game of chance. The rules were simple. One player tossed a pair of coins and caught them. If both were heads, he won; if both tails, he lost. If one of each came up, he had to go on tossing until the decision went either way.

Kacew hesitated before relinquishing the coins to Frykowski. He would sooner have tossed them himself, somehow feeling that he might stand a better chance. He didn't even watch while Frykowski balanced the coins on his thumb. Something far more arresting had claimed his attention: Karski's face. It was, he thought, the classic gambler's face. The predominant expression was one of profound melancholy. Win or lose, no issue could be forced. Either a thing happened or it didn't; all was predetermined and preordained.

From behind him, Kacew heard Frykowski give vent to a string of Polish expletives, then burst out laughing. Both reactions told Kacew that he'd won. The pain in his chest subsided.

12

Trouville

THE HOUSES overlooking the promenade were a curious medley of architectural follies: doll's houses, castles, oriental palaces in miniature. Although they had once been their owners' pride and joy, they now struck Berger as merely spooky. All were empty, with most of their windows shuttered or bricked up and loopholed for the benefit of machine gunners.

At the few open windows, soldiers were scanning the sea through binoculars. Sometimes they trained them on the solitary couple strolling along the beach below.

"Will you know the place when you see it?" Berger asked.

"I'm not sure, it's been so long."

"When were you here last?"

Jannou brushed a strand of hair out of her eyes. "August '39."

"Did you come here every summer?"

"Yes, for four weeks."

"The whole family?"

She nodded. "There were endless arguments beforehand—I mean, before my father bought the house. My mother wanted one in Deauville because it was smarter and more fashionable. Trouville wasn't smart, just quaint. She finally came to terms with the idea when she discovered there was a casino here, too."

"Your mother was fond of gambling?"

"I never saw her on the beach. She never swam or even sunbathed on the terrace—she simply waited for the casino to open."

Jannou shivered despite the warmth of the day, which was almost hot. There was surprisingly little wind, even here at the water's edge.

He had draped his jacket over his arm; she had slipped off her flimsy sandals and was carrying them by the straps.

"Perhaps we already passed it." He kept on talking because he sensed that she was becoming steadily less relaxed and more withdrawn. She had a way of conveying moods that was independent of speech. Her restlessness and impatience were like a physical emanation.

Jannou had paused and was staring at a house with turrets and oriel windows. "That could be it—yes . . . Or is it?"

She ran up the beach toward the house. She was wearing a half-length red linen coat. A patent leather bag of the same vivid red hung from her shoulder on a long strap. Jacket and bag were both brand-new, acquired before leaving Paris that morning. Berger couldn't help reflecting that they were the first presents she'd ever accepted from him. Until now, it had been impossible to give her so much as a pair of stockings. She managed to make him feel guilty whenever he offered her such things, her very silence seeming to suggest that they were loot extracted from her compatriots.

She came to a halt. Two German soldiers at one of the villa's windows waved and whistled to her. When Berger caught her up, she was looking pale and tense.

"Is that it?"

"There's no point," she said brusquely.

"Let's walk to the end of the beach." He took her arm and led her down to the sea again.

"We shouldn't have come here. Too many things have changed." She walked along the shore, following the arcs of foam deposited on the sand by waves that spent themselves just short of her bare feet or lapped over them. "Unless you liked what we saw? Perhaps you did."

From Paris they'd headed for the coast near Honfleur, not that they ever reached it. All the seaward turnings off the coast road were closed. They were brought up short by sentries or notice boards announcing that the area was mined. Concrete pillboxes guarded every access, swathed in camouflage netting. In many places, construction work was still in progress. Whenever they did catch a glimpse of the beach, it was strewn with obstacles—hideous and strangely antediluvian-looking pieces of apparatus: jagged steel triangles, barbed wire wheels, black balks of timber protruding from the sand like rotten teeth. To Berger they seemed to resemble the outward manifestations of some foul disease, doubly frightful to behold because the sea beyond these excres-

cences on the sandy white skin of the shore was as halcyon blue and
beautiful as ever.

They had reached the point where the Touques River flowed into
the sea, separating Trouville from Deauville. A dense thicket of barbed
wire barred their path, dotted with the black shapes of mines. Visible
beyond this entanglement were pillboxes and an antiaircraft tower.

They turned and retraced their steps. Jannou walked stiffly, holding
the strap of her bag taut. To the right and ahead of them, the casino
came into view. Three German soldiers had set out some gilt chairs and
a table on the terrace. They were playing cards with field glasses slung
around their necks.

Jannou paused opposite the casino. The main gaming room was built
in a crescent. Spanning the wall above its long windows was a red
banner inscribed in black. It read:

GERMANY IS WINNING ON EVERY FRONT

"What does it say?" Jannou asked curtly.

"You know enough German for that."

She frowned. "Let's go."

"I'm not responsible for such stupidities."

"Let's go back to Paris."

"Listen, Jannou." He caught her by the arm. "If you want this thing
to stand between us, it always will."

"Coming here was a mistake. It's no use raking over old memories."

"I'm not talking about memories, I'm talking about us."

"There's nothing to be said."

"You know there is. We've both been trying to say it for months."

"Silence was the only way."

"What about last night?"

She turned on her heel and walked down to the sea, hitched up her
skirt and waded in. The tide was high. A few yards farther out, some
posts jutted from the water. They carried death's-head notices in
French and German warning people not to venture beyond them. Presumably, the beach had been mined.

Berger went as close to the water's edge as he could without getting
his feet wet. "Careful, don't go in too far."

She stayed where she was, looking at him. "I'm coming," she said.
The belligerence had left her voice. It sounded almost normal.

"Wasn't the water cold?" he asked, when she rejoined him.

"You don't notice it after a while."

They walked back to the steps that led up to the promenade. The Simca was parked at the top. Jannou sat down on a step and started brushing wet sand off her feet.

"We could drive inland somewhere." He passed her a handkerchief.

"It would be the same everywhere."

"I've got another identity card with me. It's made out in the name of Pierre Hougron, sales manager of Ciment Français, Brest."

"Very inventive of you."

"Monsieur and Madame Hougron—could you carry it off?"

She shook her head. "I'm frightened. That writing on the wall last night—it opened my eyes. They're right, I'm a traitor." She laughed. "And I wanted to do something patriotic."

"It'll all be over soon."

"I've clung to that idea, and now it scares me."

"The war will soon be over, I tell you!"

"And then what? For us the end will mean two different things." She put her sandals on. The handkerchief, which was moist and sandy, she folded but kept in her hand.

They climbed the steps side by side. Pausing at the top, Jannou turned and looked back at the sea. The sun was so bright that she had to shade her eyes.

"When?" she asked. "When will it happen?"

Berger stared at the glittering expanse and asked himself the same question. He had no need to recall the tenor of Joseph's signals; the invasion was palpable, imminent, menacing—as inexorable as an act of God.

But when? The first two weeks of April had been fine—very little rain, no storms in the Channel, ideal landing weather—and nothing had happened. Then had come a cold and rainy spell that made the landing of so huge a force impossible or at least improbable. Now the weather seemed to be changing again, for the better. He'd telephoned Zossen, the Army General Staff's headquarters on the outskirts of Berlin, only yesterday. It was thought there that the invasion could be only a matter of days away. Even a date had been mentioned: May 15. That was one of his motives for coming here, an urge to see where the final act would take place.

"Don't you know," he heard her say, "or can't you talk about it?"

"No one really knows, but it has to be soon."

As though on cue, an air raid siren began to wail. The shrill, plaintive sound was echoed all along the sea front. One siren joined in right above their heads, on the roof of the fortified house across the road from them.

She clung to him, trembling, terrified by the piercing din. Sirens never frightened her in Paris. They often sounded during the day, but the city had never suffered any really heavy raids. At the film studios in Billancourt, air raid warnings provided an almost welcome respite from work. Everyone trooped outside and stood gawking at the sky, disappointed when there wasn't at least a dogfight over the suburbs.

The strident chorus died away.

"What is it?"

Berger pointed. "Incoming bombers."

Following the direction of his finger, she could see nothing at first but sunlit blue sky. Then she made out a few high-flying airplanes. They looked like a shoal of silvery minnows. She started to count them and got as far as eight.

From the river end of the beach came the staccato of a light antiaircraft gun. It sounded impotent and innocuous.

The minnows swam on, the gun fell silent. The hiss of the waves could be heard once more.

Rochebrune

ALTHOUGH THE SUN WAS HIGH, the horseman was wrapped in a thick black cloak. His gaunt face was frosted with stubble, his white hair so long that it brushed his shoulders. The mare he rode appeared to belong to some extinct breed, a heavy-bodied dapple-gray with short legs and a long tail.

He reined in beside a stream and allowed the beast to drink without dismounting. He himself produced a flat silver flask from his voluminous cloak and put it to his lips.

Not far away on his right, a fringe of trees marked the beginning of the Forêt de Perseigne. The valley ahead, a deserted expanse of long grass yellow with dandelions, was bounded by a small eminence. At its summit stood the remains of a ruined castle.

"Prepare to advance," he said eventually. With the reins in his left hand and the flask held on high in his right, he kicked the mare in the ribs. She set off up the slope. Despite his repeated cries of exhortation, a bone-jarring trot was all she could manage.

"En avant! Chargez!" The horseman's eyes were fixed on the hill. He could see the German battery near the crest, hear the thunder of

the creeping barrage laid down by his own artillery. Never had the gunfire sounded more real than it did today.

Taken aback, he dropped the reins. The mare slowed to a walk, then stopped. He stood up in his stirrups. The strangely muted explosions were not coming from the hill at all; their source was the sky overhead. Then he caught sight of the airplanes.

There were eight of them, one much closer and flying much lower than the rest. Two plumes of smoke trailed behind it. With a fierce gush of flame, a fiery mass detached itself from the left wing. One of the stricken bomber's engines had come adrift and was plunging to the ground.

Other objects fell away, disintegrating into smaller fragments as they vanished over the brow of the hill, but one remained visible: a black speck that exploded into whiteness and floated in the sky like a giant puffball. The parachute drifted slowly toward the hill. The figure in the shade of the canopy showed no sign of life.

For a moment the horseman's attention was distracted. A horse-drawn wagon had appeared on the narrow, dusty track that led to St.-Rigomer-des-Bois, the nearest village. The driver must also have seen the burning plane, because he whipped up his horse and turned off after it, straight across the valley.

The parachute was drifting down behind the hill. The horseman urged his steed forward. Its lethargy seemed to anger him for the first time. He slapped it on the rump and shook the reins impatiently. The parachute disappeared from view. Glancing briefly to his left, the horseman saw the bomber crash and burst into flames.

He caught sight of the parachute as soon as he breasted the summit, a big splash of white on a green and gold background. Folds of silk stirred gently in the breeze.

He dismounted and removed his cloak because it hampered him on the ground. There was a bulge in the middle of the white expanse. He pulled the silk away, bundling it up in his arms with surprising speed and dexterity.

At first he thought the man must be dead, he was lying there so still with his eyes closed and blood oozing from a gash on his smoke-blackened forehead. Then the eyes opened—dark, questioning eyes—and the lips shaped a single word.

"French?"

The horseman bent lower. "Jean-Marie de Rochebrune, Colonel."

"How close are they?" Every word was an effort.

"The Germans? Never fear, I'll get you to safety."

The airman nodded and shut his eyes, then opened them again. "The others, where are they?"

"It's better you don't talk now."

Rochebrune reached into his hip pocket and produced a knife. With the same deft and purposeful movements as before, he cut the airman out of his parachute harness and opened the neck of his flying suit. When he saw the wound in his shoulder, he cut a square of parachute silk and folded it into a pad which he gently inserted between the wound and the material. The airman seemed to have lost consciousness again.

The wagon pulled up at the foot of the hill. A man jumped down and came running through the grass, short in the leg but quick and agile. He was shabbily dressed. The green sweater spanning his paunch was a mass of holes, and over it hung a greasy tie.

Rochebrune's face became an arrogant mask. He ignored the approaching farmer and led his mare to within a few feet of the man in the grass. Kneeling down, he insinuated one arm under his shoulders and heaved him into a sitting position. The airman groaned.

The farmer ran up. "Let me give you a hand," he said.

"Stand clear, Ringood!" Rochebrune struggled to his feet and propped the half-unconscious man against the mare's flank. She continued to stand there, grazing placidly.

"You'll kill him."

"Stand clear, I said! No Ringood touches anything of mine."

Ringood gave a guttural laugh. In a face as broad and coarse-featured as his, the farmer's little black eyes looked like cloves stuck in a ham. "You'll kill him with those high and mighty ways of yours. He'll never last the ride."

Rochebrune looked at the airman, then at his detested neighbor. "What about the others?"

"All dead—burned to a crisp. Well, shall I fetch the wagon? The Boches will be here soon, droves of them."

"Just to the gate, then. Not a step farther."

They hoisted the airman into the wagon and laid him down flat, with the parachute under his head and shoulders. He was conscious again but too weak or dazed to talk. All he could muster was a wan smile of comprehension and gratitude.

"Take the track through the forest." Rochebrune wrapped himself in his black cloak and remounted. For a while he rode beside the wagon in silence, watching the sky, glancing back along the deserted valley to where a pillar of smoke still marked the point of impact. His eyes returned again and again to the wounded man. Although he had spoken only a few words, Rochebrune found his accent puzzling. The English spoke French with a different intonation altogether.

He drew level with Ringood, who was sitting on a plank laid athwart the wagon. "Were they British planes or American?"

"American, I think, with RAF markings."

"How many in the crew?"

"I spotted a couple of charred bodies. No sign of any others."

"Anything worth salvaging?"

"From that bonfire? You must be joking."

"A machine gun, perhaps?"

"Not even a pair of flying boots."

"What of the other planes?"

"They'll make it, with luck."

They had reached the Forêt de Perseigne. The track consisted of two deep ruts, bone-dry at this time of year. Jays fluttered into the air at their approach, chattering resentfully. It was cooler in the shade of the trees. The airman had fallen into a restless sleep and was muttering to himself. The words were unintelligible.

It took them nearly half an hour to cross the forest and regain open country. Ahead of them, grassland sloped gently down to a valley, and in the valley stood a turreted manor house with avenues radiating from all four sides.

Château Rochebrune looked imposing from a distance, but closer inspection rendered it less so. The avenue Ringood drove down was overgrown with grass and obstructed by withered branches that had broken off the ancient beech trees and hung or lay where they had fallen. What had once been a formal garden with rose beds and gravel paths was choked with vegetation, and the ornamental lake bore a film of green slime.

The château and its outbuildings formed a hollow square around a cobbled courtyard. Parts of the main house were obviously uninhabitable. The roofs had tiles missing, and the walls had been shored up with timber to prevent them from collapsing.

Ringood halted outside the big wrought iron gates, which were thick with rust and hanging askew. Plaster was flaking off the gateposts.

Rochebrune dismounted, and the dapple-gray trotted into the courtyard without waiting for him. Standing beside the fountain in the middle of the courtyard was a woman in an ankle-length blue gown. Her hair hung loose to her waist.

A crafty look came into Ringood's eyes. "It's bad enough neglecting your land," he said, "but not breeding from that daughter of yours is a crime."

"If your son shows his face here again," Rochebrune growled, "I'll give him a dose of buckshot."

Ringood chuckled hoarsely. "If he's anything like his father, that won't stop him."

The woman or girl—it was hard to tell which—had gone to meet the horse. She caught hold of the bridle and started to lead it away.

"Leave her, Yseult," Rochebrune called. "Go and heat some water. I need hot water and bandages."

She stopped short, then released the bridle and ran toward the house. Her feet were bare.

Rochebrune turned back to the wagon. The airman was awake and conscious. He gazed around him, smiling feebly, pale beneath the grime on his face. The blood oozing from his forehead had congealed and looked almost black.

They lifted him down from the wagon and laid him carefully on the ground.

"Don't be a fool," said Ringood, "let me help you. Just as far as the house."

Carrying the man between them, they made their way into the courtyard. From one of the nearby roofs, ringdoves took wing with a sound like muffled laughter.

PART TWO

13

The Vine House, Chiltern Hills

GAHAGAN TURNED LEFT off the main road at Monks Risborough. From there he drove up a smaller road to Whiteleaf, a little cluster of thatched cottages. A quarter of a mile beyond this village, down a narrow lane flanked by high hedges, he came to a sign saying "The Vine House."

The sign was a plain and unpretentious wooden board, and Gahagan had no gates or sentries to negotiate. In his neighbors' eyes, Sir Graham was the archetypal senior civil servant, a gentleman who worked in London but withdrew as often as he could to his "place in the country." That Chequers, the Prime Minister's official country residence, was only a mile away, and that Sir Graham could therefore come and go without causing comment—no such farfetched association of ideas would ever have occurred to them.

Chequers was closely guarded and inaccessible to members of the general public, whereas anyone could drop in at The Vine House for a chat with Sir Graham. Although it was rumored that he held some post at the War Office, nobody would have suspected him of handling anything really hush-hush. The notion that Britain's secret service might be headed by a man like Sir Graham would have been universally consigned to the realm of fantasy.

It was a warm, sunny day. The sight of bluebells and cherry blossom reminded Gahagan of the house in Berkshire. Now that his wife had left him, she lived there with the children. Thoughts of his broken marriage and Berkshire in springtime were painful enough, but they weren't the principal reason for the twinges in his gut.

Their cause lay elsewhere. Ever since leaving the A40 at West

Wycombe, he'd been driving through villages whose half-timbered houses and Norman churches called to mind another familiar landscape —the one in which, according to his latest information, the bomber had crashed.

He turned into the drive, a stretch of gravel bordered by trees and shrubs. A well-tended lawn came into view, and beyond it a house with vine-covered walls of mellow red brick, leaded windows, and a thatched roof. On the small paved forecourt, a man in rubber boots was busy hosing down a discreet gray Wolseley sedan.

Sir Graham belonged to England's rich and powerful elite. His wealth had accrued to him from all quarters—his father, his mother, his ex-wife—and was soundly invested. He was a major stockholder in several large corporations, owned a shoot in Scotland and a model farm in Gloucestershire, and had inherited half a dozen substantial office buildings in the City of London. Gahagan found it almost dishonest of a man like Sir Graham to live in a place as modest as The Vine House.

The chauffeur-manservant turned off the water, put the sponge on the Wolseley's roof, and peeled off his chamois-leather gloves.

"Mr. Gahagan?"

"That's right." The voice sounded like the one Gahagan had heard on the phone in London an hour ago.

"My name's Winter, sir. Would you come this way?"

Winter removed his boots before entering the house and padded on ahead in his thick gray socks. The drawing room had white walls and a parquet floor strewn with Indian rugs. The twin sofas and the armchairs were chintz-covered. The curtains were chintz, too. It was a room indistinguishable from a thousand others within commuting distance of London.

"May I offer you something to drink, sir? A dry Madeira, perhaps?"

"Thanks—I mean, no thanks. Would you let Sir Graham know I'm here?"

Winter pointed to one of the rear-facing windows. "He's attending to his bees."

"Perhaps I could join him out there. The matter's urgent."

"I wouldn't advise it, sir." Though polite, the smile conveyed that it would be pointless to go into too much detail with a layman. "It's swarming time."

Gahagan detected a faint accent. Winter confused his *v*'s and *w*'s in an unmistakable way. Could it really be that the head of the British Secret Service employed a factotum of German origin?

Gahagan strolled over to the window. It looked out on a neglected kitchen garden enclosed by a high brick wall of the same mellow brick as the house itself. Set into the wall were two tiers of beehives, one above the other.

Sir Graham was standing in front of one of the niches with his head and shoulders protected by a veil, his gloved hand holding a large white net. Gahagan felt a mixture of surprise and irritation. How could this ardent beekeeper reconcile his Arcadian hobby with supreme command of an organization whose role was so entirely functional, so utterly unidyllic?

He turned back into the room. His ulcers were giving him hell. In search of distraction, he examined the painting above the open fireplace.

It was a battle scene from World War One. Some khaki-clad cavalrymen in peaked caps and chinstraps were charging up a hill. A small bronze plaque at the foot of the frame identified them as a squadron of Life Guards. Gahagan looked more closely at the faces. They were almost identical—boyish, tense, eager—except for the squadron commander's. All the predictable emotions, all the eagerness and apprehension, had been erased from it.

"A horse painter," said a voice at Gahagan's back. "That was all that really interested him, horseflesh."

Gahagan hadn't heard anyone come in. Turning, he reflected that Sir Graham had done the painter an injustice. The hair was gray, the skin wrinkled, the set of the shoulders less square, but the face was just as impassive. Not for the first time, it reminded him of a worn old coin. The impression had faded, leaving only the hint of a face.

"Seems a pretty fair likeness to me, sir."

"Really? It's a long time ago." Sir Graham gestured at an armchair. "Do sit down."

To those aware of how much power he wielded, Sir Graham always seemed smaller in the flesh than their mental image of him. People who had known him as a young man told tales of his prowess over the hurdles and claimed that he could have become a champion jockey if his wealth and social status hadn't ruled it out.

Gahagan sat down. Sir Graham, after hovering awhile, did likewise. He was wearing an apron over his Glen check suit. Contrary to habit, Gahagan was formally dressed in a navy blue pinstripe with a pale blue shirt and regimental tie. He felt thoroughly ill at ease in it.

A peculiar smell had entered the drawing room in Sir Graham's wake. He saw Gahagan's nostrils twitch.

"Recognize the smell?"

"Ether?"

"I thought you'd know, being a doctor's son."

Gahagan digested the implications of this remark. If Sir Graham had been dipping into his personal file, he must know that he and his wife had split up, and that he'd requested permission to start divorce proceedings. Perhaps Sir Graham had denied the request himself—"for the duration of the war"—on the principle that divorced intelligence officers were a threat to national security.

"Thank you for seeing me at such short notice," Gahagan said. "It's a disastrous business, I know."

"Rather a nuisance, yes, especially at this juncture." Sir Graham folded his hands in his lap. "You're always dependent on a fair slice of luck when you build up a tissue of lies like ours. Our luck's running out, from the look of it. First Lisbon, now this. We seem to have struck a bad patch."

Gahagan wasn't deceived by his relaxed pose and casual tone. "How much detail would you like, sir?"

"Time spent on detail is seldom wasted. This copilot—what's his name?—has he been questioned?"

"Frykowski. They're still holding him. There's nothing to report apart from what I already told you on the phone. He got cold feet and started telling everyone about the bet. The security officer alerted me."

"What about the rest of the planes?"

"Six of them have made it back to Elsham Wolds—I got word by radio on the way down here. A seventh was damaged and crash-landed on the beach near Ramsgate. As for Karski and Kacew—"

Sir Graham raised his hand, which was sprinkled with old man's freckles. "Let's leave it at Frykowski, shall we? Officially, that's who was in the plane."

"If they're still alive and haven't fallen into enemy hands, their best chance is to stay put."

"Did anyone actually see the plane crash?"

"The others weren't back when I left London. All we have is a preliminary report radioed en route."

"This man Karski was an experienced pilot?"

"Over three hundred missions, sir."

"How did it happen?"

"Seems they fell into a trap. A harmless-looking freight train in a siding on the outskirts of Le Mans turned out to be bristling with antiaircraft guns. Only four of the eight Liberators escaped damage."

"Do we know where Karski's plane came down?"

Gahagan produced a map from his breast pocket, but Sir Graham waved it away. "They used the Le Mans-Alençon railroad track as a navigational aid, there and back. Karski's machine was damaged over Le Mans, like the others. In the end, only one of his engines was still functioning. He even shed weight by jettisoning some of his machine guns. According to the others, his Liberator must have come down ten or fifteen miles south of Alençon."

"Were any parachutes sighted?"

"The only signal received wasn't clear on that point."

"So we don't know whether our man is dead or alive?"

"He could be either."

"And both contingencies present us with a problem, eh?"

Gahagan, who had been wondering all the time why Sir Graham didn't twist the knife in the wound, couldn't restrain himself any longer. "I know I owe you an explanation, sir. I mean, about how he came to be aboard in the first place."

"That tomfool bet—you already told me on the phone." Sir Graham made another dismissive gesture. "The whole thing's a joke in poor taste. I never thought our operation would be put at risk by a couple of crazy Poles."

It dawned on Gahagan that Sir Graham's interest centered solely on the conclusions to be drawn from what had happened, not on the event itself. For his part, all he could think of was the moment when the call came through from the security officer at Elsham Wolds. "You know that Pole you asked me to keep tabs on? I regret to have to inform you . . ." Kacew had hoodwinked him, and the knowledge left a bitter taste.

"Cato was showing signs of wear and tear," he said. "He seemed tired and disillusioned, but I didn't find that abnormal in an active man condemned to inactivity. I had no reason to suppose—"

"He simply couldn't resist the temptation, apparently." Sir Graham shrugged. "A question of temperament. The Poles have too damned much of it."

"He was asking me only last night to help him land a field assignment. Later he got drunk and talked about the old days. I detailed someone to keep him company, but he gave her no indication of what he had in mind. It may have been a sudden whim."

"If all had gone well, we might never have known. The odds were in his favor. Seven out of eight machines came back; his didn't, worse luck." Sir Graham inspected his fingernails for a moment. "No self-flagellation, Jeremy, it only breeds more mistakes. Let's review what we have in the way of facts and leave it at that. The main thing is, how much did he know or deduce about Fortitude South?"

"He was never let into the secret, sir, but he must have guessed that his signals were designed to make the Germans believe in the existence of a phantom army. He knew the objective of that army—a bridgehead in the Pas-de-Calais—so he must also have guessed that we don't intend to land there. After all, he spent some time working in the cipher section of the Polish General Staff."

"You mean he may have deduced our real objective? If the invasion misfires, Jeremy, it could prolong this war by a couple of years. There's only one passport to success, and that's surprise—misleading the enemy into thinking he knows where our main force will land. That little advantage could tip the scales. If the Germans got their hands on a man with that kind of information . . ."

Gahagan nodded gloomily. "Even if he hadn't thought about it before, he will now—if he's still alive."

"Was Normandy ever mentioned in his presence?"

"Of course not, sir, but if the Pas-de-Calais is only a feint, Normandy becomes a fair assumption."

"We must hope he's dead, you mean?"

"Wouldn't it be preferable, sir?"

"If he's alive and finds somewhere to hide, will he lie low or embark on some new escapade? Will he try to get in touch with us?"

"Knowing him as I do, I wouldn't rule it out. I'm afraid he may try to make amends."

Sir Graham studied his fingernails again. "If he falls into German hands, will he talk?"

"He'll hold out, but for how long I wouldn't like to say."

"In other words," said Sir Graham, "putting the most optimistic construction on what has happened, we've lost our trump card at a crucial stage in the game."

"D-Day's imminent, then?"

"At the worst, Fortitude South is a write-off. Yes, time's getting short —too short for me to keep this inside the Firm." Sir Graham's voice sank to a muttered soliloquy. "I don't see how I can avoid going right to the top."

"Cato isn't the only card in our hand," Gahagan said, without conviction. "Brutus and Garbo are still operating. So is Dancer."

"Yes, but they're secondary. Let's not delude ourselves, Jeremy: the Germans trusted Cato most of all because he supplied them with the best material." Sir Graham subsided still deeper into his reverie. Then he said, "I'd like a file on that Paris controller of his."

"Berger? We don't have much on him."

"Collate what you've got and let me have it. In our trade, it doesn't pay to dwell on an enemy's motives. Human beings change their spots too quickly. I wonder, all the same . . . Has he really changed his spots?"

Sir Graham's monotonous voice was having a soporific effect on Gahagan. What did he mean? He was still debating this when Sir Graham changed the subject.

"You wondered what the ether was for?"

"Something to do with your bees, I imagine."

"An old but effective method. At swarming time, the reigning queen leaves the hive with part of the swarm to found a new colony. Swarming confuses their sense of direction. To make sure they lose it altogether—unless they do, you can't move them and populate a new hive—you give them a whiff of ether. Then they'll never find their way back to the parent colony."

"Frankly, sir, I don't follow your meaning."

"My meaning? I saw you were puzzled by the ether, that's all."

Was Sir Graham implying that the Germans might regain their "sense of direction" because Cato's function had been to keep them anesthetized, or had he genuinely meant nothing in particular? Perhaps all this talk about bees was just a verbal smokescreen, a way of concealing how shocked he was by the disaster that had befallen the Firm's most cherished operation.

"Are you really interested in bees, sir?"

Sir Graham chuckled. "In these days of sugar rationing, a little honey goes a long way." He stood up. "How do you rate our chances of finding Cato?"

"I'll have to consult the French Section, it's their department."

"Have you alerted Ian Scott? If not, do so right away. Did Cato have a transmission scheduled for tonight?"

"No, not till tomorrow."

"Is the text ready?"

Gahagan nodded.

"Very well, Jeremy, we'll meet tonight—you, Ian, and I. At ten, let's say. That should give us time enough."

"At Broadway?" Gahagan only just stopped himself from referring to the Firm's headquarters by its unofficial name, "the Beehive"—a tribute to Sir Graham's hobby. His office overlooked Birdcage Walk and St. James's Park.

"I don't want to arouse any needless curiosity. Better bring Ian to my new *pied-à-terre.*" Sir Graham gave an address in Holland Park, smiling like someone who feels a trifle guilty for having kept a secret from his friends. "I think that's all."

He led the way out. Winter, still at work on the Wolseley, was polishing the chrome. Sir Graham picked up his veil and gauntlets from the bench where he'd left them.

"You aren't too fond of the country, are you?" he said as he walked Gahagan to his car. "Pity, you don't know what you're missing."

"So my wife always said."

Sir Graham smiled apologetically. "Sorry I couldn't approve your divorce application."

Gahagan, surprised by this admission, said nothing. The irony of it was that Sir Graham himself had been secretly divorced two years ago. There were many who said that it had almost ruined the culmination of a long career.

"And don't take your agent's fall from grace so hard. We'll never solve this problem if we allow ourselves to be swayed by sentiment."

"Sentiment, as you call it, sir, is what prompts men like Kacew to fight for us. And die, if necessary."

"You worry me sometimes, Jeremy. Calmness and composure, that's the secret of this country's success . . ."

Gahagan had ceased to listen properly. His mind was already on the trip back to London. He would have to drive through verdant, unspoiled English countryside, and all the time he would be seeing the images that had haunted him ever since the news broke: a burning Liberator, men striving desperately to extinguish the flames, fuel tanks exploding, the final nosedive . . .

"Our luck's running out," Sir Graham had said. Gahagan clung to the thought that Roman Kacew was a past master in the art of survival.

14

Rochebrune

SOMETHING WAS FLITTING through the air, dark and agile, with a dry rustle of wings. There was another sound, too—bare feet on floorboards? A figure entered Kacew's field of vision. All he could see of the woman was a curtain of hair falling smoothly to her waist.

He sensed that she'd been there for some time, watching him. Now he saw her open a window and heard a high-pitched squeak. A bat darted out and was swallowed up by a darkening sky.

The woman disappeared; the window remained in view. One pane was smashed. Its jagged residue, held in place by putty, reminded Kacew of a human face in profile: Gahagan's. The pain of awakening to reality flooded through his body.

"Who's there?"

Feet padded off swiftly, a door opened and closed. Kacew sat up, surprised at his ability to do so.

The big room was bare and deserted. All it contained was the bed, a chair, and a number of receptacles—bowls, basins, buckets—dotted around the floor between him and the window. Patches of damp on the ceiling told him that they had been put there to catch drips.

The pain was centered in his left shoulder. It had been bandaged, but he couldn't remember when or by whom. He gingerly fingered his eyebrows, which had some kind of ointment on them, and discovered a dressing taped to his forehead. He looked around the room again, then back at the window. It was clear from the failing light that he'd been dead to the world for hours.

He lowered his feet to the floor and stood up. The first thing he saw when he reached the window was a girl in a long blue gown running across a courtyard, hair flying. She vanished into a big house opposite, the only building in sight with rendered walls. The plaster was dirty gray, like the shutters over the windows. The line of the roof was broken by two turrets and a row of chimneys. Wind was plucking at the smoke that rose from one of them. Perched on the ridge tiles were some doves, as off-white as the house itself.

As he surveyed the cobbled courtyard, the central fountain, and the château with its twin turrets, Kacew's mind became clearer and the pain in his shoulder more insistent.

What of Karski? What of the other planes? How many had made it back to England? And Gahagan—did he already know what had happened? What would he do—what could he do?

A man came out of the château, tall and gaunt, with a mane of white hair. He looked up at the window. Kacew had a hazy recollection of him and another man, a jolting wagon, the gloomy depths of a forest.

Kacew was sitting on the bed when the man came in, dressed in a faded blue velvet smoking jacket and a pair of black drainpipe trousers. He was carrying a bundle of clothes in his arms.

"Yseult tells me you were recalled to the land of the living by a bat. No genuine château would be complete without bats, you must admit." The gaunt face creased in a smile. "How are you feeling? How's the shoulder?"

"Where am I?"

"Not in the lap of luxury, I fear, but you couldn't have chosen a safer place."

"I didn't get your name."

"Jean-Marie de Rochebrune, known locally as 'le Colonel.' This is Château Rochebrune."

"What happened to the plane?"

Rochebrune had a well-developed capacity for forgetting what he didn't wish to remember and imagining what didn't exist. All that had lodged in his mind was the vision of this man floating down from the sky beneath a white canopy, and he had long ago persuaded himself that the stranger's arrival was a stroke of providence.

"What happened to the plane?" Kacew repeated. "Are there any other survivors?"

"I had to get you to safety, there was no time for anything else. It was hopeless in any case—nothing but flames and a big black hole in the ground."

Kacew became conscious of an odor clinging to his skin—a blend of gasoline and oily metal. It reminded him of the moment when he'd climbed aboard the bomber on the runway at Elsham Wolds. Everything inside had given off the same effluvium of steel and aviation fuel: intoxicating, almost cloying, enhancing his dizzy delight at the prospect of flying again at last.

But the smell was associated with a more immediate memory—one that made his gorge rise. The bomber shuddered as the blazing engine broke loose; smoke filled the cockpit, blue and choking. He could see Karski, dark eyes staring in a scorched face, and hear his shouted, barely intelligible words: "We'll have to jump for it, Roman, I can't hold her any longer! Get going, jump!"

"What's the matter?" The words seemed to come from far away.

"Nothing."

A hand felt his pulse. "You're feverish, but it's only a flesh wound. The collarbone wasn't touched."

Kacew fought his way back to the present. "You called a doctor?"

"A doctor could have done no better. Besides, I was sure you wouldn't want one. The presence of a doctor at Rochebrune would have caused talk. We send for the vet when the mare gets colic, but that's all."

For the first time, it really dawned on Kacew where he was. Not in England, not in London, not in Elsham Wolds. This was France, an occupied country.

"Where exactly are we?" he asked.

"I'll show you on a map."

"And the nearest Germans?"

"Two army posts, both a good ten kilometers away. The only Germans who visit this area are officers on weekend hunting trips. They drive over from Le Mans, the headquarters of their Seventh Army."

"Where did the plane come down?" The pictures returned, the smell of burning gasoline and hot metal, Karski's voice urging him to jump.

"Eight kilometers away, on the other side of the forest."

The navigator must have bailed out after him, then Karski. The rest of the crew were dead or too badly wounded.

"You saw no other parachutes?"

"No, just yours."

"Did you examine the scene of the crash yourself?"

"My neighbor did."

"No survivors?"

"None at all."

"Where's my uniform?"

"It will be better if you wear these civilian clothes, Monsieur . . ."

Kacew didn't hesitate. "Frykowski," he said.

"Polish? I guessed as much from your accent."

"The plane—may I go and see it?"

"Better not. Besides, you wouldn't find anything. The Germans have already been there and carted the debris away."

"What makes you so sure they won't come here?"

"They used to come here right at the beginning—officers in search of billets—but it wasn't comfortable enough for them. The patrols they send out now are only interested in chickens and fresh eggs and bottles of Calvados. They leave us in peace because they know there's nothing here worth taking." Rochebrune laughed. "They regularly search my neighbor's place, but his is a big, prosperous farm with a lot of livestock."

"May I stay here for the present?"

Rochebrune made a sweeping gesture. "My home is at your disposal, Monsieur. I've had some supper prepared for us. Would you prefer Yseult to bring it to you, or do you feel strong enough to accompany me?"

"I'll come," Kacew said. The thought of remaining alone in this empty room, with only his thoughts for company, appalled him.

The stairs were dark and deserted. Kacew was wearing the clothes Rochebrune had brought him: flannel slacks, a white shirt, a corduroy jacket. They were all too big for him, but at least there was room in the jacket for his bandaged shoulder.

It was lighter outside. One of the château's four avenues ran due west, and the sky above it still glowed red. Peering at his wristwatch, Kacew saw that the glass had shattered and the hands were missing.

They crossed the courtyard and entered a spacious hall with a tessellated floor and a broad flight of stairs at one end. Not a picture or stick of furniture relieved its emptiness. It was colder inside the house than out. The chill in the air seemed age-old—the kind that endures from one winter's end to the next. Rochebrune was obviously too poor to heat or maintain the place.

He opened a door on the left of the hall. The drawing room had long windows and paneled walls. Logs were burning in the big stone fireplace, but there was little furniture even here: a crude wooden table in front of the fire, a few kitchen chairs, and another, smaller table with a radio on it.

"Yseult! Yseult!"

She appeared at once, so quickly that she might have been hovering behind the inner door. Hanging in the center of the room was a large wrought iron chandelier. Rochebrune mounted a chair and inserted candles in it as his daughter passed them to him. When he'd seen her running across the courtyard, Kacew had taken her for a girl in her teens. He now saw that she was older, in her late twenties or early thirties. Nothing in her face moved, not even her eyes.

Rochebrune got down off his chair and walked over to the table. "What will you have to drink?"

Kacew wasn't sure that he wanted anything at all. "Whatever there is." He pointed to the radio. "You have electricity here?"

"Only when the wind blows, but it usually does."

Rochebrune's daughter brought two heavy cut-glass goblets and a dark green bottle without a label. She went away and returned with bread, butter, cheese, some pâté in an earthenware bowl, and the remains of a cold chicken.

"Please sit down." Rochebrune filled both glasses to the brim. He drank slowly, almost hesitantly, but Kacew was undeceived. The deliberation with which he raised the glass to his lips, and the intervals between one pull and the next, stamped him as a drinker. Kacew only sipped at his Calvados. The fiery apple brandy had a curiously medicinal flavor.

One of the candles began to drip, spattering the flagstones with yellow wax. The girl—Kacew continued to think of her as that—had laid two places only. She now sat perched on the raised curb of the hearth with her knees drawn up, watching the other two in silence. Kacew wondered if she and her father made a habit of eating separately. They were as strange a pair as the house they lived in.

Rochebrune raised his glass. "To the Poles! I admire your compatriots, Monsieur Frykowski. In my view, they're among the finest fighting men in the world."

"We were beaten pretty quickly in '39," Kacew said.

"No matter. We were beaten quickly, too, but the war isn't over yet. The Poles are bold and courageous soldiers. We Frenchmen may have lost some of our military reputation, but we possess something just as important as dash and daring, especially in present circumstances. We have a talent for improvisation, for acting off the cuff." Rochebrune drank, eyeing Kacew over the rim of his glass. "You can trust me, you know."

"Of course."

"Really trust me, I mean. A courageous Pole and a Frenchman who refuses to give up: not a bad combination." Rochebrune leaned forward. "I want to show you something," he said in a conspiratorial whisper.

Draining his glass, he rose and armed himself with a candle and some matches. His walk betrayed no sign of the liquor inside him. Kacew glanced at the girl before they left the room. She hadn't stirred.

Rochebrune set off along a passage faintly lit by some windows facing the courtyard. They came to one of the turrets Kacew had noticed, recognizable from within by a circular stairway. Rochebrune paused to light his candle before descending the steps, which led to a vaulted cellar. At the far end was a wooden door. This he unlocked and threw open. Against the limestone wall of the inner chamber stood a row of casks.

"Would you hold the candle for a moment?" Rochebrune pried up the lids, one by one. He relieved Kacew of the candle and stood back. "There!"

Two of the casks contained submachine guns. Kacew put out his hand and touched the oily steel. They were British Stens, six in all, three to a cask. The remaining cask was packed with sticks of dynamite and other explosives.

Kacew knew about the airdrops of containers filled with guns, explosives, and money for the *réseaux*, or underground networks. He knew, too, about the British agents parachuted into France for the purpose of welding scattered French Resistance units into a secret army that would count for something when the invasion finally took place.

"How long have you had these?" he asked.

"Since October of last year."

"Is there a *réseau* here?"

Rochebrune, his face flushed with pride and excitement, said, "Serge was probably meant to organize one."

"Serge?"

"That's the name he used: Serge. He posed as a Belgian to account for his accent. He came by parachute, like you. As English as roast beef, but he insisted on being called 'Monsieur Serge.' Have you come to replace him?"

Kacew caught on at last. Rochebrune assumed, or chose to assume, that he was an Allied agent. "What was his assignment?"

"Something to do with the German headquarters at Le Mans and its lines of communication—at least, that's what I gathered. I go riding every day, you see. Everyone around here knows that, so they're accustomed to seeing me. I made drawings for him—sketch maps of all the telephone lines I could find."

Kacew's shoulder was throbbing badly. "Did he have a radio?"

"No. Perhaps they were supposed to send him one—perhaps he had access to a radio elsewhere. He was only with us a week."

"What became of him?"

The candle in the old man's hand guttered. A drop of hot wax landed on the back of his hand, making him start. "He said he had to go away for three or four days. I went with him to Champfleur—that's our nearest railroad station. He never returned."

From somewhere overhead came a series of muffled heartbeats. The single naked bulb suspended from the ceiling began to glow, feebly at first. The light gained strength as the heartbeats speeded up and the rhythm steadied.

"That's the generator." Rochebrune blew out the candle and replaced the lids on the casks.

"Where's the ammunition for the guns? I didn't see any."

Rochebrune's face darkened. "It was in another container—one that drifted out of range. Later on, I discovered that my neighbor had found it."

"The man you mentioned—Ringood?"

"These airdrops are common knowledge. The local peasants go foraging whenever the moon is full—you'll find one lurking behind every hedge. Why? Because they know the cylinders contain money and cigarettes and canned food, among other things. When the Ringoods found the ammunition, I tried to strike a bargain with them. They wanted three of my guns for half their ammunition—three!"

Kacew felt uneasy. "What if the Germans turn up here?"

"I told you. They only go hunting in the forest."

"Will you come to an arrangement?"

"With Ringood? Perhaps."

"And then?"

"We'll see. Those guns may prove useful someday." Rochebrune smiled. "The Poles and the French make good allies, don't forget."

He led the way upstairs again. Lights were burning in the drawing room, too—a pair of weak and flickering wall lights. The room was filled with a swelling, fading roar of static. The girl had turned on the radio and was sitting over it.

Rochebrune refilled his glass and knocked it back. "How's the shoulder?"

"It hurts."

"That's only to be expected. I'll take another look at it before you go to bed. Stay here in the warm. I must see to my horse."

Kacew sipped his Calvados. Again he was struck by its peculiar tang.

"You shouldn't drink. It isn't good for a fever."

Surprised that the girl had addressed him at all, Kacew went and stood beside her. She was listening to the coded messages that always followed the BBC's news in French—listening as intently as if they were meant for her.

"He showed me the guns."

She nodded. "You mustn't believe everything he tells you."

"I believe my own eyes."

"Did he also mention Serge?"

She pushed back her flowing hair as if to show how pretty she really was. Her full lips curved in a smile which Kacew found hard to interpret in the dim light. He wondered exactly how much she knew. Had this silent, watchful girl seen more than her father?

"Did Serge have a transmitter?"

She turned off the radio and stood up. "Let me show you something."

He followed her out into the hall. At the front door she gestured to him to wait and peered into the courtyard, then signaled that the coast was clear.

She paused and turned when they reached the fountain. "Look," she said, pointing back at the château. "You see the pigeon?"

Scudding clouds reflected and amplified the light of the rising moon. A row of grayish white ringdoves were roosting on the ridge tiles, and in their midst was a bigger bird with darker plumage.

"A homing pigeon," she whispered. "He had three. Two of them he sent off with things clipped to their legs—little capsules. He didn't see me watching him. The third was still in its cage when he left. I fed it for a month, two months—I don't recall how long. When he still didn't come back, I let it go. It disappeared for three days, then it turned up again."

Was the story true, or did it exist only in her imagination—the same imagination that lent wings to her father's flights of fancy? Kacew found it hard to decide.

He could hear the metallic clank of the wind-powered generator, the snorting and stamping of a horse in one of the stables. As though by common consent, the birds on the roof flew off. Everything seemed unreal except the pain in his shoulder, the memory of Karski's blackened face and parting words, and his recurrent thoughts of Gahagan. Would they try to find him?

15

Les Deux Vallées, Eure

THE LANDLORD WAS CLEARING AWAY. "Sorry," he said, "this toothpick slows me down a bit." In fact, he moved quite nimbly for a corpulent fifty-year-old with a wooden leg. The inn, which had been in his family for five generations, was just outside Serquigny, a village at the confluence of the Risle and the Charantonne, hence its name: Les Deux Vallées.

"Where did you lose it?" asked Berger.

"In a trench near Beaumont-Hamel." The landlord brushed some crumbs into his palm with a napkin and straightened up. He laughed as if the recollection amused him. "A lot of men lost bits and pieces there."

His wife, as rotund as himself, was sitting at a table in the corner with some card-playing customers. The room had a low wooden ceiling and heavy oak farmhouse furniture. A log fire was burning on the open hearth. The evening had turned cool.

"Nineteen-sixteen, I bought it—November 14, to be exact. It was daybreak, cold and misty. Some confounded Boche sniper must have been wide awake, though, because he spotted me lighting a cigarette. The bullet was a dumdum." He laughed again. "I can recommend the cheese. It's local."

"We've already eaten too well—too well and too much."

"It's a Pont l'Évêque. You should try some."

Jannou was watching Berger. Ever since they'd stopped here on the way back to Paris, he'd been playing the part of Monsieur Pierre Hougron, and playing it as convincingly as if he'd never been anyone else but the sales manager of Ciment Français of Brest, a man whose car, clothes, and manner inspired universal confidence.

The landlord returned with the cheese, some more bread, and a fresh carafe of wine. He rested one hand on the edge of the table and waited while they sampled the cheese.

"Well, have you ever tasted better?"

"It's excellent," said Berger, "like everything else here."

"Only excellent?" The landlord half turned to include his wife and her companions in his remarks. "Rommel's absolutely crazy about this cheese, did you know?"

"Rommel?"

"The German."

The men at the corner table lowered their cards. They'd probably heard the same thing a dozen times before, but they listened like children enjoying a twice-told tale.

Jannou glanced at Berger. She could detect nothing in his face but polite attention and faint amusement.

"Wherever he goes these days," the landlord went on, "the first thing he asks is, 'Got any Pont l'Évêque?' He eats it till it comes out of his ears."

He chuckled. The others smiled indulgently, all except Berger, who frowned.

"You mean he was here?"

"He hasn't done us that honor, I'm afraid, not General Rommel."

"The Germans honored my brother with their presence," Berger said grimly. "He owns a farm southwest of the Vire, and they flooded his best grazing land."

The men's smiles vanished. The landlord cleared his throat. "Yes, well, they do a lot of bad things, there's no denying."

The tension in the room communicated itself to Jannou. Why? she asked herself. Why must he carry the joke too far?

Everyone was staring at Berger. Suddenly, his face cleared. "Know what?" he said. "We ought to feed all their generals on Pont l'Évêque. By the time the Allies land, they'll be too fat to fight."

The tension disappeared in a flash. The landlord laughed. "There wouldn't be enough to go round," he quipped. "They've got too many generals, the Boches." He hobbled over to the other table and sat in on the game.

Berger poured some more wine and smiled across at Jannou. "We were really lucky to find this place."

She sipped her wine. Her tension, too, was slowly subsiding. "Was that necessary?"

"Maybe not. What shall we do, drive straight back to Paris?"

"Have you played many parts like this?"

"A few."

"And do people always tell you their life story on the spot?"

"The landlord makes a habit of it, I'd say."

"The way he spoke of Rommel—it made him sound nice."

"One day," Berger said, "that's just what it will be, a nice little anecdote."

"No matter how bad things get, time heals all, is that what you mean?"

"I mean he'll tell his customers the story as if it were his own—as if nice General Rommel used to patronize this place in person." Berger pushed his chair back. "We could always stay the night. What do you think?"

Jannou thought of Trouville and the fortifications along the coast; of the long, dark drive ahead of them; of the inevitable checkpoints; of Paris itself, dark and deprived of light; of the apartment in Rue Guynemer and the words daubed on the wall. Paris kept them apart, drove a wedge between them. No one here knew them or knew who they were.

"Yes," she said, "let's stay."

They were given a room on the second floor. It was crammed with furniture; even the carpets were two or three deep. The landlord's daughter, who lived in Paris, had moved her "best pieces" here for fear of air raids.

One of the windows overlooked an orchard full of apple trees planted in dead straight rows. With the light off and the window open, they leaned on the sill side by side. Voices could be heard. The landlord was saying good night to his customers in front of the inn. There was a final burst of laughter, then silence.

The air smelled of woodsmoke from the chimney overhead, wafted down to them by the night wind. A boat was chugging along the river, probably some small barge traveling under cover of darkness rather than risk attack by Allied fighter bombers during the day.

"Aren't you cold?" Berger said.

She recalled his telephoning in the lobby while the landlord's wife got their room ready. "Who did you call just now?"

"The Lutétia. I left this number."

"Why?"

She felt him stir beside her. Whether or not he'd intended to put his arm round her, he didn't.

"Force of habit, that's all."

"Does Monsieur Hougron really exist?"

"Yes."

"Where did you learn your French?"

"In France."

"Do you realize I know nothing about you? Nothing, after two years."

"There isn't much to tell."

"When were you in France before?"

"Back in the twenties."

"What were you doing here? Don't make it so difficult for me."

"I drove a cab to earn some money. In Paris."

"Is that all?"

"I wanted to be a painter once. I dropped the idea when I saw how many good artists there were in Paris." He gestured at his eye. "This didn't help, either. That's why I don't like reminiscing. I've abandoned too many things in my time."

The apple trees were in full leaf. Blossom time was over, but the moonlight gilded their foliage so brightly that they seemed to be flowering all over again. Jannou savored the illusion in silence for a while.

"There must be something you don't mind talking about—your parents, for instance. Are they still alive? I've never known you to get a letter or write one. You haven't been on leave once in the past two years."

"My father called himself a cigar manufacturer. The truth was, my mother and a couple of poor relations sat at home rolling cigars while he hawked them around the district in a clapped-out Ford. He's a big man now. Huge factory, three hundred workers turning out smokes for the Army. Still interested?"

"Very. Berger, cigar manufacturer . . . Wouldn't that make a good part for you to play?"

"You think it would be in character?"

"To be honest, yes. You're respectable and reassuring—the kind of man a woman feels safe with. The kind that works hard, takes his job seriously, doesn't cheat on his wife—the kind any parents would want their daughter to marry."

"My wife wouldn't agree."

"You're married?"

"I used to be. She wanted me to do just like you said, work hard and get ahead; I wasn't interested. As soon as I found that out, which didn't take long, it was over between us. I chucked my job and went off to Paris."

"What about your other women?"

"Meaning what?"

".What were they like? Younger? My age?"

"Most of them were older and married."

"Why?"

"Married women seldom want to marry their lovers. Besides, I think I enjoyed the element of secrecy."

Jannou laughed. "That I can believe." She paused, serious again. "Are you shy with women?"

"Well, am I?"

"You are with me." Abruptly, she added, "I'm getting cold."

He leaned out of the window, pulled the shutters to and latched them, closed the window, and drew the curtains. She heard him groping for the lamp beside the massive brass bedstead. He switched it on and stood facing her.

Jannou strove to read his expression but found it as hard as ever, perhaps because of his sightless eye. She started to remove her red jacket. He half raised one arm to help her, then let it fall and stood quite still. The desire she'd felt for him was there again, even stronger than the night before.

The room was anything but conducive to intimacy, but the intimacy she craved was physical rather than emotional. She couldn't help thinking of the other two men in her life. Both of them, Julien and Roman, had prided themselves on their ability to arouse her sexually whenever they chose. The choice had been theirs. She'd always bowed to their wishes, never ventured to express any of her own; indeed, she hadn't even been aware that women were capable of sexual volition. With Berger she felt different. It was she who did the choosing, she whose wishes and desires were paramount.

She put her jacket at the foot of the bed. She unbuttoned her black silk blouse, took it off, stepped out of her skirt. She undid the bra and let it fall, stood there with her breasts provocatively bare. Watching him, she realized that her attention had always been so riveted by his voice that she'd never really looked at his mouth. It was surprisingly soft and shapely.

She came closer and ran a forefinger over his lips. He flinched, but it only heightened her desire for him. Picking up her jacket, she draped it over the lamp and lay down on the bed. She felt a mixture of impatience and apprehension. Theirs was a relationship with no foreseeable future, she knew, and deepening it would only bring her sorrow, but she wanted this moment to the exclusion of all else.

Once he was beside her, though, her reservations vanished. As she bent over and kissed him, kissed his neck and shoulders and felt him flinch again at her touch, she realized that, here at least, she was the stronger. She reveled in the sense of power that overcame her—not an aggressive emotion, but a quiet certainty that she could give him pleasure.

He raised his head and looked at her, puzzled. "What are you smiling at?"

"Myself."

Naked, he was someone else, not the German she'd known for two years. Naked, she could conceive of him as a man she might have met in other, earlier times.

She knelt over him. He surrendered himself to her, her hands and lips. His breathing quickened. Then, not roughly but with sudden, impulsive haste, he thrust her off him and entered her.

Was she happy? She might have been, she thought vaguely, in another world and another age, but she had never known that world and had no real idea of it. She had grown to womanhood in an age when mutual destruction seemed the purpose of human existence. Having accepted that, she found that happiness could be hers after all, if only for now, for the moment.

She waited until his breathing told her he was fast asleep. Once she was sure, she said softly, "It might have been so different."

But that was when she heard footsteps on the stairs. Even before they stopped outside the door, and even before someone knocked, she knew that the moment was already past.

Paris

ALL JANNOU COULD SEE over the top of the high stone wall were some trees and a roof with an aerial on it.

Berger had disappeared into the Montmartre villa half an hour before, letting himself in with a key of his own. He hadn't said anything, neither then nor on the drive back to Paris. It was the landlord who'd knocked and called Monsieur Hougron to the telephone. When Berger returned, he merely said, "Get dressed, we're leaving."

He remained silent the whole way, apparently concentrating on the road ahead. She realized how edgy he was when they had to stop at checkpoints, as they did again and again. He controlled his impatience with an effort every time.

Now she saw him step out into the street and lock the gate behind him. The night was cold, and she was shivering in her light linen jacket.

"You should have started it up and left the engine running."

"I wasn't sure, because of the gasoline."

He leaned into the Simca and switched on the ignition. After peering at the fuel gauge, he opened the hood and filled the tank from a reserve can in the trunk. The car reeked of gasoline when they drove off.

"Mind if I open my window?" she asked.

"You'll be even colder."

She wound it down just the same. The streets were completely blacked out, and the Simca's headlights, reduced to slits with layers of insulating tape, had little effect. She was surprised he could see anything at all. He was an idiosyncratic driver at the best of times. Even in daylight, he steered with abrupt little jerks of the wheel. She suspected it had something to do with his relative inability to see things in perspective.

"Thanks for not asking any questions," he said eventually.

"I knew you wouldn't answer them."

"I'm not so sure."

"That house—do you go there every night? It's got an aerial."

"Forget you ever saw the place."

"Was the phone call about Roman?"

"Now you *are* asking questions."

They rounded the dark and deserted Arc de Triomphe. The Simca picked up speed on the long descent to Place de la Concorde.

"Look out!" She'd seen the barrier, the uniformed figures, the winking red lights. Instead of slowing, he accelerated and drove straight at the road block.

"No!" she shouted. "Please don't!"

He braked hard, hurling her against the dashboard. She only realized what had happened when her numb lips began to smart and she tasted blood in her mouth. There were flashlights and loud voices all around her. One of them was Berger's, raised in anger. She reached for a handkerchief and pressed it to her lips. Someone shone a flashlight full in her eyes, dazzling her so painfully that she clamped them shut.

Then the Simca moved off again. Berger's only comment was a single word in French. *"Crétins!"* she heard him mutter.

Leaving the checkpoint behind, they skirted Place de la Concorde. Without lights, Jannou thought, the huge square lost all its beauty and became a gloomy void, nothing more. Berger made for the bridge, which was also in darkness, its old-fashioned globe lamps unlit. The river beneath resembled an underpass, a ribbon of black asphalt.

Berger pulled up as soon as he reached the Left Bank. He leaned over, removed the bloodstained handkerchief from her mouth, and inspected the cut with the aid of his cigarette lighter.

"It's nothing," she said. "I bit my lip, that's all. What made you do it, though? Didn't you see them?"

For want of an answer, he took her in his arms and kissed her. She resisted at first, not wanting him to taste the blood.

"The instant before you stopped," she said, "I was sure they'd open fire on us." She felt her lip begin to bleed again and took the handkerchief back.

He sat there beside her, hesitating. She thought he was about to speak, communicate, confide in her, but he started the car and drove off in silence.

The Left Bank was dark and devoid of life. One thing I'll never forgive him for, she told herself, focusing her resentment on Berger alone: I'll never forgive him for blacking out our city.

When he stopped outside the house in Rue Guynemer and she got out to open the gate, she noticed that the inscription beneath the fresh paint was showing through again.

16

London

THEY WERE TOO EARLY, so they sat killing time in Scott's Lagonda. The cul-de-sac ended in a blank brick wall. A tree overhung the wall and the narrow street, and visible beyond it in the moonlight was the gutted east wing of Holland House, a former royal residence in the park of the same name. It had been bombed during one of the first heavy raids on London.

Ian Scott, though also in his early forties, could not have been less like Gahagan. Scott's athletic frame radiated vigor, and his sandy hair was close-cropped for at least two inches above his rather prominent ears. Not even a dapper tweed suit could disguise the soldier beneath.

"Let's get something straight, Jeremy: I can't spare you any of my people. I'm not risking a single one of them to clear up your mess."

"Please, Ian, I'm beat."

"Have you any idea how tired *I* am of gambling with agents' lives for the benefit of you and your hocus-pocus?"

"Then tell him so yourself. Spell out exactly what you can or can't do for us."

"The operative word is 'can't.' "

"It's time we went."

They got out of the Lagonda and made their way past Gahagan's government-owned Morris sedan, which was parked in front of it. Both were carrying briefcases, though neither was likely to need one. If they had anything in common, it was a good memory.

The house was at the end of the mews, a onetime carriage house converted into an apartment with a double garage beneath. A car stood outside, but it wasn't Sir Graham's Wolseley. This one was a dark blue Bentley.

"Since when has he been driving that?" mused Scott. "Come to that, since when has he had this hideaway?"

Gahagan was in no mood for idle speculation. When he rang the bell, it was Sir Graham himself, not Winter, who came to the door.

"Good evening, sir."

"Evening. On the dot, I see. I like punctuality."

The place was newly converted and incompletely furnished. Crates were stacked in the downstairs hall, and there was a smell of fresh paint. In default of anywhere to hang it, Gahagan draped his duffel coat over a packing case.

"Follow me, gentlemen." Sir Graham led the way upstairs and into a low-ceilinged room with small windows. "This is my den, or will be."

The room looked more spacious than it was because the built-in bookshelves were still empty. A fire was burning in the grate, with some comfortable leather armchairs in front of it.

Seated in an armchair a little apart from the rest, legs elegantly crossed, was a silver-haired man in a double-breasted gray suit of immaculate cut. Gahagan and Scott glanced at each other, faintly surprised to find an outsider present.

Sir Graham didn't introduce him by his full name. "Gerald is my buffer," he said. "When I collide with the powers that be, he absorbs some of the impact."

The man smiled blandly and adjusted the snow-white handkerchief in his breast pocket. "It isn't an official function," he drawled.

"Gerald, this is Jeremy Gahagan—you know what he does. Colonel Scott here heads the French Section."

"I used to play golf at Dornoch with a namesake of yours," said Gerald. "Fine course, Dornoch. Ever played up there?"

"Not lately." Scott made no effort to sound polite.

"Never mind the social chitchat, Gerald," Sir Graham said. "In the first place, charm is wasted on Ian. Secondly, we don't have the time."

Gerald was unruffled. "In that case, I shall simply sit here and observe in admiring silence, as usual." He raised his right hand and inspected the palm as if it might help him do a vanishing act.

"Fine," said Sir Graham, when everyone was seated. "Let's kick off with you, Ian."

"Suits me, sir. I'm expecting two Lysanders back from France tonight with agents aboard. I've got to be at Manston to meet them."

"Did Jeremy outline our problem?"

"He did."

"And?"

"There's not much to go on. We don't even know if your man's alive."

"The bomber crews were debriefed on their return," Gahagan said, "but nothing new emerged." He hesitated. "It doesn't look as if anyone survived the crash."

Sir Graham leaned forward intently. "Even that would be a help, knowing whether he's alive or not. Well, Ian?"

"We don't have any organized Resistance group in the area where the plane came down. Airdrops were made until recently, but we've discontinued them."

"I want this man located, dead or alive. If an individual can do it, so much the better. I'm not asking you to mobilize an army."

Scott shrugged. "I don't have anyone there. At your request, we're holding our teams in reserve until the invasion. The area is taboo until then. 'Don't alert the Germans in the Normandy hinterland,' those are my instructions. Ferreting around there now would present us with a lot of problems."

"Forget your problems for a change and help us with ours. I thought you inserted an agent in the Le Mans area."

"We did, sir, with orders to prepare to disrupt the Seventh Army's communications on D-Day." Scott paused, then went on even more curtly. "Sam Hopkins—Serge, I should say—was captured. He committed suicide to escape further interrogation by the SD."

Sir Graham frowned. "So what's the answer?"

"We don't have an agent in the area who could trace your man, sir. That's the short answer."

"What about Double?" There was a hint of impatience in Sir Graham's tone.

"He's living up to his name," Scott said wryly. "The Abwehr turned him. One of our reasons for sending Serge was to check on him. We lost Serge in the process. Double is still active, but he'd be useless to us for present purposes."

Sir Graham looked at Gahagan. "I hoped you'd make it clear how much importance we attach to this matter, Jeremy. You don't seem to have had much success."

"As you say, sir, Ian doesn't respond to charm." Gahagan secretly admired Scott at this moment. If only I could grow a skin as thick as his, he thought, I mightn't have ulcers.

Nobody spoke for several seconds. Nothing broke the silence except a whisper of wind in the chimney. Gahagan had meant to say as little as possible, but his resolution cracked. "Can't you send someone out from here?" he asked.

"To do what?" said Scott. "Traipse around from door to door and ask if—"

"Damn it all!"

Coming from a man as preternaturally calm as Sir Graham, this was an emotional outburst of such magnitude that the other three stared at him in surprise.

"Since when do I have to climb on my high horse and give you a direct order, Ian? Where this business is concerned, we're all in the same boat. Act at your own discretion, but locate that man. Trace him and be quick about it."

Gahagan studied Sir Graham with covert fascination. His posture and expression remained unchanged. All that betrayed his anger was the edge to his voice and a curious twitching of the scalp.

Scott said, "Our best hope might be to use Julien in Paris. He couldn't afford to get involved himself, but he does have a wide range of useful contacts."

"Then use him."

"Do I have your permission, sir?"

"Yes, damn it! You want that in writing?"

"No, sir, two witnesses will be good enough." Scott's tone became more formal still. "If we locate him, what then?"

Sir Graham gestured at Gahagan as if his outburst had left him too debilitated to answer the question himself.

"If you do discover his whereabouts," Gahagan said, "and he's still alive, get him out. I don't care how—air, sea, any way you can—but get him back here. We need him badly. And don't forget it's Jerzy Frykowski we're after, not Roman Kacew."

Scott looked at Sir Graham. "Will you be needing me anymore, sir?"

"No, but report your progress every twelve hours."

"Very good." Scott rose.

"One more thing, Ian. You know what's happening in Paris better than any of us. Those latest reports of yours about the feud between the Abwehr and the SD—which bunch would you put your money on?"

"The SD, sir, no doubt about it. They wield the real power, or will do once the invasion takes place and there's a serious threat from the Resistance. To keep order, as the German authorities understand it, they'll use the SD to—"

"Yes, yes, no need to go into detail now." Sir Graham drew a deep breath. "Draft me a report on the current situation in Paris—all you've got on every aspect of it, and that includes personalities. That's all, Ian. No one's keeping you from your fun and games any longer."

Gahagan thought he detected a kind of envy in the old man's voice. Was he envious of men like Ian Scott—even, perhaps, of himself—because they could go off and *do* something, whereas he had to sit and vegetate with "Gerald," who had Foreign Office written all over him and was doubtless breathing down his neck? If it wasn't envy, it was certainly regret. Sir Graham's oft-repeated maxim was that the Firm must steer clear of politics; he himself was up to his neck in them.

While Sir Graham was seeing Scott out, Gerald carefully smoothed his silver wings and leaned toward Gahagan with a confidential air. "Tell me," he said, echoing Scott's question of twenty minutes before, "how long has he had this place?"

"I wouldn't know," Gahagan replied. He wondered idly if Gerald tinted his hair.

"That Pole has really dropped you in the dirt, eh? Don't we have enough people of our own?"

"Using foreigners has its advantages." Gahagan's gut gave a violent twinge.

"They're a necessary evil, you mean?"

Sir Graham returned. He went over to the fire and silently put another log on.

"Don't you ever offer your people a drink?" asked Gerald. "A drop of brandy wouldn't come amiss."

"Brandy and ulcers don't mix." Sir Graham straightened up and subjected Gahagan to a searching stare. "Isn't that right, Jeremy? How are they, by the way?"

"Acting up a bit, sir." Gahagan wished he'd been able to leave with Scott.

"What are you doing about them?" When Gahagan merely shrugged, Sir Graham went on, "Let me see what you prepared for Cato's next transmission."

Gahagan put his briefcase on his lap, opened it, and produced three sheets of typescript stapled together.

"Good, very good . . ." The brown blotches on the backs of Sir Graham's hands showed up more than ever as he turned the crisp white sheets, then turned them back again. "No wonder you think such a lot of him . . ." He looked up, still turning the sheets back and forth, but not at Gahagan. His gaze was on the fire. "We'll have to make a decision, won't we? Damned awkward, but there it is. He hasn't been in touch with Paris every night, has he?"

"No, not every night. At intervals."

"What sort of intervals?"

"They vary. When he changes his location, three or four days. When he's away 'gathering intelligence,' as much as a week—it makes his work seem more difficult. The longest gap was two weeks. We threatened to cease transmitting altogether—Cato did, I mean—because he felt his services weren't sufficiently appreciated."

"That was at an early stage, though, wasn't it?"

"True, but it isn't exceptional for us to suspend transmissions. Provided Ian finds him quickly enough . . ."

Sir Graham sighed. "What does 'quickly' mean? How quickly, Jeremy? We can't afford to silence Cato at this juncture."

"Except that I don't see how—"

"Whispering lies in the ear of an enemy who believes them to be true—that's worth whole armies, eh, Gerald?"

Gerald spread his hands. "I'm only an observer, remember?"

"Couldn't you stand in for him, Jeremy? You've been working together for over a year."

"They wouldn't swallow it, sir. Our 'handwriting' isn't the same. His opposite number would smell a rat at once."

"You mean it's too risky?"

Sir Graham's incomprehension exasperated Gahagan. "Not just risky, downright impossible. Maybe Ian will find him sooner than we think." Who, he wondered, was Julien? The name was new to him.

"Maybe so, maybe not. One thing's certain: we can't let Cato die."

"We've invented some subagents for him. In the last resort, we could try 'promoting' one of them, get him to deputize. We'll have to concoct some explanation in any case, if Cato's really dead."

Sir Graham shook his head as though unable to accept the possibility. "I wonder," he said, and his voice was little more than a whisper, "—can *he* afford to lose him? When I cast my mind back, when I recall the plan as a whole, there always was an element of ambiguity . . ."

The silence that followed was intense. Gahagan experienced a mixture of uneasiness and curiosity. Sir Graham continued to sit there, outwardly impassive, but the firelight bathed him in a glow that seemed to come from within. Gahagan had the absurd notion that, if he opened his mouth, flames would dart forth. When he did eventually speak, his words were accompanied by a pensive smile. "There's no solution, from the look of it—none that's likely to satisfy us all." He held out the sheaf of typescript.

Gahagan replaced it in his briefcase and took out a slim red folder. "That's all we have on Berger."

"Berger? Ah yes, thank you." Sir Graham put the folder on the arm of his chair. "Any news of the man from Lisbon?"

"Nothing, sir."

"Who's taken over the paymaster's job?"

"Luis Chavero, a Mexican employed in the embassy here."

"Did Cato get in touch with him?"

"This morning, sir, by telephone."

"They arranged to meet?"

"I assume so."

"When?"

"Cato didn't have a chance to inform me."

"This Mexican chap—have him watched."

"I ordered surveillance as soon as the signal arrived from Paris."

"Good, Jeremy. I think that's all for now."

Gahagan shut his briefcase and rose. "Can I reach you here if something comes up?"

"I'll be at the office." Sir Graham stood up too. Gerald made an airy gesture and remained seated.

Sir Graham accompanied Gahagan downstairs to the front door. "What about Lieutenant Mills—Alison Mills, isn't it? She'll wonder what's happened when her 'guest' fails to reappear. We can't afford any idle talk, even inside the Firm."

Gahagan put his duffel coat over his arm. "She's on a night train to Scotland. Tomorrow she'll be catching a boat from Mallaig to Stornoway, in the Outer Hebrides."

"Poor girl, what a godforsaken spot! Still, you have to take the rough with the smooth in our business. Watch those ulcers, Jeremy."

Sir Graham let Gahagan out and went upstairs again. He glanced at a door at the end of the passage and sighed before rejoining Gerald in the den.

The Foreign Office man was standing in front of the fire, looking as if his observer's role had palled at last. "Prickly customers, those two," he said. "They don't toe the line too readily."

"Good men, though. They may curse me under their breath, but they pull their weight."

Gerald looked around the room. "You really haven't any brandy?"

"Sorry, I'm not properly organized yet." Sir Graham cocked an eyebrow. "Well, you asked to sit in on that session. Are you satisfied?"

"Not entirely. Why are you so interested in the rivalry between the Abwehr and the SD?"

"That's a long story. Can't we call it a day? It's late, and I still have work to do." Sir Graham picked up the red folder.

"Who's Julien?"

"You're treading on dangerous ground, Gerald."

"And you're being evasive. The Firm thrives on mystery, doesn't it? Daylight destroys its magic. All right, who's Julien?"

"A Frenchman based in Paris. His contacts are important to us."

"Contacts with the Germans?"

"With one particular German, yes, but this is a delicate matter. I'd sooner drop the subject."

"I hope you aren't poaching on our preserves again."

"This has nothing to do with politics. You know I'm allergic to the very word."

"But not too allergic to attend a secret meeting with Donovan and Canaris in Spain."

"My God, must we go into all that again! Every well-informed secret service maintains certain contacts with the enemy."

Gerald toyed with his silk handkerchief. "The Foreign Secretary won't just raise his eyebrows and leave it at that, not a second time. No communication with the enemy: Mr. Eden is adamant on that point."

"Don't worry about Canaris. He'll be lucky to survive the next three months."

"You seem sorry."

"Canaris had some sound ideas. Yes, it's always sad to see a good man bite the dust."

"He didn't by any chance mention Cato when you saw him at Santander? He didn't take you aside and—"

"You're fantasizing, Gerald."

"I simply want to make the official position clear: no more flirting with the enemy."

"I do my job, that's all."

"I keep forgetting. You may have a romantic streak, but you're a double-barreled realist at heart. Unloading your wife like that . . ."

"Please, Gerald, let's call it a day." Sir Graham led the way downstairs.

Gerald gave a last glance over his shoulder. "Cozy little place."

"It will be, if I ever find the time to furnish it."

"You live here under your own name?"

Sir Graham made a noncommittal gesture. "Good night, Gerald."

He switched off the hall light and stood at the open door until the Bentley was out of sight. Instead of returning to the den, he walked quickly to the door at the end of the passage, knocked, and went in. The room was fully furnished. Two small bowl lamps shed a warm glow on the double bed and the girl in it. She said, "I thought they'd never go."

He smiled down at her benevolently. Her round and rather doll-like face, framed by a mass of blond hair, was a little flushed.

"Sorry, Rona."

She was wearing the lace negligee that had looked so chic in the store window, but on her made a somewhat tarty impression, just as he'd hoped it would.

"Are you coming to bed now?" She laughed rather nervously. "I'm so bad at waiting, I had a teeny drink. You don't mind, do you?" Either her lisp was natural, or the drink hadn't been as teeny as all that.

"Fix me one, too. I'm just going to check the fire."

"Brandy?"

"And water. Very long."

He felt a trifle guilty, thinking of Ian Scott and Jeremy Gahagan as he raked the remains of the fire to the back of the grate—especially Gahagan, with his chronic stomach ulcers. Good men, both of them.

He felt a trifle guilty, too, because he was transgressing the moral code whose strict observance he demanded from others, but he knew his pangs of conscience wouldn't last. The world of secrets was a strange place. Living in its perpetual twilight was like suffering from some physical or mental disorder. The events he set in motion, their byproducts and ramifications, sometimes proved too much, even for him.

They could never be forgotten altogether, but from time to time, he reflected on the way back to the bedroom, even a man like himself was entitled to a thoroughly mundane existence complete with thoroughly mundane pleasures.

17

Paris

THE SILENCE IN BERGER'S OFFICE was unbroken except by the faint staccato of a typewriter in the room next door; Hermine had defied his ban on weekend working. The window behind him was open, but the streets were almost empty of traffic because Parisians were forbidden to drive on Sundays. The Lutétia might have been in the depths of the country.

As a rule, Sunday was the day when Berger caught up on his official mail, drafted memos, and reread the agents' reports that had come in during the week. His desk was usually strewn with papers; today there was nothing on it but Chavero's brief message from London.

The signal had been received last night. Looking at it now, by the light of day, he felt that he had overreacted, that his return to Paris had been precipitate and unnecessary. Joseph had made an appointment with the Mexican and failed to turn up; that was the sum total of the information that had caused him to panic like a man in the path of an avalanche.

Why, he wondered, should everything look so different now? Perhaps because he was sitting at his desk, where he could still marshal his thoughts and master his doubts about the double role he'd played for so long.

He went over to the window and stood looking down. Anonymous figures were climbing and descending the steps to the Métro station, cyclists pedaling past in the direction of the Seine, old men sunning themselves on benches, children skipping. Everything looked normal and unremarkable, yet Berger had a feeling that all he could see was possessed of some significance which, like the message on his desk, had only to be interpreted aright.

Something intruded on his thoughts. He took a moment to identify it, then realized that Hermine had stopped typing. He could hear voices in the outer office, one of them hers, the other a resonant baritone. Hermine laughed, a phenomenon so unusual that he guessed at once who the visitor was. In times as grave as these, his secretary considered it permissible to laugh only when the instigator of her mirth was a priest.

He shook his head as soon as she came in. "I've no time for him now."

"It's Father Ebert." Hermine was wearing her Sunday best, presumably because she'd been to early Mass.

"I know who it is." Berger was seldom as impatient with her. "I don't want to see him—or you, for that matter. I told you to take the day off. Personally, I've got work to do."

"I think you ought to."

There were times when Berger suspected the pair of them of engaging in a sort of conspiracy to shepherd him, a lapsed Catholic, back into the fold. To Hermine, saving her boss's soul would have more than justified her decision to join him in a sink of iniquity like Paris.

"It's very inconvenient, honestly."

She continued to stand in front of his desk, mutely insistent.

Berger capitulated. "Five minutes," he said. He opened a drawer and put Chavero's message inside. "That's all I can spare him."

Ebert was a red-haired colossus who propelled his massive frame along at a ponderous shuffle, scarcely lifting his feet off the ground. His peculiar gait was said to be a legacy of frostbite from the first disastrous winter of the Russian campaign.

"There isn't much demand for priests at the moment, not in this godforsaken city." Ebert pulled up a chair and squeezed into it uninvited. His army chaplain's uniform was adorned with several medal ribbons and a pectoral cross on a chain.

"That's not what I've heard." The uniform, Berger noted, had been made by a first-class tailor. "They say it's the height of fashion to confess to you, like patronizing that clairvoyante at the Ritz."

Ebert had become something of a celebrity in Paris, but not so much in his capacity as the chaplain responsible for prisons under German administration. He was a frequent visitor to the Palais Rose, the Military Governor's private residence, and had von Stülpnagel's ear—or rather, lent him his own.

Berger's gibe left Ebert unruffled. He gave a bland smile. "I hear you're interested in knowing what's become of a certain Abwehr officer. Schneevogel, right?"

Berger lit a cigarette, his first of the day. Till then, he hadn't noticed the envelope in the chaplain's hand. He said nothing, but again he had the feeling that an avalanche was bearing down on him.

"Your boss asked General von Stülpnagel for a legal inquiry. Odd, considering how wary Steinberg tends to be." Ebert put the envelope on the desk. "This is a copy of an autopsy report."

Berger opened the envelope with studious deliberation. The single sheet inside bore an itemized list of findings and was signed "Ulitzky." He barely glanced at it. The precise details seemed remote and unimportant now.

"I hope I'm the bearer of good news."

Berger looked up. There was no discernible expression on the chaplain's plump, pallid, clean-shaven countenance. "One of our men is killed by the SD, and you call that good?"

"Schneevogel was brought to Paris for questioning. The interrogation never took place. Whether that's good news or bad, only you can judge."

He's dead, thought Berger, and he didn't talk. Any regret he might have felt was swamped by a sense of relief.

"How did you come by this?"

"I happened to be present when Gürtner submitted his report to the general. A fortunate coincidence."

"Whom did Gürtner interview?"

"Everyone concerned."

"Including Standartenführer Reckzeh?"

"Of course. The Majestic takes a very grave view of this affair."

"Which means, in my experience, that it'll go no farther."

"The general's legal advisers consider the SD's explanation satisfactory."

"What about the body?"

"They're releasing it to the next of kin."

Berger replaced the report in the envelope. "Thanks. May I keep this?"

"I had it made for you specially." Ebert adjusted the chain that supported his cross—like a woman adjusting a piece of jewelry, thought

Berger. Even his medal ribbons, genuine though they were, looked like fashion accessories. "May I ask you something in return? A small favor . . ."

Berger got up and went over to the safe. He dialed the combination, swung the door open, and leafed through the contents of a folder on one of the shelves inside. He returned to his desk bearing a log sheet of the type used for Abwehr surveillance reports.

"On April 28 last," Berger said, paraphrasing, "a certain military chaplain visited the Hôtel Raphael, Avenue Kléber, between 1830 and 1920 hours. In the hotel bar he met a Major Voss. Voss, just back from the Eastern Front, reported that—"

"Look, Berger—"

"Voss reported that the SS were engaging in 'wholesale extermination in the East,' quote unquote. The chaplain declared, and I quote again, that it was 'time to take some form of political initiative.' Major Voss inquired if General von—"

"Please, Berger, I've heard enough." Ebert was looking more surprised than perturbed. "Is that how you spend your days, delving into such things?"

"This office is *my* confessional," Berger said quietly.

"And your conscience never pricks you?"

Berger could feel the chaplain's eyes fixed on him, probing and appraising. That was his chief reason for keeping Ebert at arm's length— Ebert, who was forever putting out feelers and inviting confidences. He handed him the typewritten sheet.

"You can keep that. There aren't any copies, either. I know you've got some influential friends, but don't put too much faith in them. And now, if you'll excuse me . . ."

Ebert pocketed the piece of paper but made no move to rise. "Actually, I wanted to ask you something else."

"Another time."

"I'm trying to locate a man, an Allied airman. His plane was shot down. Your people keep an eye on underground escape routes, don't they?"

Berger hesitated, then sat down again.

"The plane, a four-engined RAF Liberator, was badly damaged during a raid on Le Mans. It crashed about fifteen kilometers south of Alençon and burned out."

"Any idea when?" Berger picked up a pencil and drew a memo pad toward him.

"Early yesterday afternoon, around one-thirty. The man I'm after is a flight lieutenant, nationality Polish, name Frykowski—Jerzy Frykowski."

Berger didn't look up. "Spell it for me, would you?" Although he couldn't recall hearing the name before, the pencil seemed to twitch in his hand like a dowsing rod as he wrote it down.

"Can you describe him?"

"Early thirties, medium height, dark hair, brown eyes, swarthy complexion, no distinguishing marks. Speaks French, but with an accent. I'd appreciate your help."

"What do you want me to do?"

"There are three possibilities: either he didn't survive the crash, or he's alive and in custody, or he's alive and in hiding. It all depends which."

"Stranded Allied airmen are the Luftwaffe's baby, not ours."

"You could make inquiries, though."

"What's so special about this man?"

"I'm in the business of helping people. They don't have to be special."

Berger finished writing and looked up. "You're playing with fire," he said mechanically, but his mind was elsewhere. Frykowski, Frykowski . . . What was it about the name?

Ebert extricated himself from his chair with difficulty. "Thank you for this." He patted the report in his breast pocket.

"Only one thing puzzles me," Berger said. "A British plane is shot down. Twenty-four hours later you waltz in here and make inquiries about a possible survivor. Note the time factor: twenty-four hours. How did they contact you so quickly?"

Ebert toyed with the cross on his chest. "I quite understand," he said. "You have a reputation to maintain as a man who gets people to talk. Spare a thought for my reputation as a man who can keep his mouth shut. If you decide to help, you know where to find me."

Berger sat motionless at his desk for some seconds after the chaplain had lumbered out. The inference was blindingly obvious: no such inquiry could have been transmitted to Paris except by radio. Cross-Channel radio links were few in number and dangerous to maintain. The British never used them without a very special reason.

He opened the safe again and took out a copy of Joseph's latest signal, the one received on Friday night. Then he shut the window and resumed his seat. With the two texts spread out in front of him, Joseph's and Chavero's, he proceeded to absorb them word for word.

Berger had never found paperwork tedious. Much as he enjoyed his excursions into the field, his approach to it was methodical and precise. Paperwork was the basis of all counterespionage. Most of his successes had originated here, at his desk.

He tore the top sheet off his memo pad, put it aside, and started on the next:

Friday: Joseph takes up new appointment as liaison officer RAF/HQ Polish Armed Forces in Britain. Requests cash payment Chavero.
Saturday: Joseph scheduled visit Polish-manned RAF base, Elsham Wolds. Fails keep appointment Chavero. No transmission from London, though none expected.
Sunday: Ebert inquires after Polish airman J. F.

Even the simple act of wielding a pencil, the mere sight of his impeccably neat handwriting, helped to clear Berger's head. He picked up the phone and called the villa in Montmartre. Gehrts took a while to answer. When he did, his rapid breathing suggested that he'd been in the middle of a workout.

"Anything more from Chavero?"

"No. Are you expecting another signal from him?"

"Just call me at once if he comes through again."

Joseph had been insistent on more cash—he'd even threatened to suspend operations unless he got it—so why hadn't he kept his appointment with Chavero? Why hadn't he fixed another?

Berger reread his notes and burned them in the ashtray before going to the safe and locking the two signals away. He could hear Hermine's typewriter clattering in the next room.

Leaving his office by the outer door, he walked the few yards that separated it from Schmidt's. His assistant wasn't there. The poky little office, which overlooked a yard at the rear of the building, was gloomy even by day. Its furnishings were bleak and barracklike; no one had even troubled to remove the washbasin and mirror dating from the Lutétia's days as a hotel. Berger knew the room well. It was the one he himself had been allocated after his transfer from Brest to Paris.

A note was lying on Schmidt's tidy desk. Berger leaned over and read it.

He passed no one on his way downstairs to the ground-floor canteen. On Sundays, full-scale activity was confined to the Lutétia's attics, where the men of the Monitoring Section sat hunched over their sets, jotting down enciphered signals from London to Resistance groups in France—mysterious messages of which it was assumed that one would sooner or later herald the long-awaited invasion.

When? Berger asked himself. How much longer? Could he hold out till then? If he'd never realized it before, he did so now: he was attached to his present function. For the first time ever, he identified with himself. The youngster who'd hawked cigars from door to door with his father, the romantic who'd gone off to Paris to become a painter, the numerous other Bergers who'd roamed around, forever embarking on new ventures, never seeing them through—how glad he'd been to bid them all farewell.

Berger the intelligence officer: that was the role that had fulfilled him. He liked the rewards associated with it, the sense of self-importance, the stage he played on, the Lutétia, Paris, France. He'd never pretended to himself that his motives were any more exalted or profound than they were in reality. He had an affection for this role, *this* Berger, because it was the only one he could see that suited him.

Lights burned day and night in the Lutétia's restaurant, now reduced to the status of a canteen. The big windows facing the street had been boarded up six months ago, after a bomb exploded on the sidewalk. One of the tables was occupied by a foursome, two officers and two switchboard girls. They were laughing at something when Berger walked in.

"Over here, Captain."

Schmidt was alone at a corner table. Like his uniform, his civilian suit looked a size too big for him. The artificial lighting lent his gray face a translucent, parchmentlike quality.

Berger sat down. A waiter came over, but he shook his head and lit a cigarette.

"Ever since they got rid of the French chef," Schmidt said, "even the coffee's been a disaster."

"I didn't even know we had a French chef." Everything was grating on Berger's nerves: the laughter from the other table, the room itself, the claustrophobic, subterranean atmosphere. "Have you heard when Steinberg's expected back?"

"Nobody seems to know."

The officers and their girls got up. Berger watched them go. "A formation of RAF Liberators raided Le Mans yesterday. One of them came down south of Alençon. Find out all you can about it. Try to contact someone who investigated the incident."

Schmidt's expression had a soothing effect on Berger. He never had to be told when something was important. He still looked like a worried spaniel, but he seemed to fill out his suit better.

"I need maps of the area," Berger went on. "Which is our nearest outstation?"

"To Alençon? That would be Weber's office at Sées."

"Weber? Good. Tell him to drop everything else and concentrate on this. He's to inspect the scene of the crash and make discreet inquiries in the neighborhood. What's his usual cover?"

"French railroad inspector."

"I want him to phone in as soon as he's run a preliminary check—no later than this afternoon, say between five and six." Berger paused. "By the way, does the name Frykowski ring a bell?"

He could see Schmidt probing his memory like an oil prospector, bringing up core samples and discarding them until he found what he was looking for.

"Jerzy Frykowski?"

"You mean we've got something on him?" Berger found it hard to keep the excitement out of his voice.

"General Records don't. You do, though, in the Joseph file."

"You're sure?"

"When we searched the Rue Vercingétorix apartment after Kacew's arrest, we came across a snapshot—a photograph of Kacew himself, Frykowski, and another man. All Poles, all fliers. The names should be down somewhere. I can dig them out for you."

Berger rose.

Schmidt carefully folded his napkin. "I'd better make that call first and start the ball rolling."

Berger couldn't remember seeing Schmidt smile in quite that way before.

18

Rochebrune

KACEW STOOD AT THE GATE and watched the girl cycle off. She waved goodbye, keeping her balance with difficulty because of the rutted surface and the long skirt bunched up beneath her. On second thoughts, the idea of sending Yseult to St.-Rigomer-des-Bois seemed pointless and unwise, but he made no attempt to stop her.

Three tethered ponies were grazing nearby in the shade of the beech trees. Behind him, doves fluttered back and forth across the courtyard. From the forest came sporadic shots and the barking of dogs, but the sounds were muted by distance.

Two airplanes had flown over the château that morning—small, low-flying machines with spindly undercarriages. Kacew surmised that they were ferrying German officers to neighboring units for Sunday lunch.

He'd woken to find a washstand in the corner of his room, complete with razor, shaving brush, and soap. None of these things had been there the night before, though he hadn't heard anyone come in. He felt refreshed after his long and dreamless sleep. Even the pain in his shoulder had eased.

The room was chilly, but the sun was shining outside. Halfway through shaving, he'd heard a clatter of hoofs on the cobbles. He put the razor down and went to the window. Rochebrune, wrapped in a voluminous black cloak, was mounting his horse, though "horse" was a flattering term for such a decrepit old nag. He said something to his daughter, who'd been holding the bridle, and she nodded, brushing a strand of hair out of her eyes. Rochebrune nodded back, arranged his cloak over the horse's rump, and rode out of the courtyard. Once past the gates, the animal broke into a slow, lurching trot.

By the time Kacew made his way over to the main house, Yseult had breakfast ready for him. She was wearing another long gown, not blue but cream-colored, and she'd done something to her hair. It was gathered into a bun on the nape of her neck, but there was almost too much of it for the pins to cope with.

"Good morning," she said. "How are you feeling?"

"Better, thanks. Your father should have been a doctor."

"Is that what he told you—that he wanted to study medicine but his father wouldn't let him?" She put two jugs on the table. "I'm sorry, the coffee's very weak. It's scarce these days."

"Don't worry. Why, isn't it true?"

"Father never seriously considered anything but the Army."

She sat down opposite him, though she hadn't laid a place for herself. The bun made her look older. She watched him while he ate and sipped his coffee. Her unabashed stare was faintly disconcerting.

"Where has he gone?"

"It's the same old story. I do the work while he goes chasing his memories."

"Is it Sunday today?" Kacew's sense of time was at a standstill, like his watch.

"It's always Sunday to him, when he's out on that horse of his."

"Where has he really gone?"

"Courtilloles, a ruined castle on the other side of the forest. Didn't he tell you about it? If he hasn't, he will. He storms it at the head of his regiment and holds it against German counterattacks. It's his way of reliving the battle of the Marne."

"Your father sounds a happy man."

She tossed her head. "Wait till you've heard the story a hundred times."

"What's the name of your nearest village?"

"St.-Rigomer-des-Bois." She started to remove the pins from her hair, one by one.

"How big is it?"

"There's a church and a café." A thought seemed to strike her, because her eyes grew bright. "And a village hall. They have dances there sometimes."

"Is there a pharmacy?"

"No, just a dispensary at the doctor's house."

"What about shops? Does anyone sell nails, wire—that sort of thing?"

"Old Monsieur Richet does."

Kacew had been taught, while training for his original assignment in France, how to build a radio out of simple components obtainable in any hardware store. Batteries would be the main problem, but it seemed better to make a start—better to occupy himself than sit around waiting for something to happen.

"How far is it to the village?"

"Half an hour on horseback, a little longer if you cycle there."

"Do you have a bicycle?"

She nodded, all attention.

"I could make a list of the things I need."

"Expensive things?" She sounded alarmed.

"No, cheap, everyday things. There was some money in my flying suit, French money for emergencies."

"I don't know where your clothes were put, but I have a little money of my own. When would you like me to go?"

"Why not now, while your father's out?"

She had risen at once, Kacew recalled, as though afraid he might change his mind.

"I'll get the bicycle out while you make your list."

Now he saw her reach the end of the beechwood avenue and pedal unsteadily out of sight. Had she guessed what the things were for? With an imagination as vivid as hers, perhaps she had. What would she tell the doctor and old Monsieur Richet if they started asking questions?

He sheltered beneath the trees as another stork-legged monoplane droned past the château. Although it was a reminder of his predicament, he had often felt far closer to danger in London when the bombs rained down. It seemed impossible that this remote and isolated spot would ever be touched by war. His predominant feeling was fatalistic rather than frightened or resentful. All had hinged on the turn of two coins, the success of his bet with Frykowski.

Again he heard shots and dogs barking. The Germans must be hunting in the forest, as Rochebrune had said. Tired of staring along the deserted avenue, he went back into the courtyard and then, after some hesitation, into the big, empty house.

St.-Rigomer-des-Bois

THE FARM TRACK was dry and dusty, white as chalk. It wound its way through the fields until it joined another track, little wider or less rutted. By the time the wagon reached the intersection, they could see the church tower and rooftops of St.-Rigomer.

Camille Ringood straightened up and flicked the horse into a trot. His wife, seated beside him, held out the black felt hat that had been lying on her lap.

"Better put it on now."

Ringood hawked and spat. "I've been working in the fields without a hat for forty years, and it hasn't done me any harm."

"I don't care what you do in the fields, you're not going into the village without a hat on."

Their son, who was lolling in the back of the flatbed wagon with his knees drawn up and his hat tipped over his eyes to shield them from the sun, laughed. "Everyone wears a hat on Sundays," he said, mimicking his mother's voice. "It's no use, Papa, you won't change her."

They were all dressed in churchgoing black. For a while, nothing could be heard but the creak of harness, the rumble of the wheels, and periodic squeals from an axle starved of grease.

"That'll change," the son said eventually. "The first thing I'm going to do when the war's over is buy myself a car."

Camille Ringood turned his head and spat again. "You'll never earn that much money in your life." Two more wagons debouched from the fields and joined the road ahead of them, trailing clouds of dust. Ringood's next words were a scornful aside to his wife. "He can't even get near a girl like Yseult, that's how smart our Hugues is."

Hugues pushed his hat back. "You're after Rochebrune, that's all. Nothing else matters to you, just that moldering old ruin."

"You're right." Ringood guffawed. "I'll get it, too. I'll get the château before you get the girl."

"I was pretty close before that confounded Englishman turned up."

"Shotgun range," sneered Ringood, "that's as close to her as you ever got. To think you call yourself my son!"

"And you're helping her old man hide that Polish airman, that's how smart *you* are."

"Who'd want to live there?" Ringood's wife broke in. "I wouldn't, that's for sure."

"But I would, and I'm damn well—"

"Please," she said, "not before Communion."

They had reached the outskirts of the village. When they turned into the main street, at the far end of which stood the church, with the village square and war memorial in front of it, they found the place humming with activity, not peaceful and deserted in the usual way. Vehicles stenciled with black and white crosses were parked in line outside the café, and beside them stood German soldiers. Some were holding dogs on leashes, others tinkering with shotguns.

The tables and chairs beneath the plane trees, which had been trimmed into neat cubes and gave little shade, were occupied by a dozen-odd German officers, some of them wearing the carmine-striped breeches that denoted senior rank. The proprietress of the café, with her red ringlets and red dress, was outside serving drinks.

Just as the Ringoods' wagon passed them, the Germans raised their glasses in a noisy toast.

"Getting drunk *before* they go hunting," Ringood growled. "Only the Boches would be daft enough to do that."

They skirted the war memorial, a small bronze obelisk enclosed by stone posts and rusty iron chains. The names of those who had died in World War One were illegible; the latest additions petered out in 1940.

Ringood pulled up near the church. More wagons and carts were standing in the dusty square, left there by other farmers who attended church on Sundays and played *boule* or patronized the café after morning service.

Ringood tethered his horse to one of the plane trees, which were pollarded like those outside the café and gave just as little shade. As he turned, he caught sight of a figure in the distance—a girl on a bicycle.

"Yseult," he said. "I'm surprised the old man let her out by herself." She dismounted outside the doctor's house, which was bigger than its neighbors. Ringood registered grim satisfaction. "The Pole must be worse. Rochebrune's a bungler."

"We'll be late," his wife warned.

Hugues hung back. "I'll catch you up," he said. "Got to see someone for a minute."

"You're coming with us," said Ringood. "Yes," his wife chimed in, "no drinking before Communion!"

Hugues took his hat off, rubbed it on the sleeve of his jacket, and slammed it back on his head. "Do this, don't do that," he said, white with rage. "Sometime it's got to stop."

He stomped into church ahead of his parents. From behind them came the shrill barking of dogs. They could hear it even when the verger closed the door.

19

Paris

"WHAT'S THE TIME?" Berger still hadn't found his watch.

"Just after five." Schmidt was sitting across the desk from him, where the chaplain had sat that morning.

"Why hasn't Weber phoned?" Berger rose and went over to the map that now adorned his wall. A red cross marked the spot where the bomber had crashed.

"You said between five and six."

Restlessly, Berger walked back to the desk. Staring down at the papers on it, the snapshot and the newspaper clipping, he again had the feeling that everything was there—that the puzzle was complete, and only incompetence prevented him from fitting the pieces together.

Schmidt's memory hadn't played him false. The photograph had been on file, a snapshot showing three men in front of a sports plane with a hangar in the background. Under interrogation, Kacew himself had disclosed where and when it had been taken: at Le Bourget in 1938, during a flying competition in which three Polish pilots took part. The other two he identified as Jan Karski and Jerzy Frykowski.

Frykowski's name hadn't turned up anywhere else in the files, but Schmidt had come across a newspaper clipping on Karski. A brief announcement in *The Times*, less than a year old, stated that Squadron Leader Jan Karski had been awarded the Distinguished Service Order.

Berger picked the clipping up. He had underlined one phrase in red: *". . . at an investiture at Elsham Wolds, Lincolnshire."* The place name should never have slipped past the British censor, but there it was, staring him in the face.

He forced himself to think logically. What were the facts? Kacew,

Karski, and Frykowski were fellow fliers from way back. Kacew had reported a forthcoming visit to Elsham Wolds air base, where Karski was apparently stationed. An RAF bomber had been shot down over Le Mans. Kacew was supposed to rendezvous with Chavero the same night but hadn't shown up. Twenty-four hours later, Ebert had inquired about an airman named Frykowski.

That was a lot of coincidences—too many not to seem suspect. There had to be a connection, but what was it?

The office was quiet. Hermine Köster had left at midday. Schmidt continued to sit there like a statue. It occurred to Berger that he knew nothing about his assistant's private life. They'd never exchanged a word on the subject in almost three years.

"Ever been married, Schmidt?"

The sergeant seemed taken aback. He scrutinized his hands as though looking for a wedding ring. "No," he said eventually.

"You've never told me where you come from." Berger lit a cigarette, noticing as he did so that the second and third fingers of his left hand were orange with nicotine.

"With my Swabian accent? I'd have thought that was obvious, Captain. I'm from a village on the Neckar near Stuttgart. My father's a winegrower."

"Is that what you did prewar, pick grapes?"

"I've got three elder brothers and the vineyard's only a small one. It wouldn't have suited me anyway, I'm not the outdoor type."

"How did you get into this outfit?"

"I worked for a government office in Stuttgart. Our job was keeping in touch with German nationals abroad and trying to persuade them to come home—we circularized them with propaganda leaflets. I was responsible for France and the French colonial territories. When war broke out, I wound up in the Abwehr as a matter of course."

Berger's eyes strayed to the outside phone. He lifted the receiver and blew into the mouthpiece to satisfy himself that it was in working order. "Anything on your mind, Schmidt?"

"No, Captain."

"In general, I mean, not at this particular moment."

Schmidt inspected his hands again. At length he said, "Do I look Jewish?"

"What on earth do you mean? Who says so?"

"It's never crossed your mind?" Schmidt laughed abruptly, a little uncertainly. "I had to produce a certificate of Aryan descent when I joined the Abwehr. They were all Aryans, my ancestors—all winegrowers for generations back. My mistake was, I got too interested in the subject. I went back farther than I need have, back to 1722. That was when I came across the name Schwob, Salomon Schwob, a cooper from down by the Swiss border."

"What did you do?"

"I tore up my notes and stopped looking."

The telephone rang at last. Berger reached for it, glad of the interruption.

"Weber here. Is that you, Captain?" Berger remembered Weber as a brisk-mannered man, but his voice was surprisingly thin and reedy.

"Where are you calling from?"

"Sées. I only just got back."

"Sorry to spoil your Sunday."

"That British bomber—the Luftwaffe people say there isn't a chance that anyone survived. The crew tried to bail out—some did, at least—but they jumped too late and got their chutes snarled up in the tail unit."

"We already have a report to that effect. What about the bomber's point of departure? Any indication of where it was based?"

"None in the wreckage. You've never seen such a mess."

"So there weren't any survivors?"

"One moment, Captain. The nearest village is St.-Rigomer-des-Bois. Do you have a map handy?"

Berger repeated the name and Schmidt ringed it on the wall map. "Yes, got it."

"It so happens a German hunting party was there today. The woods nearby are popular with officers from Le Mans—they rendezvous at a café, the only one in the place. I came across something there this afternoon—something that seems to conflict with the Luftwaffe's theory."

Berger had forgotten Schmidt. Nothing existed for him but the voice in his ear. He drank in the words it uttered, and the words translated themselves into images so graphic that the village street, the crowded little café, sprang to life.

"The son of a local farmer came in. He started drinking, shooting his mouth off, bragging that he knew of certain people in the district who sheltered Allied airmen."

"He said that in so many words?"

"You know how it is, Captain. My information's only secondhand. I got it from a corporal in the hunting party—one of the beaters. He was in the café at the time, but no one thought he knew enough French to understand. He simply overheard something that made him think twice, and my questions jogged his memory."

"What about the villagers?"

"Whenever I raised the subject—it's on everyone's lips, naturally, with the scene of the crash being so close—there was something about their reaction, I can't quite define it . . . Forgive me for not being more precise. Instinct tells me that your information about a survivor may be correct, that's all."

"Not information, Weber, just a hunch."

"I understand."

"Did you get the boy's name?"

"Hugues Ringood." Weber spelled it out. "I checked his file at police headquarters. Age twenty-four, a labor conscript in Germany until a year ago."

"Escaped?"

"No, formally discharged, which doesn't give us any leverage. If you'd like to question him, though, we could always bring him in on the pretext that his papers need updating."

"Not at this stage, Weber. It's all too vague."

"Want me to follow the matter up?"

Berger studied the wall map, gauging distances. "I'll drive down myself tomorrow. I'd like to take a look around."

"I could meet you somewhere."

"Let's make it St.-Rigomer. Pick me up at the café." Berger's face relaxed a little. "I'll be using the name Maurice Flandin, head office, Société National des Chemins de Fer. That'll tie in with your cover."

"What time?"

"Around midday. I'll call you before I leave."

Berger replaced the receiver with a slow, deliberate movement. He got up and walked over to the map. The village Schmidt had ringed was on the edge of a large wooded area, the Forêt de Perseigne.

"May I ask you something?" he heard Schmidt say. He knew what the question would be: the one he himself had put to Ebert that morning. "Of course," he said.

"What's so special about this man Frykowski, Captain?"

He turned and looked into Schmidt's worried, weary, prematurely wrinkled face. Schmidt wasn't one of the last-ditch fanatics who still raved about final victory and pinned their hopes on Hitler's secret weapons. There, thought Berger, was yet another person he could have confided in.

"Our colleagues across the Channel have asked us to help get him out of the country." Similar instances had occurred in the past, so the lie sprang quite spontaneously to his lips.

"No connection with Joseph?" Schmidt sounded faintly disappointed.

"That's the danger in our trade," Berger said, "seeing connections everywhere."

"Do you need me anymore?"

"No. Good work, Schmidt." Berger wanted to say more, but he knew the time wasn't ripe, nor would it ever be. "What do you plan to do with the rest of your Sunday?"

"I thought I'd take in a movie," Schmidt said, rather forlornly.

Berger knew he oughtn't to let him go—he should have offered to keep him company and picked up the thread of their earlier conversation—but all he said was, "See you tomorrow, then."

"You'll be looking in here before you leave?"

"Yes, of course."

"Right, Captain. Till tomorrow."

Alone again, Berger gathered up the papers on his desk and replaced them in the folder, which he locked away in the safe. Karski, Frykowski, Kacew, Elsham Wolds, Le Mans, Chavero, Ebert . . . The pieces fitted together somehow, but what pattern did they form?

He looked out of the window. The wreath was still propped against the railings of the Métro station, but the sentries had been withdrawn. Back at his desk, he dialed the Rue Guynemer number. Even before he finished dialing, he visualized a telephone ringing in an empty apartment. He let it ring for a long time, but no one answered.

Berger returned as he had come that morning, on foot. Few people passed him on the way, and the food stores were without their weekday lines of depressed, apathetic-looking shoppers. But for the occasional German patrol, the city might have been at peace.

Yet there was something spurious and contrived about the atmosphere. Berger felt more keenly than ever that Paris and the Parisians were being strained to the breaking point, and that their tensile test was nearing its climax. The one thought uppermost in every mind was survival.

Why not speak to her? Why not simply tell her the whole story?

They could make a joint escape, quit Paris, quit France altogether. With his knowledge and resources, it wouldn't be difficult. Money was no problem, and he could easily procure false papers for them both. He knew the routes into Spain and Portugal. The risk would be minimal. The worst that could happen was a death sentence passed *in absentia,* a meaningless entry in his personal file. The man Berger would have to die in any case, if he fled . . .

He entered the Jardin du Luxembourg by the main gate. A bunker had been embedded in the ground in front of the palace—thousands of tons of hideous reinforced concrete. The camouflaged armored car stationed beside it resembled a toy.

The park beyond, of which only the far end had been plowed up and sown with potatoes and cabbages, looked idyllic to the point of unreality. The stretches of grass and the plane trees separating it from Rue Guynemer were so intensely green as to seem theatrical. The sun itself might have been installed by a stage electrician.

Visitors to the park were sunning themselves on the curb of the ornamental lake and watching children sail boats. Berger had to make a detour around their outstretched legs. His sense of unreality persisted as he walked on. Even the statues of the queens of France looked whiter than usual.

If he found Jannou anywhere, the puppet theater would be the likeliest place. The open-air benches were occupied by children, old folk, and a scattering of German soldiers in uniform.

He spotted her at the end of the back row, wearing a sleeveless cotton dress and a pair of red sandals. Her legs were bare. It was two summers ago, when she moved in with him after Kacew's escape, that he'd first seen her "painting stockings," as she called it. She'd been standing at an open window overlooking the park, one foot on the sill, brushes and boxes of powder laid out on a chair beside her. She hadn't heard him come in, and he watched her for quite a while. Without actually seeing her face, he could picture the expression so typical of her—half intent, half abstracted, smiling faintly.

Now as then, the sight of her stirred something in him. All the women who'd meant anything to him had been as slim and deceptively fragile. He stood behind her, dominated by the thought of how much he needed her.

Jannou, still unaware of his presence, was concentrating on the stage. Two puppets were in action, a Gallic Punch and a pug-faced figure with a cigar and an English accent.

"Jannou?"

Unsurprised, she made room for him on the bench and continued to watch the stage.

He squeezed in beside her. "What's it all about?" he asked, but she merely said, "You'll see."

The show claimed less of his attention than she did. From the side, he could see her lower lip was still swollen. The compulsion to speak was so strong that he made up his mind to tell her everything.

She applauded enthusiastically when the curtain fell. "That puppet with a face like a bulldog," Berger said as they headed for the side gate, "was he meant to be Churchill?"

"Yes, the villain of the piece. There always has to be a villain." She smiled. "Till 1940 he had a German accent and a toothbrush mustache."

"I tried to call you."

"Well, now you've found me." She sucked in her lower lip, smiling no longer.

He took her arm and forced her to walk more slowly. "Some nights, when I get back from the Lutétia and climb the stairs, I think I'm going to find the apartment empty, without even a note on the mantelpiece. By the time I put the key in the door, I'm ready to bet you've gone for good."

He felt her arm stiffen, every sinew transmitting tension. She paused and looked at him, and the arm went limp, becoming as soft and girlish to the touch as it had been a moment ago.

"I've never had the courage," she said.

"You sound sorry."

"Perhaps I am."

"We could go away together. It wouldn't be too risky if I made the necessary arrangements."

"Go where?"

"Spain, Portugal."

She shook her head. "Why should you want to?"

"Survival's a great incentive."

"What if I said yes?"

"Say it."

"You'd never suggest such a thing if you hadn't already decided against it. I'm right, aren't I?"

He hesitated before replying. "Yes."

"My God," she said bitterly, "then why suggest it at all?"

Not that he could have put his finger on the reason, the time to speak had passed. Perhaps it was because they were too alike, too apt to feign self-assurance when they felt least secure. It alienated them just when they needed each other most.

She set off for the side gate, walking fast. He followed her out into the street. The apartment was almost opposite. Lit by the sun's slanting rays, the inscription on the wall could easily be deciphered beneath its coat of fresh paint.

20

Paris

THE STREETS bordering the Jardin du Ranelagh formed part of an opulent neighborhood. Set in spacious grounds and screened by trees, the houses had façades ranging from ivory to pink like the rouged and powdered cheeks of elderly dowagers. Whenever he drove through this part of Paris, Reckzeh fell prey to an emotion that transcended mere annoyance: he nursed a personal hatred for its wealthy residents.

Although it was early Monday morning, he had already visited his office in Avenue Foch. Pulling up outside a palatial mansion enclosed by a chest-high wall and railings with gilded spikes, he reached for the package on the Mercedes' passenger seat. Those who knew about such things would have recognized from the wrapping paper that it came from Cambourakis, one of the best men's outfitters in Paris.

A woman was walking down the gravel drive. She wavered at the sight of Reckzeh's uniform, then walked on. She was wearing a long black dress and coat, a black felt hat, and an embroidered shawl.

Reckzeh waited until the last moment before opening the wicket gate. "Good morning, Madame," he said in German.

She glared at him from under the brim of her hat. Her eyes were blue and a little shortsighted, like her son's, but there the resemblance ended. Gino's eyes had none of the hauteur and disdain that burned in them whenever she looked at Reckzeh. They rarely met because, although the house was hers, she lived in a secluded side wing. When they did, she pointedly ignored him. This time, though, she did more than confine herself to silent scorn.

"You feel at home here, it seems."

"Thoroughly at home, Madame."

The look in her eyes changed, and a malicious smile appeared on her wrinkled, heavily powdered face.

"How you Germans are going to miss Paris!"

"We're still here, Madame, as you see."

She shook her head so fiercely that the hat slipped sideways. The streaks of gold in her white hair showed that it had once been the color of Gino's.

"I don't wish you to come here anymore! I want these parties to stop! I want you to leave my son alone!"

"Why not tell that to Gino?"

"Leave my son alone, I implore you!"

Her undisguised contempt had always left Reckzeh cold, but this sudden note of entreaty made him see red. His face hardened.

"Save your breath," he snapped. "Gino fully appreciates the value of our friendship." Instantly regaining his composure, he gave a little bow. "May I drop you somewhere, Madame?"

"In a Gestapo car? Only at the nearest jail!"

It would have been futile to explain that he belonged to the Security Service, and that his principal function was counterespionage. The French had never mastered the difference between Gestapo, SS, and SD; to them, the first term covered all three.

She walked on without another word. Reckzeh watched her cross the road, a thin, frail figure in black. He guessed her age at sixty or more. She'd given birth to her son very late, when she was nearly forty, and had been widowed soon afterward. Her maiden name was Charlotte de Marillac, hence the "Rillac" which Gino had adopted as his stage name.

The pillared portico was flanked by rhododendron bushes heavy with pale violet blossom. Reckzeh made his way through it into the entrance hall, which had a chessboard marble floor and neoclassical cupids smirking in vaulted niches.

He always found it hard to conceive how two people could live alone in so vast a house. His own parents had reared six children in two tiny rooms and a kitchen, a wretched little apartment that would have fitted into this lobby three times over. Perhaps that accounted for the sado-masochistic quality of his visits to the mansion, their combination of pain and pleasure.

Voices were coming from the dining room. He opened the double doors and looked in. Two servants, an elderly couple with graying hair, were busy clearing away the debris of last night's party, the dismembered suckling pig and pheasant carcasses. The floor of the big room was littered with empty burgundy and champagne bottles.

Reckzeh's thoughts returned to Gino's mother and her stubborn refusal to accept favors. Although he saw to it that the household received a special allocation of coal in winter, the old woman kept her radiators turned off; the most she would allow herself was an open fire. She declined to ride in the car for which Gino held an official permit and spurned the delicacies that came by truck from the SD's central depot.

He could picture her now, tiptoeing into the church she attended every day of the week. His own mother could never afford to go to church on weekdays; she was too busy scrubbing floors. Her husband had left her penniless when a shell blew him to bits on the Oise bridge at Guise in the opening months of World War One.

Reckzeh slammed the doors behind him and marched off down a paneled corridor lined with paintings and mirrors. At the end he turned left down another passage. The windows looked out on the grounds, where horse-chestnut trees were in full flower.

The room was large, with silk-lined walls and an ornate molded ceiling. The curtains were still drawn, and a light was burning beside the enormous bed. A film script lay open on the floor with paper tabs protruding from it, presumably marking Gino's lines.

Gino himself was in bed, bare shoulders above the covers, the rest of him sprawling belly-down. His hair, grown long for his latest part, was almost unbelievably blond. His lips were full and soft. All that saved his face from effeminacy was a deceptively firm, resolute-looking chin. Reckzeh recalled what Oberg had said about him. Gino's Nordic looks would more than have fitted him for the role of Siegfried.

Reckzeh stooped and picked up the screenplay. Going over to the window, he drew the lacy white curtains and opened it. Then he threw the shutters wide.

"Ah non, Érik, je t'en prie!" Gino struggled up in bed, shading his eyes.

"It's almost eight. Aren't you filming today?"

"If you can call it filming. The trash they give me!" Though pale from the effects of last night's binge, Gino's face wore an anguished expression that had nothing to do with drink or lack of sleep.

"Tu es mignon!" Reckzeh laughed long and loud. "Vraiment mignon! That sad, tormented look—is that from your latest epic? You're never better than when you're lying wounded in the arms of la Dar-

rieux. Someday they ought to give you a part that requires you to die—
a deathbed scene. There'd be no one to touch you. Now get up and
order yourself some breakfast."

Gino threw back the covers and disappeared into his dressing room.
Reckzeh pulled a table and two chairs up to the window, sat down, and
started leafing idly through the script. Gino returned, wearing a white
bathrobe. He had a glass in one hand and a bottle of Veuve Clicquot in
the other.

"Rather early for champagne, isn't it?" Reckzeh said.

Gino put the bottle on the table, then the glass, and stood looking
down at him.

"For you." Reckzeh pushed the package from Cambourakis across
the table.

Gino's eyes fastened on the script. "All they ever offer me is trash,
vulgar trash."

"That's what audiences like to see you in."

"And you do nothing about it!" Gino reached for the bottle and
poured himself a glass so hurriedly that champagne cascaded over the
rim. The expensive gold watch he was wearing slid down his wrist as he
picked up the glass. "This new Jeancoles movie—my part in it is simply
ridiculous." He raised the glass to his lips but put it down again at
once, his hand was trembling so much.

Reckzeh opened the package himself. He lifted the lid of the slim
box inside and folded back the tissue paper to reveal a fringed white silk
scarf.

Gino pouted. "You haven't been to the studio for a month."

"You always say I put you off your work. Where are you shooting?"

"Billancourt."

"Maybe I'll drive out and take a look. Come here."

"Promise?"

"Closer—bend down." Reckzeh shook out the scarf and put it
around Gino's neck. "For tonight."

"Tonight?"

"The reception at the German Center—don't say you'd forgotten.
I'm sure you're dying to meet some of your fellow stars from Germany,
not to mention Dr. Goebbels. It's the Propaganda Ministry that fi-
nances your films, after all."

Gino picked up the glass again. This time he drank it—drained it at
a gulp. "I can't afford another late night. I need my sleep."

"But Gino, everyone knows about us anyway. They see us together at the best restaurants, they . . ." Reckzeh saw Gino raise his hand to remove the scarf. "Leave it on," he said, "it suits you." His voice was ice-cold.

The hand froze; so did the handsome face with the china blue eyes. Gino struggled for words. "Sometimes," he said, "I think my mother's right about you."

"Of course she is. It's just that you don't have her guts."

"Perhaps we should end this thing, Érik." Gino's attempt to sound belligerent was obvious but ineffectual.

"If you've really made your mind up." Reckzeh smiled sardonically.

"You'd never let me go, not without making me pay."

Reckzeh threw back his head and laughed. "Melodramatic as ever! This isn't one of your movies."

Someone knocked at the door. Gino went to open it. A haggard face peered into the room over a laden tray, torn between apprehension and curiosity.

"All right, André, I'll take it." Gino relieved the old butler of his burden and put it down on the bed, cleared the table and laid two places.

Reckzeh, who had risen, was staring out of the window. "I learned a valuable lesson once—one you've still to learn. I was under eighteen at the time, serving with the Legion in Morocco. We'd arrested two suspected Arab rebels. Suspected, not convicted, but that was good enough. They were to be shot at daybreak."

"If this is another of your macabre stories . . ."

"Then along came this Arab boy. There was a big, sandy square in front of the jailhouse. At first he hung around in the blazing sun, then he wandered over to us. Six years old or thereabouts, shaven-headed, bare feet, ragged clothes. He came over and started pleading for his father's life."

"Must you, Érik? I don't enjoy your reminiscences."

"There were two of us guarding the jail, a sergeant and myself. I tried to talk him into letting the boy's father go. He wouldn't hear of it, but I was so set on the idea that I engineered his escape during the night."

Reckzeh sat down and poured himself a cup of black coffee.

"Two days later—my court-martial had been postponed—we stormed a mountain village in the Djebel Baddou and shot everyone in sight. It was a reprisal raid for a rebel ambush. That evening, when we were counting the dead, I came across the two of them together, father and son. They had their arms around each other—you couldn't tell who'd been protecting whom. Beautiful spot, that village—way up in the Atlas. I'd love to show it to you sometime."

Gino shivered. "My mother's right, you're a cynic."

"I was young, Gino. Short of eighteen and brimming with the milk of human kindness, and it didn't matter a damn—didn't change a thing. I spent two months in jail at Sidi-bel-Abbès. Later they pinned a decoration on me. That Legion of yours was a great teacher. Within a year I found I could kill without a second thought."

"I'd never get another part, would I? You'd see to that."

"You misunderstand me, Gino."

"You wouldn't put any obstacles in my way?"

"Never fear, you'll find someone else to take you under his wing. Of course, if the day ever comes when we aren't here any longer . . ."

"My parts have never had any propaganda value."

"Grow up, Gino! Everything has. This is total war, Dr. Goebbels says so himself."

"You see? Now you're threatening me."

Reckzeh laughed. "You nailed your colors to our mast."

"What ought I to do?" Gino licked his lips. "What else is there?"

"There's a French SS contingent. You've got a perfect SS physique." A spiteful note crept into Reckzeh's voice. Amused and sardonic no longer, it was cold, arrogant, and cruel. "You could die for real, not just for the camera."

"Please, Érik!"

"My name is Erich. Say it: E-rich! You've had plenty of time to learn it."

"Please, Erich. I'm feeling lousy, honestly."

Reckzeh stood up. He took hold of the silk scarf and pulled, compelling Gino to stand up too. "All right, say something. Let's hear what really goes on inside that handsome head." He twisted the scarf like a tourniquet, pulling Gino even closer. "Whose side are you on, ours or theirs?"

Gino groped for his hands and tried to pry them loose. He fought for breath, and the words issued from his lips in little disjointed gasps. "You . . . You can't believe I'd . . ."

Reckzeh released the scarf and laughed deep in his throat. "You never act better than when you're scared." His expression changed to one of concern. "Are you really feeling bad?"

Gino nodded mutely.

Reckzah took his arm and led him over to the bed. "Take it easy, I'll fetch you a nice cold facecloth. Forget what I said just now."

Gino sank back against the pillows. As soon as Reckzeh had turned away to go to the bathroom, he smiled with the complacency of a spoiled child.

21

Billancourt

THEY WERE WATCHING the latest batch of rushes. The atmosphere in the darkened projection room was strained, Jannou noticed, and the quality of the takes flickering across the screen did nothing to improve it.

It had all begun that morning, when there was still no sign of their promised consignment of raw stock. The remaining negative had sufficed for only two short scenes: No. 14, in which the girl Sophie, played by Danielle Darrieux, stole a doll from the toy department of the Bon Marché, and No. 15, in which the son of the proprietor, Gino Rillac, caught her in the act.

The picture was a period piece with a Christmas 1896 setting. Jannou, poised to record the director's comments, paid less attention to the screen than to the shooting script on her reading stand, which was lit by a small shaded lamp.

"She isn't *into* her part. Not a hint of fear or compulsion. If she doesn't *have* to steal the damned thing, there's no story."

In the normal way, Pierre Jeancoles was a director who radiated phlegm rather than frenzy. He was sitting in front of her now, a mournful-looking, black-sweatered man with a pair of horn-rims dangling from a cord around his neck.

Jeancoles turned to her, nervously plucking at his grizzled mustache. "When she grabs the doll, cut!"

"You're cutting just what the public adores—that dreamy expression." Jeancoles' assistant tried hard to copy his dress and mannerisms, but his attempt at the director's bass voice was a miserable failure.

Jannou noted the cut. Jeancoles wasn't in the habit of reversing his decisions, and she knew it.

"Scene 15," he asked his assistant. "How many takes?"

"Three."

"What a waste."

The rest of the Scene 14 takes unfolded on the screen, silent and grainy. Jannou turned a page. She hadn't read the whole script, but there was no need. All the Jeancoles pictures she'd worked on were much the same.

For a moment the room went completely dark except for the desk lamp over her script. Then the projector's silver beam reappeared above her, alive with the smoke and dust that floated in it.

Jannou loved that silvery shaft of light as much as anything else to do with films. She could recall emerging from movie theaters as a girl with little recollection of the picture itself, only of the motes dancing overhead like fireflies. She could also recall imagining that this was how it must be when you lay in bed asleep and dreams appeared in your mind's eye.

Take 1 of the next scene passed without any comment from Jeancoles, though Jannou saw him fidget and shake his head. It showed the proprietor's son covertly watching the girl steal the doll.

The lights went up, then dimmed again. From somewhere at the back of the room came a sound that didn't belong there. The clapper boards signaled the start of Take 2. This time Jeancoles exploded. "Look at the way he's watching her—like a block of wood. He doesn't project a thing in front of the camera. I'll be damned if I let them foist him on me again!"

The take ran its course. "That's it," said Jeancoles. "I think we can dispense with the last one."

Again they heard the alien sound behind them—a movement, nothing more. This time it was followed by a voice.

"Let's see it all the same."

Part of Jannou must have recognized the voice; a vile, nauseating taste filled her mouth.

Jeancoles stood up and turned to look, scalped by the beam from the projector. He shaded his eyes.

"Who the devil? Is that you, Gino?"

"Carry on," said the voice. "Don't let us disturb you."

The second take drew silently to a close.

"Lights!"

Jannou stared fixedly at Jeancoles. She didn't want to see the owner of the voice in the background. It was all she could do to choke back the foul taste in her mouth.

The wall lights came on again. In their subdued glow, Jeancoles peered at the back row of seats. "I'm sorry," he said, "but it isn't customary for actors to see rushes."

"We're wasting time. Carry on."

Jannou was sure now. She knew the voice only too well, the icy courtesy, the overtones of mockery and menace. It amazed her to see how quickly Jeancoles lost his habitual poise and self-assurance, but his reaction was as nothing to her own inner turmoil.

She forced herself to turn around, told herself that he had lost all power over her—that she could look him in the face unafraid because there was no form of terror she had not already met and overcome.

Three men were sitting in the back row, one of them Gino Rillac. Reckzeh was in uniform. He sat there just as she remembered him, utterly motionless, head slightly cocked in an attitude of sympathetic attention. For a moment she watched him, hypnotized.

"What exactly would you like to see?" she heard Jeancoles ask.

"Everything you've shot in the last few days."

She neither expected nor wanted Jeancoles to argue; the return of darkness was her only wish. As the lights dimmed—reabsorbed, so it seemed, by the walls—she leaned forward. She only just summoned up the strength to speak, and even then she was afraid she might vomit if she opened her mouth.

"You don't need me anymore, do you?"

The bulky figure in front of her didn't stir. Jeancoles had retracted his head like a tortoise on the defensive. She stood up. Hugging the script to her, she edged along the row of seats, step by step, with her eyes glued to the green exit light on the right of the screen.

She fumbled with the door handle, expecting every moment to hear the voice call her back. Once outside, she lost control over the vile taste forcing its way into her mouth. She retched again and again, her whole body convulsed with the effort, but the act of vomiting made her feel better.

Longing for a drink of water, she walked quickly across the yard. Stagehands were streaming out of the main studio and joining other workers clustered admiringly around the black Mercedes convertible parked outside the projection room. The sight of it turned her stomach again.

The studio was as big and high as an aircraft hangar. She entered by one of the side doors and made her way to a washroom, where she ran the cold water as hard as she could. Still clutching the script, she bent over the basin and tilted her head so the jet played over her lips. She filled her mouth with water, spat it out, took another mouthful, and rinsed repeatedly until the foul taste became less pronounced.

An iron stairway like a fire escape led to a gallery with numerous doors opening off it. The higher she climbed, the better her view of the various sets. One of them was the toy counter where Scene 14 had been shot. Another, still unfinished, was the office of Monsieur Boucicot, the Bon Marché's owner.

Normally the building was filled with the sound of voices, of sawing and hammering; now there were only the familiar smells of paint and glue and raw wood. Jannou felt better because the studio gave her a sense of belonging.

Her office was at the end of the gallery. She left the door open so as to be able to hear the others returning from their afternoon break. The office, too, enhanced her sense of security. Every feature of it—the cutting tables, the shelves laden with cans of film, the shooting schedule pinned to the wall—was like a tacit guarantee that her life would go on as before.

She laid the script aside and went to the window. It looked out over Billancourt, a bleak industrial district whose air of decay had not been improved by Allied bombing directed at the Renault works, which turned out tanks for the German Army. Billancourt seemed an incongruous choice of site for the filming of costume dramas. Studios Cinéma Billancourt were housed in a group of buildings belonging to a factory closed by order of the Germans on the grounds that its products were "inessential to the war effort."

The black Mercedes was still parked in the yard. It looked even longer and more sinister from overhead. The open roof gaped like a reptile's jaws. The crowd around it had dispersed, but Jannou saw Reckzeh and Jeancoles come out of the projection room, followed by the other two. They stood beside the car, talking, then shook hands.

Jannou sat down at her desk and dialed the Lutétia.

"Captain Berger, please."

She waited, marveling at her own composure. Perhaps it sprang from her previous certainty that Reckzeh would cross her path again, sooner or later, and that she wouldn't survive the encounter. She'd always felt that, if her memories of Avenue Foch returned in full measure, she would simply give up the ghost. Now they had, and she was still alive.

"That's right," she said, "Captain Berger. Please try to find him."

Berger was the one person who would understand. Perhaps the thought of him had helped, too. Even while she'd stood there outside the projection room, retching miserably, she'd known she could turn to him. He was there and would understand, and because of his capacity for understanding she might even, someday, grow to love him. She should have said yes when he asked her to go away. Perhaps he'd expected her to. That was something else she wanted to talk to him about.

"Yes?" She listened to his secretary's voice in the earpiece. "I see," she said. "You don't know when he'll be back? I see. No, no message. Thank you."

"You speak German?" Jeancoles was standing in the doorway, looking pregnant in his bulging black sweater. The smile left his face as soon as he closed the door behind him. His features seemed to disintegrate as if only the smile had been holding them together.

"What's the matter?" she asked.

He took a can of film off a shelf and put it back. "That batch of negative will be here in an hour," he said eventually.

"I apologize for walking out. I couldn't help it."

"Actors never see rushes. I've been in the business over twenty years, and it just isn't done." Jeancoles paused. "I'd no idea you knew him."

"Reckzeh, you mean?" She felt proud of herself for uttering the name at all.

He nodded, lumbering awkwardly around the room. "Look, was there something between you? I'm only asking. I'll quite understand if you don't want to talk about it."

"Ten toenails." The words slipped out before she could stop them, though she knew they'd be meaningless to him.

"I'm sorry. I don't follow."

"Why not just tell me what happened? Aren't we going on with the picture?"

"Of course. The script's got to be rewritten—Gino's part, that is—but who cares? Substituting one load of corn for another doesn't bother me."

"Who was the other man?"

"Someone from the Tobis Corporation—you know, the people who are financing and distributing the picture. It's the old, old story: they want a say in the finished product, but that used to happen long before the Germans came. It isn't just my job that's at stake. I'm responsible for the whole team, Jannou—for everyone working on the picture. We're a good team, wouldn't you say?"

"Yes," she said, dry-mouthed.

"You only joined us on a short-term basis in the first place, didn't you, more or less?"

"More or less."

"All my jobs are short-term." Jeancoles flopped into a chair. Either it was too small for comfort or he found he could communicate better on the move, because he got up and resumed his elephantine pacing. "I've been asked to replace you."

Half surprised, half hurt, she didn't speak for a moment. Then she said, "I ought to feel flattered, I suppose, an insignificant creature like me."

"Please, Jannou, I haven't agreed yet."

"But you will."

"Do you really need the job?"

"I'll miss it." Surely he didn't expect her to make it easier for him?

"They'll replace *me* otherwise, don't you see? Cross them once and they never forgive you. Maybe they'd let me finish the picture, but that would be the end. I know I shouldn't knuckle under, but what can I do?"

She stared at the script. The cover was tear-stained with splashes of water from the washroom. "You'll find someone else who'll fit in. The team won't suffer."

"You're still so young."

"When do I quit?"

"Hell, I'm sorry. I feel really bad about this, but you know how it is."

"I'll need my papers."

"Papers? Oh yes, of course. We'll go on paying you till the picture's in the can. At least you won't have to worry for a few weeks."

"Thanks," she said, because that was what he wanted to hear.

"Come out and see us whenever you like. Call me first, though. Promise?"

As though by chance, Jeancoles' perambulations had brought him within reach of the door. He stood there with his hand on the knob, groping for something else to say, but his script had run out of lines. She sensed how relieved he must be feeling—"bad" as well, perhaps, but mostly relieved.

"Promise?"

"Yes, of course." Jannou felt a sort of emptiness when the door closed behind him. She had to force herself not to look out of the window to see if the Mercedes had already driven off.

For a moment the scene came back to her: Reckzeh in the twilit projection room, sitting back with his arms folded and his hands encased in gray doeskin gloves. The details seemed far more vivid in retrospect than they had at the time.

How could he have guessed that such a fundamentally unimportant thing as her dismissal would hurt so much? Why should he have gone to such trouble for the sake of such a cheap little satisfaction? Anyone would think he was afraid of her.

A car drove into the yard. When she looked out of the window, some studio employees were unloading cans of film and carrying them across to the main building.

22

St.-Rigomer-des-Bois

"YOUR FRIEND'S LATE." The redhead behind the counter was polishing a glass. She held it up to the light before adding it to the rest of the glasses, which were kept in a mirror-backed cabinet. Then she took a drag at the cigarette smoldering in the ashtray beside her. The end was gooey with lipstick.

"He's driving over from Sées."

"Does he work for the railroad, too?"

"Yes, in the local office."

They were alone in the café. The most recent customers, a couple of farmers, had downed their wine in silence and departed. Theirs were the glasses the redhead had been polishing so assiduously.

Berger was sitting at a window table near the entrance. He pulled the grubby lace curtain aside and peered out at the street with its mutilated plane trees.

"Why do they trim them like that?" he asked. "They give less shade."

The woman laughed. "Who needs shade in this dismal hole? The more sun we get, the better."

He turned. The barroom was painted a sad, dirty ocher. On the counter stood a glass case filled with cheap brands of cigarettes. The bowl in the center contained a handful of hard-boiled eggs that looked as old as the tattered newspapers beside them. In such surroundings, the woman with her dyed red ringlets and crimson dress resembled an exotic plant.

"Is this the only café in the village?"

"What do you think?"

"If you'd like to close for lunch . . ."

"No, this place is like a morgue when it's shut."

"You don't come from around here?"

"I'm from the south, from Marseille. I got married and buried here." She laughed. "Anyone can make a mistake—that's life. Hungry?"

"Not very."

"There's some stew. The Germans hunt here most weekends. They always leave me something. It's made—I'd only have to heat it up."

"If it isn't too much trouble."

She disappeared through a doorway beside the counter. A moment later he heard her clattering pans and singing in the kitchen. Although her voice sounded coarse when she laughed or spoke, she sang with a natural sweetness of tone.

Berger felt uncomfortable. He wasn't enjoying himself. Tension usually enhanced his pleasure in an assumed role, but today he found it hard to enter into the charade—hard to grasp what he was doing here at all.

What did he hope to find? Was he making a fool of himself? Last night, while waiting in the attic in Montmartre, he'd felt the same when the radio remained silent and Joseph failed to make contact. He seemed to be losing his grip on the situation, drifting at the mercy of forces beyond his control.

The woman returned with a tray. She laid the table, brought him bread, wine, and a bowl of stew, and retired behind the counter again.

"You really weren't hungry, were you?" she said after a while.

"It's excellent. Wild boar, isn't it?"

She nodded.

"Don't the locals mind the Germans hunting here?"

"The farmers only leave them the wild boar and the few hares and pheasants they don't manage to shoot themselves. The Germans bring money into the district. The farmers claim compensation for damage to their crops, and they pay up without batting an eye." She lit another cigarette but left it to smolder in the ashtray. "If you ask me, they behave pretty well."

"I hear there was a plane shot down near here."

"Yes, poor devils. Burned alive, they were. What a way to go!"

"No survivors?" He watched her closely, but she reacted like someone who'd often been asked the same question before.

"I've heard rumors, but I doubt if there's anything in them. Nothing ever happens here, you see. If I dye my hair a different color, that keeps tongues wagging for a couple of months: Has she found herself a new boyfriend? et cetera. A local farmer's son has been dropping hints about someone in the neighborhood with an Allied airman hidden away, but it's probably just spite. He's after the daughter of the house and his father wants the land. Old feuds die hard."

"Is the other man a farmer too?"

"Monsieur de Rochebrune? He wouldn't answer to the description. Rides around on a broken-down nag and calls himself 'le Colonel.' "

"So it's only a rumor?"

"That's all." The woman reached for a swab and mopped the counter. "I'd be glad to offer you some coffee, but there isn't any. When the war's over I'm going to buy myself a sack of it, a whole hundredweight of best Brazilian." She smiled. "It's one of my dreams."

From outside came the sound of an approaching car. It pulled up behind the Simca. Berger got up and walked over to the counter. "How much do I owe you?"

"Aren't you going to ask your friend in?"

The corners of her mouth turned down, and it was suddenly impossible to tell whether she was pretty or ugly, young or old; she was just a weary-looking Southerner stranded in the North. Berger noticed for the first time that her hands were rough and chapped from washing too many glasses.

"We've got a long drive ahead of us."

"Pity. I'd have liked to give the neighbors something else to gossip about."

He paid her. Mechanically picking up a glass and a cloth, she came out from behind the counter and accompanied him to the door. "Looks like rain," she said. "Drop in again sometime."

The wind had freshened; conscious of it as soon as he emerged into the street, Berger pulled his coat on while walking to the other car. Weber wound his window down.

"Drive somewhere quiet," Berger told him. "I'll follow you."

"You said you wanted to see where it crashed."

"All right." Berger went to the Simca and opened the door. The woman was still standing in the café entrance. He waved to her but she didn't move, just stood there with the glass and the cloth in her hand.

He let the low-slung Citroën take the lead and tucked himself in behind it. The sky was heavy with racing gray clouds. It started to rain, but the windshield wipers only smeared the glass.

He was so close behind the Citroën when it stopped that he nearly ran into the back of it. A farm track intersected with the road at this point. A rusty sign marked the site of what had once been, or still was, a bus stop.

Weber got out. Berger stayed put. "What is it? Why are we stopping?"

"We'll have to walk from here, the cars won't make it. I hope I didn't keep you waiting long."

"It's all right. Let's get going."

Weber led the way. A couple of hundred yards along the track he turned off into a field. Many feet had trodden a path through tall grass silver with hemlock and cow parsley.

Berger's sense of futility returned. Irritably, he now recalled why Weber had been banished to the provinces: for carving himself a cozy little niche in the black market. He still cultivated the same brisk and forceful manner, still had the same reedy voice that failed to match his rather raffish exterior.

"This is the spot, Captain." Since they were both dressed as French civilians, the military form of address sounded absurdly inappropriate.

The environs of the big black crater had been churned up by the vehicles used to haul the wreckage away. What they hadn't removed was the stench of gasoline and burning. Berger was reminded of the woman's epitaph on the crew: "What a way to go!" In the café it had sounded merely banal; here it made him feel queasy.

Hearing a sound, he looked up and saw a row of telegraph poles flanking a railroad track in the distance. A freight train was trundling slowly northward, boxcar after boxcar.

"Doesn't look as if anyone survived that," Berger said. He knuckled the raindrops out of his eyes. "Anything new to report?"

"I'm afraid not."

"Let's get back to the cars." Berger didn't speak again until they reached the intersection. Then he said, "Show me this area on the map."

Weber spread out a large-scale map on the Citroën's hood. The rain had stopped, but the wind was so strong that they had to hold it down four-handed.

"There's the point of impact, there's the nearest farm, and there's the local château." All three places were ringed in pencil.

"And we're here?" Berger couldn't wait to get rid of Weber and be by himself.

"That's right, Captain."

"I'll take this." Berger refolded the map and stuffed it in his pocket. "The proprietress of the café thinks it's all a rumor."

"If someone wanted to hide, the château would be the logical place."

"Someone? After what we've just seen? Personally, I think the woman's right."

"Would you like me to show you the way?"

Another squall hit them. "Pity the weather didn't hold," Berger said. "This would have been a nice little outing. No, don't bother. If anything else crops up, I'll call you in Sées. Thanks, Weber."

Weber gave a rueful laugh. Like his voice, it didn't go with his bandit's face. "And I thought this might be my chance of a recall to Paris. Am I still in the doghouse, Captain?"

"I don't follow you."

"Because of those stockings—a gross of silk stockings, remember?"

"Oh, that." Berger couldn't raise any sympathy for the man. He climbed into the Simca and put the map on the passenger seat. Weber continued to hover outside in the rain, mourning his blighted career. "Sées isn't such a bad place to be," Berger said, "the way things are going."

"You think so?"

"Better than Paris."

"Maybe you're right, Captain."

Berger backed into the mouth of the farm track and turned. The Simca was getting old, and he could hear the exhaust beginning to blow. He kept his eyes on the rearview mirror until the Citroën had driven off in the opposite direction.

The rain came down in sheets, stopped altogether, started again, and finally settled into an incessant drizzle. Berger went astray twice and had to consult the map before he saw a beechwood avenue in the distance and, looming at the far end, a group of buildings surmounted by twin turrets.

Rochebrune

He stopped beside the fountain in the courtyard and sounded the horn before switching off. The thin, wavering note suggested that the Simca's battery was on its last legs.

He got out and looked around. Although there was no sign of life, he sensed that someone had heard the car and was watching him. Nothing happened, so he leaned through the window and tooted again.

At length he walked slowly over to the main house. He had no plan, no idea of what he would say or hoped to find. It was an effort of the will merely to put one foot in front of the other.

The rain was coming down harder again. He hadn't realized it until he saw streams of it pouring from holes in the gutter and bouncing off the steps. For a moment he wondered if there would be dogs. He had never overcome his ingrained childhood fear of them.

The big door had inset glass panels. They changed color as he watched: the door was opening. Automatically, he scraped his shoes on the iron grid beside it. There couldn't be any dogs in the house, he felt sure, or they would have started barking long ago.

"Mind if I come in?" All he could see of the man in the hall was a lanky figure with shoulder-length hair.

"What do you want? Is something the matter with your car?"

Berger thought of his father, the cigar salesman. You didn't insinuate yourself into people's houses by answering direct questions. He scraped his shoes again and said, "It really took me by surprise, this rain. Mind if I come in for a minute?"

The man in the worn velvet smoking jacket said nothing, so Berger edged past him into the hall. "Thanks. I apologize for turning up unannounced." He was enjoying this entrance far more than his role in the café.

"Have you driven far?" The man led the way into a big drawing room almost as bare of furniture as the hall. On a low table in front of the fireplace stood a bottle and two glasses. Some logs were burning on the hearth.

"Fancy! May already, and still cold enough for a fire." Berger unbuttoned his coat and produced a calling card. It bore his own name and the Rue Guynemer address.

The man took the card and examined it. "I'm Jean-Marie de Rochebrune," he said, without shaking hands.

"Le Colonel?"

"We haven't met, have we?" Rochebrune's tone was less guarded than curious.

Berger pointed to a telephone lying on the floor beside the fireplace. "I couldn't call you. It isn't the sort of subject one discusses on the phone."

Rochebrune gave a smothered laugh. "Even if you'd tried, it's been cut off for years. Would you mind telling me why you're here?"

It had all been easy so far—easier than expected. Berger had been waiting for something to come to his aid, a lead of some kind. He was still waiting.

"Some friends of mine have been in touch with me. I'm acting on their behalf."

He saw the old man's expression change, becoming alert as well as curious. His eyes flickered toward a door in the background. Berger's sole emotion was relief: he hadn't come on a wild-goose chase after all. There was no point in pulling his punches.

"My friends are interested in the whereabouts of a Polish airman named Jerzy Frykowski. Can you help them?"

"There must be some mistake. Why should your friends imagine I can help them? Who are they, anyway?" Rochebrune broke off, startled by a sudden commotion.

It was a composite sound: a door opening, a woman's voice exclaiming "No!" and a man's voice.

"Don't bother, Rochebrune, he knows."

Berger recognized the accent and intonation at once, yet he couldn't accept their authenticity. Even when he turned and saw the well-remembered face, he couldn't immediately accept that it belonged to Roman Kacew. His hair was wet. A drop of rainwater trickled down his neck, cold and repellent. For an instant, all of his attention was focused on its snail-like progress.

"You know this man?" said Rochebrune.

Berger waited for Kacew to answer in the irrational hope that, on second hearing, the voice would prove him an impostor.

Kacew nodded. "Yes, it's all right."

Berger pulled out a handkerchief and mopped the back of his neck. So that's the end of Joseph, he thought, but what really shook him was something else: his lack of perception—his blindness. All the pieces had been there from the start, and he'd failed to fit them together. "Can we talk somewhere?" he said at last.

The girl, who'd been clinging to Kacew's arm, ran to her father. "Why should he trust him?"

Kacew looked at Berger. "You came alone, didn't you?"

He'd hardly changed in two years. Berger noted the singed eyebrows, which made his eyes seem even darker and bigger, the dressing on his forehead, the bulge of his injured shoulder in the oversize corduroy jacket. "Yes," he said, "there's no one with me."

Kacew nodded gravely. "You always were a lone operator." He turned to Rochebrune. "It's all right," he repeated, "you can leave us alone together."

"But who are these friends of his?" Rochebrune was obviously loath to be left out.

"Please," said Kacew. His voice sounded edgy, and Berger saw his jaw muscles tighten. "Please!"

Berger and Kacew stood where they were, even when the door had closed. They said nothing, just eyed each other like players embarking on a game whose rules had yet to be agreed. Both were tense and uneasy, but in different ways. Kacew's uneasiness could readily be detected from the set of his jaw, a vein throbbing in his temple, fingers fumbling with the buttons of his jacket. In Berger the uneasiness lay at a deeper level. Its only outward sign was a subtle transformation in his sightless eye. It looked less immobile, less blank, more revealing of what went on in his mind.

Kacew was the first to move. He filled one of the goblets on the table and drained it without even trying to conceal how badly he needed a drink.

Berger put his handkerchief away. His coat collar felt clammy against the back of his neck, so he turned it down. "You're sure we can talk here undisturbed?"

Instead of replying, Kacew poured himself another glass. He held it in his left hand, still trying to button the jacket with his right.

"Are you badly hurt?"

"No, it's nothing serious."

Berger took out his case and slowly selected a cigarette. "How did you get out of the plane alive?"

"You've seen where it crashed?"

"Yes. The wreckage has been removed, but it was bad enough. What happened?"

"I bailed out and hit my shoulder on something, that's all I know. I've tried to remember the rest, but my mind's a blank." Kacew had no need to ask the obvious question.

"No," said Berger, "no other survivors."

"Did they identify the bodies?"

"It wasn't possible."

"How did you find me?"

"Three old friends: Roman Kacew, Jan Karski, Jerzy Frykowski . . . Does that remind you of anything?"

"It reminds me of the interrogation room at Fresnes," Kacew said bitterly. "You asked a lot of questions and answered none yourself."

"How did you come to be on board?"

"There you go again." Kacew gulped his second glass.

For a moment or two, Berger's grasp on reality slipped. All that possessed him was a sense of betrayal. Kacew had betrayed him, reneged on their deal and returned to the enemy fold. He genuinely forgot that this had been allowed for—indeed, that the whole plan depended on it. Rage overcame him.

"You realize what this means?" he said eventually. "It's the end of Joseph."

Kacew gazed at his empty glass. "Two years in London—two years, I stuck it. That's a long time for any agent."

"Longer than most," said Berger. "Three months is an agent's normal life span in England, then they string him up. Unless, of course, he's prepared to work for them."

Voices could be heard outside in the courtyard. They seemed to remind Kacew of something. "What put you on my track?"

Berger finally lit his cigarette. "Luck, and the fact that your friends in London were so anxious to find this man Frykowski."

"My friends in London? How would you know?"

"Why don't we stop playing games, Kacew?"

"Meaning what?"

"What code name did the British give you? How about Brutus? It must be something of the kind."

Kacew stared at Berger long and hard, still unable to fathom what was going on, still perplexed by Berger's role. Either that, or he was incapable of accepting the truth, just as Berger had at first been incapable of accepting his presence.

"You surely don't think . . . Look, Berger, you've had my signals, hundreds of them. What more proof do you want?"

Berger hesitated. He had often yearned to break his silence. Now that he could speak out at last, he found it hard to remove the mask he'd worn for so long. "When we made that deal at Fresnes," he said, "did you seriously think we counted on being able to buy your allegiance?"

"The signals," Kacew repeated. "You had my signals!"

"Yes," said Berger, "and they were worthy of my plan. Now, however you came to be on board that plane, you've ruined the whole operation."

"What is this, a double bluff?"

"We aren't the only ones to have lost an agent. Your friends in London have lost one, too." Kacew would have to go back where he came from, Berger thought suddenly—it was the only answer. Aloud, he said, "You realize you'll have to go back?"

Kacew's glass fell to the floor and smashed. He seized Berger by the coat collar and shook him fiercely with his one good arm. "You goddamned liar! If you think you can fool me, you're wrong. Lies, that's all they are, goddamned lies. You'll never convince me—never!" His voice took on an agonized note. "*Your* plan, was it? Why should you do such a thing?" He let Berger go.

Berger didn't move, made no attempt to straighten his clothing. "You mean it never occurred to you?"

"Never!" Kacew said. Another wave of doubt assailed him. "Never, and I don't believe you."

"Wouldn't you like to go back?"

"You still haven't answered my question. Why? I had my reasons, but you? A firing squad is a good incentive, but what incentive could you have?" Whether because his fury had spent itself or because the truth was dawning on him, the belligerence—even the hostility—had left Kacew's voice. "Why, Berger?"

Berger made no reply. What could he say? How could he answer a question so complex and intricate that he'd always shirked it himself? There was no simple answer, he knew, nor was there only one. Methodically, he straightened his shirt and tie. The room felt cold, but the cold seemed to come from somewhere inside him.

"A traitor . . ." Kacew said wonderingly. He filled the remaining glass and cradled it in his hands. "I hated you at Fresnes and I've hated you all this time in London. If I ever get back to England, I'll hate you even more."

Berger read the next question in Kacew's eyes. All that surprised him, given its inevitability, was how long the man had succeeded in holding it back.

"What about her?" Kacew asked. "Is she in on this?"

Again Berger said nothing. Knowing the rules, Kacew must also know the answer.

"You've never told her? Does she really think I'm Joseph, then?

Joseph the master spy, the Germans' prize possession in England—is that what she thinks?"

"Did you promise her you'd double-cross us?" Berger answered the question himself. "Of course you did."

Kacew put the glass down untouched. "Is she living with you?"

"Yes."

For one brief moment, Kacew looked as if he might launch himself at Berger again, but all he said was, "Is that why, because you wanted her to yourself? Was that your lofty motive?"

"You knew what you were doing when you left her behind. The choice was yours. Whatever promise you made her, you must have known you wouldn't be able to keep it."

"You sound just like . . ." Gahagan's name was on the tip of Kacew's tongue. He gave a wry laugh. "You ought to tell her the truth —I mean, what a hero you really are. Jannou has a soft spot for heroes."

Berger looked round the room in search of a clock. He'd left the café in St.-Rigomer a little after one, so it must be between two and half past. Allowing three hours for the drive back to Paris, he might still reach Billancourt in time to collect Jannou from the studio.

"I think we should get down to practicalities," he said.

Kacew shook his head. "Us two working in harness? I can't say the idea appeals to me. What about London? You really think they'll buy it?"

"They'll have to decide for themselves," Berger said wearily.

"But will they go on playing the game?"

"I'm not even sure I want them to. Has it ever occurred to you?"

"Really? What about your career? I remember you at Fresnes. Don't tell me your career didn't matter to you then."

"What would I have to lose? A valuable agent, a little professional kudos. Then I'd be what I was to start with, an insignificant cog in the Abwehr machine. Insignificance is an aid to survival, Kacew, and I want to survive. Intelligence officers don't get shot for losing an agent. Treason is another matter."

"How can you get me back?"

"That'll be up to your friends."

"As long as it's not by air." Kacew's attempt to be jocular fell painfully flat.

"I'll notify London."

"How?"

Berger ignored the question. "I'll need some proof that I've really located you. Give me a clue—something known only to yourself and London."

Kacew thought for a moment. Then he said, "Ask them this: 'How are the white canaries?' " He seemed to have run out of hostility. "Like some Calvados?"

"Thanks all the same." After a long pause, Berger added, "You've done a good job in London."

"So they keep telling me over there—how important I am and so on, but . . ." Kacew shrugged. "It's been nearly two years, Berger, know what I mean?"

"Yes, it's seemed a long time at this end, too."

"That's why I was in that plane: I simply couldn't resist it. Now, all I can think of is Karski and the others."

"They'd have died anyway. The fact remains, more people will die unless you go back."

Some of Kacew's hostility revived. "What do you keep in your veins, Berger, ice water?"

"You chose this trade. It isn't for the squeamish."

"All right, you win. What happens next? Do I stay put?"

"Do you feel safe here?"

"Yes, I think so."

Berger wondered whether to mention the rumors, but housing Kacew elsewhere would complicate matters. The less he moved around the better. "Lie low, then. Is your uniform still in existence?"

Kacew nodded.

"Keep it just in case. I'll get you some papers."

"Do you have a photo of me?"

"On file, yes."

"When will I hear from you?"

"As soon as I've been in touch with London."

"Sure you won't have one for the road? It's damned good Calvados."

Berger smiled for the first time. "Know something, Kacew? You must have been born under a lucky star. Of all the places you might have wound up in, you pick on a château owned by a French patriot with an attractive daughter and a cellar full of liquor. Let's hope your luck holds."

It was still raining. Water dripped and ran from the château's leaking gutters in counterpoint to the rain itself, a curtain of unbroken gray threads suspended from the overcast.

"Stay inside," said Berger. He buttoned his coat and turned the collar up.

"Will you tell Jannou I'm here?" Kacew asked.

"I'd better go."

"What shall I tell Rochebrune?"

"Anything except the truth."

Would it be raining in Paris, too? It was going to be a long, lonely drive. Berger hared across the courtyard, dodging puddles. Although he saw no one, he again felt sure that someone was watching him.

23

Paris

I CAN NEVER GO BACK TO BILLANCOURT . . . It was silly, but she couldn't stop herself. The words went round and round in her head like a prayer wheel, ousting every other thought. Even her visions of Reckzeh receded into the background, became blurred and less horrific.

It was stuffy in the apartment. She had opened the windows overlooking the park and taken her dress off as soon as she got back. She was in the bathroom, washing her hair in the basin, when the storm broke and the rain came down in sheets.

Running from room to room, she captured the swinging shutters and closed the windows again. Lightning danced in a charcoal gray sky. Rue Guynemer's plane trees, usually visible from four floors up as a series of static green hummocks, swirled like a river in full flood.

I can't go back to Billancourt tomorrow, she thought again. I won't be there when Jeancoles shoots the scene in Monsieur Boucicot's office. I won't see old Boucicot walk in and find his son with the girl and fall in love with her himself . . .

She heard someone open the front door and ran out into the passage. When she saw Berger standing there with his wet coat over one arm, rings under his eyes and chin dark with the strong growth of beard that obliged him to shave twice a day, all thoughts of Billancourt vanished.

"You're wet." She took his coat and hung it up.

"How long have you been back?"

"Awhile."

"I missed you at Billancourt."

She was so glad to see him, she decided not to say anything.

"You called the Lutétia. What did you want?"

"Nothing special. You look tired."

"I must get out of these clothes."

"I'll make some coffee."

"Damn, I forgot it again."

"I managed to get some."

Why, she thought, did people condemn banalities when they served such a useful purpose? She returned to the bathroom, combed out her wet hair, and put on her blouse. Then she went to the kitchen and started making coffee.

He had shaved by the time it was ready. His face, which seldom showed much emotion, looked frozen and expressionless. She put it down to fatigue, though she knew it was something more than that.

He sat down at the kitchen table and wrapped his hands around the cup. "I think I'm getting a cold."

"Which would you prefer, an aspirin or some cognac in your coffee?"

"Cognac, I think. Where did you get the coffee?"

She fetched the bottle from the living room. It was still raining heavily, but the storm had moved on.

"The concierge. There's nothing she doesn't deal in."

"She always looks so pathetic in her little glass box."

"That little glass box is a gold mine. She'll probably own the whole building by the time the war's over." Jannou paused. "Do you have to go out again?"

Simple though it was, the question seemed to take him aback. He poured a dash of cognac into his coffee and sipped it in silence. The rain died away and the kitchen grew lighter.

"It'll be nice and fresh outside, after that storm," she said.

"You've washed your hair, haven't you? Don't you mind it being so wet?"

"I don't think I've ever caught a cold in my life." Suddenly, she could restrain herself no longer. "I won't be going back to Billancourt."

"Why, is the studio closing down?"

"You know how I've always sneered at their pictures? The one they're making now is cornier than most, but I was roaming around the apartment before you came in, thinking of the ludicrous scene they'll be shooting tomorrow, and it was awful, knowing I wouldn't be there."

He watched her silently, waiting for her to go on.

"I liked the job. Only this morning in my office I was thinking to myself, You could be doing this ten years from now. I don't know how to explain it."

"So what happened?"

"Ten years . . . Normally my mind doesn't work that way, but the job seemed important to me—something permanent in the midst of so much uncertainty."

"You still haven't—"

"Oh, I was fired." She laughed, trying to make light of it. "Jeancoles can't employ me anymore. I'll be paid up to the end of the picture. It means I'm my own boss again." She got up and went into the living room, which still felt stuffy. She opened both the windows. The air that streamed in was cool and fresh, and the sky had cleared. "Could we go for a walk?"

Berger had followed her in. "What happened?"

Two quick steps closed the gap between them. She hugged him tight with her head burrowed into his shoulder and her arms around his waist.

He took her wrists, pried them away, and forced her to look at him.

"Sorry to make such a drama out of it," she said. The blood had returned to her cheeks. "That's what I wanted to tell you on the phone. It was Reckzeh—yes, I was as surprised as you are. He came to the studio." She winced. "You're hurting me."

He gave a little start and released her.

"Somehow I'd always reckoned with the possibility of our meeting again. I thought I'd drop dead at the sight of him, but I didn't. You see? I'm already more worried about losing that silly job."

"What did he want?"

"It's a relief to be able to talk about it."

"Was it he who got you fired?"

"Yes, but why should he have bothered?"

"How did Jeancoles react?"

"You know how easy it is for someone like Reckzeh to throw a scare into people. It's over, anyway. I'm through the surf and out the other side. There used to be a spot on the beach at Trouville that scared me —I meant to tell you when we were there—and because I was scared, I always got a mouthful of seawater and thought I was going to drown. One day I plucked up my courage and plunged into the surf head-on. After that it was easy. Give me a couple of minutes to dry my hair and we'll go for a walk."

"No, wait. Listen to me."

"Yes?" she said, but instead of replying at once he went back to the kitchen. She followed. "More coffee?"

He nodded. "The thing is, there's a chance of getting you away from here. Out of Paris, out of France altogether."

She poured some coffee into his cup and pushed the cognac bottle toward him. "Careful, don't tempt me. After what happened at Billancourt, I was sorry I didn't jump at the idea yesterday."

He nursed the cup between his hands. "I've considered all the alternatives: renting another apartment in another part of the city where nobody knows you—where nobody knows about us . . ."

"Why?"

"Think of that writing on the wall downstairs. The liberation of Paris won't be an easy time for anyone."

"Easier than now."

"But what happens in the meantime? No one can guarantee your safety. Not even I can do that."

"You're a strange man."

His smile was almost imperceptible. "Listen, Jannou. An Allied airman was shot down over France last week. The British have been in touch—they want him back. You could hitch a ride to England with him."

She recoiled at the sound of her own laughter. "Are communications between Paris and London that good?"

"The opportunity only just came up. You'd be safe in England—safe from Reckzeh and all that's going to happen here in the next few months."

"If I said yes, at least I'd know if you meant it this time." She knew, even as she spoke, that he was in earnest, but she wondered if he'd have broached the idea if she hadn't told him about Reckzeh. Something was wrong, and it irked her not to be able to put her finger on it.

"I don't know exactly when the pickup will take place," he went on, "but you'll have to decide right away."

It was hopeless trying to read his thoughts when she wasn't even sure how she felt herself. "I've never asked you, have I?" she said eventually.

"Never asked me what?"

"To confide in me. What are you up to? Perhaps I've never asked because I doubted if you'd tell me. Perhaps I wouldn't believe you whatever you said, but why not try?"

"You'd be safe in England," he repeated. "You could breathe freely. The war will be over soon, then you can think again. There are too many things between us here, you said so yourself. Over there you'd know your own mind."

"Do you know yours?"

"Yes."

"You love me, is that what you're saying?"

"Grab the chance while you can."

"And in the same breath you tell me to go."

He thought for a moment. "We'd be separated anyway, when the end comes. It's the best solution."

"What makes you think the British will let me in?"

"Don't worry about that."

"You're holding something back."

"You'll know all the answers once you're in England."

"Won't you tell me before I go?"

"You'll know."

"Couldn't we both go?" She looked at him pensively. "Did you know I was en route to England when the accident happened that killed my father? He was driving me to Le Havre to catch the ferry. We were almost on the outskirts."

Berger reached across the table and took her hand. "We'll have to buy you some things for the journey."

"Some solution!" she said. "I'll be in England, safe and sound and worried sick about you."

His face relaxed at last, as though her departure were a foregone conclusion and the knowledge reassured him. "Would you mind repeating the last part?" he said.

The streets were dry again by the time he turned off the boulevard into Rue de la Santé. A lot of Parisians were out and about, enjoying the freshness that had followed the storm.

It had taken him less than fifteen minutes to walk here from Rue Guynemer. He was familiar with the district because the Santé Prison, like the Cherche-Midi, was used by the Abwehr. At this hour, however, he passed none of the vans with barred windows that ferried prisoners between the Santé and the Lutétia or the Avenue Foch.

An ambulance overtook him and swung into a hospital entrance. There were many hospitals in the quarter, as well as homes for the old and mentally ill. To supply all these institutions with staff, a number of religious orders had established convents in the vicinity. Some, like that of the Dames Augustines, which he was just passing, were big and sumptuous; others occupied dilapidated old buildings with frontages that looked as if they themselves were riddled with disease.

Berger paused outside one of these less prepossessing convents. St. Vincent's was a leprous gray building hemmed in on both sides by others of its kind. The two tall Gothic windows were protected by rusty grilles and caked with grime, the belfry looked more like a water tower than an adjunct to divine worship. Through the belfry's wooden slats a bell could be heard tolling faintly. Pinned to the oak door was a faded notice announcing the times of Masses. The door itself was held open by a sort of leather cuff.

Berger strolled on, crossed the street, stopped to light a cigarette. He did so not only to satisfy himself that no one had followed him; his hesitation was a symptom of uncertainty. Was this really what Canaris had meant by an extreme emergency?

It had happened last year, after the Santander meeting. Canaris, who was visiting Paris, had given a dinner at the George V. Everyone was there: the Military Governor, General Oberg, Reckzeh, Colonel von Steinberg, and—basking in his newfound glory because Joseph's signals had been coming in for three months past—Lieutenant Berger.

He was seated near the bottom of the table, far from Canaris and the other bigwigs, but after dinner, when everyone repaired to a private room for coffee and cigars, he found the Admiral beside him for a moment.

"Congratulations, Berger!" That was intended for general consumption. Then the voice sank to a confidential undertone. "Keep Joseph alive at all costs. And listen: here's how you get in touch with London if I can't be reached, but only in the last resort, Berger. Only in an extreme emergency."

Berger dropped his half-smoked cigarette in the gutter and ground it out with his heel. Three women in black shawls were making for the church door. He crossed the street and followed them inside.

He could see almost nothing at first, the grimy windows admitted so little of the evening sunlight he'd left behind. There were no pews in the nave, just a few rows of plain wooden chairs. Most of the men and women who occupied them were old and shabbily dressed. A scattering of candles burned in front of the Virgin and Child. A nun was kneeling on the worn red carpet covering the stone altar steps.

Berger walked slowly up the right-hand side of the nave, which was emptier. He paused near the altar but couldn't bring himself to kneel and cross himself. It occurred to him that he hadn't been inside a church since his wedding. The realization made him feel uneasy. It seemed such a bad omen that he nearly turned tail.

Someone began to intone a prayer. The voice sounded startlingly crisp and incisive in comparison with the answering murmur from the rows of chairs. Berger spotted the side door and reached it in three or four swift strides. He opened it quickly and closed it behind him.

The room, an octagonal chamber paneled in some dark wood, was even gloomier than the church. Berger guessed it must be the sacristy. Then he saw something that made him smile despite his jangling nerves. A nun was standing at a table, immersing the inner tube of a bicycle tire in a bowl of water. Several ancient bicycles were propped against the wall.

"Excuse me, Sister."

She slowly turned her head. "Yes?"

"May I speak to the mother superior?"

She removed the tube from the bowl and put it down on the table beside a puncture repair kit. "You're speaking to her." Like rabbits diving down a burrow, her hands disappeared into the voluminous sleeves of her blue habit.

"You are Mother Célestine?" From the little Berger could see of her face beneath the projecting hood, she seemed surprisingly young for her rank.

"As I already told you."

According to his inquiries, the convent housed nuns belonging to a nursing order that worked in hospitals and tended private patients at home. Although nothing suspicious had come to light, Berger couldn't help wondering—given that anything was possible in the world of deception he inhabited—if Mother Célestine was really a nun.

"I should like to call on your services."

The congregation had started singing.

"Our services are available to all," she said, "in urgent cases."

"In an extreme emergency, you mean?"

He sensed her hesitation, her mistrust. She crossed her arms without exposing her hands. Her face seemed to retreat still farther into the shadow of her hood.

"We very seldom take private patients."

"This one is—how shall I put it?—a person of importance. His condition is grave. I was told in confidence that you might be able to help him."

She waited. The singing had gained strength. Berger wondered how the undernourished old men and women he'd seen could sing so lustily.

"This patient," he went on, "requires special treatment. Perhaps you'd be good enough to obtain the necessary drugs."

"I'm afraid I don't understand."

He produced an envelope from his pocket. "I've made a note of the details. All I ask is that you should pass them on. This is a genuine emergency."

"There must be some mistake, Monsieur . . . ?"

"Berger. You'll also find a telephone number and a list of times when I can be reached in the event of your receiving an answer to my request. I think it would be better if I didn't come here again."

"I'm sorry, I still don't understand."

Berger experienced a momentary feeling of panic. The sacristy's paneled walls seemed to be closing in, converging on him, constricting his chest. What if she were telling the truth? A year had gone by—perhaps the link with London no longer existed. Perhaps it had never existed at all, save in the Admiral's fertile imagination.

Putting the envelope on the table beside the tire and the repair kit, he indicated the door behind him. "Is there another way out?"

"The other door leads to our living quarters, and the rule of our order does not permit men access to them."

Was she smiling?

Although there was no reason for him to linger, Berger waited for some gesture, some sign of acquiescence. He felt he couldn't leave without knowing for certain that his message had reached its proper destination. "Strange times make strange Allies," he said, "don't you agree?"

She resumed her place at the table. "If you'll excuse me. Bicycles are essential to our work. We have patients all over the city."

"I apologize for disturbing you."

She turned to face him once more. "All that disturbs me is the possibility that our tires may not last the war."

This time, somewhere deep inside the starched hood, Berger detected an unmistakable smile. She folded back her sleeves, picked up the inner tube, and started feeding it through the water. The envelope had disappeared.

He left the sacristy by the same door. The chairs were empty and in
some disarray. A nun was busy straightening the rows. She looked up as
he passed her, surprised at first, then with a smile that puzzled Berger
because it struck him as a little too worldly.

24

London

GAHAGAN PEERED UNCERTAINLY through the downpour. His windshield wipers and masked headlights were fighting a losing battle with the rain and the blackout. "Corner of Wimpole and Queen Anne Street," Ian Scott had said. "Pick me up there. What's the matter with my car? Don't ask daft questions, just get there. You can tell something's up from my voice? Damn it, Jeremy, it's 2 A.M. I always sound like this at two o'clock in the morning."

Gahagan slowed to a crawl, one hand on the wheel, the other wiping his condensed breath off the inside of the windshield. Catching sight of the tall figure and waving hand at the last moment, he braked hard to avoid drenching Scott from head to foot.

Scott furled his umbrella and wrenched the door open. Gahagan was glad to see him, relieved that his phone call had put an end to the suspense. It could only mean that a signal had come in from Paris.

"You took your time," said Scott. He deposited the dripping umbrella on the floor beside him.

"Why did you have to wait in the open? Where are we going, anyway?"

"At this hour? Where the hell do you think?"

Gahagan turned right and headed for Wigmore Street. The first call had been from a woman with a dark brown voice. Ian was in the garage, she said, trying to get his car started, so Gahagan might have to pick him up. "Why not come over anyway?" she added. "I can promise you a drink."

"What's wrong with your bus?" Gahagan asked.

"No idea. It wouldn't start. They never do when you really need them."

Gahagan had felt something close to envy when he heard the woman's voice on the phone. He knew next to nothing about Ian Scott's private life.

"The girl who called me," he said. "She's got an unusual voice."

"What are you, a talent scout?"

"I'd guess she's a brunette. Dark hair, dark eyes . . ."

"Save it, Jeremy." Scott produced a pipe from his pocket and smacked the bowl against his palm with a sound like a cork popping. He always smoked pipes so big and heavy that it was a wonder any set of teeth could support their weight.

Gahagan took another right into Wigmore Street. If Scott didn't want to talk, it was useless to try and draw him out, but the sight of Portman Square and the aerials on the roof of Braille House proved too much for Gahagan's self-restraint.

"Have you located him?"

Scott continued to stare straight ahead with the unlit pipe clamped between his teeth. "Albatross," he said. "Mean anything to you?"

"What is it, a code name?"

"Never heard it before?"

"No. Have you found him? Is he alive?"

"Oh yes, he's alive all right, but your outfit won't like the implications."

"What does Sir Graham say?"

They crossed Oxford Street and drove down Park Lane. On their right, rain and darkness transformed Hyde Park into a desolate infinity.

"It wasn't us who found him, Jeremy. In case you didn't know, France is still under German occupation."

"But you said . . . You mentioned Frykowski on the phone. It is our man your people have found, isn't it?"

"All right, get ready for a shock. It's the Germans who've found him. I haven't heard a word from my contacts." Gahagan started to say something. "No, wait, there's worse to come. You told me Cato's German controller was a man called Berger. Apparently, it's Berger who's got him."

"What do you mean, 'apparently'?"

"We've received a signal signed Albatross. It could only have come from him."

"Berger?"

"Yes, damn it. He's offering your outfit a chance to retrieve Frykowski from France."

"Why us?"

"Because it's your little game. I'll tell you something else I shouldn't: M.I.6 maintains a direct radio link with Paris. It's sacrosanct, so to speak—the safe house and transmitter can only be used with Sir Graham's express permission."

"Where in Paris?"

"A convent run by a nursing order—nine nuns and a mother superior. The transmitter's installed in the belfry, in a cubbyhole above the sacristy, and the Germans have never located it. I'm only telling you now because the transmitter's probably defunct. Berger used it to pass his message."

"And he's offering us Frykowski back?"

"Yes, how do you like that?"

"But . . ."

"Exactly, Jeremy: but! It means he knows that Cato has been in our hands all the time. Look out, are you trying to kill us?"

The car skidded so wildly as Gahagan rounded the Victoria Memorial that he almost hit the curb. He regained control of it and drove more slowly. St. James's Park, too, was shrouded in rain.

Bombs had demolished one of the buildings on Broadway. The rubble had been cleared and the site leveled to form a parking lot. Only two cars could be seen, one of them Sir Graham's Wolseley.

"He's there already," Gahagan said.

"Old men need less sleep, they say," Scott observed dryly.

"Your lady friend sounded wide awake."

"That's another cross I have to bear, a woman who only comes to life after midnight. It's worse than an ulcer."

"What the hell would you know about ulcers? We'd better hurry. How did he take it?"

Scott didn't answer. He opened his umbrella and held it over them both. Side by side, they picked their way across the parking lot to the street, trying to avoid the worst of the puddles.

Everyone in the Firm asked the same question: Why did Sir Graham, an outdoor type who preferred to live in the country, keep his office hermetically sealed? The windows were never opened and the air inside was stale. Even the tea he dispensed to visitors had a musty flavor.

Winter deposited the tray on the edge of Sir Graham's desk. "How do you take your tea, sir?"

The question, as Gahagan rightly guessed, was a pure formality. Winter asked it even when the milk and sugar had run out. A handful of crackers lay forlornly on a willow pattern plate, as stale and insipid as the tea.

When Winter withdrew, the silence in the room was so intense that Gahagan balked at replacing his cup on the saucer for fear of the noise it would make.

"It's China," Sir Graham said eventually. "I'm sorry, there isn't any Indian to be had at the moment." Opening a desk drawer, he almost furtively produced two lumps of sugar. These he dunked and popped into his mouth before they could disintegrate.

On the wall behind him hung another picture of the Life Guards in action. It didn't match the quality of the one above the fireplace in his country house and had recently been restored. The khaki-clad horsemen were charging through a morass of gleaming varnish.

Scott had brought along a copy of the signal and put it on the desk. Sir Graham picked it up, studied it by the light of his antiquated desk lamp, and put it down with a sigh. He said nothing, merely bent an inquiring gaze on the other two.

Gahagan wondered who was expected to kick off, himself or Scott. Scott had refused a cup of tea and was nursing his empty pipe. He would obviously do his best to stay out of the firing line.

"Please smoke if you wish," said Sir Graham.

Scott shook his head. "Thank you, sir. I never smoke before breakfast."

"Very creditable." Sir Graham targeted on Gahagan. "Did you have any inkling of this? It must have come as a shock to you."

Why to me, thought Gahagan, why not to him? Sir Graham looked a trifle jaded around the eyes but otherwise quite his usual self. Gahagan coveted Scott's pipe. Any form of distraction would have been welcome.

"Well, Jeremy? Did it ever cross your mind that Cato might not be our agent—exclusively ours, I mean?"

"No, I had no reason to suspect any such thing. It doesn't add up."

"What doesn't?"

"I just don't see a German playing Berger's role. It conflicts with all I've ever felt about the German mentality."

"There have been one or two exceptions," Sir Graham said vaguely.

"Yes, a few anti-Nazis who came to grief because they went off half-cocked, but this man? He's been stringing us along for the past two years."

"It's a blow to your pride, I can understand that."

"My pride?"

"Very well, ours. We preened ourselves on our finesse, and now it turns out we needn't have bothered because we had a"—Sir Graham selected his words with care—"a secret ally all the time."

"It could be a trap," Gahagan said. "We send in a rescue team for Kacew, alias Frykowski, and they have themselves a field day."

Scott knocked some imaginary dottle into his palm. "Will you want me to handle the pickup?"

Sir Graham evaded the question. "This Berger—he got onto our man damned quickly, Ian. Quicker than your people. Any idea how?"

"I could only guess."

"Carry on."

"I'd sooner not, sir."

"I've always admired your spirit of cooperation, Ian." Sir Graham turned back to Gahagan and pointed to the message form. "This phrase—'How are the white canaries?'—what does it mean?"

"He kept two of them, a male and a female. He bought them a few months back."

"Odd fish, these agents. Do you take it as proof that Cato has been picked up? You're in no doubt at all?"

"No one could have forced him to divulge such a thing—no one would have tried. I mean, it's too unimportant, too incidental."

"You never reported it."

"Reported what, sir?"

"That he'd bought these birds."

Gahagan glanced at Scott, whose jug ears looked redder than usual. "You mean I should have submitted a memo on the subject?"

"Never mind, Jeremy, it isn't worth getting het up about. So we must assume that Berger has found Cato, that Cato is alive, and that he's showing a certain willingness to cooperate." Sir Graham held the sheet to the light again. "What about Berger's suggestion, Ian? This spot on the coast where he wants us to make the pickup, Lock some-thing—I can never get my tongue round these French names."

"Breton, sir, actually. Locquirec's a Breton name. The beach itself is called Les Sables Blancs, meaning 'The White Sands.' "

"Thanks for the language lesson, Ian. I'd sooner hear what you think of the location."

"I've checked it on the map. It's a definite possibility—if you're thinking of bringing the man out."

"We are, and I propose to make it your job." Sir Graham succumbed to a moment's irritation. "Why don't you smoke that thing?"

Scott stuffed the pipe in his pocket. "Personally, I'd favor a seaborne operation. If we had to plan days ahead, a plane would make us too dependent on the weather. Mind you, it's a long way by sea. We'd probably have to go from Portsmouth."

"I'm glad to see you've already given the matter some thought."

"It would mean using a fast launch and running ashore in a rubber dinghy. I've a fair idea of the coastline: cliffs, narrow beaches, biggish breakers—not too easy."

"Berger doesn't say it's going to be a picnic."

"On the other hand, I don't think the area's too heavily defended. I recall some agents' reports to that effect."

"Brittany, eh?" mused Sir Graham. "How far from Brest, would you say?"

"Forty or fifty miles."

"That figures. Jeremy's file on Berger mentions that he was stationed there before they transferred him to Paris." Sir Graham smiled. "He'd be bound to choose an area he knows, for safety's sake. I don't suppose he aims to get caught red-handed."

"However well he knows that stretch of coast, he'll be running a risk."

"He sounds pretty confident."

Gahagan continued to marvel at Sir Graham's sangfroid, more puzzled than ever by his complete lack of surprise, let alone dismay. He actually seemed to be relishing the situation.

"This pickup," Gahagan said, "—why not let me handle it?"

Sir Graham poured himself another cup of tea. There was a repeat of the sugar routine: the opening of the drawer, the surreptitious removal of two lumps, the dunking of each in turn. "You'll be needed at this end, Jeremy. Your presence here is essential."

"Will we resume transmissions when he's back?"

"One thing at a time." An uncharacteristic note of impatience had entered Sir Graham's voice. "What about this second person Berger mentions in his signal?" He picked up the sheet and read aloud. " 'Request transportation for two, impossible give particulars.' Can you explain that, Jeremy? Any idea who he means?"

"Himself, maybe."

"Berger? Why? The man has stuck it for two years without losing his nerve."

"Perhaps this foul-up has scared him—perhaps he wants to come over to our side of the fence." Gahagan put his cup down with sudden vehemence. "Or perhaps the situation has gone to his head. 'Impossible give particulars . . .' Kacew hated him, and I'm beginning to understand why."

Sir Graham subsided into the high-backed leather armchair, cradling his cup in both hands. He sighed. When he spoke, his voice was almost inaudible. "Scared or overconfident, which? Any man would feel confident after getting away with it for two whole years, but is he scared underneath?" He took a sip of tea. "We'll have trouble with him either way—you always do when you're dealing with someone who's afraid or complacent. How can we play it safe, Jeremy? That's the most important question of all. Fortitude South must be kept alive, but with Berger?"

"We'll know more when Cato's back."

Sir Graham sat there with a brooding, ruminative expression on his face, as certain as any man could be that no one would dare to interrupt his reverie.

What was going on in his head? For a moment, Gahagan felt almost sure that the answer was nothing, that he was just a tired old man whose brooding silence was merely an act designed to simulate profound thought.

Sir Graham replaced his empty cup on the desk. "If Berger dropped out, who'd take over the Paris end?" He sighed again, so deeply that the pale blue shirt drew taut across his chest. "We'll have to give him an answer. What do you suggest, Ian?"

"You approve Locquirec, sir?"

"Yes, let's follow his plan. You gave it your blessing too, more or less."

"I'd have to clear it with the Naval Section. When do you want us to bring your man out?"

"As soon as you're ready. No, wait, let's fix the timing now. The night of Thursday-Friday—does that give you long enough?"

"It's pretty tight."

"I'm lunching at the club tomorrow—today, I mean. Call me there around two."

"Which club, sir?"

"Hellions. If you confirm the timing, we'll signal him after that."

"Over the M.I.6 link?"

"It's what he'll be expecting. Any other form of contact may make him suspicious. Let's hope he doesn't get cold feet at the last minute. I want him to feel secure, completely secure, especially on the beach."

"Will that be all, sir?"

"Your people have reported nothing so far?"

"The time was too short."

"Not for Berger, though. Amazing, really amazing. I'd like to have met the man . . . Are you dashing off?" Sir Graham seemed almost resentful of their departure. "Winter will bring you your coats."

"No need, sir."

Sir Graham remained seated at his desk. He picked up the signal and glanced at it again. "Jeremy?"

"Sir?" Gahagan turned.

"Find a safe place for Cato when he's back. I don't want him joyriding off to France again. The same applies to whoever comes with him."

"I'll submit some suggestions."

"What happened to his canaries?"

"Lieutenant Mills took them with her."

"To the Hebrides?" Sir Graham frowned. "Isn't the climate up there a bit harsh for canaries?"

Was it a genuine question? Gahagan decided not. He said good night and closed the door behind him. Scott was halfway to the elevator and beckoning impatiently.

A minute later they were standing in the entrance with their coat collars turned up, reluctant to venture out into the rain, which was still teeming down.

"He didn't seem particularly shaken by the news," Gahagan said.

"Him? He's as unflappable as the Mona Lisa."

"And not a word about Albatross—I was waiting for it the whole time."

Scott opened his umbrella with a decisive click. "It's late, Jeremy."

"Shall I drive you straight home?" Gahagan felt another pang of envy when he thought of the woman's voice and then of his bleak apartment in Harewood Avenue, where the furniture removed by his wife had yet to be replaced.

"Via the office, if you don't mind. I've a couple of things to pick up."

"You think it's a certainty, the night of Thursday-Friday?"

"The old man wouldn't want to spoil his weekend."

"I wish I were coming, too."

Scott had stepped out into the rain, so Gahagan was compelled to follow suit or forgo his share of the umbrella.

PART THREE

25

Paris

IT WAS ALREADY LIGHT OUTSIDE, but the lobby of the Ritz still blazed as if in demonstration of its luxury and opulence. Although there were few places in Paris that filled him with greater revulsion—he regarded the hotel as a nest of parasites and conspirators—Reckzeh had turned up early for his appointment.

He was armed and in uniform—surprisingly, in view of the private nature of his business, but quite deliberately. The same deliberation had governed his choice of a seat in the lobby, one of the deep velvet armchairs near the hotel's Place Vendôme entrance.

It amused him to see how, every time German officers walked in from the street and saw him sitting there, their faces became tinged with uneasiness. Even the ones who didn't know him stole a surreptitious glance at the uniform greatcoat on the chair beside him, the belt and holster, the package on the table in front of him. All who could afford to stay at the Ritz or eat there at inflationary prices were bound to identify the contents of the package as caviar from Petrossian's, and none could fail to be impressed by its size.

At present the lobby was almost deserted. The only sound was a hum of conversation from the crowded breakfast room.

May they choke on their croissants, Reckzeh thought savagely. As a boy he had watched in fascination while his grandmother clamped a struggling goose between her legs, squeezed its neck, inserted the little piece of wood that held its beak open, and thrust the mash down its throat with her fingers. In his native Alsace, the production of goose liver was a cottage industry.

"Herr Standartenführer? Madame Gurdyev will see you now."

It was the head receptionist himself, a pallid, white-haired man in a shabby cutaway.

Reckzeh rose and buckled on his belt, patting the holster into place. "How the devil do you remember all our ranks?"

The man construed this as a compliment. "This is the Ritz," he said with a little bow. "Kindly follow me."

Reckzeh draped his coat over his arm and picked up the package. Half a pound of caviar! Koch, who'd bought it and fixed the appointment, had been unmoved by his look of outrage. "It's far less than her standard charge," he said. "You're getting an SD discount, so to speak."

The receptionist ushered Reckzeh down a long corridor lined with illuminated showcases displaying photographs of an exhibition entitled "German Art in Paris." When they reached the elevator, he pressed the button for him.

"Fourth floor, Monsieur. Suite 403."

"What do you think of her?" asked Reckzeh.

"She has a waiting list a mile long."

"Is she really Russian?"

"They say she's the daughter of a White Russian general."

Reckzeh laughed. "Paris has more White Russian generals than the White Russian Army had soldiers."

Something about Reckzeh's laugh must have activated a sense of timing acquired in thirty-odd years of professional experience, because the receptionist said, "Here at the Ritz one forms the same impression of the German Army: more generals than soldiers—more colonels than corporals, anyway."

Reckzeh laughed again. "Would you say it was worth half a pound of caviar to have your future foretold by Madame Gurdyev?"

The receptionist looked down at his worn black shoes. Beneath their thick glaze of polish, the uppers were cracking badly. "Personally, Monsieur, I'd settle for the caviar. It would guarantee *my* future for a month or two."

The elevator door slid open. On the way up, Reckzeh studied the menu hanging on the wall with an air of disgust. He got out at the fourth floor and was scanning the room numbers when a colonel in the Luftwaffe accosted him. His uniform was impeccably tailored, Reckzeh noted, but unadorned with any medal ribbons worth mentioning.

"My name is Engels," he said. Slim, with graying fair hair, Colonel Engels was a man who strove to look younger than his age. His tone was studiously brisk and youthful. "Follow me, please, Madame is expecting you. Did you come on General Oberg's recommendation?"

"Is he a client of hers, if that's the proper term?"

"Madame has a very considerable following—that might be a more appropriate description—particularly in SS circles. She has even been consulted by Reichsführer Himmler. Here we are."

The walls of the anteroom were lined with pale blue silk. The colonel took Reckzeh's coat and held out his hand for the package. "You'd better leave that with me, it would only spoil her concentration."

Reckzeh had done some research. Engels was one of Göring's minions and belonged to a small "advisory staff" based in Paris for the purpose of buying up paintings for the Marshal's collection. That left him ample time to play impresario to Madame Gurdyev, who lived with him here at the Ritz. Reckzeh surmised that a percentage of her fees found its way into the colonel's pocket.

He surrendered the package. "She must get pretty sick of caviar."

"She never touches it."

"So she not only foretells other people's futures, she takes care of her own, eh? How much does a pound of caviar fetch on the black market?"

Engels gave a thin smile. "It's your time you're wasting, Standartenführer." He indicated a door behind him. "Madame's next appointment is in half an hour."

The two large interconnecting rooms were curtained and unlit except by a lamp on the table where the woman was sitting. The air was heavy with a scent that grated at once on Reckzeh's nerves.

"Come in."

The voice was strongly accented. All he could see of the woman at the table was a bulky figure dressed entirely in black, even to the turban on her head.

"What is it? Come closer, where I can see you. Is something troubling you?"

Reckzeh hadn't moved since the door closed behind him. "The incense," he said, and walked slowly toward her.

She remained seated at the table, erect and motionless. A long rope of pearls encircled her throat several times, perhaps to conceal the wrinkled skin. The front of her turban, too, was embellished with pearls —a huge brooch resembling some order of chivalry. Her face was massive, the withered flesh so thickly coated with powder that it looked icebound.

"You dislike churches? They hold some unpleasant memory for you?"

There was an empty chair across the table from her. Reckzeh came to a halt behind it and rested his hands on the back.

"You dislike incense? Why?"

She was right. It reminded him of Prague and the church where Heydrich's assassins had taken refuge, of the six-hour gunfight that had left seven enemy agents and twice as many SS men dead. It was a Czech Orthodox church pervaded by just the same aroma of incense and candle wax.

"Who researches your clients for you," he said, "that colonel of yours?"

"Why come at all, if you're so skeptical?" One of her hands emerged from the robe, the fingers laden with rings deeply embedded in soft white flesh. She pointed to the chair. "Please be seated. It distracts me, your standing there."

Reckzeh sat down with his hands flat on his thighs.

"So why have you come? About the future, I suppose." She gave a full-throated, sensual laugh. The icebound face seemed to melt. "No one cares about the past these days. I fail to understand all this interest in the future."

Reckzeh couldn't help it: he was transfixed by the rich, deep voice— by the woman herself. Apart from his wife, the few women he'd had sex with had been girls with the bodies of young men, but the sensuality emitted by this creature was so overpowering that he had a sudden vision of himself engulfed by her warm, mountainous body.

"I'm told you take a rather gloomy view of the future."

"One doesn't require my powers to do that."

"In other words, you spread defeatist propaganda?"

"One need not be a defeatist to sense that things will get worse. It isn't that I wish them to; I simply say what I see. That is why I prefer the past to the future."

"I don't see a crystal ball anywhere."

"Did you expect one? Would it make you less suspicious of me?"

"I don't know."

"Were you told to bring something with you, some object you carry on your person every day?"

Reckzeh unbuttoned the breast pocket of his uniform jacket and took out Berger's wristwatch. He'd been meaning to wear it ever since

Koch produced it, but he couldn't bring himself to. He put it on the table in front of him and waited.

"Hold it in your hand for a moment."

"I'm sorry?"

"Hold it for a moment and think of what is in your heart, then give it to me."

Her body remained immobile as she put out her hand and took the watch. The smell of incense became stronger, or seemed to. Reckzeh's head had begun to ache. He struggled to concentrate on what the woman was doing. She rested her fingertips on the watch face. Although he could detect no change in her expression, he sensed that part of her was elsewhere. When she spoke, her voice seemed to come from far away.

"I see water, waves, spray . . . It must be the sea. Not a river, not a lake—yes, the sea . . . Cliffs, steep cliffs, a sandy shore . . ."

The invasion, he thought—everyone in Paris was talking about the invasion. Was that what she meant?

"It is night . . . A light is flashing on the water—a signal? Out of the darkness comes a boat . . . Three figures are standing on the shore, waiting—yes, three . . . What's this? Suddenly, it's daytime—everything is as bright as day." She broke off, looking bemused. "Your skepticism makes it hard for me."

Reckzeh's headache had become intolerable, viselike. He would have urged her to continue, but his throat was too dry.

"No, not as bright as day, but light enough—as light as it would be at sunrise. Wait . . . This is somewhere else. The sea has gone . . . Some trees, a clearing—that's it, a clearing in a wood at dawn . . . In the middle of the clearing, a lone tree . . .

"I hear a sound. It comes nearer, stops . . . A truck, uniforms, soldiers armed with rifles, leaping to the ground . . . A coffin of raw, white wood . . . Another vehicle, a smaller one . . . An officer, a priest, a man with his hands tied behind his back . . ." Her voice rose. "No, no, you're asking too much of me!"

"Please," said Reckzeh, unconscious of having spoken. He only knew that he wouldn't be able to endure it if she stopped now.

"The tree in the clearing . . . They take the man and strap him to it . . . The priest begins to say something, but the man . . ." Again her voice rose in pitch. "It's agony for me, this. Don't force me to continue."

Reckzeh ran a finger round his collar and loosened his tie. The pain in his head pulsated like a glaring light switched on and off at regular intervals. "No," he said, "please go on!"

"A red card . . . They pin it to his chest . . . The size of a playing card . . . They pin it over his heart . . . The soldiers line up and raise their rifles, the officer steps aside . . . Black dots on the red card . . . Five little black dots . . . Blood . . ."

She pushed the watch away, breathing hard. Her bosom undulated beneath the black taffeta gown. She looked at Reckzeh alertly, back in the present again. It was he who seemed to be stranded in another time and clinging to it with all his might.

"Now do you see what I mean," she said, "about preferring the past?"

"What you described was an execution."

Standing on a small table at her elbow were a carafe and a tumbler. She poured some colorless liquid into the glass, hesitated, and added a little more. After only a few sips, she put the glass aside.

"You don't seem very alarmed," she said.

Reckzeh's headache had gone. He picked up the watch in one swift movement, almost as if he feared it might vanish before his eyes.

"Where was this?"

"I beg your pardon?"

"You described a clearing in a wood. Where was it?"

"I've forgotten."

"Can you tell me when?"

"In the future. Sometime, I don't know."

"The tree—you mentioned a tree. You remember the tree in the clearing? A lone tree, you said."

"I may have."

"What time of year? Did it have leaves?"

"Leaves? Yes, pointed green leaves."

Reckzeh replaced the watch in his breast pocket and buttoned the flap. He rose. "Thank you for seeing me."

"Is that all?" She smiled. "You haven't used up all your time."

"I'm impressed, Madame. I shall recommend you in the warmest terms."

She still didn't move, but her smile became sardonic.

"Only, I'm sure, if I prove to be right."

26

London

WHEN HELLIONS was gutted by incendiary bombs in the middle of November 1940, not a few of its members believed that the club's destruction portended the imminent collapse of the British Empire itself.

Barely a year later, Hellions reopened on its original site just off St. James's. Now that the tide of war had turned and the Empire was saved, the members had regained their habitual pigheaded optimism.

The firm of architects commissioned to restore the interior had worked wonders. Everything looked exactly the same, even the paintings, which had been copied from photographs. The mediocrity of these copies was gladly accepted for the sake of their familiar appearance. Most miraculous of all, the club's atmosphere remained as formal and fusty as ever.

Sir Graham and Gerald Foote were seated at a table in the small room normally reserved for the playing of chess, the only game permitted on the premises, but which the committee allowed members to use for lunch when they wished to entertain in private. The elderly waiter had cleared away and served coffee. He had also, with a pained expression, brought a glass of Remy Martin for Gerald.

"What's he got against brandy?" asked Gerald, who wasn't a member.

Sir Graham dipped a lump of sugar in his coffee and popped it into his mouth. He seemed averse to talking. Most of his guest's conversational gambits had been countered with stubborn silence.

"Restoring this place must have cost you people a pretty penny."

"A fortune," Sir Graham replied tersely.

From his offhand tone, Gerald gathered that Sir Graham, with the unconcern proper to a wealthy man, had forgotten the exact sum.

"How much is a fortune?"

"You've had a fixation about money ever since I've known you, Gerald."

"I'm a pessimist. A pessimist needs more money than other people, otherwise he feels insecure."

"You've got a well-paid job, a Bentley in the garage, and a house in Belgravia. On top of that, you married an American heiress. What more do you want?"

"Maybe that's the trouble, the money's hers." Gerald sipped his brandy. "Why did the waiter give me a dirty look?"

"Nothing stronger than sherry or port is served here before six in the evening."

"So how come I got served?"

"Guests are allowed their vices. What time do you make it?"

"Half past one. You've found Cato, is that why you asked me here?"

"Yes, sooner than expected."

"Do you plan to bring him back?"

"Scott's working on it." Sir Graham's shepherd's pie had left him feeling unpleasantly bloated. He wasn't a big eater, but he'd recently been putting on weight for no discernible reason. I'm growing old, he told himself, and promptly offset this thought by recalling his night with Rona and her multiple orgasms, though in his present mood he suspected she might have been playacting to cheer him up. He sighed. "No one should grow old, Gerald."

"Depends how well-heeled you are. I think I could endure old age with the right kind of bank balance."

"You aren't a pessimist, you're a crypto-optimist—I've always thought so. Remind me to propose you in my will."

"Propose me?"

"Hellions only has a hundred members. You can't get in till one of them kicks the bucket."

Gerald looked quizzical. "First old age, now death. What's eating you?"

"You Foreign Office chaps usually phrase these things more gracefully."

"All right, what's the problem?"

Sir Graham passed a copy of Berger's signal across the table and took it back when Gerald had read it.

"Who's Albatross?" asked Gerald.

"You realize it's the Germans who've found Cato?"

"Look, Graham, you'd better put me in the picture if you want me to help."

"When I went to that meeting at Santander, Canaris asked me in confidence if there was some way he could get in touch with me in an emergency."

"You never told us."

"I'm telling you now."

"So Albatross is Canaris?"

Sir Graham frowned. What he found even more irksome than Gerald's questions was the mood of depression that so often assailed him these days, like a black cloud descending out of a clear blue sky. There was an unfinished game of chess on the next table. He stared at the pieces as if they held the answer to all his problems.

"Graham!"

"Yes, it's Canaris, but according to our latest information he's under house arrest."

"So who's using his code name?"

"The man who controlled Cato—or whatever the Germans call him —from the Paris end."

"I'm not sure I follow you."

"It looks as if the Abwehr always expected Cato to switch sides again. It was part of their plan."

"But that's high treason—from their point of view."

"Which means there can't be many people in the know. That's the one bright spot."

"Were you expecting this?"

"I had a hunch, if you like. My God, I've studied Canaris and his methods for years. It's got his handwriting all over it."

"So our best double agent turns out to be a treble agent—a German plant. Some people aren't going to like this."

"Last night, when the signal came in, Gahagan said he couldn't visualize a German in the role. It's hard to accept, I grant you."

"May I see that again?" Gerald reread the text and handed it back. "Scott's organizing the pickup, you said. How soon can it be done?"

"By the end of the week, I think. He's going to call me here."

"So we won't be losing Cato after all?"

"No."

"Then I don't see your problem. Hurt pride apart, everything's fine. It'll be business as usual—the perfect solution."

"On the face of it, yes."

"Meaning there's a snag?"

"Human nature." Sir Graham felt his depression dwindle, as it always did when a decision was forced on him. "The name of the problem is Berger."

"If the Germans have never had any doubts about Cato, why should they suspect this man Berger?"

"He now knows the location of the Paris transmitter, which is a damned uncomfortable thought. That transmitter is vital to us. We planned to use it to issue operational orders covering most of the sabotage to be carried out on the eve of the invasion. Its detection at this stage would be a near disaster."

"But do you have any reason not to trust Berger? He's on our side, in a manner of speaking."

"Trust doesn't come into it. Albatross, Cato, the transmitter . . . That's too much, Gerald—too much inside information for any one man. One false move on his part, one little blunder . . ."

"He hasn't put a foot wrong in two years, according to you."

"He's an amateur—didn't join counterintelligence till the war broke out."

"Nor did you."

Sir Graham ignored this. "You once said I had a blind spot about Canaris, but at least I can adjust to the realities of a situation. Assume that Berger comes under suspicion. Further assume that the source of the suspicion is a personal rival who happens to head the SD's Paris office—one of Himmler's smartest young operators. How would you rate Berger's chances then?"

"I'm not a betting man." Gerald stared at his empty glass.

"Now do you see the flaw in your business-as-usual solution?" Sir Graham always enjoyed discussing things with Gerald. The Foreign Office man had an india-rubber psyche; everything bounced off it. Scott and Gahagan were less resilient.

"What other solution is there?"

"I don't know." Sir Graham couldn't sit still any longer. He got up and went to inspect the unfinished game of chess. There was a solution, of course—a pretty hard-boiled one for a man who didn't consider himself a cynic. On the other hand, it was the best solution under the circumstances—one that would restore the situation at a stroke.

There was something different about his walk when he returned to the table. His swift little strides reminded Gerald that Sir Graham had once been a cavalryman.

"White's in a hopeless position." Sir Graham nodded at the chessboard. "If I know old Arthur, though, he won't resign till it's staring him in the face. Like another brandy?"

"Think he'd bring me one?"

"If you're prepared to blight your chances of membership."

"Have you found the answer?"

"You can't afford to let yourself be swayed by sentiment in my job. If you do, you end up in a loony bin."

"Sounds ominous."

"I'll need your help."

"As if I didn't know."

"It'll take some arranging, Gerald. What I need for Cato, when he's back, is some really high-grade information—something bigger than any material he's leaked to the Hun so far." Sir Graham hesitated, but only briefly. "I want him to inform them of the time and place of the invasion—six hours before our troops actually go ashore."

"Are you out of your mind?"

"Six hours, Gerald. It can't do much harm, and even if it does, the gains will far outweigh the losses."

"Why, for God's sake?"

"Because Cato will be the only German agent to predict the invasion correctly: not only the time but the place, which is far more to the point." Sir Graham's voice sank to a whisper. "The object of Fortitude South is to convince the Germans that our main force will be landing in the Pas-de-Calais. What'll they think when we go ashore in Normandy? They'll discount anything Cato tells them from that moment on. Now do you see what I'm driving at? Cato will reveal the focus of the invasion but simultaneously warn them that it's just a diversionary maneuver—that the main landing will still take place in the Pas-de-Calais."

"I do see, yes, but it won't be easy to sell the idea."

"It'll make our troops' task easier if the Germans continue to deploy their crack formations in the Pas-de-Calais. Cato will be more important than ever during the consolidation phase."

"You make it all sound very convincing."

"The person I've got to convince is the man who'll be controlling Cato from the German end." Sir Graham sat back and studied his hands. He took a lump of sugar, broke it in half, and dunked one of the fragments in the dregs of his coffee. "Some things become inescapable," he mused. "They develop a momentum of their own."

"Now you're being enigmatic. You cultivate your mystique, don't you?"

"Do I? I told you, Berger knows too much for his own good and ours —he's too vulnerable. There's only one answer: I'll have to take Cato off his hands."

Gerald gave an uneasy laugh. "Meaning what, exactly?"

"Meaning that success is all that counts."

"What do you have in mind?"

"Something rather distasteful."

"If you can stand it, so can I."

The waiter, an ex-guardsman with a waxed mustache and a back like a ramrod, coughed discreetly to signal his presence. "A call for you, Sir Graham."

"Thank you, Fletcher. And please bring Mr. Foote another brandy. He's suffering from indigestion."

Fletcher stiffly inclined his head. "Very good, Sir Graham. I took the liberty of having the call put through to the writing room. It's unoccupied at present."

"Thanks for the white lie," Gerald murmured as Fletcher departed and Sir Graham rose. "I really could use another."

There were only two members in the smoking room when Sir Graham passed through. Even while pausing to exchange a few words with them, he pondered his decision. If Berger had been on the same side all along, was it really necessary to sacrifice him?

The writing room was still empty, the receiver off the hook. Distasteful, he thought again, but his conscience ceased to prick him as soon as he heard Scott's voice, ragged with fatigue. His own voice, he knew, sounded cool and impassive, and he confined himself to the barest essentials.

"How's it going?"

"I've checked his suggestions out, sir. The place and time look good. He knows what he's doing."

"So we proceed as planned?"

"Yes, but we'll knock a few miles off the trip if we operate from Swanage instead of Portsmouth. The Naval Section could make a trial run tonight, for timing purposes."

"That's up to you."

"Couldn't you let Jeremy come along for the ride, sir? It would boost his morale."

"Did he ask you to ask me?"

"You know he wouldn't, sir."

"Tell him he can go to Swanage, but only to take delivery."

"I will."

"And signal Albatross in the affirmative."

"By the same route?"

"Yes."

"We've a flight going to Compiègne tonight, with a consignment for Paris. That way we'd avoid using the convent."

"No, no, I don't want him rattled. Another thing: Will Julien be handling the Compiègne flight?"

"Yes, sir."

"What about that contact of his? You say he keeps complaining there isn't enough in it for him."

"That's his feeling, apparently. We've made six flights to the Paris area this year, all courtesy of the SD, all without incident. According to Reckzeh, the courier correspondence he gets to see in return is less informative than he hoped."

"I've got something for him, Ian." Sir Graham was pleased with his choice of words and the casual way he uttered them.

"It would certainly make Julien's position easier."

"Just as long as it doesn't look too easy. Where are you calling from?"

"My office."

"Then let's discuss the details there. I'll be with you in half an hour. And Ian, this is just between us. Not a word to Jeremy, since you're so concerned about his morale."

Sir Graham hung up, feeling wrung out. Although he'd said what he meant to say, he couldn't repress a flicker of guilt and uneasiness. He was getting old, he told himself again—old and sentimental. It was time he retired to his bees and abandoned the pretense that his was a profession in which a man acquired close friends and agreeable memories to sustain him in his declining years.

He left the writing room with the bland smile that customarily concealed whatever emotions might be stirring within him. Fletcher, who had evidently delivered the second brandy, was returning with an empty silver salver in his hand. It wasn't his habit to initiate a conversation, but this time, with puckered brow and considerable reluctance, he made an exception.

"I'm sorry about the gentleman's dyspepsia, Sir Graham, but you did hear me: I expressly warned him against the baked beans. Some of this American food is highly indigestible."

"That's all right, Fletcher. Mr. Foote is a big man at the Foreign Office, and the Foreign Office always knows best. You've no need to reproach yourself."

Fletcher's face brightened, and for one brief moment Sir Graham felt less alone in the world.

27

Paris

HE WAS ALREADY AWAKE when he heard the faint sounds of movement downstairs that heralded Léon's arrival. It had been two o'clock when he got back from Compiègne, so he couldn't have slept for more than four hours.

He groped for the bedside light and switched it on. The girl beside him rolled over, grumbling in her sleep. He directed the light away from her in the hope that she wouldn't wake up till he'd gone. The money he could leave her in an envelope. Only one girl had ever supplemented her fee by stealing an item from his collection. Another had actually left hers behind and scrawled *"Imbécile!"* on the envelope. As one who believed that everything in life had its price and should be paid for, Julien Dargaud had found this rather touching.

While he was pulling on his bathrobe, the Siamese cat walked in through the half-open door, jumped onto the bed and from there into his arms. He absently tickled the animal's head, his eyes still on the girl, her bare shoulders, her blond hair going dark at the roots. Then he switched off the light, put the cat down, and left the room.

There was a door at the end of the passage. The hum of a vacuum cleaner could be heard when he opened it. He made his way down the steep flight of stairs to the bar. The cat came bounding after him.

Few of the lights were on, so the red-draped walls looked almost black. Chairs were upended on tables, and the stench of mildew and stale tobacco smoke was as strong as ever.

"Léon!" The vacuum cleaner expired with a low moan. Léon, skinny and frail-looking in his grimy overalls, came over to the counter. "Morning, *patron.*"

"The people from Mareuil will be delivering some champagne this morning. Check the cases and tell them payment as usual. I'll be out all morning."

"Very good, *patron*."

Going back upstairs, Dargaud retired to the bathroom to wash and dress. Shaving he always deferred until the nightclub opened in the evening. The bathroom was chilly because the window had been left open for the cat's benefit. By the time he'd breakfasted in the kitchen and fed the cat, it was seven o'clock.

The apartment's two main rooms were connected by an archway. One was a drawing room with an open fireplace, pale green walls, green and white curtains, and Directoire furniture, the other a sort of library in which bookshelves had been replaced by illuminated display cases containing a collection of antique bronzes. The contrast between these elegant rooms and the nightclub's sleezy eroticism was startling.

Dargaud paused in front of his desk, one hand on the telephone. The cat, which had selected a chaise longue and settled down there, was gazing at him with its forepaws crossed. He dialed the number of a hotel near the Étoile and waited for the switchboard to connect him. The cat's unwinking gaze reminded him of Reckzeh.

"Julien here," he said. "Can I see you?"

"Anything of interest?"

"I haven't processed it yet."

"How soon?"

"I could meet you at ten. The gym, as usual?"

"Yes. I hope you made it clear to our suppliers that we can't continue to do business on the present basis."

Dargaud hung up without answering Reckzeh's implied question. He lingered over the cat for a while, caressing it with the same abstracted air as before.

"It's getting harder every day," he said. He might have been addressing a human being.

The room at the far end of the passage was white and empty save for a low plinth, some spotlights, and a pair of cameras mounted on tripods. The photographic blowups on the walls were all nude studies.

Like the nightclub, the studio had been Ian Scott's idea—an additional form of cover. In time, however, Dargaud had become so attached to both occupations that he half intended to pursue them after the war.

He crossed the studio and entered the cramped little darkroom, where he took his white smock from the hook and put it on. The nude shots he'd taken of the girl were hanging in a row on the line. He unclipped them without a second glance and set out the materials he needed, including the three rolls of film he'd been handed at Compiègne, which were in the chemicals cabinet. Last of all, he put on a pair of glasses with circular lenses. They altered his appearance completely, making him look reserved and professorial.

Switching off the overhead light, he began to develop the films by red light. He hung them up to dry by normal light, cut them up, copied the negatives, and enlarged each one in turn. The first two rolls yielded twelve messages ranging in length from half a dozen words to four pages. Enciphered orders from London to agents and networks in the Paris area, they were serially numbered and adorned with symbols.

Again he switched off the overhead light. The third roll of film lay before him in the fixing bath. He noticed the difference at once. It was a message in clear, he could tell that even before enlargement. He removed it from the milky solution with a haste that was very unlike his usual slow, deliberate movements.

His work had become routine: arranging the dates of the clandestine Lysander flights with Reckzeh, taking delivery of courier mail from England, developing films and forwarding copies to the SD in return for Reckzeh's continued cooperation, delivering other copies to various "mailboxes." Although he had ceased to associate his work with danger, his skin sometimes crawled at the thought that he might be consigning some fellow agent to a Gestapo jail for the sake of an elaborate game whose purpose eluded him.

He removed the message from the enlarger and read it through. If Ian Scott had drafted it, its chill and impersonal tone was oddly uncharacteristic. Having inserted the enciphered messages in a dozen different envelopes, he picked them up, together with the message in clear addressed to himself, and bore them off to his desk.

The cat jumped down off the chaise longue and stretched luxuriously. As though to attract his attention, it chased an imaginary mouse across the carpet. Fascinated by its predatory antics, Dargaud kept glancing at it while he read the message through again and again. The more he did so, the less likely it seemed that the plan had been conceived by Scott.

He took off his glasses and stared into space for a while. Then he got up and went over to the fireplace, where he burned the print and negative and stirred their ashes into the remains of a log fire. Then, and not before, he drew the curtains. The sky was overcast, and a light drizzle was falling.

The girl stirred when he tiptoed back into the bedroom. She rolled over and sleepily opened her eyes.

"You're up already? What's the time?"

He put the envelope on the table on her side of the bed. "There's no hurry. You'll find some coffee in the kitchen."

She stretched, smiling coyly. "How did the pictures come out? May I see them?"

"Another time. Call me first." At the door, he turned. "The bathroom window," he said, "—open it a crack before you go, for the cat."

Berger was woken by a chirping sound. He lay there in total darkness, unsure of its source. Then he remembered that Jannou had put a pillow over the telephone.

He started to clamber across her. One arm came up and clasped him. He couldn't tell whether she was awake and trying to detain him or merely stirring in her sleep.

"It's the phone," he said softly. "It could be the message from London."

She was hot with sleep, bathed in sweat. It was strange how much more exuberantly female her naked body felt in the night, as if distended by the warmth of the bed.

He was still trying to reach the telephone when its muffled ringing stopped. Jannou whispered something in his ear. Her lips felt swollen too—almost twice their normal size. The word became clearer and more intelligible.

"*Viens . . . Viens!*"

It was uttered with such urgency and passion that he felt a stab of jealousy at the thought that she might be talking in her sleep to someone else, not him.

How could he ever be sure that she loved him? Persuading her to go away had been a crazy idea, a noble gesture whose sole effect would be to rob him of her. A picture took shape in his jealous imagination: a stretch of coastline, waves breaking, a boat pulling away from the shore. The picture went into close-up and froze: Jannou and Kacew side by side in the stern, smiling, their arms around each other, gazing back at a dot on the narrow strip of sand—himself.

"*Viens . . . Viens!*"

Again the voice in his ear sounded alien. He thought his jealousy would stifle him, paralyze him, but it only intensified his desire for her. He felt her body splayed beneath him, ripe and open. He felt the moist warmth of her. His jealousy waned and died.

He had no idea how long it was before the smothered chirping began again. She was lying quietly in his arms, relaxed and at peace, as close to him as any stranger could be.

This time she made no attempt to stop him when he got out of bed and groped his way to the telephone. Once he removed the pillow, the bell shrilled like a fire alarm. He picked up the receiver and said his name.

"You were inquiring about a special course of drugs."

The mother superior's voice sounded harder than he remembered, but it was definitely hers.

"Did you manage to get them?"

"They're promised for the night of Thursday-Friday."

"Are they the ones I asked for?"

"Yes, we've just had confirmation."

He started to thank her, but the line went dead.

"Jannou?"

She didn't answer. Could she really have failed to hear the bell? He went to the window and drew the blackout curtain far enough to admit a little daylight before tiptoeing back to the bed.

She was lying with her head turned aside, one arm draped protectively over her eyes, breathing deeply. Her lips were moving and her face wore a strained, almost pained expression. He thought again how little he knew her.

"Jannou? London came through."

Restlessly, she averted her face and covered it with the other arm. He bent down and kissed her on the cheek, but still she didn't wake.

The weather had broken. It was drizzling when he left the apartment, and the sky was dark with cloud. Men and women were cycling to work bent low over their handlebars, legs laboriously pumping up and down. They looked as if they were pedaling into the teeth of a gale.

A long line had formed outside the bakery in Place St. Sulpice, housewives and old folk who had probably been there since curfew ended. They waited in silence, huddling together for warmth in the dank morning air.

Even while climbing the stairs, Dargaud could hear the smack of leather on flesh and the instructors' bellowed exhortations. The noise rose to a crescendo when he pushed the swing doors open.

The big hall had once been the cutting room of a Jewish-owned fashion house, and remnants of machinery were still bolted to the overhead beams. There were six brightly lit boxing rings in all, each occupied by a pair of men engaged in hitting one another with what, to Dargaud, looked like murderous intent. Others, in the background, were belaboring canvas bags suspended from the ceiling like corpses from a gibbet.

Dargaud lingered just inside the door. The thud of boxing gloves and the stench of sweat made him feel slightly sick.

"Over here, Julien!"

He hadn't immediately identified Reckzeh as one of the men in the ring. He was far less muscular than he looked in uniform. His chest, pink and hairless, resembled that of a doll whose designer had been undecided about the sex of his finished product.

The French trainer held the ropes apart for him to duck through and the instructor removed his head guard. Reckzeh took a hand towel from the corner of the ring and draped it around his shoulders. His breathing was unhurried, his skin barely moist.

Dargaud followed him to one of the benches ranged against the wall. They sat down, Reckzeh with his gloved hands on his knees. The nut-brown leather caught the light.

"Isn't it a bit unfair?" Dargaud said. "Your opponents must know who you are. Do they have the guts to wallop you properly?"

"You have a well-developed sense of humor, Julien—for a Frenchman. I hear everything went off without a hitch at Compiègne last night."

Dargaud had put the briefcase between his feet. He pushed it across to Reckzeh, wondering where to begin. He found it harder than ever to believe that the plan was Scott's.

"That's the sixth flight this year," Reckzeh said. "Our arrangement called for give-and-take on both sides."

"There won't be any more flights for a while."

"Really? Any reason?"

"None that I know of."

"The invasion?"

"Could be."

"I feel I've been getting a raw deal. Did you make that clear to your friends?"

Dargaud nodded. "I think they got the message." He resolved to take the plunge and get it over. "I've got something on Captain Berger of the Abwehr," he said, "something you can nail him with."

Reckzeh neither moved nor spoke. He stared at the boxing gloves on his knees. A thin film of sweat had formed on his face and chest. The strange thing was, thought Dargaud, it seemed entirely odorless.

"The lives of two of our agents in exchange for the lowdown on Berger. My friends thought you might be interested."

Reckzeh raised his head at last. He still said nothing, but his dark eyes gleamed like the leather of his gloves. He held one out. "Would you mind undoing that for me?"

Concealing his repugnance, Dargaud leaned over and undid the lace. Reckzeh clamped the glove against his chest and pulled. His well-manicured hand slid forth, moist and rosy.

"Why should I be interested in 'nailing' a colleague in the Abwehr, as you put it?"

Dargaud did not feel called on to answer; the rivalry between the two men was common knowledge. Scott's message had warned him not to make it look too easy.

Reckzeh unlaced his other glove. "Why, Julien? Why should London make such a suggestion? I'm not so foolish as to believe that your allegiance"—he drawled the word derisively—"belongs to us. We came to an arrangement, yes, but I've never had any illusions about it. Whenever you give me a handout, I look for the hidden catch. There always has to be one."

"As I understand it, London wants Berger eliminated."

"And the British call us ruthless! If there's one thing I hate, it's hypocrisy."

"They made the offer. I'm only passing it on."

"To repeat: Why, Julien? The Abwehr's run by a bunch of aristocrats. The British Secret Service has always preferred to deal with them on a gentleman-to-gentleman basis."

Scott, or whoever it was, had foreseen this question and supplied Dargaud with an answer. "The Paris Abwehr, meaning Berger, has an agent in England. London is finding his activities inconvenient, to say the least. All attempts to track him down have failed."

"What difference would it make if Berger dropped out? His agent would be taken over by someone else."

"It would alarm him. Nervous agents panic and make mistakes. They're easier to detect."

Reckzeh idly watched his sparring partner, who was still in the ring, shadowboxing. "What makes the British think I'd lend myself to such a scheme? Do they really believe I'd risk losing one of our most valuable agents, just because of friction between the Abwehr and the SD?"

Was Reckzeh's lack of interest genuine or feigned? Had London miscalculated? Dargaud almost relished the possibility. He said, "Berger is preparing to sneak two enemy agents out of the country."

"It's been done before."

"He's acting on his own initiative."

"What are they giving him in return?"

"Nothing, as far as I know. Perhaps he's hoping for a good word after the war."

"So are a lot of people. There seems to be an epidemic of it at the moment."

"These agents are extremely important to my friends," Dargaud said. "I've been instructed to tell you where and when the transaction will take place, in return for a promise not to intervene. As soon as the agents are safely away, you can do as you please."

"Very well. Where and when?"

"You promise not to touch them?"

"You trust my word?"

"Yes."

Reckzeh turned and looked at Dargaud. "It's dangerous, knowing as much as you do. I could get the information out of you for nothing. We specialize in mind reading in the SD. Our methods are very effective, if not infallible."

Dargaud almost shivered as he met the German's coldly appraising stare. Rather than betray fear, he looked down at the overlength black gym shorts, the pallid, rather bandy legs, and managed a smile.

"That's the proposition."

Reckzeh knotted his gloves together and hung them around his neck. Taking the briefcase, he rose. "Wait for me here," he said.

Dargaud watched him go, and the spectacle gave him another injection of courage. Reckzeh padding along in flat-soled, high-laced boxing boots looked very different from Reckzeh striding out in his glossy riding boots.

The gymnasium noises, which had barely impinged on his consciousness for the past few minutes, regained their full intensity. Bellowed instructions, the squeak of resined soles on canvas-covered boards, the smack of leather buffeting flesh—these, combined with the sour smell of perspiring bodies, became too much for him.

He left the gym, crossed the inner courtyard, and stepped out into Boulevard de Latour-Maubourg. The drizzle had ceased and the sky was blue again—streaked with cloud but blue for all that. It was the same color as the shop front across the street. Petrossian's, thought Dargaud. Only the Germans would have sited a gymnasium opposite a gourmet's paradise.

The delicatessen shop was just about to open. Official German cars were already parked in line down the nearest side street. A big Opel coupe, yellow and black, with a long hood and German Embassy license plates, appeared from the direction of the Pont des Invalides and pulled up right outside the shop. The chauffeur got out and started polishing raindrops off the windshield.

Dargaud heard brisk, confident footsteps coming up behind him. It was Reckzeh, uniformed and booted once more. His cheeks were a trifle flushed.

"Is it really true they still sell caviar there?" Dargaud asked innocently.

"Why do you think we're putting up such a fight for the Don and the Dnieper?"

"So that's what the war's all about. I've often wondered."

Reckzeh set off toward the Seine. His Mercedes, with an SS driver at the wheel, followed at a walking pace.

"Tell me something, Julien. Do you have a personal interest in this proposition?"

"Why?"

"That French girl who lives with Berger—am I right in thinking she used to be a friend of yours?"

"A man in your position seldom gets his facts wrong."

"What will she do without Berger?"

"Survive. It's what we've all learned to do." Dargaud had asked himself the same question, but he thrust it aside. "Are you interested?" he said, still unsure.

They had reached the Seine. Across the river, swastika banners were fluttering from the Grand Palais. Reckzeh beckoned his driver, who pulled up alongside. He planted one glossy boot on the running board.

"How is Berger planning to get them out? You can afford to tell me that much."

"The British are sending a boat."

Reckzeh looked down. An offending speck of dust seemed to have landed on his boot, because he flicked the leather with his doeskin gloves. "And they're picking them up on the coast?"

"That's the plan."

"At night?"

"Of course."

"At night, somewhere on the Channel coast."

Dargaud was puzzled by Reckzeh's sudden excitement. He'd broken out in a sweat at last—Dargaud could actually smell the rankness erupting from his skin.

Reckzeh opened the door of the Mercedes. "Very well," he said, "get in. Let's talk about your proposition. Your friends were right: I'm interested."

28

Paris

THE LUTÉTIA'S DINING ROOM was crowded at this hour of the morning. The white-jacketed waiters were grouchy and the tablecloths slopped with coffee. Berger helped himself to a cup from one of the big metal pots on the table just inside the door. The bread was fresh but the butter had a slightly rancid flavor. He ate one slice as a pretext for his first cigarette. Even that one lacerated his throat and tasted worse than usual.

He drank a second cup of coffee, smoked another cigarette to see if it tasted any better, and left the canteen. Night shift personnel were coming off duty, gloomy and gray-faced with fatigue. Passing them in the lobby, he was struck yet again by the contrast with earlier times.

Instead of going straight to his office, he went downstairs to the basement. The equipment store had just opened for the day. He put down the canvas grip he'd brought along and filled out a requisition for the things he needed: binoculars, flashlights, wristwatch, radio, skeleton keys, and large-scale maps of the northeastern part of Finistère, including the coastline.

Although it was hot and stuffy belowground, the storeman wore woolen gloves with the fingers cut off. His own fingers protruded from them, ivory-yellow like those of someone in the early stages of frostbite.

Berger signed for the things and stowed them in his grip. He left the store satisfied that it wasn't too heavy for comfort. Somehow, the feel of it in his hand was like a first real intimation of what the phone call had meant. Two A.M. Friday was the agreed time. Three more days and half a night: at last he had something definite to focus on.

He found Hermine Köster dusting his desk with the windows wide open.

"Morning, Hermine."

"This place is going to the dogs," she said grimly. "It's a scandal, the way those cleaners skimp their work these days. Good morning."

He walked to the window behind his desk. The wreath near the subway entrance was withered, its inscribed ribbon faded and shrunk by the rain. Shutting the window, he lit a cigarette.

"Well, where's the morning report?"

Hermine put her hands on her hips. "I know I shouldn't say it, but I'm worried about you."

"Don't say it, then."

She stood there frowning at him, a dogged, matronly little figure. "You're looking worn out."

He pointed to the grip, which he'd dumped on the visitor's chair. "I'm taking a few days off—going to Brittany to do some fishing. No phone calls, no crises, nothing. Happy now?"

She brought a clean ashtray and put it on his desk. "The colonel wants to see you."

"Is he back? Since when?"

"He's asked for you a couple of times already. He sounded—I don't know, funny. Are you really taking a few days off?"

He nodded. "Now be a good girl and bring me the morning report."

She brought it and left him in peace. He sat down and skimmed through the stenciled sheets without really reading them. Steinberg's return was good news; it would make things easier.

There were three main reasons for suggesting Les Sables Blancs as a rendezvous, one being his firsthand knowledge of the area. The rivers and streams that flowed into the Baie de Lannion were well stocked, and he'd often fished them while stationed at Brest. In the second place, no one expected the Allies to land there, so the coastline was only lightly defended. The third and most important reason of all concerned Steinberg.

Hermine put her head round the door. "The colonel knows you're in the building. His secretary just called."

"Tell her I'm on my way."

Alone again, he opened the safe. He took out two envelopes, one containing French money and the other a thousand pounds in Bank of England fivers. Placing them in the canvas grip with the rest of his things, he stowed the whole lot in the safe, which he locked again.

Concealed behind a curtain in one corner of the office was a washbasin with a mirror over it. He drew the curtain aside and inspected himself critically. Hermine was right, he looked tired. His face was puffy, and the whites of his eyes had a yellowish tinge that reminded him of the storeman's bloodless fingers.

They would have to toil across miles of sandy terrain before they reached the sea. Picturing their arduous trek through the night, he made a halfhearted resolution to give up smoking for the next few days.

A young lieutenant from the Monitoring Section was leaving Steinberg's office as Berger entered. The colonel was standing at a window with his hands behind his back, staring out.

Berger fended off the dachshunds, which had scampered to meet him and were busily sniffing his legs.

"Berger, Colonel. You wanted me?" He might have been addressing a statue. He walked right up to the desk and repeated his name.

Very slowly, the colonel turned to face him. If Berger hadn't examined himself in the mirror a few minutes earlier, the shock would probably have been greater. As it was, the change in Steinberg's appearance merely surprised him. His eyes were red-rimmed, his cheeks gray and sunken, but there was something else, something deeper, underlying his obvious exhaustion.

"Dogs are an awful nuisance." The gray face puckered in a laborious smile. He shook hands. "Thank you for coming."

He's only six years older than I am, Berger thought—only forty-six, and we both look like old men.

"May I offer you something, Berger?"

"No thanks, Colonel."

"A glass of champagne, perhaps?"

Berger didn't reply. Steinberg seemed to have lost track of time.

"We'll have to be quick if we want to use up our stocks. Have you read the latest intelligence digest? The Monitoring Section reports a steady increase in enemy radio traffic. Yesterday's aerial reconnaissance flights paint a similar picture. Big concentrations of men and equipment in the southeast, the Thames Estuary choked with landing craft, transport gliders lined up on the airfields. It can't be long now, can it?"

"I haven't studied the reports in detail yet."

"Our Calais outstation picked up two British officers last night. Apparently, they'd been assigned to plot the extent of our minefields on the beach at Cayeux. That ties in with Joseph's reports. The Pas-de-

Calais must be the Allies' main objective. I was thinking of sending you there to interrogate the prisoners."

Berger noticed a narrow black ribbon in Steinberg's buttonhole. It looked almost too smart for a mourning band—more like a decoration of some kind. He wondered involuntarily what had become of the colonel's son and why he hadn't mentioned him.

"I've a problem I'd like to discuss with you, Colonel," he said. "A request from London."

"The dogs need an airing, if you wouldn't mind accompanying me." Steinberg took a leash from the back of the chair behind his desk. "It's silly, really, keeping dogs when you live in a hotel and have to take them to the office every day. You really don't mind?"

They hadn't exchanged a word on the way to the Quai Voltaire. The dachshunds had governed their progress, their stops and starts, by straining at the leash or pausing to investigate alluring smells. They now towed Steinberg across the road and down the steps to the river bank, panting hoarsely. He suffered himself to be dragged along as though he hadn't the strength to resist.

The Seine was swollen with rain, Berger saw. Discounting a handful of fishermen sitting under the Pont du Carrousel, they had the water-front to themselves.

Steinberg let the dogs off the leash. They scurried ahead on their bandy little legs, tails wagging furiously and ears brushing the ground.

"Do you believe in God, Berger?"

Berger had been prepared for anything but that. The question was so unexpected and uttered with such emotional intensity that he was too taken aback to reply. Steinberg came to a halt and caught him by the arm.

Berger looked at the silk shirt, the polka-dot bow tie, the crepe band in the buttonhole of the gray flannel suit. He caught a whiff of the colonel's rather sickly cologne. Even his customary condescension would have been preferable to his present air of desperate entreaty.

"We've courted his anger once too often. Now he's taking his revenge." Steinberg licked his lips. "The boy—my boy—is dead."

Berger's surprise was too great and his recollection of the colonel's son too vague for him to muster any real sympathy.

"No one really liked him, you know," Steinberg went on. "He was always in trouble. You couldn't help him, though—he wouldn't let anyone near him. Forgive me, I had to talk to someone, and the Lutétia isn't the place. I have my reasons for saying that."

Above them, hidden by the embankment wall, an occasional vehicle drove along the Quai Malaquais. A barge came chugging down the river. It lay deep in the water, laden with ammunition boxes.

"What happened, Colonel?"

"He refused to see me—imagine, I went there to help him and he wouldn't even see me. Then, after sentence had been passed, he hanged himself in his cell. Eighteen, that's all he was—imagine!" For a moment, Steinberg's face conveyed the full horror of his sense of loss.

"They sentenced him to death because of that foolish remark?"

"He was transferred to a punishment battalion, which amounts to the same thing. The boy must have thought so, anyway."

Berger recalled their last conversation the night before Steinberg's departure. "You said you knew someone who would put in a word for him."

"Yes, but someone else brought pressure to bear from this end—from the Avenue Foch. It sickens me to think the boy had to pay such a price for being my son."

"The Avenue Foch? Reckzeh, you mean?"

"He must have an informant at the Lutétia—my driver, probably. No one else knew where I was going."

"I did."

Steinberg brushed this aside. "Listen, Berger, there's something I want to ask you in the strictest confidence."

They had reached the next bridge over the Seine, which led to the Louvre. Steinberg broke off. Three men pounded past in army track suits emblazoned with the eagle and swastika, arms pumping rhythmically, faces puce and sweating. Berger got in first.

"Did you speak to the Admiral?"

"He was reluctant to get involved."

"So you got through to him?"

"Yes, at the third attempt. He sounded rather—well, embarrassed. Said I should have kept a closer eye on the boy, advised me to put my faith in the court's good judgment."

"Nothing else?"

"Only the usual things. We talked about the weather, his state of health, our dogs—his and mine come from the same kennels. It was obvious to both of us that our conversation was being monitored."

"Is he still at Burg Lauenstein?"

"Yes. The fact is, he couldn't help. I suspect he'll be needing help himself before long." Steinberg paused and looked Berger full in the face. "Has he ever discussed his ideas with you?"

"What ideas?" Berger said warily.

"Maintaining a dialogue with the British and Americans, keeping in touch with them by devious means. Don't pretend you still believe we can win this war. To me, my son's death was the writing on the wall. He was right: it's got to stop. Hitler is dragging us all down to perdition —he doesn't care what happens. If he goes down, he wants the entire nation to go down with him. It's madness, Berger, and someone must put a stop to it."

"Now I see why you wanted to talk out here."

"Yes, because you're in a position to do something—something positive."

"I am?"

"I'm talking about Joseph, Berger. You must cut off his flow of information."

He knows something! That was Berger's first thought, and it jolted him. At the same time, the irony of the situation almost made him laugh out loud.

"You know how vital his intelligence reports are," Steinberg went on. "Each one helps to prolong this war. Do something—put him out of commission in some way. You've got to, I implore you!"

Berger was tempted to tell him everything. The temptation was all the keener because Steinberg had unwittingly shown him a way out: do nothing, let things ride, break off contact with London, leave Kacew in Rochebrune. He even had a fleeting recurrence of the jealousy he'd felt at the prospect of losing Jannou if he let her go, too.

"What makes you think you can trust me?" he said.

"No one can be sure of anyone. Will you think it over?"

"I'm sorry about your son." The words sounded trite and meaningless. Berger wished he'd either left them unsaid or expressed himself differently.

Steinberg unbuttoned his jacket and took out a gold fob watch with a spring lid. He glanced at it, snapped the lid shut, and replaced it in his vest pocket. "I intend," he said, "to resign my post."

"With respect, I don't think this is the proper time."

"You've never thought I was particularly good at my job, have you? You felt I owed it to my connections, my name."

"I only know you shouldn't quit at this stage," Berger said stiffly.

Steinberg might have stepped out of character, but he couldn't bring himself to do likewise.

"You'd sooner have a commanding officer who shuts his eyes to what goes on behind his back, is that it? Is that my principal recommendation?" Steinberg called the dogs and put them back on the leash. "You said something about a request from London, I believe."

"Yes, from M.I.6. They want us to hand someone back."

"An exchange? At this juncture?"

"Not an exchange, Colonel. The man's an air force officer. He was shot down over Le Mans." Berger had resolved to steer as close to the truth as possible. "They propose to send a boat for him."

"Why the risk?"

"It's only a guess, but I think he must be the son of some prominent figure. The request came right from the top, from the head of M.I.6 himself."

Steinberg seemed to throw off his apathy. "Any chance of building up a connection there?" The words came tumbling out as he warmed to his theme. "Couldn't we send a message by this flier of yours? The war's lost, Berger. The only remaining question is, how soon will it end and what can we do to speed things up?"

"You shouldn't make such remarks, Colonel, not even in private."

Steinberg forced a smile. Four birds with dark plumage and white throat patches glided past. The dachshunds towed him to the water's edge, yapping and scrabbling at the cobbles. "Very well," he said meekly, "what can I do to help?"

"The handover is scheduled for the night of Thursday-Friday, on the Brittany coast." Berger hesitated. "It's an inaccessible spot, a rocky headland bounded by cliffs. I'm not worried about minefields, not with mines in such short supply. Sentries are going to be the problem."

"Where do I come in?"

"The local commander is a Major Seidl."

"Armin Seidl? Is that why you chose the place?"

"I thought you might like to call him. He's based at the Château de Kergan, near Locquirec."

"What do you want me to say?"

"Simply that we're planning an operation in his sector during the night of Thursday-Friday." Berger hesitated again before continuing. "The handover will take place at Pointe de Plestin. Ask him to withdraw his sentries between 2400 Thursday and 0400 Friday. I hardly think you'll have to give him your reasons for mounting an Abwehr operation."

"I didn't know Seidl had landed up there. Still a major, eh?" Steinberg's smile was genuine this time. "Closed the enlisted men's brothel in Deauville on moral grounds, that's Armin Seidl for you! The result was, his men flocked to the one in Trouville and swamped it, which brought violent protests from the garrison commander there. That was back in '41—ruined his career. Very well, I'll phone him."

"But not till late on Thursday itself, Colonel, and preferably not from the Lutétia. It might be unwise, under the circumstances."

"When do you plan to leave here?"

"Early Thursday morning. Subject to your approval, I could officially be visiting Calais to question those British officers."

"You always were careful, Berger, but why go to such lengths? Why is this business so important to you?"

"I already gave you my reasons, Colonel."

Steinberg shook his head. "I've seen you in a dozen different roles over the past three years. I still don't know who or what you are."

"Perhaps you're looking for something that isn't there."

"Whatever it is, I haven't found it."

"I'll report to you before I go and run through the details again."

"You're quite sure we don't share the same, er—objectives?"

Berger was assailed by a weariness so overpowering that it seemed to permeate his skin and proliferate until it took the place of flesh and bone. It was a warning to tread carefully, to check and double-check every aspect of his plan; above all, to bring it to fruition alone. He'd always drawn strength from revealing as little of himself as possible, and it was too late now to change his spots.

Steinberg sighed. "I think we'd better return separately. Under the circumstances, as you put it."

He walked back along the waterfront and climbed the steps. The dachshunds governed his rate of progress as before.

Berger waited awhile before setting off in the same direction. The bookstalls on the Quai Voltaire were open now, but the only prospective customers he saw were Germans in uniform.

29

Paris

RECKZEH LOOKED DOWN at Avenue Foch, with its tree-lined central thoroughfare and twin subsidiary roads. He had been lunching at the round table that occupied a window recess in his fourth-floor office.

The orderly poured him a second cup of coffee. "There are fresh strawberries, Standartenführer. The first of the season."

"No, thanks. Bring me a bottle of mineral water, a big one, not fizzy, and tell Koch I want him."

Reckzeh continued to sit there surveying the avenue. Three vehicles were driving down from the Étoile in convoy: two black Citroën sedans and, sandwiched between them, a blue, boxlike prison van with barred windows. When they turned off the main road and into the side street, Reckzeh picked up a pair of binoculars and rose to his feet.

There was a knock at the door. He ignored it. The convoy had halted in the forecourt immediately below him. He adjusted the binoculars and trained them on the three uniformed men who were getting out of the lead car. Focke, Herwig, and Patzig looked pale and preoccupied, he noted with amusement. Again the knocking came, and again he ignored it. Finally, Koch marched in and clicked his heels.

"The prisoners for Ravensbrück and Buchenwald are ready to leave, Standartenführer. Eight enemy agents, four men, four women. We've assembled them in the conference room."

Reckzeh lowered the binoculars but went on looking out of the window. "Did you give them a decent meal?"

"They only wanted tea—they're English, all of them. We gave them tea and fruitcake. Naturally, I instructed the mess sergeant to use our best Sèvres china." Koch laughed.

Reckzeh swung round abruptly. Koch stiffened to attention and thrust his chest out.

"Have you returned their belongings?" Reckzeh walked over to his desk. He laid the binoculars aside and sat down.

"Yes, all they had on them at the time of their arrest. You should have seen the women. They couldn't wait to get at their makeup—started painting their faces right away."

"I hope you remember to put some lipstick on when your time comes."

Koch grinned uncertainly but kept his arms clamped to his sides. "Will you sign the movement order now?"

Reckzeh opened the folder in front of him and ran his eyes over the typewritten sheet inside. The names meant little to him. Although he'd seen and questioned all the prisoners at one time or another, his recollection of them was hazy. Years of interrogation tended to reduce all faces to a common denominator.

He took an ordinary pen from the bronze holder on his desk. It scratched harshly as he put his name to the document. "What a palaver," he said. "In the old days, enemy agents were shot out of hand."

Koch stood ready with the blotter poised. "Would you like to see them before they go?"

Reckzeh didn't appear to have heard. He sat back, staring past Koch at the room beyond. The décor was just as its erstwhile owner had left it: molded ceiling, parquet floor, ornate furniture, Louis Quatorze chandelier, mauve carpet of vast dimensions. The only alien feature was Reckzeh's Foreign Legion citation, which had replaced a picture on the wall behind his desk and was too small to conceal the rectangular patch on the elaborate wallpaper.

"It's time they were leaving," Koch murmured. He was usually adept at gauging Reckzeh's mood of the moment, but today he felt utterly at sea.

"Sit down and shut up." Reckzeh pushed a memo pad and a pencil across the desk. "Are you keeping a close watch on that house in Montmartre?"

"Twenty-four hours a day, as you instructed."

"Good, make a note. Have a squad standing by on Thursday night. Three or four men should be enough to take the place over."

"To do what?"

"You heard me. I want everything seized: radio operator, transmitter, code book—everything, and don't forget the code book whatever you do. Go easy on the operator, we'll be needing him. I'll tell you exactly when to move in."

"But the Lutétia—"

"Install the transmitter here—clear one of the attics—and fix the operator some temporary quarters on the premises. He's to be held under guard."

Koch, with the pad on his knee, hesitated. "Berger will raise the roof," he said eventually. "The Abwehr, Steinberg . . ." His voice trailed away.

Reckzeh opened a drawer and took out Berger's wristwatch. He wound it, slowly and carefully, and laid it flat on the desk in front of him. Koch, who was watching him with covert curiosity, found it impossible to analyze the expression on his face.

"Send another half pound of caviar to Madame Gurdyev at the Ritz, with my compliments."

Koch started to make a note but thought better of it. Reckzeh picked up the watch and strapped it on. In some strange way, it struck him as significant that his wrist and Berger's were the same size. "The British have offered us Berger's head on a plate," he said abruptly. "Name me one good reason."

"Joseph?" hazarded Koch. "He must be quite a thorn in their side."

"But why? Why would the British want to eliminate Berger? Surely not for love of us?"

Koch stared at his hands and made no attempt to answer. "Anything else?" he asked.

"Yes, Locquirec." Reckzeh rose and walked to the window, spelling out the name as he went. "It's a place in Brittany. I want to know who commands that coastal sector: name, rank, unit, location of headquarters. I'll also need half a platoon of handpicked SS men for a special operation. Got that?"

"Yes, Standartenführer."

"Now comes the most important item of all, Koch. Captain Berger is abetting the escape of two enemy agents, so he must have them hidden somewhere. He must be in communication with them and he's got to get them to the Channel coast." Reckzeh turned and walked back to the desk. "From now on, I want to be informed of his every move, every last thing he does, however trivial. I also want to know what he's been up to in the past few days—the past week, let's say. Has he been out of Paris? Who has he seen, met, spoken to? I want as full a report as possible."

Koch looked up. "Sneaking enemy agents out of the country isn't so unusual. I mean, it could be part of a deal."

Reckzeh's face darkened. Sorry that he'd spoken at all, Koch hastily readdressed himself to his pad and started doodling. Reckzeh gave a sudden smile and said, "One last thing: I want a list of all the places in and around Paris where executions are carried out. A full list complete with photographs of the places in question."

"There's a ban on such photographs, Standartenführer."

"It doesn't apply to us."

"Very good." Koch tore off his two sheets of notes and stood up. "Did you really mean it about the caviar?" he asked. His boyish face was flushed with mental exertion.

Reckzeh brushed the question aside with an impatient gesture. It signified, quite unmistakably, that he wanted to be left alone.

He could feel another headache coming on. Shaking two of the pills the doctor had prescribed into his palm, he chewed them briefly and washed them down with a glass of mineral water. Then he opened the window and returned to his desk. Traffic in Avenue Foch was sparse, and all that came to his ears was a distant hum.

He worked for a while, studying reports and looking through the latest batch of official correspondence. From time to time, as though still unused to the feel of it, he glanced at the watch on his wrist.

A sudden commotion broke out down below. Reckzeh grabbed his binoculars and hurried to the window. A dozen SS men had formed up in the forecourt, machine pistols at the ready. The eight prisoners were led out. Handcuffed in pairs, they filed past the guards on their way to the blue van with the barred windows.

Reckzeh focused his glasses on the procession. One pair of prisoners had slowed and come to a halt. They were women. He saw them turn and look back, look up. All at once, before the guards could stop them, they raised their manacled hands above their heads.

For a second or two, the binoculars brought their magnified faces within arm's reach. Both women were carefully made up, as Koch had said. To his surprise, Reckzeh saw them smile. The smile endowed them with an almost twinlike resemblance. Stubborn and defiant, scared but triumphant, their faces might have been carved in stone.

Had they spotted him at the window? Was their demonstration aimed at him? Reckzeh lowered the binoculars and stepped back a pace —quickly, like a boxer on the defensive. His eyes smarted, his ears rang with the guards' angry shouts.

Prodded along by their captors, the prisoners disappeared into the van. Herwig and Patzig slammed the doors and locked them.

The convoy got under way. Before long, all Reckzeh could see of it was an occasional glimpse through the trees that lined the avenue. The pain in his head was wearing off.

30

London

GAHAGAN WAS SITTING at a window table on the lookout for Scott's car. Harewood Avenue was less an avenue than a gray street lined with gray houses, and Gibbon's wasn't the kind of place where anyone would normally have invited anyone else to eat. Gahagan used it mainly for convenience' sake—his apartment was in the building next door—and because an elaborate menu tended to increase the difficulty of choosing something his stomach could cope with. Gibbon's solved that problem by dispensing with a menu altogether.

Few of the tables were occupied, but the bar was as crowded as usual at this hour. Most of the regulars were office staff from the railroad depot at nearby Marylebone Station. They drank their thin wartime beer at the counter and offset its meager alcohol content by talking and gesticulating with forced vivacity.

"You aren't looking too chirpy today. Anything the matter?" Nora Gibbon was a plump little woman with soft and soulful eyes. "Can I bring you a sherry?"

Gahagan tapped his stomach. He could still taste the white pig swill he'd been made to swallow before his X-ray that morning. "Just a pot of tea, if it isn't too much trouble."

She stared at him and shook her head. "It must get you down, having to sort out other people's problems all the time."

Like the rest of the local inhabitants, Nora thought he was a lawyer. Gahagan had, in fact, studied law at his father's insistence, and his wife had never forgiven him for abandoning a career at the bar in favor of the Army and an obscure job with the Firm.

"Divorces must be the worst thing, I shouldn't wonder."

He smiled at the curiosity on her face. "No worse than most cases."

"Is your wife still in Berkshire?"

"Yes, on account of the children. The food's better, too."

"There's fish pie today. You should be able to manage that."

"Fish pie will do fine."

I ought to move, Gahagan thought. He'd always balked at the sheer complications of moving house, and anyway, it hadn't seemed important while Kacew was in London.

He resumed his watch on the street. The rain had stopped, and a watery sun was shining. A man with a limp was cranking down the candy-striped awning that was Nora Gibbon's sole attempt to lend her so-called "café restaurant" a touch of class. Outside the movie house on the corner, someone was changing the stills in the display cases.

Ian Scott was over half an hour late. Gahagan wondered if he would turn up at all—if his promise to meet had been simply a way of gaining time. They were cooking something up behind his back; he'd taken two days to admit it to himself, his pride was so badly hurt.

Nora brought him some tea and a plate of fish pie. He ate without relish, one eye on the street. The place began to empty. It looked even shabbier without customers. Just as the last of them were leaving, Scott appeared.

"Sorry I'm late." His face showed signs of strain. Fatigue had made inroads into his healthy tan, and Gahagan noticed a tiny muscle twitching, almost imperceptibly, below his left eye.

Nora bustled up. Scott seemed at a loss, so Gahagan told her to bring him a sherry. When she'd gone, he said, "All right, why are you keeping me in the dark?"

"Steady on, Jeremy! All I've done this past couple of days is lose sleep on account of your damned section."

Nora returned with the sherry, cleared the table, and retired behind the counter. Scott watched her go, then extended his appraisal to the rest of the establishment.

"Is this where you usually eat?"

"What's going on, Ian?"

"No wonder you've got ulcers."

"Who said anything about ulcers?"

"Ashbury X-rayed you, didn't he? Three nice, ripe duodenal ulcers." Gahagan stared at him. "You paid a visit to Battersea Hospital this morning."

"I was arranging new quarters for our man when he gets back."

"Funny, I heard something about ulcers."

"I thought a man's ailments were a secret between him and his doctor."

"Not when he uses a doctor on the Firm's payroll. Don't be so damned naïve."

"Where did you get your information?"

Scott raised his glass, avoiding Gahagan's eye. "Cheers," he said.

"Where, Ian?"

"At the Beehive, of course."

Gahagan leaned across the table. "I've been trying to contact Sir Graham for the past two days, ever since our last get-together. Either he's in conference and can't be disturbed, or he'll call me back as soon as he's off another line, or he's halfway between the office and the club. Why, Ian?"

"Search me."

"What about you, then? Why are you always out when I call?"

"I'm here now, aren't I?"

"You haven't answered my question."

"Which one?"

There was no warmth in Scott's voice. In spite of the rivalry between their sections, the two men had never prevaricated or lied to each other in the past. Gahagan found Scott's cold and guarded manner wounding. For a moment, he almost gave up the struggle.

"You were going to call Sir Graham at the club on Monday," he said.

Scott nodded. "I not only called him, I suggested delegating the pickup to you. He wouldn't hear of it—said it was my job to pick them up and yours to take delivery of them at Swanage."

"Swanage?"

"Yes, it's more convenient. We carried out a trial run last night, to check the timing. We got back at 0600. If the weather in the Channel doesn't deteriorate too drastically, that'll be our ETA: Swanage 0600 Friday, No. 3 Jetty."

"Berger's plan has been accepted, in other words?"

"We've signaled him to that effect."

"So what else has changed, Ian? I may be naïve, but I'm too old a hand not to sense when there's something in the wind. You're planning something I don't know about—something I'm not supposed to know about. Why freeze me out?"

"Ask Sir Graham." Scott's manner remained frigid. He sounded hostile or tired or both.

"Some of the old man's ideas are unconventional, for want of a better word."

"It's in the nature of the trade."

"I've always gone along with him, even when I didn't like what he was doing—even when it went against the grain. Why all this secrecy?"

"You know his motto, Jeremy. Once a thing's decided, no more arguments."

"But what has been decided?"

"Even if I were keeping something under my hat, what would it matter? We're both on the same side, aren't we? Well, aren't we?"

Gahagan hadn't the energy to go on butting his head against a brick wall. "Is he putting me out to grass?" he asked at length. "Doesn't he think I'm up to it anymore? Are my X-rays being circulated to all sections?"

"What did Ashbury say?"

"He told me to take it easy."

"So why not try?"

"Is that your last word?"

Scott finished his sherry and stood up. "I really must go now."

Nora came out from behind the counter. "I hope you enjoyed your sherry. It's like liquid gold these days."

"Eh? Oh, the sherry—yes, excellent. What do I owe you?"

"I expect Mr. Gahagan would prefer me to put it on his account." She dimpled at Gahagan. "Your advice doesn't seem to have gone down very well."

Scott waited till they were outside. Then he said, "What did she mean?"

"As far as she's concerned, I'm a divorce lawyer—Grenfell, Grenfell, and Gahagan. She thought you were a client of mine."

Gahagan recognized Scott's car on the other side of the street. The Lagonda's roof was down, and he could see a woman in a white hat on the passenger side. Presumably, she was the one who'd spoken to him on the phone the other night.

"Thanks for sparing the time."

"See you at Swanage, then." The relief in Scott's voice was unmistakable.

Gahagan felt a mixture of resentment, disappointment, and anger. Instead of waiting for the car to drive off, he disappeared into the apartment house next door. There was no elevator, so he climbed the dark, creaking stairs to the third floor.

He was glad when the door closed behind him. He went into the sitting room, which was empty save for an armchair, a table, and a mass of books. Every indentation in the carpet, every pristine patch on the wall where a picture had hung, reminded him of his wife and children.

There were no curtains over the windows, only some dirty green Venetian blinds. The mechanism didn't work properly, so he parted the slats and looked down into the street. A few olive-drab figures were lounging outside the movie house on the corner, which was popular with GIs because most of its programs consisted of Hollywood imports. The latest included a reshowing of *Road to Singapore*. Gahagan had seen all the "Road" pictures.

The first performance started at two o'clock, and the house was never full on weekdays. Gahagan decided to take another dose of Crosby, Hope, and Lamour. Actually, he reflected, Harewood Avenue wasn't such a bad place to live after all, with Gibbon's and the movies so close. Even the apartment wasn't so bad, or wouldn't be if only he could bring himself to rid it of memories.

He went into the kitchen and brewed himself a pot of tea. As he carried the tray into the sitting room, he was reminded of the tea Alison Mills had insisted on making him before he drove her to the station last Saturday. On impulse, he extricated the telephone from a litter of old newspapers, dialed the Beehive switchboard, and told the operator to call him back when she got through. While waiting, he remembered how he'd sat and waited for Alison to pack, sipping tea in the kitchen of the Paddington house and brooding on Kacew's perfidy. When the waiting became too much for him, he'd gone upstairs to check on her progress.

Her things were packed, but she was standing in front of the bedroom mirror, tucking a few last strands of hair into place beneath her uniform cap.

"How much longer are you going to be?"

"I'm ready now." She dropped a comb into her khaki canvas grip and zipped it shut. The lipstick and powder were overdone. They looked incongruous on her fresh, schoolgirlish face.

He bent and picked up the bag. "Is this all you've got?"

"I've moved around a lot lately. It teaches you to travel light."

"This shouldn't have happened, you know."

"I'm sorry. I had no idea he'd do such a thing, or I'd have reported it."

They walked downstairs together. The sitting-room door was ajar. "The birds," she said, pointing. "Who's going to look after them?"

"Only that damned Pole would have saddled himself with them in the first place."

"Mind if I take them with me?"

Gahagan surfaced with a start: the telephone was ringing on the floor at his feet. He lifted the receiver. The noises in his ear sounded like an infinitude of storm-tossed sea.

"Hello? Hello?"

"Mills speaking."

"Alison? Gahagan here." He suddenly didn't know what to say. "Jeremy Gahagan."

The pause that followed was so long, he thought they'd been cut off. Then he heard her voice again.

"Hello, is that London? They said it was London."

"Yes, London. Gahagan here. How are you?"

"You sound so far away—really like London."

"How are you settling in?"

"What a nice surprise. I wasn't expecting you to call."

"How are the birds? Did they survive the journey all right?"

"They're fine. This isn't such a bad spot. Plenty of fresh fish and no air raids."

"If I fall from grace, I'll apply for a transfer."

He heard her laugh. "You'll never fall this far."

"I wouldn't bet on it."

"Bad news?"

"No."

"Have they . . . Have they found him?"

"Yes, but I only called to know how you are. Anything I can do for you?"

"Thanks, no . . . Yes, you can call me again sometime."

"I'll do that."

Gahagan replaced the receiver and drank the rest of his tea. He had an inexplicable sense of relief, of liberation. The knot in his stomach relaxed. The whole apartment seemed lighter, more spacious, less confined.

Rochebrune

THE ATTIC WAS EVEN EMPTIER than the room they'd given him as a bedroom. Rain drummed loudly on the tiles immediately overhead. His makeshift workbench under the dormer window consisted of a plank laid crosswise on two crates.

Kacew had always felt better when his hands were occupied. He trusted his hands far more than his thoughts and emotions. That was why he'd taken up flying, because survival in the air depended on dexterity and coordination. That was why, although he'd chafed at them a few days ago, he now felt almost homesick for his midnight sessions at the Morse key in London. And that was why he now sat spinning out his work on the radio, deliberately prolonging it, continually dismantling components and reassembling them on the crude wooden base he'd fashioned out of an old cigar box.

It was a pointless task. He had no battery and little prospect of obtaining one, but doing something with his hands was an antidote to thoughts of Berger. He still hoped vaguely that he wouldn't need him; with luck, another solution would present itself.

He was alone in the attic, having sent Yseult off on the pretext that he needed some tool or other. She'd spent most of the day at his side, silently watching him at work with a mixture of emotions: childlike disbelief that this primitive contraption could ever send messages winging through the ether, and resentment at the suspicion that, if he succeeded in making it work, he would vanish from her life as swiftly and mysteriously as he had entered it.

Kacew heard noises outside: hoofs and a clatter of wheels. He stood up and looked out of the window. The wagon that had transported him to the château was standing in the courtyard, piled high with straw. Beside it stood Rochebrune and the farmer, Ringood. After some discussion, they unearthed a wooden box from the straw and carried it into the house between them.

Yseult was nowhere to be seen, but a moment later Kacew heard her running up the stairs. Fleet-footed and nimble, she darted from place to place like a dragonfly, as though compensating for the utter stillness that descended on her when she came to rest.

Kacew resumed his post at the bench and waited for her to reappear. She handed him the tool and stood watching. "Well?" she said, when he didn't move.

He gestured at the window. "What's going on out there?"

"My father and Ringood. They've come to an arrangement."

"An arrangement?"

"About the guns and ammunition."

"So they're sharing them after all?"

"Yes." She peered at the radio. "Is it finished? Will it work?"

The attic was so dark by now that he could hardly see her face. "Maybe, with a battery."

"That man who said he came from your friends—you don't trust him, do you?"

"What gives you that idea?"

"When is he coming back?"

"I don't know."

"Will you go away with him when he comes?"

Kacew thought of the men across the way, the guns and ammunition, the Calvados; they'd be bound to seal their bargain with a glass or two. "Let's go," he said. "I've done as much as I can."

"You don't like being alone with me. Why not?"

"We've been alone up here all day."

"And last night? What about last night?"

He knew what she meant. He'd heard her softly open his door in the middle of the night, slip into the room, tiptoe over to the bed. Presumably, she'd stood there watching him, because it was a long time before he heard the door close behind her.

"You pretended to be asleep, but you knew I was there, didn't you?"

He stared at her, longing for a Calvados—itching to get away from this weird young woman and her weird fancies.

She laughed. "What would you have done?"

"When?"

"If I'd climbed into bed with you?" Her laugh gave way to another sound, harsh and full of pain. "You find me ugly!"

"Nonsense," he said helplessly.

"Say it, then! Say I'm not ugly!"

"No," he said. "I mean . . ."

But Yseult hadn't waited for an answer. She was already out of the door and racing downstairs.

Kacew followed her, feeling hunted. Rochebrune had seemed so peaceful, such a perfect hideaway; now he wasn't so sure. Much as he disliked the idea of cooperating with Berger and being dependent on him, he couldn't wait for the man to reappear.

31

Paris

THE DESK LAMP carved a cone of light out of the surrounding gloom. It shone on the plan he'd drawn up, half schedule, half sketch map, complete with symbols, arrows, circles, times. On the floor beside him, ready packed, were the two canvas grips, one for him, the other for Kacew.

There was a knock at the door. Berger folded the plan and put it in his breast pocket. His new leather jacket was stiff and unyielding, so the buttonhole put up a hard fight.

"Come in."

"I finally got you a room." Hermine Köster put a slip of paper in front of him. "At the Meurice. Calais is booked solid."

Berger sat back so that his face was in shadow.

"Oh yes," she went on, "and there's a problem with your car."

"What kind of problem?"

"The garage called. They're still working on it." She pointed to the bags on the floor. "I phoned the motor pool. One of their duty drivers will take you home."

"What's the matter with the Simca?"

"The carburetor, I think they said."

"I see." He thought for a moment. "What's the right time?"

"Gone eight," she said, peering at her wrist. "Eleven minutes past."

He set the army-issue watch he'd drawn from the equipment store. "My own watch has never turned up, I suppose?"

"I'm afraid not. There's been so much pilfering lately."

"Never mind, it wasn't a good one."

"Shall I let the colonel know?"

"Know what?"

"That you'll be staying at the Meurice?"

"Yes, of course. Did he ask?"

"His secretary did."

Though only momentary, the mistrust he felt was enough to set his antennae vibrating. "Get off home now, I won't be needing you anymore. I'll call the garage myself when I'm through."

She removed the ashtray from his desk. It was only half full. "You're improving."

Berger said nothing. He knew Hermine's gambits of old, and he didn't want to be drawn into conversation.

"Have a good trip, then."

Her dejection was undisguised. What did she expect him to do or say? He was only visiting Calais on official business and taking two days' leave.

"See you on Monday. Don't work too hard while I'm gone."

"It'll seem like ages."

"Ages? Honestly, Hermine!"

"I . . ." Her voice trailed off. She went to empty the ashtray and brought it back. Then, with a muttered good-night, she made a final exit.

Berger switched on the overhead light and started tidying his desk. He looked through the drawers and sorted out some papers for the shredder. Next, he turned his attention to the safe.

The documents he'd obtained for Kacew and Jannou were already packed. The English money, a thousand pounds in fivers, he'd given Jannou that afternoon with instructions to sew it into the lining of her coat. He wondered if she'd already done so.

There was no sound from the outer office; Hermine had evidently gone home. He put both bags on the desk, which was now clear, fed his unwanted papers into the shredder, and turned it on. With the machine humming in the background, he called the garage.

A mechanic answered. Yes, he'd found the cause of the trouble: the float valve was defective. He was still waiting for a replacement. No, he definitely wouldn't knock off till the Simca was back in running order.

"Why should it have acted up?"

"Search me, Captain. One of those things."

"My secretary booked me a pool car. Tell the driver to meet me out front in five minutes."

He switched off the shredder and dialed another internal number.

"Weather Room here, Fischer speaking." From the sound of his voice, Fischer had been enjoying a joke.

"Berger. What's the forecast?"

"Just a minute . . . Cloud expected to increase in the course of tomorrow. Wind freshening too, but remaining dry."

"Channel coast?"

"Present wind strength six to seven knots, variable, which simply means a moderate breeze. Visibility good, if you're hoping for a ringside view of the Allied invasion fleet." Fischer laughed merrily.

"Night temperatures?"

"Around fifty degrees. The five-day outlook talks of a substantial deterioration. Wind veering westerly, gusting to twenty knots, which isn't a breeze any longer. Intermittent squalls, cloud base very low."

The weather was holding up pretty well, Berger reflected. It would be an advantage if they could dispense with flashlights on the final trek to the coast.

He picked up the bags and walked to the door, where he turned and looked back. What had changed since he first moved into this room? What had he done there? Wielded a little power, walked a tightrope, worn a mask. But beyond that?

The smile that flitted across his face was curiously detached. He might have been surveying the office of a stranger.

The night sky accorded with the meteorologist's description. Only a scattering of clouds marred its clarity, and Vega was winking just above the black bulk of the Cherche-Midi.

It felt warmer than fifty, but the temperature was always a degree or two higher in Paris than on the coast. Or perhaps it was his leather jacket. As he walked out past the sentries, Berger had a sudden fear that it might be too conspicuous, too youthful for him, but he hadn't been able to resist it when buying the things for Kacew.

The car, a four-door Renault sedan, was waiting at the curb. Berger knew all the Abwehr motor pool drivers, but this one was new to him. Despite his close-cropped, iron gray hair, he moved with the speed and agility of a much younger man.

Berger dumped the bags on the rear seat and climbed in beside them. "Know your way?"

"Of course, Captain."

There was little traffic on the streets apart from the ubiquitous cyclists. Once they overtook a motorcycle-sidecar combination with a couple of MPs on board. Berger lit a cigarette, his first for an hour. Hermine was right: he really had smoked less in the past two days.

The driver wound his window down. Berger detected a certain belligerence in the gesture. The wind on his face was like a warning.

"You're new, aren't you?"

"Yes, Captain."

"Since when?" Berger had the man's neck dead ahead of him, hard and chunky as a block of granite.

"Since today."

"Where were you before?"

The driver removed one hand from the wheel and plucked at his ear. It was stunted and misshapen, like a boxer's. "Military Police, Captain, based at the Hôtel Métropole."

Although it sounded plausible enough—the Lutétia and the Métropole worked closely together—Berger's uneasiness persisted. Careful, he told himself, but caution was in his blood, his second nature. It was caution that had dissuaded him from confiding fully, even in Steinberg. Not only during their stroll beside the Seine but an hour ago, when taking his leave, he had deliberately given him the wrong spot on the coast. Should anyone take an active interest in his plans and the scene of the operation, he would find Pointe de Plestin deserted.

The car slowed to a halt outside the apartment house in Rue Guynemer. Berger noticed again how nimbly the driver moved when he got out and opened the door for him.

"Let me help you upstairs with your bags, Captain."

Berger smiled. "Thanks, I'll manage. What's your name?"

"Schimanski. Shall I pick you up later?"

"Are you on night duty?"

"On standby."

"I may need you for a trip to Calais tomorrow, if my own car isn't ready."

"You won't have cause to complain of my driving, Captain. I was three years with the same officer."

"I'll phone if I need you. Good night."

Light was coming from the living room when Berger let himself into the apartment. He carried the bags along the passage and pushed the door open with his knee. The place was just as it had been when he moved in, anonymous and impersonal.

In the middle of the room stood a cheap brown fiber suitcase. Jan-

nou's new fur coat, a marten which the saleswoman in the Place Vendôme had tried to pass off as sable, was draped over an armchair. She
hadn't finished work on it. The lining was still unstitched along the
hem. On the coffee table, lit by a single lamp, lay her sewing things and
the wad of crisp white five-pound notes.

"Jannou?"

There was no reply. He deposited the bags beside the suitcase. It was
only then that he noticed the table in the corner, resplendent with
gold-rimmed china, glasses, candles—things he'd never seen before,
probably resurrected from the landlord's big black sideboard.

He stood there rather at a loss, staring at the table. Then he bent
over one of the bags. Unzipping it, he took out the envelope containing
Jannou's documents and travel permit, together with a small leather
case. For want of any paper to wrap it in, he concealed it in one of the
napkins on the table.

He switched off the light, felt his way to the nearest window overlooking the park, and lifted a corner of the blackout curtain. Peering
down into the street, he half expected to see a loitering figure or an
unfamiliar car discreetly parked a couple of doors away, but Rue
Guynemer was deserted. The side gate into the Jardin du Luxembourg
was locked.

Then he caught sight of her, slim and long-legged in her tightly
belted raincoat. He watched her until she disappeared into the entrance immediately below, and even then he continued to scan the
street for some sign that she might have been followed. There was
none.

He readjusted the blackout and switched the light on, pulled off his
leather jacket and put it down beside the fur. They looked incongruous
together—as ill assorted, perhaps, as their wearers.

Berger felt old.

She covered her glass with her hand and shook her head when he
reached for the champagne.

"I think I'll leave it at one glass."

The bottle in the ice bucket was still three-quarters full, and neither
of them had done more than pick at the food she'd bought.

"Silly of me," she said. "It was a waste of money."

He lit a cigarette and looked at her across the table. "Shall we run
through the whole thing once more?"

"No need, I've got it straight."

"Just to be sure?"

She was wearing the black pleated skirt and the black silk blouse with the embroidered rose. He'd always thought that black was her color. Seen against her skin, it acquired a luminous, iridescent quality that set off her complexion and her eyes. Mourning was the last thing he thought of when Jannou wore black.

"What is it?" she asked.

"I was thinking how well black suits you."

She rose and blew out the candles. Gathering up the coat and her sewing things, she sat on the floor with her back against the armchair. He peeled off some fivers and handed them to her.

"How much is it?" she asked. "I mean, how much is it worth in England, all this money?"

"Enough to live on for a year at least."

"A year! You think it'll be a year before I'm back?"

"You aren't there yet." He split the rest of the fivers into equal bundles. "Carry on."

"My train leaves Montparnasse at six forty-eight. I'm going to Roscoff on medical grounds. My doctor says I'm in urgent need of sea air." She laughed, but it was a laugh that conveyed how tense she was— tense or simply frightened.

"You have a reserved first-class seat, but you'd better be there half an hour in advance."

"The express gets to Guingamp just before three. That's where I leave it and catch a railcar. There are three possible connections. You'll be waiting for me at Luzivilly." She broke off. "Is it really out of the question for us to travel together?"

"What happens if you miss the last railcar?"

"A bus leaves the Place du Centre at seven-thirty. Our fallback rendezvous is the Café Brest in Plouégat-Moyson."

"Phone number?"

"Luzivilly 593. I can leave a message there for Jean Paturel. When are you leaving, before me?"

"Yes, very early." He felt an urge to go to the window and check the street again, but he suppressed it rather than add to her uneasiness.

"I'm dreading it, all those hours in the train."

"Try to sleep. Use the journey to get some rest."

"Trains make me queasy."

"What about boats?"

"I—I throw up if there's the slightest movement."

"I've brought you some pills."

"What?" She looked up from her sewing as if it had dawned on her at last that she was really going. There was fear in her eyes but no hysteria. "Let's call it off," she said.

He glanced at her bare legs. "You'll need a pair of warm stockings. Some walking shoes, too. They're essential."

"I want to stay here. I don't want to leave Paris."

"Do you have any good strong shoes?"

"No, not by your standards."

"We've got a four-hour hike ahead of us. It'll be tough going in the dark—long grass, moorland, sand dunes . . ." He bent down and handed her the last sheaf of bills.

"What if I refuse to go?" She'd reached the stage she remembered from her time in prison, the point at which the craving to speak became so potent and irresistible that it banished every other consideration. "Ever since you suggested this scheme, I've been thinking it over, and it doesn't make sense. There's something wrong with it. Most of all, there's something wrong with your part in it."

His gray face remained expressionless. "We've been through all this before," he said at length. "You're in danger here."

"I've been in danger ever since the war broke out, like most people."

"What are you trying to prove, Jannou? That you could take another spell in one of our jails, another dose of torture? That I couldn't do anything to prevent it—that I'd be powerless to help?"

She laid the needle and thread aside. "Are *you* in danger?"

"That's different. I'm not without resources. My chances are better. They'll be better still when I know you're safe."

"In other words, you're giving me no choice."

"You chose when you said yes. I don't think you should change your mind now."

Jannou stood up before he could help her and put the coat on. She rotated in front of him like a mannequin, with a mannequin's frozen, artificial smile, turned the collar up, and plunged her hands deep in the pockets.

"Is England really so cold? Is that why you bought me this thing?"

"You'll be glad of it on the boat. It's a long trip."

"I don't want to go."

"What size shoes do you take?"

"Thirty-eights." Her smile became natural again. "This is our last night together. You aren't being very romantic."

He went to the table and came back with the leather case. "This isn't a very romantic present," he said, "just useful."

"What is it?"

"The key to an apartment near here, on Rue Notre Dame des Champs. It's rented in your name, and the rent's paid for a year in advance."

She seemed to shrink into her coat. "When did you . . . ?"

"Today. It's only two small rooms on the fourth floor. No pets, no gentlemen visitors after ten o'clock at night. The landlady was most insistent on that point."

"She accepted a year's rent in advance?"

"Yes, but not in francs. She didn't trust sterling either, only dollars. The Americans have always had a soft spot for Paris, she said. 'They'll liberate us very nicely,' were her actual words."

"But why?"

"You'll be back before me."

"What about you?"

"It'll take me a little longer, but I'll make it. Then I'll know where to find you."

"You expect me to believe that?"

"Please! Go on, take it. The address is on the tag."

Jannou weighed the case in her hand for a moment. "I got you something too." She laughed. "They weren't so particular—they didn't mind taking English money."

Still wearing the fur coat, which swirled about her even more luxuriously because of the bills sewn into the hem, she left the room and returned with a little package. "Now I'm embarrassed," she said.

He removed the wrapping. When he saw the jeweler's name on the box and guessed the contents from its size, he was too disconcerted to open it at once. Gold cuff links, which could be converted into cash in an emergency, were standard issue for Abwehr agents operating in enemy territory.

"You've guessed already!"

He opened the box and took out the links. There was a *B* engraved on each rectangular plaque.

"They're gold," she said helplessly. "God knows why I hit on a present like that. It must be my middle-class blood coming out."

"I'll wear them," he said, thinking how odd they'd look with his leather jacket.

"The fact is, I couldn't think of anything else."

He kissed her. "I promise I'll wear them tomorrow," he said. His eyes strayed to the window.

"Why do you keep looking over there?" Her voice was unafraid and matter-of-fact.

"I wonder what the weather's doing, that's all."

He switched off the light and went to the window, aware that Jannou had followed him. He drew the inner curtain aside, then the blackout. Nothing suspicious met his eye; the street was still deserted. There were many more clouds in the sky. Lower and faster-moving than before, they sent moon-projected shadows scurrying across the Jardin du Luxembourg.

He continued to watch the street with Jannou at his side. "See them?" she said.

"Who?"

"Over there on the right. In the nursery garden—I mean, where the nursery garden used to be."

Following the direction of her gaze, he saw a number of figures bending low, with sacks on the ground beside them. Then he understood: they were scavengers who'd managed to scale the fence and were raiding the municipal vegetable beds.

Neither of them spoke for a while. He put his arm around her. Even through the fur, he could feel the tension leave her body, feel her relax against him.

"I'll chance it," she said eventually.

He knew what she meant. "There's a saying: Find happiness in Paris and you'll never be happy anywhere else."

"I know a different version," she said, matter-of-fact once more. "Find happiness in Paris, and you'll never be happy again. Not even in Paris."

32

St.-Rigomer-des-Bois

THERE WERE ONLY TWO MEN in the café, and both looked as old and worn as their deck of cards. They didn't play, just shuffled and cut, shuffled and cut, waiting for their friend to turn up.

The drizzle outside was so fine that it enshrouded the village street like mist and made the square-cut plane trees look even more like boxes on sticks, the interior of the café so dark that even the hair of the woman behind the counter had lost its artificial brilliance.

One of the men swiveled on his chair and addressed her. "How about making up a threesome?"

"I don't understand the games you play in this part of the world." The proprietress glanced at her watch and turned the radio on. It was time for the eleven o'clock news.

"How long have you lived here? Long enough to learn, anyway. Your Émile was an ace at cards."

"He never had a chance to teach me. He was in too much of a hurry to climb into uniform and get himself shot."

"It's been four years. You could have found another husband long ago."

"Too choosy," said the other man.

"Every village should have a landlord with time for a hand of cards . . . Ah, here's Albert."

The first speaker pushed the dirty lace curtain aside. A man was cycling up the deserted street. He reached the café and dismounted. Then he cocked his head and looked back.

They could hear the drone of engines inside the café now. It grew louder, drew nearer. A black Mercedes convertible appeared, and behind it a closed truck with gray-green paintwork.

"Since when have the Boches come hunting here in the middle of the week?"

The news had just started. Turning the volume down, the proprietress sucked at her cigarette and put it in an ashtray. The men had risen to their feet and were peering through the flyblown window. She joined them.

The Mercedes—they knew the make from the newsreels they saw in Alençon—had stopped right outside. A uniformed arm emerged from the window, beckoning. Visible beyond it were the head and shoulders of a German officer in a peaked cap.

The man called Albert swung his cycle around and wheeled it over to the car. They spoke for a while, the officer and Albert. Steadying the handlebars with one hand, Albert used the other to point in a westerly direction and sketch a route in the air. At length he nodded and stepped back. The window slid shut and the Mercedes drove off, its black paintwork glistening with moisture.

The truck followed. Nothing could be seen through the misted windows of the cab, and the rear of the vehicle was enclosed by a tarpaulin, but someone inside lifted one corner of the canvas and peered out. It was a steel-helmeted soldier in field gray with a rifle between his knees.

By the time Albert came in, the proprietress was back at her usual post and pouring him a beer. He mopped his bearded face, shook himself like a wet dog, and walked up to the counter. The other two trailed after him with their empty glasses in their hands.

"Where are they off to?"

"Thanks." Albert picked up his beer and took a long pull. "Know anything about a German who was here at the beginning of the week?" He looked at the proprietress. "Monday, it was. Ring a bell?"

She reached for her cigarette. Most of it had smoldered away, so she mashed it out and added the remains to the other lipstick-smeared butts in the ashtray.

"The Germans only come here on Sundays, for the shooting."

"That's what I told the officer. According to him, this one would have been inquiring about a flier from that bomber they shot down."

One of the first arrivals raised his eyebrows. "You mean they're still looking?"

The woman filled the others' glasses. Her expression was thoughtful. "Was that all he wanted to know?"

"More or less. He asked the quickest way to the château. Very polite —spoke French like you or me."

"They've been here long enough," said one of the others.

"Are you thinking what I'm thinking? If anyone's daft enough to hide an English flier, it's Rochebrune."

"I heard it was a Pole."

"Whichever . . . He'll land us in trouble yet, you mark my words."

"If you ask me," said the woman, "it's just a rumor."

"Serve le Colonel right if it isn't. He's always treated the village like dirt."

The men retired to their table beside the window. Albert shuffled the cards and dealt a hand. "Really polite, that officer," he said. "Didn't act like a damned Boche at all."

The woman started rinsing glasses. Outside, as the rain died away, the sky slowly brightened.

Rochebrune

THE SUN HAD COME OUT, and clouds of vapor were rising from the avenue.

"Speed it up, can't you?" Reckzeh said impatiently. "We've got a lot to do today."

His driver glanced at the rearview mirror and jerked a thumb over his shoulder. "It's all these overhanging branches, Standartenführer. The truck can hardly get through."

A low branch brushed the windshield on Reckzeh's side, showering the Mercedes with droplets and momentarily blotting out the light. Ahead of them, at the end of the avenue, the château's twin turrets loomed above the trees.

"The grander the name, the shabbier the place." Reckzeh turned to the man in the back. "So Berger came here on his own? He didn't want you with him?"

"He didn't actually say so." Weber, flushed and tense, was sitting on the very edge of his seat, with one hand on each of the back rests. "But why, er—I mean, why has your outfit stepped in?"

"It's the shape of things to come," Reckzeh said coolly. "There's a general feeling that the SD does a more effective job than the Abwehr."

"So one hears, even out here in the provinces."

"You used to be based in Paris, didn't you, at the Lutétia?"

"I'm still hoping for a transfer back there."

"Anything's possible."

"That's what crossed my mind this morning, when you phoned."

Weber laughed. It was a high-pitched, nervous laugh. Reckzeh sat back with a look of contempt on his face.

They had reached the gates. The driver slowed, crouching a little as if he expected an ambush, then circled the fountain and pulled up facing the gates. He switched off but kept his hands on the wheel. The truck, after unsuccessfully trying to negotiate the gateway, reversed and maneuvered to and fro until it, too, was facing the way they'd come. The sound of its engine died away. Under the tarpaulin, nothing stirred.

Reckzeh wound his window down, very deliberately, and sat back again.

There was something catacomblike about the silent and deserted courtyard. Its air of desolation was accentuated by the sound of water dripping from the eaves and gutters. The May sun came and went, alternately bathing the scene in radiance and plunging it in gloom.

In the back of the Mercedes, Weber mopped his clammy forehead and endeavored to wriggle out of his raincoat. Reckzeh continued to sit there, his dark face impassive.

The driver fidgeted with the horn button. Reckzeh gripped the man's arm and shook his head. He surveyed the courtyard building by building. The first sign of life came, not from the main house, but from a stable opposite. It was the faint whinny of a horse.

The stable door opened and a man appeared. Tall, with long white hair and a black cloak over his arm, he paused for a moment, looking disconcerted. Then he neatly refolded the cloak, straightened his jacket, and walked over to the car. If he noticed the truck outside the gate at all, his sole reaction was to hold himself a trifle more erect.

He was so tall he had to bend almost double to address Reckzeh through the open window. "If you're looking for billets," he said, "you're wasting your time. You couldn't have picked a worse spot." His self-assured smile was that of a man confronted by a familiar situation.

Reckzeh saluted. "Are you the owner?"

"Your pardon, Monsieur. I am Jean-Marie de Rochebrune. We've often been visited by prospective tenants, but they always go away disappointed. You won't find any home comforts here."

"I've a couple of questions, that's all." Reckzeh made no move to get out. He rested one gloved hand on the edge of the lowered window.

Rochebrune made a gesture of invitation. "Why not see for your-self?"

"I'm sure your premises would be comfortable enough for a fugitive from the German authorities."

"No doubt, Monsieur. Someone in that predicament would be less interested in comfort than safety."

Reckzeh sized up the supercilious smile, the condescending manner. The old man's arrogance was too ingrained for him to be easily intimi-dated. He got out of the car with an air of regret. "We're wasting time," he said. "You know the penalty for sheltering enemy airmen. Do you have one hidden here?"

The driver got out too and stationed himself a pace to the rear. He was blond and blue-eyed and a head taller than Reckzeh.

"Good heavens," said Rochebrune, "don't you people ever give up? Have you seen where the plane came down? No one could have sur-vived that inferno."

"Just answer my question."

"Would you believe me if I said no?"

"You're making things needlessly difficult for me. I'll ask you once more: Are you hiding someone? Have you hidden anyone here in the past few days?"

"I've just returned from my morning ride and I wish to go and change. The answer is no."

"And no one visited you last Monday?"

Rochebrune, in the act of turning on his heel, paused. "We have so few visitors here, one can hardly forget them."

"Well, yes or no?"

"Yes, a man came."

"What did he want?" When he'd learned of Berger's visit to Rochebrune on Monday, Reckzeh's instinct had told him that he was on the track of something important. The rendezvous on the coast and Berger's hectic search for a survivor from the plane could hardly be coincidental. "Wasn't my question plain enough for you?"

"He wanted the same as you," Rochebrune said grudgingly.

"And did he get it?"

"I already told you—"

"What was his name? Berger? Or did he call himself something else?"

"It doesn't seem customary to introduce oneself these days." The smile returned to Rochebrune's face, the relieved and complacent smile of someone who has avoided a pitfall. "That's to say, I don't know his name any more than I know yours."

He was lying, Reckzeh felt sure. Had he lied to Berger, too, or had Berger managed to gain his trust? Reckzeh recalled what Oberg had said that morning in the Bois de Boulogne—his allusion to Berger's gentle-sounding name and mellifluous voice. Although Rochebrune's defiance had left him unmoved, the thought of Berger sent him into a towering rage.

He raised his right arm and pumped it up and down, twice in quick succession, with a violence that seemed to rape the quiet air. Someone barked an order, and the truck belched soldiers in field-gray uniforms and steel helmets. They ducked under the tarpaulin and sprang to the ground, two by two, left and right, until there were fifteen or twenty of them. Doubling in through the gateway, they fanned out in all directions. The whole thing smacked of long practice.

The courtyard resounded to raucous words of command and the clatter of hobnailed boots. Reckzeh's face, so recently convulsed with fury, relaxed.

"Stay where you are," he said, not that Rochebrune had moved. The old man was watching the scene transfixed, white to the lips. His only discernible emotion was utter disbelief.

The soldiers split up. Four small parties occupied the corners of the yard and stood motionless with their rifles ported; others, operating in pairs, proceeded to search each building in turn. Apart from the muffled crash of doors being kicked open, the silence was as profound as before.

"You brought this on yourself," Reckzeh said. "If my men don't find anything, well and good, but first I want a few straight answers. Who else lives here?"

Rochebrune readjusted the cloak over his arm. The color was slowly returning to his cheeks. "I live with my daughter, but you're mistaken if you think you'll fare any better with her because she's a woman. That's all I have to say."

Nothing happened for a while. Then, prodded along from behind by two soldiers, a man and a woman came out of the château.

"Raus! Schnell!"

The woman or girl—Reckzeh found it hard to guess her age—was wearing a curiously old-fashioned gown that swept the cobbles, and her hair was gathered into a bun. She looked demure at first glance, but closer inspection seemed to bear out what the old man had said. Not only did she have her father's haughty cast of feature, but there was an abstracted look in her eye that seemed to dismiss the very existence of the German soldiers at her back and the German officer in front of her.

Her companion was obviously a peasant, thickset and barrel-chested, in a baggy black suit that flapped around him as if its pockets were filled with pebbles. He grinned at Rochebrune, exposing a clutter of strong yellow teeth.

"Who the hell's this?" Reckzeh controlled himself with an effort. He was slowly losing patience. Everything combined to fray his nerves: the renewed silence, the heat of the sun, which felt oppressive, and the soldiers' stolid, bovine faces.

It was Weber who stuck his head out of the car window and supplied the answer. "Ringood," he said, "a local farmer. His son started the rumor about a survivor." After debating whether to get out and say more, he cautiously sat back again.

Reckzeh was finding the situation more and more intolerable. He wanted to wind things up and move on, but he didn't know how to without losing face. Berger had been there, he told himself—Berger had been there and gained their trust, whereas he was handling them like a crass amateur. Again he felt hatred bubbling up inside him, and the prospect of a confrontation on the beach in a few hours' time seemed too remote, too indefinite, to appease him.

Something had to be done to breach the trio's wall of silence; he couldn't simply beat a retreat. He eyed each uncommunicative face in turn, trying to gauge where best to begin. At last he turned to the farmer.

"Got any rats on your place?"

Ringood just stood there, a squat and burly figure with a pair of fists as black and chunky as farm implements. He seemed disposed to answer, but a gesture from Rochebrune silenced him.

"I know a way to get rid of them—a surefire way. Perhaps you'd be interested to hear it. Where I come from, the farmers catch a rat alive, just one rat, and torture it . . ."

The girl shivered and Ringood put his arm around her shoulders. Reckzeh gave no sign of having noticed.

"They inflict as much pain on the beast as they can—they even put its eyes out with a red-hot skewer—but the one thing they don't do is kill it. They let it live, they let it run free, and guess what? All the other rats take to the hills! It's an absolutely guaranteed method—far more effective than strychnine, believe me."

Ringood hugged the girl to him. Then he looked at Rochebrune as though courtesy prescribed that he should have the first word. When Rochebrune still said nothing, Ringood turned back to Reckzeh. "Your method sounds like an old wives' tale," he growled.

"Shall we try it?"

The SS sergeant in command of the detachment had marched up and was trying to attract Reckzeh's attention. His pallid features registered supreme devotion to duty. Unterscharführer Witte was a conscientious young man.

"Excuse me, Standartenführer."

"Well, what is it?"

"We've found nothing, not a soul."

"Nothing suspicious? No discarded bits of uniform, no parachute silk, nothing at all?"

"Nothing, Standartenführer."

"What about the stables, have you searched them thoroughly?"

"All we found was a horse, if you can call it that."

Rochebrune gave a little start. The cloak slid off his arm, and he stooped to retrieve it. Reckzeh, trying to analyze the look on his face, couldn't decide between anger and dismay. "Bring it out here," he commanded, watching the old man closely. Now he could sense it, the apprehension, the vulnerability—the opening he'd been waiting for all this time.

"No!" Rochebrune said. "No one touches that horse."

"Stay where you are. Witte!"

The name was enough. With almost lustful alacrity, Witte leveled his gun at Rochebrune.

"And now fetch that horse. You two, move!"

Two soldiers set off at the double. They kicked the stable door open and disappeared inside. Weber hung his head out of the window of the Mercedes, half expectant, half relieved that the whole affair seemed to be ending on a farcical note. Reckzeh smiled at human nature in general, and, in particular, at the thought that a man could be more concerned about his horse than his daughter. Rochebrune's face was twitching. Ringood's arm tightened around the girl's shoulders.

From inside the stable came a whinny of protest. Sunlight slanted through the doorway, illuminating the cloud of dust scuffed up by the soldiers' boots.

The horse appeared, first its head and pricked ears, then its flea-bitten flanks and stumpy legs. The soldiers, one on either side, tried vainly to urge it into a trot.

Weber began to laugh, shrilly, almost hysterically.

And then, from one moment to the next, the focus of attention was transferred to another part of the courtyard by a shout—by two voices shouting at once.

"Guns! Sten guns! Guns!"

Distorted by excitement and triumph, the words were not immediately intelligible to the group outside the stable. An incredulous silence followed, then more shouts—or were they only the echoes of the first?

Everyone stood rooted to the spot, including Reckzeh, who looked less startled than irritated by this unwelcome distraction from what had promised to be an amusing psychological experiment.

Only Rochebrune and Ringood reacted. A glance passed between them—a flash of mutual understanding. Ringood let go of the girl and Rochebrune dropped his cloak. They broke into a run. Surprisingly, it was the thickset farmer who proved faster over the first few yards. Then Rochebrune overhauled him with long, loping strides. It was he who reached the soldiers first.

They had propped their rifles against a wall and were advancing with the captured submachine guns triumphantly cradled in their arms. Their belated reaction was quite instinctive: they dropped the guns and ran for it.

Rochebrune snatched up one of the Stens and Ringood reached for another, but by then it was already too late. As Rochebrune turned, still struggling to cock his gun, a ragged volley rang out.

The shots went home, jolting both bodies and freezing them in mid-movement. As the men had run, so they fell: Rochebrune, with his arms outflung, seemed to plummet from a great height; Ringood subsided heavily, ponderously, almost without falling at all.

Silence returned. Everyone stared at the two inert bodies as though uncertain what to do next. But this was just another interlude. A moment later, the girl gave a piercing scream and dashed across the courtyard.

Her hair came unpinned and tumbled down, her legs became entangled in her skirt. This time only two shots rang out, dry and crisp as whiplashes—negligible sounds compared to the volley that had gone before. But for them, an onlooker might have thought the girl had merely tripped over her skirt and fallen headlong. She lay quite still, halfway between her starting point and the other two lifeless bodies.

This time the silence persisted. Even the doves seemed to trust it. They had been circling the château, alarmed by the unwonted din; now they settled on the roof again and folded their wings.

"*Merde!*" said Reckzeh. He sounded more annoyed than anything else. Bending down, he picked up Rochebrune's cloak and handed it to Witte. "Make sure they're dead, and bring me one of those Stens."

He turned back to the stable and the horse that had started it all. The soldiers were still flanking the beast, but they had no need to hold it. It stood there unmoved and unmoving, like a veteran charger inured to the sound of battle.

Witte returned. He nodded, and then, as if he might be misunderstood, shook his head. Reckzeh took the dun-colored submachine gun from him and removed the magazine. He indicated the rounds inside. "We could all have stopped one," he said. "I thought your men were supposed to be good."

The soldiers had clustered around the bodies. The group beside the girl was the bigger of the two. They were leaning on their rifles shoulder to shoulder, as if physical contact were what they needed to restore their sense of security. Embarrassed rather than upset by recent events, they resembled tourists who had strayed into a red-light district by mistake.

Reckzeh handed the gun back to Witte. "Get those men moving," he said, "and collect up all the guns they've found."

Witte hesitated. "What about the bodies?"

"Dump them in the stable and set fire to it, but don't waste too much gasoline on them. We've still got a long way to go." Reckzeh removed his cap, mopped his brow, and put it on again. He turned to his driver. "Fetch me a glass of water. Let it run till it's good and cold."

The courtyard sprang to life. Reckzeh started to walk back to the car, then changed his mind. Taking the horse by the halter, he led it into the stable. Soldiers busied themselves with the bodies, using the old black cloak as a litter.

A few feet inside the stable, Reckzeh halted. So did the horse. Stroking its neck with one hand, he opened his holster with the other—rather awkwardly, because of his glove. Then he stepped back and, holding the Walther at arm's length, placed the muzzle beneath the animal's ear. With ritual deliberation, like an officer administering the coup de grace after a firing squad has done its work, he squeezed the trigger.

The horse, eyes dilated, convulsively turned its head and trembled all over. Reckzeh had already turned away. He passed the first of the bodies on his way out.

The driver was waiting beside the Mercedes with a glass of water. Reckzeh put his pistol away, buttoned the holster, and took the glass from him. He drained it without drawing breath. The driver was gazing across at the stable when he went to hand it back. Instead of reprimanding him for inattention, Reckzeh strolled over to the fountain and balanced the tumbler on the lip of the basin.

Soldiers came running out of the stable. The gasoline ignited with a dull roar. Flames shot up, pale and scarcely visible at first in the sunlight. Sparks soared into the hayloft, setting fire to the tinder-dry grass.

Reckzeh walked back to the car and got in. A voice behind him said, "Why?"

"I couldn't leave the beast to burn to death."

"Why the girl?" There was real hysteria in Weber's voice. "Why kill the girl? Why?"

Reckzeh half turned in his seat. For a man with skin as dark as his, he looked uncannily pale. "Shut your mouth!" he said, and then, as the blood returned to his cheeks, "What a damnfool question!"

Smoke and flames were erupting from the stable. The driver started up. Beyond the gates, the last of Witte's men could be seen scrambling aboard the truck and disappearing under the tarpaulin.

St.-Rigomer-des-Bois

THE CARDPLAYERS had finished their game and were standing outside the café, chatting. The proprietress had followed them as far as the door. Now that the puddles in the village street had evaporated, the sun's heat was extracting a stench of tar from the pitted asphalt.

The three men were just about to go home when one of them stopped and stared, then pointed. West of the village, smoke was billowing into the sky.

"My God," said Albert, "that must be the château."

"Rochebrune," said one of his companions. "What did I tell you? Sooner or later he was bound to do something crazy and land us all in trouble. I knew it!"

Albert mounted his bicycle and rode off. The other two went their separate ways, hurriedly, without another word.

Only the woman continued to stand in the doorway, staring at the column of smoke. It steadily rose higher, like the smoke that had marked the spot where the bomber crashed. She shielded her eyes from the sun with her hand. Out here in the open, her hair looked as glaringly red as ever.

33

Lanleya

THE HOUSES had petered out fifteen minutes ago. So had the road. They were now driving along a muddy track that meandered through the flat countryside like the little river whose convolutions it followed so faithfully. The riverbank was overgrown with reeds on their side and densely wooded on the other.

Even the track petered out when Berger left the river. The plain, featureless except for an occasional stunted copse, had a primeval appearance. Gunmetal clouds raced low overhead, and the air was dank.

Berger, grateful for the breeze on his face, had wound his window down. It was well past midday, which meant that he'd been at the wheel for nine hours, the first two or three of them in darkness. He was too tired to want to talk. As for Kacew, he hadn't opened his mouth since leaving Rochebrune. His stubborn silence was an unspoken ban on any form of intimacy between them.

They had passed three checkpoints. Since then, Kacew's silence had acquired an even deeper and more oppressive quality. From time to time, Berger sensed that he was being eyed askance, as if the Pole's mistrust of him were increasing with every mile that brought them nearer the coast.

Hazel bushes had grown together into a ragged hedge on their left. Beyond it lay a stretch of open ground pockmarked with craters. On either side of this expanse, enclosed by semicircular banks of earth, were the skeletal remains of aircraft that had been shot to pieces in their dispersal bays. Grass and young bushes sprouted from the ruins of a concrete control tower. At one end of the field, beside a clump of trees, stood a hangar. Most of the roof had collapsed, and the sliding doors had been blown in. The entrance was waist-high with nettles. Berger drove in and parked beneath what remained of the roof.

"We'll have to walk from here," he said.

He climbed out, stiff-limbed, and rubbed his aching back. Kacew watched him remove the bags from the trunk as if in two minds whether to help, then made his way outside without a word. He had already set off by the time Berger emerged.

"Not that way," Berger called. He put the bags down and gestured in the opposite direction. At the foot of a gentle slope on their right, a winding ribbon of reeds and brushwood marked the course of the river they'd left a few minutes before.

Kacew paused. For the first time, his dark and impassive face registered interest. "What was this, a fighter base?"

"We'd better get going." Berger scanned their surroundings. There was no sign of life anywhere, not even a bird in the sky.

Kacew pointed north to where the clouds thinned and gave way to a band of blue with a single mountain of cumulus silhouetted against it. "Is that the coast?"

Berger nodded. In his imagination, he could already taste salt on his lips.

"How far from here?"

"As the crow flies, six or seven miles."

"When do we have to be there?"

"Rendezvous time is 2 A.M."

"I didn't know."

"You didn't ask."

"You call the tune. You always did."

"Please," Berger said wearily. "This time we're on the same side."

"Yes, more's the pity. Don't keep reminding me."

Berger picked up the bags again. Tall grass, still wet with rain, obscured what had once been a narrow path leading down to the river. He walked as fast as the heavy grips would allow. Then, to his relief, he saw the hut.

Tucked away beneath a group of willows on the bank, it was built of stone salvaged from the ruins of an old mill a few yards upstream. The heavy wooden shutters and door looked relatively modern. The flat roof, a thick slab of reinforced concrete, would have graced a gun emplacement.

Berger dumped the bags outside and felt in his pocket for the skeleton keys. Discounting periodic gurgles from the river, absolute silence reigned here, too. The lock yielded at once and the door swung open. The interior smelled damp and musty but was otherwise unchanged, with its crude peasant furniture and open fireplace. Even the board with the pike's head nailed to it still adorned the chimney breast.

He opened the windows and shutters of the living room and the room next door, which had nothing in it but two camp beds. Then he fetched the bags and proceeded to unpack them.

Kacew stood watching with his hands in his pockets. He was wearing a dark blue suit with a striped shirt and tie. The jacket was too small for him—Berger had misjudged his breadth of shoulder—but that was all to the good. Its effect was to make him look as young as the out-of-date photograph Berger had used for his identity card.

Putting the radio set on a shelf, Berger took Kacew's uniform into the inner room and hung it up. "I'm just going back to the car," he said. He'd had to leave the blankets behind, and the Simca's tank needed topping up from the reserve can.

"Anything I can do?" Kacew asked grudgingly.

"There should be some firewood in the shed around the back. If not, we'll have to gather some. Water you can get from the river. You'll find a pitcher in the cupboard." Berger paused. "And keep to the trees."

By the time he returned, Kacew had built a fire and was about to light it. Although it was cold inside the hut, Berger said, "No, better wait till nightfall." Taking the blankets next door, he came back and seated himself at the table. He opened two cans of meat and sliced some bread. Kacew had filled the pitcher and put it on the table. "As soon as it's dark, we'll make some coffee and fix ourselves something hot to eat."

Kacew sat down opposite him but as far away as possible. They ate in silence.

"Got anything stronger than water?" Kacew asked. He shrugged when Berger shook his head. "I should have begged a bottle of the old man's Calvados. Why did we have to leave so damned early?"

No one had followed Berger when he collected the Simca from the Lutétia's garage well before dawn—tailing him would have been impossible, with the streets so empty. It was only when he left Paris and headed north, in the direction of Calais, that he spotted two men watching him through binoculars from a car parked at the entrance to the military gas station on the outskirts of the city. They made no attempt to follow him, even then, but he hadn't turned off west for another fifteen miles.

"Someone seems interested in our operation," he said.

Kacew stared at him. His expression was thoughtful rather than hostile. "We were followed, you mean?"

"All I said was, someone's interested."

"Who?"

"Who matters less than why."

"All right, why?"

They both raised their heads and listened. Berger picked up a pair of binoculars and went to the door. He peered at the sky, then trained his glasses on something in the distance. The hum grew louder, developed a monotonous, throbbing rhythm, and died away.

Berger sat down again. "Just a Storch," he said. "A courier or a local CO, probably." He unbuttoned the breast pocket of his leather jacket and produced the plan he'd made at the Lutétia. "Here," he went on, spreading it out on the table and using the binoculars as a paperweight, "better familiarize yourself with this. We're here, and there's Lanleya, the nearest village. We'll be leaving around 2130, when it's properly dark. The dotted line marks our route."

"We'll be going together, though, won't we?"

Kacew's question remained unanswered. "We have to cross the river, the Dourduff, here. There's only the one bridge, but it's said to be unguarded. That's the main road from Morlaix to Lannion. It's continuously patrolled after curfew, so we'll have to keep our eyes peeled. Once we're safely on the other side, it's just a two-hour trek across the moors, keeping this smaller river on our left. If it rains heavily, steer clear of the bank—the level can rise in no time."

Kacew smiled sardonically. "You're a glutton for detail, aren't you?" He only just stopped himself from adding, "Like Gahagan," but wondered why he'd bothered.

"The river joins the sea here, at Moulin de la Rive. We turn off here, three quarters of a mile from its mouth. This stretch of coast is really rugged, all cliffs and inaccessible beaches. See this barn I've drawn in? That's where we head due north for the sea."

"You're the boss. Why tell me all this?"

Berger looked up. "Just in case you have to go it alone. It's a standard precaution. I want your friends to get you back."

"Very altruistic of you," said Kacew, but his tone was less acid than before.

Berger turned the sketch map over and indicated the large-scale drawing on the reverse. "This is Les Sables Blancs, the beach itself. If we're too early, we'll wait halfway down."

"The circle marks the pickup point?"

"Yes."

"And those are German guard posts?"

"Yes, one at Moulin de la Rive and the other at Poul Rodou. By day they patrol the beach with dogs. At night they focus their attention on the sea, though no one seriously expects the Allies to land here."

"It's risky all the same. Those guard posts are pretty close."

"Does it worry you?"

"It wouldn't if we had a couple of MGs."

"No need for fireworks." Berger tapped another spot on the map. "Everyone will be concentrating on Pointe de Plestin. The Abwehr is planning an operation there tonight—an exchange of agents timed for 2 A.M. precisely."

"So what?"

"So the garrison commander will be notified in advance and instructed to withdraw all sentries for the relevant period. Our security being as poor as it is, everyone for miles along the coast will know about the operation in no time. They won't be able to resist hiding in the dunes for a grandstand view, the garrison commander and his staff least of all. Les Sables Blancs will be deserted. By the time they get sick of waiting for something to happen, you'll be halfway to England."

"What do you expect me to do, applaud?" Kacew said, with some of his old belligerence.

Berger carefully folded the sketch map and held it out. "Here, take this. It's for you."

Kacew looked thoughtful suddenly. "What about you? Will you come back here afterward?"

"Of course. It'll be easy enough."

"So why all these precautions?"

Berger gestured as if to convey that the question was out of court. He started clearing the table.

"Have you used this place before?"

"Not for an operation like this."

"How did you find it?"

"The fighter base you saw was a decoy. The Luftwaffe built it to take the heat off their airfield at Morlaix."

"And the planes?"

"Dummies, a whole squadron of them. Very convincing, especially from the air. The RAF bombed Lanleya several times."

"How far away is Morlaix?"

"Less than ten miles. The airfield there was an important base during the Battle of Britain; that's why the Luftwaffe went to so much trouble and expense. Morlaix was blacked out at night; here they left runway lights burning to divert the enemy." Berger inserted candles in some candlesticks on the mantelpiece. "The maintenance staff were billeted in this hut."

"I still don't see the connection."

"Morlaix was bombed to blazes just the same—three heavy raids. No one could fathom why, so they called the Abwehr in. I was stationed in Brest at the time, which made it my baby."

"Espionage?"

"Yes."

"Did you find the people concerned?"

"There was only one: Yves Morel, the proprietor of a photographic firm in Brest. The German authorities were rash enough to employ him to reproduce the plans and drawings of their installations at Morlaix."

"You even remember his name?"

"Yes, Yves Morel, captain of the reserve, age thirty-one, married, two children. He was sentenced to death and executed a few weeks after I arrested him." Berger returned to the table. He looked Kacew straight in the eye. "That little coup earned me my transfer to Paris."

"How did you feel about it? All part of the job, I suppose."

Berger took out his cigarette case. He lit a cigarette and put the case and lighter on the table. "You could say that. If I manage to get you back to England, that'll be part of the job, too."

Kacew stared at the cigarette case. "Remember your big entrance when I was arrested? 'My name is Berger. Make a note of it.' I thought you were a megalomaniac."

Berger smoked in silence.

"You were hellbent on pulling it off, weren't you? You had to turn me somehow—your whole career depended on it. I became the biggest feather in your cap. What am I, a form of atonement? Do you weigh me against the others—the Yves Morels? Is that why you're so anxious to get me back alive?"

"When we had our first interview, the plan didn't exist."

Kacew glowered. "You seriously thought you could recruit me. I hate you for that—I always will."

"I can't blame you."

"Shut up, damn you! Don't be so mealy-mouthed!"

From outside came the sound they'd heard before, the drone of a low-flying aircraft. Berger picked up the glasses again and walked to the door. Screened by the willows, he stood watching the sky, waiting for the throb of the engine to fade.

"What are you really afraid of?" Kacew asked when he came back.

Berger glanced at the army-issue watch on his wrist. "I think I'm going to try and sleep awhile."

"How many people know about the pickup?"

"Only the two of us." Berger thought of Jannou and debated whether to broach the subject now.

"So what's worrying you?"

"How many would know on your side?"

Gahagan, for one. Would he be on board the boat? He'd insist on coming, Kacew felt almost certain. "I don't know," he said. "My controller and maybe one other, not more. I honestly don't know, I'm only an agent. They never tell an agent more than they need." He sounded almost self-pitying.

Berger said, "About my signal to London. When I asked you for something that would convince them you were alive and in touch with me, you said, 'Ask them how the white canaries are.' "

"And you did?"

Berger nodded.

"Is there really nothing to drink in this place?"

"You'll need to keep a clear head."

"No allowances for the human factor, eh?" Kacew swore in Polish. "You're all brothers under the skin. To you I'm just a cipher. I'm Joseph to you and another code name to them. Beyond that, agents don't exist. They change their names and locations because they have to eat and sleep somewhere, but they never stop being ciphers."

Berger produced a bottle from his grip and put it on the table. Kacew ignored it.

"Do you reckon I'll be Roman Kacew again when the war's over, or will they invent another name for me? I think that's why I lost my head at Elsham Wolds when the chance came up. Being back among plain, honest-to-God, crazy Poles, that's what did it."

"White canaries," Berger said. "Are there such things?"

"That's what he sold them as. John Stockton, Dealer in Domestic and Exotic Birds, Lavender Hill, S.W.11. There were two of them, a cock and a hen. I bought them while I was waiting to pick up some cash from Schneevogel's man. He'd suggested the shop as a rendezvous." Kacew still hadn't touched the bottle. "I don't feel like drinking alone."

Berger reached behind him and took two stoneware mugs off the shelf. "Only a drop for me, please."

"Why, got a weak stomach?"

"No." Berger smiled. "Does *he?*"

"You could be a goddamned Englishman." Kacew splashed some cognac into the mugs and pushed one across the table. "While I was waiting for my contact to show, this Mr. Stockton sidled up. I asked what kind of birds they were, but he told me they weren't for sale. 'I thought you were a dealer,' I said, which made him furious. 'I'm not selling any birds,' he said, 'not to you.'"

"Why not?"

"Because I was a foreigner, he said, and no bloody foreigner knew how to treat birds. Only the English did. When I told him I was a Pole and the English and the Poles were fighting on the same side, he said, 'We can win our wars without any help from the likes of you!'"

"But he sold them to you after all?"

"Yes, eventually. He riled me so much, I came away with a pair of birds I'd never meant to buy in the first place."

"You still had them?"

"Yes."

"Who's looking after them?"

"How in hell would I know? As far as—as *he* was concerned, it was just the kind of crackbrained notion you'd expect from a crazy Polack."

They drank in silence. Although the hut was in a dip, they could hear the wind getting up. It had started to rain again. Berger consulted his watch. "If I really do drop off, make sure you wake me by four at the latest."

Kacew looked at the bottle, then at the room, then out of the window. "It's going to be a long wait," he said.

There was a drawer on Berger's side of the table. He pulled it open. Inside, shrouded in dust and cobwebs, lay a snarled line, a sinker, and a couple of rusty hooks. "You could always try catching us something for supper. I'm going to have to leave you on your own for an hour or two. Don't worry if I'm not back till after dark."

"Where will you be?"

Berger stood up and busied himself with the radio. He unwound a length of aerial from a cleat on the back of the case and strung it over a nail near the ceiling, switched on, and waited for the set to warm up. Then he adjusted the frequency and switched off again. "If you can't get good reception on 373 meters, try 1500. The BBC's next transmission to France is at 1930."

Kacew stared at him and said nothing.

"After the news they'll read out the *messages personnels*. Listen to them carefully. There should be one for us, either then or after the late news at 2115."

Kacew put his mug down impatiently. "All right, tell me what to listen for and leave it at that."

"Just pray they come through."

"What's the message, for God's sake?"

"*Les canaris blancs vont bien.* That'll mean the pickup's still on for tonight." Berger picked up his cigarette case and lighter. On the threshold of the inner room, he turned. "Don't forget," he said, "four o'clock."

He closed the door, then the shutters and the window. Spreading a blanket on one of the camp beds, he lit a cigarette and stretched out on his back, convinced that he wouldn't be able to sleep. Although he'd smoked very little, the cigarette stung his throat. He stubbed it out on the concrete floor.

The wind was still rising, the rain getting heavier. He lay there with his hands behind his head.

Les canaris blancs vont bien . . . The white canaries are well. With luck, he'd be back in time to hear it himself. He fell asleep after all.

34

Guingamp

THE TRAIN SLOWED and stopped on an open stretch of track. She kept her eyes shut and feigned sleep, snuggling deep into her fur collar rather than meet the gaze of the blue eyes that were almost certainly fixed on her, even now.

He had occupied the first-class window seat opposite hers ever since Paris, a young lieutenant with a chestful of ribbons and a disfigured face. The multicolored skin grafts on his right cheek and lower jaw were separated by welts of scar tissue. The sight of him not only horrified her but aroused an unwelcomed sense of compassion.

The train continued to stand there. Jannou could feel how chill and damp it was outside, even through the window pane at her elbow. Three more German officers were sitting on her side of the compartment, oldish men with morose expressions and spreading waistlines. Opposite her, beside the lieutenant, sat a French traveling salesman who persisted in questioning him about his decorations. The other two occupants of the section were a stiff, silent French couple. Jannou could picture them all with her eyes shut.

Without warning, a gust of air buffeted her cheek and the window began to vibrate. Instinctively opening her eyes to look, she saw a freight train clanking past: boxcars, refrigerator cars, tank wagons filled with gasoline. Just when it seemed that the procession would never end, the window stopped trembling as abruptly as it had started. She could see little of the countryside even then, just threads of moisture streaking the glass as the train continued on its way.

A helpful hand wiped the film of condensation away. She recoiled, burrowing still deeper into her fur.

"You have rested a little? You are feeling better?"

She nodded, resigned to the fact that her admirer tried to strike up a conversation whenever her eyes were open.

"May I offer you some chocolate?"

She shook her head. The order on his chest that irritated her most was a heavy red star with gilded points and a swastika in the middle.

"I've seen you eat nothing since Paris." He proffered the bar of chocolate.

"Really not, thank you." Then, because she'd rejected every one of his overtures to date, she added, "I'm thirsty, that's all."

"Then you're going to the right place. I mean, in Roscoff you'll find nothing but water. The sea, the aquarium, the spa, hundreds of people with glasses of water in their hands."

The transplanted skin extended past the corner of his mouth, permanently distorting it into the semblance of a bashful smile. How, she wondered, was she going to leave the train at Guingamp? Till now the thought had been only vague and intermittent; suddenly it alarmed her.

"Are you feeling unwell? Would you like to change places with me?"

"No, really not, thanks."

They'd been asked to show their papers several times, though the lieutenant's sponsorship—"This lady is traveling to Roscoff with me" —had usually been accepted as sufficient proof of her bona fides. Berger could not, however, have foreseen that she would be so steadfastly squired by a susceptible young German who'd discovered at the first ticket check that her destination was ostensibly the same as his own.

Jannou stared out of the window. Although there had been no air raids, they'd left Paris an hour late and lost another hour since then. She'd hoped the train would make up for lost time, but now it was going too fast for her liking—hurrying her toward the moment of decision.

She saw a church spire, some houses, a way station, and a horse-drawn cart waiting at a grade crossing, the driver with a sack over his head to keep the rain off.

How much longer?

The train sped past another crossing and a signal cabin. A road converged with the tracks and ran parallel to them. Houses appeared, singly at first, then in clusters. The tracks divided. Jannou felt the brakes go on. The passengers thronging the corridor began to stir. The couple opposite lifted their luggage down off the rack.

Whatever happened, she had to get out at Guingamp and take the railcar. She slipped her arms into the sleeves of her coat and got ready.

The sidings were a mass of wagons guarded by German soldiers with dogs. She saw a signal tower, some warehouses, then the station itself, covered platforms crowded with passengers sheltering from the rain, uniformed police and plainclothesmen at the exits. She stood up.

"We don't have to change here," she heard the lieutenant say behind her, "only at Morlaix."

In the act of reaching for the fiber suitcase on the rack, she let her arms fall. The train stopped with a jerk. She leaned against the window, feeling sick.

"I must get something to drink," she said.

"Permit me, Mademoiselle. Stay here, you cannot go outside in this rain."

Although his French was poor, he spoke it without the arrogant harshness common to many Germans. It sounded gentle and diffident, like the look in his very blue eyes, but all it did at that moment was fill her with terror. A shiver ran down her spine. Unable to look him in the face, she stared at the hideous, ostentatious decoration on his chest. "Stop pestering me!" she snapped.

The lieutenant's French neighbor grinned broadly. One of the other German officers said, "Incorrigible, these French."

She flushed. The couple and their baggage were blocking the doorway. She squeezed past them and joined the procession shuffling slowly along the corridor.

At last she was out on the platform. As she straightened her coat, which had slipped off one shoulder in the crush, she could feel the weight of the bills sewn into the hem. On the far side of the station, people were lining up at the exit to have their papers examined by French police and a brace of trench-coated civilians, probably Germans.

"Be quick, one never knows how much time there is."

Turning, she saw the lieutenant. He had lowered the window and was leaning out, heedless of the rain that spattered his ruined face.

"Please hand me my suitcase," she said.

In spite of his unchanging smile, she caught the look of hurt incomprehension in his eyes.

"My suitcase, please!" Though tempted to walk off and abandon it, she remembered the men at the exit. She was conspicuous enough already in her new fur coat; without luggage, she would be even more so.

He lifted the suitcase down and rested it on the sill, then beckoned to someone behind her. "Hey, Corporal, over here! Give this lady a hand, will you?"

"Certainly, Lieutenant. My pleasure, Mademoiselle."

The corporal must have been fifty at least, with grizzled hair and gaunt cheeks. He was already laboring under the combined weight of four valises, one in each hand and two slung over his shoulder on a strap, but he tucked Jannou's suitcase under his arm and set off along the platform. Down the steps he trudged and through the underpass, which the rain had partly flooded, turning every now and then to make sure she was following. Each time he did so, his pinched face broke into a beaming smile.

They joined the end of the line. On the far track, the train had already begun to pull out. The lieutenant was still standing at the open window, motionless as a statue. Jannou watched the train until it disappeared from view.

They were now beneath the canopy and out of the rain. Her mascara had run. Opening her shoulder bag, she took out a handkerchief and mopped her face, put it back and got her papers ready.

The French policeman gave them a cursory glance. He was about to return them when the trench-coated man behind him withdrew a hand from his pocket and held it out.

"May I see, please?"

His pale, colorless eyes scrutinized her from under the brim of his fedora. Coolly appraising, they flitted from her face to her identity card and back again. His thin lips barely moved when he spoke.

"No luggage? Wait over there."

She went cold. The mascara had made her eyes sting, but the pain was almost welcome. The gray-haired corporal stepped forward. "I've got the lady's bag," he said in German. "She's with me."

The man in the trench coat did a double take. He eyed the corporal with a sarcastic grin. "All right, Casanova, on your way."

Jannou had an urge to laugh and retch at the same time. She bit her lips till they hurt, knowing that if she once started laughing, she wouldn't be able to stop; she would laugh and laugh until her lungs were drained of air.

Retrieving her identity card from the outstretched hand, she made her way into the booking hall. She scanned the faces of the people waiting there. Berger wouldn't be one of them, but she looked for him just the same.

Luzivilly

BERGER PULLED UP in front of the station. Built of stone and far too grand for such a little place, it stood on the outskirts like an abandoned dream.

He got out, turning up his coat collar as he went, and hurried inside. The booking hall was cold and deserted. He walked straight through and out onto the platform.

Arrayed in a siding were some boxcars and a few four-axle flatbeds laden with steel girders. Men were toting sacks from a wooden shed to an open wagon. Farther away, almost obscured by the fine drizzle, a locomotive was busy shunting.

Berger sheltered beneath the overhanging roof. The platform and twin tracks were separated from some willow trees in the background by a hawthorn hedge. The hedge had been trimmed in such a way that its foliage spelled out the name of the village: LUZIVILLY.

A man in black dungarees strolled over from the shed. He was short, with a round face and the beginnings of a dirty beard. "Not bad, eh?" He indicated the hedge. "It's a hobby of mine."

"Looks like a lot of hard work," Berger said. "It must grow fast here, with all the rain you get."

"I'm not short of time. Waiting for someone?"

"Any idea how late the Paris–Brest express is?"

"It came through about twenty minutes ago. Two hours late is pretty good going for these days. It doesn't stop here."

"What about the railcar from Guingamp?" Berger looked at his watch. Even if she was two hours late, Jannou would just make the second connection. "Will that be here on time?"

"Maybe, maybe not. It's due in half an hour, but I wouldn't count on it."

"Where do I find the post office?"

"In the main street, or what we call the main street." A bell rang somewhere. The man made a gesture of apology. "See you later," he said.

From outside, the sandstone post office bore some resemblance to a toy fort. The interior consisted of one gloomy room with small barred

windows. It smelled as much like a schoolroom as the black-clad, ane-
mic-looking postmistress looked like a schoolmarm. She peered at Berger over her glasses.

"Jean Paturel," he said. "Has anyone phoned and left a message for
me?"

She shook her head. She must have heard him drive up, because he
saw her staring past him at the Simca parked outside. Private cars were
bound to be a rarity in this part of the world.

"Can I make a call from here?" He handed her the slip of paper on
which he'd noted the number of the Hôtel Meurice.

"Calais?" she said. "I hope you aren't in a hurry, Monsieur. It could
take some time." She got up and went over to the antiquated switchboard. There was something wrong with her hip, he noticed.

"No, not at all." He sat down to wait on a narrow wooden bench
outside the booth. He felt relieved that Jannou hadn't phoned, that
Kacew was safely installed in the hut, that his visit to Major Seidl at the
Château de Kergan had passed off so smoothly.

The postmistress manipulated her plugs with deft little fingers.
While setting up the connection, she adjusted her language to each
exchange in turn, switching effortlessly from unintelligible Breton to
textbook French.

"I have Calais for you," she said at last. She sounded faintly surprised at her own success.

He felt a touch of claustrophobia as soon as he entered the cramped,
dark little booth. The only light came from a small glass panel set in
the door. He picked up the receiver.

"Berger here, Captain Berger. You're holding a room for me."

"I'll put you through to Reception."

"Captain Berger? We thought you'd be here by now."

"My car's been giving trouble. I'm at a garage in Boulogne, and I
don't know how much longer I'll be."

"Anything we can do at this end?"

"Nothing, thanks, but make sure you don't let my room go."

"There were two calls for you, Captain. From Paris."

"Any messages?"

"It was the same caller both times. The gentleman only left his
number. May I give it you?"

"One moment." Berger opened the door of the booth. The postmistress was sitting at the switchboard with her headset off. He said,

"Could you take down a number for me?" He put the receiver to his ear, repeated the number for her benefit, and hung up.

"That's a Paris number," she said, impressed. "Shall I get it for you?"

"Please."

He sat down on the bench again. The number meant nothing to him. It wasn't the Lutétia's, but that was all he knew for certain. Listening to the woman's voice as she progressed from one exchange to another, he was more than ever reminded of a teacher giving her class a language lesson.

"Paris," she said eventually. Her anemic face was flushed with triumph.

This time he wedged the door open with his foot.

"Hôtel Voltaire," said a voice. "Hello, Hôtel Voltaire here. Hello?"

Berger was momentarily at a loss. Then he had a vision of a man in a pale gray flannel suit walking two dachshunds beside the Seine.

"Is Colonel von Steinberg there?" He withdrew his foot and the door swung to. The booth was so small he could barely turn round.

"Steinberg."

"Berger here, Colonel. I was puzzled for a moment. Are you staying at the Voltaire?"

A long silence followed. Berger began to think they'd been cut off. Overcome by the dizziness that always afflicted him in confined spaces, he yearned to hang up.

"When I couldn't reach you in Calais, I didn't know where else to try."

"They said you phoned twice."

"Can you speak freely? God, am I glad you've called! Is everything all right?" The dogs started yapping in the background. Berger heard Steinberg shushing them. Then he caught one muffled word: "Terrible . . ."

"I'm sorry?"

"Simply terrible, Berger."

The colonel didn't elaborate, so Berger said, "Thanks for calling Seidl. I've seen him. He was most cooperative—no problem there."

"Seidl? Oh yes, of course . . . The thing is, I had a call from Weber. Something quite awful has happened."

The walls of the booth seemed to close in, compressing Berger's shoulders, squeezing the breath from his lungs.

"This man you're handing over—is he identical with a certain Polish airman who survived when his plane was shot down?"

"Did Weber tell you that?"

"You visited the place. Rochebrune, isn't it?"

"There were no survivors. It was only a rumor."

"No, Berger, listen. I'm talking about the Avenue Foch—Reckzeh. He knows you were there. I don't know how he found out or why it should interest him. He phoned Weber this morning—pumped him dry." The next words came out with a rush. "He went there himself, Berger. There was a massacre—they gunned them down, two men and a woman. Do you understand what I'm saying?"

Berger recalled the scene in the courtyard just before sunrise that morning: Rochebrune embracing Kacew, reluctant to let him go; and the girl, Yseult, barefoot in spite of the dew on the cobblestones, shrinking into her shawl rather than submit to Kacew's ritual double-kiss of farewell. He even recalled her parting words: "You won't come back, I know it."

"Are you still there, Berger?"

"Yes."

"Weber didn't get in touch with me for four hours."

"Was he there, too?"

"It happened around midday, but it was four hours before he screwed up the courage to phone me. He said he simply had to confide in someone and begged me not to give him away. I don't know which weighed more with him, fear of Reckzeh or horror at what he'd seen. He said there was no need to kill the woman, none at all."

"Did he tell you what actually happened?"

As Berger listened, his mind's eye re-created the scene in every detail: the overgrown avenue, the rusty iron gates, the courtyard enclosed by dilapidated buildings, the fountain. With an immediacy that gripped him by the throat, he saw the black Mercedes, saw soldiers spewing from the back of the truck, saw Reckzeh, saw—more vividly than anyone or anything else—the old man, the farmer, and the girl. He winced as he heard the shots ring out, saw the three figures fall, heard the thud as they hit the cobblestones, found to his surprise that he could feel the pain of the impact himself.

Silence fell at the other end of the line, deep and unbroken. The phone booth felt more than ever like an upended coffin. Berger forced himself to breathe evenly.

"What happened to the bodies?" he said at last.

"Reckzeh had them dumped in a stable and set fire to it."

"Rochebrune and the farmer—did they talk before they died?"

"Not according to Weber. That's what made Reckzeh so—so wild."

"Where was Weber calling from?"

"Sées. I informed General Oberg as soon as I heard. Oberg says he can't comment till he gets a report from Reckzeh. He'll cover for him as usual, of course. The worst of it is, they found a cache of arms—British submachine guns. Did you know about them?"

"No. Did Weber have any idea of Reckzeh's next move?"

"The subject wasn't mentioned."

"Is he back in Paris?"

"He certainly isn't at his office—Oberg couldn't reach him there. The business of the guns will let him off the hook. In any case, I don't know that Weber would repeat his statement if it came to an inquiry. Where are you now?"

Berger hesitated. "A service station in Boulogne. My car's been giving trouble. I'll drive on to Calais as soon as it's repaired."

"You intend to press on regardless?"

"Regardless of what?"

"Why should Reckzeh have gone to such extremes? Remember our talk beside the Seine!"

"I have to go now."

"Very well, but be careful."

Berger flung the door open. It was all he could do not to rush straight out of the post office and into the street. His heart pounded. Although he was sweating from every pore, he felt ice-cold inside.

"They're going to be expensive calls, Monsieur."

"What? Oh yes, of course. How much do I owe you?"

But he had to wait for the charges to be phoned through. He sat down on the bench, his sense of time in abeyance. It came as no surprise to discover, pinned to the notice board on the wall opposite, a mobilization poster dating from 1940. It seemed neither more nor less unreal than the idea that Jannou would shortly get out at the station down the road, or that Kacew was uneasily awaiting his return, or that, somewhere on the south coast of England, a fast launch was preparing for a cross-Channel dash.

Nor, he reflected, was it any more unreal than his recollection of the voice beside the windmill in the Bois de Boulogne: "The question, of course, is this: Are you willing and able to see it through?"

For the first time ever, he wondered if he was.

The train consisted of a single railcar with hard wooden seats. Jannou's fellow passengers were farmers and farmhands. They made her feel like a bird of paradise in her fur coat, silk stockings, and flimsy sandals, the more so because their Breton dialect was wholly incomprehensible.

All she could see of the countryside was a broad, bleak plain with a muddy road running through it. If the rain went on much longer, her sandals wouldn't last a mile. The thought didn't perturb her. On the contrary, her present mood was so relaxed that she derived a perverse satisfaction from picturing the scene that night: Berger, wondering what on earth to do, and herself, swinging the sandals by the straps and laughing at him.

She was tired after her long journey, tired but inwardly serene. Only another few minutes, and she would see Berger again. That prospect alone was enough to alleviate her nagging sense of loss at having left Paris with no certainty of when she would return.

The railcar's horn gave a sudden blast. The road, now flanked by telegraph poles, had converged with the track. Only two other passengers, peasants redolent of rain-sodden earth, prepared to get off.

The first Jannou saw of Luzivilly was the station itself. Berger was sheltering under the canopy with the collar of his leather jacket turned up. There was something novel and surprising about the pleasure she felt at seeing him.

He ran to meet her through the rain. When he was close enough for her to see his face clearly, all her fears revived.

"What's happened?" she said. "Something's wrong, isn't it? Tell me!"

He took the suitcase and put his free arm around her. "Quick, let's get out of this rain."

Berger nodded to a man whose broad, flat face was sprinkled with stubble as grimy as his black dungarees. He smiled as he did so, but the smile only intensified her alarm at what she'd seen in his eyes.

"Come on, I've got the car outside. How was your journey?"

He opened the door for her, stowed her bag inside, and settled himself behind the wheel.

"Please," she said, "you still haven't told me. It's something that affects us both, isn't it?"

"Wait," he told her. "We'll be there in half an hour. Wait till then."

He started the car and turned on the windshield wipers. They drove down a deserted street. Outside a building rather like a toy fort, a woman in a black dress was locking up for the day. She turned as they passed and stared after them.

At the far end of the village, the road forked. Berger headed north.

35

Château de Kergan

EVENING HAD DESCENDED on the Channel coast out of a sky so gray and overcast that, although it was only seven o'clock, the light was already fading. A strong wind was blowing from the sea. Helmuth, Major Seidl's thirty-six-year-old adjutant, detested this kind of weather because it made him breathless.

He owed his present post to the medical officers who had recommended a transfer on the grounds that sea air would be good for his cardiac asthma. Little did they know, he thought bitterly. The Abwehr operation sounded rather fun. If the weather didn't improve, it would even spoil his enjoyment of that.

Second only to the weather, Helmuth detested Seidl's soirees—"cultural evenings," as the major called them—because of all the work and worry they entailed. He left the basement kitchen, where he'd been checking on the chef's progress, and made his way upstairs to the tapestried hall. It was empty. The chairs that usually lined the walls had been carted into the drawing room to supplement the seating there.

Helmuth paused to listen. From the drawing room came the sound of a woman's voice raised in song. At least she'd finished maltreating Schumann and moved on to the Italians; her program listed arias from *Madame Butterfly* and *Tosca*. If there weren't too many encores, the latest of his ordeals would soon be over.

Gingerly, he opened one of the double doors an inch and peeped in. The big room was brilliantly lit. A platoon of chairs had been drawn up, parade ground fashion, on the gleaming parquet. In the front row, between the Marquis and Marquise de Kergan, sat Seidl. The chairs behind him were manned by officers belonging to his coastal defense sector. The soprano, a well-upholstered blonde, had a thin voice quite at odds with her Wagnerian figure. Poor thing, thought Helmuth, feeling almost as sorry for her as he did for himself.

He eased the door shut, appalled at the thought of what must be happening to the chairs. They were old and frail and had not been designed for men who found it impossible to sit through such soirees without fidgeting. Previous damage had led to a breach between the marquise and the major which only he, Helmuth, had managed to heal by finding a cabinetmaker in Seidl's command and assigning him to the château full-time.

He crossed the hall and went outside in search of fresh air. The rain had stopped, as luck would have it, and the wind had suddenly dropped as it sometimes did at this hour, but there was no guarantee that the weather would continue to behave itself. The barometer in the hall was still falling, Helmuth noted gloomily, and he could hear the muffled roar of the surf.

The château stood just off the coast road that ran round the bay a few miles east of Locquirec. On fine days it commanded a view of the entire bay, but only from the servants' attics at the rear. As though mistrustful of wind and weather, the builder of Kergan had turned his back on the beauties of the coastline and planted a windbreak of thuyas which had, in the course of time, developed into massive trees.

There was nothing very imposing about the château itself; like the family from which it took its name, it belonged, so to speak, to the petty nobility. Built of local sandstone, the house had two stories and a slate roof, though its multitudinous chimneys lent it a faintly baronial appearance. The marquis and marquise lived upstairs, Seidl and his staff on the ground floor.

Helmuth was about to go inside again when he saw the masked headlights of a car turn in at the gate. A quick mental check on the guest list told him that no one else was expected.

The car, a black Mercedes convertible, drew nearer. Intrigued, Helmuth descended the broad flight of steps and stood waiting at the bottom.

With a soft, crunching sound, the Mercedes circled the expanse of fine gravel in front of the château and came to a halt. The officer who got out wore a uniform that fitted him like a second skin, as immaculate as his gleaming boots. Only his face, olive-skinned, with a somewhat weary and preoccupied look in the eyes that were its dominant feature, betrayed how far he had driven in the past few hours.

"My name's Reckzeh," he said. "Is this Major Seidl's headquarters?"

"That's right. Allow me to introduce myself: Helmuth—I'm his adjutant. Is he expecting you? I'm sorry if I wasn't informed."

"May I have a word with the major? I'm the one who should apologize, incidentally, but it wasn't possible to warn you of my arrival." Reckzeh gestured at the château. "Nice place."

"Well . . ." Helmuth tapped his chest and grimaced. "The climate could be better. Do come in, won't you?"

A burst of applause issued from the drawing room. The brief silence that fell when it died away was followed by a piano introduction and more singing.

"Only an encore," Helmuth said. "Perhaps you'd like to wait in the major's office."

He led the way along a paneled corridor, opened a heavy oak door, and ushered Reckzeh inside. The office was a big room with an antique desk and a few high-backed chairs ranged against the walls, which were hung with family portraits in ornate gilded frames. Red velvet curtains completed the décor.

"I'll inform the major as soon as he's free," Helmuth said. "Thursday nights are devoted to the arts."

"I saw a lot of cars outside."

"Yes, attendance is voluntary, but the major expects all his officers to turn up."

"And do they?" There was nothing jocular about the question. It was uttered in the same cold, detached tone as before.

"Oh yes. Nothing ever happens in this godforsaken spot. Besides, they know that whatever they have to sit through—song recitals, string quartets, poetry readings—they'll get a damned good dinner when it's over. Which reminds me: May I offer you something? Have you come far?"

"Paris."

"I see." Helmuth's breathing had become a little labored. "Are you here, er—officially?"

A malicious smile appeared on Reckzeh's face. He followed the direction of Helmuth's gaze, which had fastened on his sleeve and the thin black arm band bearing the letters "SD" embroidered in silver. "Strange how jumpy people get when they see that little scrap of cloth."

Helmuth was wheezing in earnest now. "Sorry, it's the sea air." He tapped his chest again. " 'Reckzeh', you said?"

"Yes, and you can set the major's mind at rest: the reason for my visit is quite innocuous."

"You're sure I can't get you something? Or your driver?"

"Really not, thank you."

Reckzeh removed his cap when the adjutant had gone. He peeled off his gloves and massaged his forehead, fingering the furrow left by the rim of the cap. Then he put the cap on the desk with the gloves inside it and went to the window. It overlooked a terrace and a rose garden. The wind had snapped dead twigs off the trees and scattered them over the rose bushes, which were in leaf. Reckzeh noted all these details as though they held some special significance.

He was not so much tired as strangely overexcited and alert. Although the confrontation with Berger was only hours away, he devoted no thought to the form it would take or the way it would end. Speculating on the inevitable was a waste of time. It would simply happen, just as the Rochebrune business had happened.

His immediate reaction to the incident had been rage. It had seemed so completely unnecessary—an exasperating mishap, that was how it had struck him at first. With the passage of time, though, he'd begun to see it as something predestined and ineluctable. He now believed with superstitious certainty that events could have taken no other course.

The oak door behind him opened. Reckzeh turned to see a slightly built, bespectacled man with a mild, donnish face. Seidl was fifty-one but looked older. He strode across the room with his hand held out. "I'm Seidl. Sorry to have kept you waiting."

"Not at all. The arts take priority."

"So Helmuth told you about our cultural evenings? He isn't too keen on them. A taste of home on a foreign shore, that's all they're meant to be."

"Foreign shores aren't everyone's cup of tea." Reckzeh gestured at one of the portraits. "Is that a de Kergan?"

Seidl nodded. "I've been here so long, and looked at those faces so often, I sometimes feel I'm beginning to resemble them—or vice versa. You're from Paris, Helmuth tells me. Have you driven all the way today?"

"Yes."

"Without incident, I trust."

Reckzeh scanned the major's meek and professorial countenance, but the question seemed quite genuine. "The RAF were kind enough to leave us in peace," he said.

"And what can I do for the Security Service?" Seidl sat down at his desk. "I hope you'll stay for dinner, by the way."

"I'm not sure I can."

"Do try. It would be an honor, Standartenführer—that is your rank, isn't it? I'm not an expert on SS insignia."

"Yes. Very well, if it won't upset your arrangements."

"Absolutely not." Seidl picked up an internal phone and dialed a number. "Helmuth, have another place laid for Standartenführer Reckzeh. Put him on the marquise's right—and Helmuth, that Steinway is a disgrace. There must be a piano tuner somewhere in our sector. Get on to Personnel." He replaced the receiver with a long-suffering smile. "You have problems of a different order, I imagine."

Everything about the major—his meek face, mild voice, and gold-rimmed spectacles—conspired to get on Reckzeh's nerves. The very look of him sounded an alarm bell in his head.

"It's about an operation in your sector," he said. "I'd appreciate your help."

Seidl had removed his glasses and was polishing them. "You mean it's a joint effort by the SD and the Abwehr?"

Reckzeh, who had been leaning against the window with his arms folded, sprang to life and pulled up a chair. The alarm bell had become loud and insistent. "An exchange of agents," he said.

"Yes, so I was informed. I've taken all the measures they thought necessary."

Reckzeh was grateful for the fading light. He ran a hand over his sleek black hair. "Who contacted you? Paris?"

"Steinberg himself. The colonel and I are old friends—personal friends. He warned me to expect a visit from Captain Berger. We discussed the whole affair in detail. By local standards, this is a red-letter day."

"When was this?"

"The call? It came through around three. As for Captain Berger himself, let's see . . . I was out for most of the afternoon, checking on the shoreline defenses at St. Barbe. I got back in time to welcome our musicians." Seidl nodded to himself. "Five o'clock, it would have been."

"The musicians or Captain Berger?"

"They arrived at the same moment. Rather awkward, but duty comes first, eh? Berger and I inspected the rendezvous together."

Reckzeh digested this news. The British had represented Berger's operation as ultrasecret when they confided it to him, and now the handover seemed to be an official Abwehr undertaking—not planned by Berger on his own initiative, but personally sanctioned by the head of the Abwehr's Paris bureau. That changed the picture entirely.

Seidl cleared his throat. "Any problems, Standartenführer?"

"No, no." Reckzeh would have sold his soul for a glass of water, but he didn't want to ask for one now. "Precisely what measures have you taken?"

"The sentries will be withdrawn between midnight, two hours before the handover, and 4 A.M., which is when they normally relieve each other. In addition, Captain Berger has asked us to clear the beach for fifty yards on either side of the pickup point. We're dismantling the obstacles at this moment, it being low tide."

Reckzeh looked round the room. "Do you have a map?"

Seidl got up from his desk. What had looked like a section of paneling turned out to be a concealed bookcase. A light came on automatically, illuminating a map on the back of the door.

"May I show you? This is the coastal sector I'm responsible for, from Pointe de Séhar in the west to Pointe de Primel in the east. We're here, roughly midway, and there's the spot where the handover's due to take place, Pointe de Plestin."

"Pointe de Plestin," Reckzeh repeated. He suddenly found it hard to breathe.

"You get the finest view of the bay from there—when the weather's kind."

First Les Sables Blancs and now Pointe de Plestin . . . Reckzeh's mind was racing, his head throbbing. Had there been a last-minute change of plan, or was someone trying to mislead him? The British? Berger? He stared at the map until his eyes hurt.

"Might I have a glass of water?"

"Of course, but I can offer you an excellent Mouton-Rothschild from the marquis's cellar. It's his regular contribution to our Thursday night dinners."

"Just water, thanks."

"If you're sure . . ."

While Seidl was telephoning, Reckzeh tried to unravel his thoughts. He could always call Dargaud in Paris and ask him if there'd been a change of plan. On the other hand, if it was the British who were trying to hoodwink him, would they have let Dargaud into the secret?

"It's just coming."

"Thank you."

And Berger? What if Berger was trying to cover his tracks?

"The shoreline defenses—are they continuous?" Reckzeh steadied his voice with an effort.

"As continuous as we've been able to make them, using all the bits and pieces we could find. They haven't exactly improved the scenery."

Reckzeh pointed to the map. "These *P*'s beside Moulin de la Rive and Poul Rodou, do they indicate guard posts?"

"Yes, permanently manned posts, and the numbers after them indicate their strength. The *B*'s stand for bunkers."

"What about this stretch of beach between them, Les Sables Blancs —isn't it guarded?"

"It's overlooked by cliffs several hundred feet high. The guard posts at Poul Rodou and Moulin de la Rive are sited at the top. Their machine-gun nests command the full length of the beach. If it would interest you, and if you're still here tomorrow, I can take you on a conducted tour." Seidl broke off. "Yes?"

A uniformed orderly entered with a carafe and a glass on a tray.

A guarded stretch of beach overlooked by cliffs . . . Why should Berger use that, when Pointe de Plestin was deserted?

"If anyone tried to land there, would the sentries open fire?"

"Of course, open fire at once and sound a general alarm. We may have our cultural evenings, but you mustn't think we aren't on our toes. Curfew time in this sector is nine o'clock. After that you won't find so much as a dog on the streets. Your water, Standartenführer."

Reckzeh picked up the glass, but only at the second attempt. His hand was so stiff and numb he had trouble holding it.

"Dinner's served, Major," said the orderly. "The others have already gone in."

"Thank you." Seidl gave Reckzeh a glance of polite inquiry. "Shall we?"

Reckzeh put the glass to his lips. They felt anesthetized, and he found it hard to swallow. He nodded.

Seidl shut the map away. "I've invited a few of my officers to watch the handover from a discreet distance, I hope you don't mind. Nothing of interest has happened here for years, you must remember. So your people planned this operation in conjunction with the Abwehr?"

"We're supervising it, yes."

"Here, give me your glass." Seidl took the tumbler from Reckzeh and replaced it on the tray, then handed him his cap. "This way, Standartenführer."

Reckzeh followed Seidl back along the passage and into the hall. Conversation and laughter drifted through the dining-room doors, which were open. Inside, a long table laden with cut glass and silver sparkled beneath an elaborate chandelier. The officers had formed two groups, one around the bosomy Valkyrie and the other, more numerous, around a dumpy little woman, gray-ringleted and heavily powdered, in a long pink evening gown. Most of the laughter emanated from the second group.

"That's the marquise," Seidl murmured. "Be warned, she's what the French call *délurée*. She tells stories that would make a seasoned campaigner blush."

Reckzeh paused in the doorway. "Would you excuse me for a moment? My driver's waiting outside."

"He can eat with the orderlies."

"Thanks, but there's something I want him to do for me."

The driver was standing beside the Mercedes, smoking a cigarette. He ground out the butt with his heel and swung the door open.

"I'm staying to dinner." Reckzeh unbuckled his pistol belt and handed it over. "You can join the others. Tell Witte to pick a nice, quiet spot. I don't want anyone sneaking off to Locquirec for a beer. His men are to stay put and eat their rations, then get some sleep. They're going to need it."

"When shall I pick you up, Standartenführer?"

Reckzeh glanced back at the château. Seidl, a slight figure in the gathering dusk, was waiting on the steps. Orderlies could be seen drawing the curtains over the long, brightly lit windows of the dining room.

The British or Berger: Whom should he distrust more?

Reckzeh's stomach churned with such an intensity of hatred as he walked back to the house that he doubted if he would be able to eat anything at all.

36

Lanleya

BERGER DROVE into the ruined hangar and switched off. Before she could ask, he said, "That was the easy part. From here on, we walk." He peered at his watch. "Two hours. That gives us time to eat and get some rest."

Although he hadn't spoken during the drive from Luzivilly, his face had gradually relaxed until it revealed nothing of what was going on inside him. Jannou was thankful, because the shock and dismay she'd read in it had infected her. If he was afraid, how could she master her own fear? Now she felt more tired than anything else.

He opened the passenger door, took her arm, and guided her out of the hangar. It was neither dark nor light outside. She was struck by the quality of the silence that enveloped them. All she could hear was the distant hum of a small, low-flying aircraft. It came into view for a moment, lights winking on its wingtips and tail, before disappearing over the skyline.

"How far is it," she said, "—to the sea, I mean?"

"On foot? Four hours, more or less."

"And the crossing, how long will that take?" She was beginning to take the idea seriously.

"Depends on the boat—another four hours, maybe. Let's go."

"What about my suitcase?"

He shook his head. "That was only for the train. I'll take it back to Paris with me."

"What do you expect me to wear in England?" She tried to sound flippant.

"You'll have to buy yourself a wardrobe when you get there."

"Tweeds? Can you see me in tweeds?"

"Careful." He took her hand. "The path gets steep here."

Mist was rising from the valley below them. Nestling in a clump of trees beside a bend in the river Jannou saw a stone hut with a curiously slablike roof. A man was standing under one of the trees, watching them through binoculars.

"Is that him?" she asked. "Is that the agent I'm going with?"

"Yes."

As they drew nearer, she saw the man lower his glasses and go on staring in their direction. She felt no kind of presentiment, just a lively interest in the person who would be sharing the dangers of the journey with her. She stopped short when she recognized him, but it was Berger she stared at, not Kacew. The silence around them seemed to deepen.

"I thought it better you shouldn't know till now," Berger said at last.

She was too stunned, too bewildered, to speak. It was only when she saw that Berger was preparing to leave them alone together, without further explanation, that the knot in her throat relaxed.

"You're crazy if you think I'm going with him."

"Talk to him." Berger walked stiffly toward the hut. At the door he turned and looked at Kacew. "Did the message come through?"

Kacew seemed to awake from a dream. "You bastard," he said hoarsely. "You goddamned bastard. Are you satisfied now?"

Berger didn't answer. He opened the door and disappeared into the hut.

Jannou turned. Kacew's dark eyes were fixed on her. He blinked once or twice, like someone who had really been jolted out of a dream. Then he smiled—uncertainly, as if he found it hard to recognize her. They stood there in silence for a while.

"So you're still working for him," Jannou said bitterly.

He shook his head. "I never have."

"You can't fool me, either of you."

"He never said anything?"

"He didn't have to. I've been aware of your joint successes for long enough—I've observed their effects at close quarters."

"You're wrong," Kacew said. "Why would I be here now? Why would the British be sending a boat for me?"

"Who says it's a British boat? Why shouldn't you travel back courtesy of the Germans?"

"Those days are over. A German spy wouldn't stand a chance, he'd be picked up right away. There'd be no point. Use your head, Jannou."

Hearing him speak her name redoubled the shock it had given her to see him again after so long. One reason was simply that he had been her lover, and she realized that nothing remained of what she had felt for him as a man; their reunion was merely an embarrassment. The other reason was stronger and more compelling. Her bitterness at his treachery revived and grew like a cancer.

"How could you do it?" she said. "How could you betray everything you believed in?"

"I never did."

"You'd be bound to say that, naturally."

Kacew looked toward the hut as if seeking support, then back at the woman in front of him. The fur coat puzzled him because it didn't match his mental picture of her.

"I don't blame you," he said eventually. "It's been a long time. I kept my promise, though. All the information he got was false."

"So what are you doing here?"

"It was an accident. I lost my head, hitched a ride with some friends who were raiding Le Mans, a Polish bomber squadron. Our plane was shot down."

"And you got in touch with Berger."

"No! It wasn't me—he tracked me down. I was just as surprised as you are now. He suggested handing me back, that's all I know."

She was beginning to believe him, but not enough to admit it. "It doesn't make sense," she said. They were the words she had used to Berger only days before.

Kacew said, "You heard him just now: 'Did the message come through?' He meant the French service of the BBC. The message did come through, and it could only have come from my people in England. Don't you understand? I never broke my promise to you, believe me. I'm not *his* agent—I never was."

"It's too late," she said after a while.

"You still don't believe me?"

It really was too late. The cancer of bitterness and disillusion was too deep-seated to be dispersed. Besides, another thought had struck her, a notion so insane and fantastic that it took her breath away. She looked at Kacew, whose face had almost melted into the darkness.

"Tell me something. What is Berger's role in all this?"

"He never discussed it with you?"

She came closer, eager to interpret Kacew's expression and catch every word, every inflection. "His role—what is it?"

"He said it was planned that way." Kacew's voice had sunk to a whisper.

"Meaning what?"

"Meaning that he counted on my going over to the British again—his plan was based on it. I supplied him with just what he wanted: an agent in England who would misinform his own High Command."

"How long have you known this?"

"Only since I saw him again."

"And you believe him?"

"He's a lousy traitor!"

"In other words, you believe him."

"But I don't see why he's doing it. What reason could he have? Why did you stay with him—why, Jannou?"

Slowly, the truth sank in. It came as even more of a shock than her unexpected reunion with Kacew, except that it was a different kind of shock. It didn't numb her, it exhilarated her because it meant that the only thing that had always stood between her and Berger no longer existed.

"In other words," she repeated, "he's on our side."

Kacew made a vehement gesture. She heard him say, "You realize we *have* to believe that? Apart from anything else, our lives depend on it."

She looked at the hut. It was very dark beneath the trees, but she could see that the shutters were closed. Only a hint of daylight lingered behind the clouds floating in the western sky. The air took on a different smell. Then she saw smoke rising from the chimney. There's no reason to leave him, she thought, not now.

It was warm inside the hut, thanks to the logs burning on the hearth. Berger was in the smaller room, shaving by candlelight in a mirror hanging from a nail. The living room, too, was only lit by candles.

Jannou stood in the doorway. "Anything I can do?"

He didn't turn round, but she saw his eyes reflected in the mirror. He'd taken off his jacket and rolled up his sleeves.

"I've put some water on for coffee. We should eat now. Kacew knows where everything is."

She went back into the living room. Glad to get out of her heavy fur coat at last, she pulled a chair up to the fire and hung it over the back to dry. A pair of stout black shoes lay beside the hearth. They were women's walking shoes and looked as if they would fit her.

Kacew was sitting at the table. He made no move to help, just pointed to things without speaking. When Berger joined them, they ate in silence.

There was an almost tangible quality about the tension between the two men—or rather, about the antagonism that emanated from Kacew. Jannou's fears revived, but in a different form; now it was Berger she feared for. One thought alone consoled her: both men were professionals, and both knew their trade. If they couldn't make a success of the operation, who could?

It was Berger who spoke first. When he'd finished eating, he sat back and lit a cigarette. "Well," he said, eyeing Kacew across the table, "did they transmit the message?"

Kacew nodded and rose to his feet. "I think I'll shave, too."

Berger smiled. "And put your uniform on, for safety's sake."

Jannou started to get up and clear the table, but Berger caught her by the arm. "Leave that, I'll be coming back here. Relax while you can." He consulted his watch. "We've only got another half hour."

Kacew had shut the door behind him. She glanced at it meaningfully and said, "Why couldn't you have told me yourself?"

"It would only have made things harder."

"Harder, when you confide in someone?"

"Yes, it multiplies the fear you have to contend with. It means debating every step twice over, looking at every idea from two angles." He hesitated for a moment. "Loving someone makes this job twice as difficult, if not impossible. Ask Kacew, he knows."

"You've the strangest way of saying the nicest things."

"I promised I'd tell you everything before you left."

"Except that I'm not going. Not now."

He looked at her without a trace of surprise, as if he'd known she would say just that. "You're being illogical. We already discussed your reasons for going, and they're still valid. Nothing has changed. On the contrary . . ."

The hut felt snug and warm. She laughed. "Don't ask me to be logical."

Although she'd expected stronger opposition on his part, he preserved a thoughtful silence. He finished his cigarette, got up, and started to pack a small knapsack.

She watched him calmly and methodically stowing things inside: a pair of binoculars, two flashlights, the remainder of the coffee, which he poured into a vacuum flask with the dregs of the cognac from the bottle on the table. Last of all, he put a compass and two boxes of glucose tablets in the outer pocket.

Kacew reappeared in an RAF uniform with Polish shoulder flashes. His dark hair was slicked back, and he smelled of soap. Jannou, who hadn't expected Berger to raise the subject again, heard him tell Kacew, "She thinks she should stay."

For a moment, some of the hostility returned to Kacew's face. Then he shrugged. "That's up to her," he said.

"Did you tell her where you hid after the plane was shot down?"

Kacew shrugged again. "There wasn't time."

"Tell her now."

"What does it matter?"

"You spent the best part of a week there," Berger insisted. "Tell her about the place, tell her about Jean-Marie de Rochebrune. Describe him, and describe the girl—Yseult, wasn't that her name?—with her long gown and flowing hair. Go on, give her a detailed description, and don't forget Rochebrune's farmer neighbor, Ringood, and the horse, the poor old nag he was so fond of . . ."

Kacew and Jannou stared at him. Berger had never been a man of many words. More a listener than a talker, he seldom uttered more than one sentence at a time, even during interrogations.

"What in hell are you getting at?" Kacew said at length.

Berger tied the drawstring, lifted the knapsack off the table, and deposited it on the floor near the door. When he straightened up, he said, "They're all dead."

It was very quiet inside the hut. Embers settled on the hearth with a flurry of sparks. Kacew sat down and reached for the cognac bottle, saw it was empty, met Berger's eye at last. "What happened?" he asked.

"Now do you see why she's got to go?"

"What happened? Tell me, damn you!"

"What's the difference? They're dead. Rochebrune and his daughter and the farmer. He shot the horse as well."

"Who did?"

To Berger, only Jannou mattered at that moment. Looking at her, he saw that she knew or guessed the answer. He hadn't meant to speak about it, but it was better for her to feel frightened now and survive than to luxuriate in the deceptive security of her newfound affection for him.

"When?" Kacew said.

"Midday today. Those people paid a high price for sheltering an Allied airman. Only an airman, Kacew—they didn't even know what you really were."

"It was Reckzeh, wasn't it?" Jannou said.

Berger nodded.

"How did he find out?" Kacew asked.

"It wasn't difficult. The question is, what's he after and why?"

Kacew said, "He hasn't gone back to Paris, I take it?"

"No."

"Shouldn't we call the whole thing off?"

"There's only one lead he can follow, and it points in the wrong direction." As if eager to convince himself—as if yielding to a moment's weakness or doubt—Berger went on, "He'll be looking for us in a place where we won't show up." He went over to the fireplace and started raking the embers.

"I still want to stay," Jannou said quietly.

Berger straightened up with a jerk. "This is your only chance," he said urgently, sounding apprehensive for the first time. "The boat won't come again." He glanced at his watch. "It's time to go."

Kacew put out a hand and touched Jannou's arm. "You should trust him," he said, and stopped short, surprised at himself.

Berger bent down again. He ground out the embers with his heel and pushed them to the back of the hearth. Then he struggled into a black sweater and put his jacket on. Shouldering the knapsack, he adjusted the straps until it was comfortable. Finally, he took the fur coat from the chair.

Jannou hadn't moved. "I have to freshen up first."

"Please," he said, holding the coat out.

"You shaved, after all. I only want to comb my hair and fix my makeup."

"No mascara," Berger said.

"It isn't raining anymore."

"You'll be sweating like a pig by the time we get there."

She turned to Kacew. "Charming, isn't he?"

Kacew laughed. There was a new note in his voice—a hint of relief. They all sensed the change in the atmosphere. As tension drained away, its place was taken by excitement and expectancy; suddenly, they were all in a hurry to go.

Jannou put the coat on, then the shoes that had been lying beside the hearth. She took a few experimental steps, smiling at each man in turn. Unable to part with her last reminder of Paris, she carried the sandals by the straps.

Berger went to the door. As soon as Kacew had blown out the candles, he opened it. He waited for the other two to brush past him, then locked it with the skeleton key.

It was very dark except above the river itself, where the mist was so dense that it gave an impression of light. Even Berger paused for a moment to get his bearings. Then he set off. Jannou followed and Kacew automatically brought up the rear.

Something about them, about the very way they walked, conveyed that they were at one.

37

Les Sables Blancs

RECKZEH WAS STANDING on the cliff top with his binoculars trained on the sea. The height of his vantage point inspired him with a mixture of excitement and vertigo. Every now and then, when buffeted by a particularly violent gust of wind, he almost timidly retreated a step.

The only patch of lightness to be seen was the deserted beach below him. Although he was too high up to hear the surf properly, his view through the glasses gave some idea of the force with which the breakers were pounding the shore. The open sea, a dark and featureless expanse, looked calm by comparison.

Dense clouds hid the moon, but even had the sky been clear, it would have given little light. The moon would be new in two days' time. Reckzeh wondered if Berger had taken that into account.

Still debating the question, he lowered his glasses and took a pace to the rear. On his left, some fifty yards away, he could make out the Poul Rodou observation post, its concrete roof just visible above the marram grass.

His squad of picked men were drawn up behind him, steel-helmeted, chin straps down. He could sense how restive they were, how impatient for him to reach a decision, but still he hesitated. Turning to face the sea again, he peered down at the beach—without binoculars this time, as if an overall view of it might bring him enlightenment. He smiled despite himself, or thought he did; in reality, his face was contorted with the effort of making up his mind. Did he have any option? Was there anything at all he could do? Had Berger wrecked his chances?

He recalled the curiosity, the note of admiration, with which Berger's name had been uttered by the officers at the Château de

Kergan. Above all, he recalled the general departure half an hour after midnight, when Seidl and a dozen or so of his officers had girded themselves for the drive to Pointe de Plestin. Already wined and dined to repletion, they'd continued drinking, clustered around the fire or seated at a couple of card tables, until it was time to go. Then they trooped outside, armed against the night air with rugs and flasks of Calvados. It was a cheerful, boisterous exodus. Even the quiet major was in unusually high spirits, his bland face pink with anticipation.

Reckzeh and his driver had followed the erratic convoy, the driver in a car on loan from Seidl, he himself in the Mercedes. On reaching the coast road, the convoy swung right. They headed left, in the direction of Locquirec, but turned off just before they reached the little fishing port. Reckzeh trailed his driver's borrowed car along winding lanes that grew steadily narrower, staying up close because of the darkness. They passed a solitary building, a chapel standing by itself in the fields. A moment later he caught sight of the truck with Witte's SS men bivouacked around it.

Even then his decision had been only halfhearted. Calling for a map, he spread it out on the hood of the Mercedes and gave Witte his orders by flashlight.

"Take twelve men and go to Pointe de Plestin. Spread out and keep your eyes open." The sergeant had infuriated him by asking if that was all. "Just do as I say!" he snapped. "And don't go sticking your oar in or you'll ruin the whole proceedings. This is an Abwehr show. I want a full account of what happens, nothing more. Yes, damn it, that's all!"

They would be there by now, Reckzeh thought. He could picture the scene vividly: Witte and his men strung out along the headland, Seidl and his officers comfortably ensconced among the dunes with their rugs and their Calvados, handing the flasks around, swigging, smoking, and, ever and again, scanning the sea through binoculars.

That was why he was here at Les Sables Blancs, standing on the cliff top in an agony of indecision. Here at least there was a chance; at Pointe de Plestin he would simply have to do as the others did: look on impotently while Berger embarked his agents for England.

But what could he do even here? Arrest Berger? On what grounds? This was an official Abwehr operation, mounted with the knowledge and approval of Paris and carried out by courtesy of the local garrison commander.

Abruptly, Reckzeh turned away from the sea and rejoined his men. There were half a dozen of them, selected by instinct. The corporal in charge was a man with a curiously naked-looking face and eyes as round and expressionless as buttons. He seemed to have no lashes or eyebrows.

Reckzeh indicated the observation post. "Relieve the sentries there and escort them back to their billet in Poul Rodou." He'd forgotten the noncom's name, but he now recalled seeing him open fire on the girl as she ran, screaming, across the courtyard.

"No rough stuff," he added. "They're fellow soldiers, don't forget. Show them this." He handed over the written authority Seidl had given him.

"Understood, Standartenführer."

"Leave two men at the billet. Then take the other three and watch the cliff path—inconspicuously. Don't challenge anyone. Let them pass and report to me at once."

Reckzeh watched the men go. They padded off in single file, inland at first, then left along the trench that led to the observation post. All he could see in the end were their bobbing steel helmets, which looked buglike and disproportionately large.

For the first time, Reckzeh became aware of the wind knifing through his uniform jacket. He felt hot inside, though—burning up. He turned and walked back to where the Mercedes and the borrowed sedan stood parked at the end of a farm track. His driver followed in silence.

"My coat," Reckzeh said, then changed his mind. "No, forget it. Open the trunk."

He waited, glancing back at the observation post. He saw the helmets reemerge and counted them. Nothing could be heard but the wind.

The driver reached into the trunk and handed Reckzeh the gun, a sniper's rifle in a canvas case. Reckzeh himself took out the leather cylinder containing the telescopic sight. He peered at Berger's watch, forgetting that the dial wasn't luminous.

"It's one-ten," said the driver, who'd noticed the gesture. He lowered the lid of the trunk and closed it very gently, as if the noise might disturb someone.

Fifty minutes, thought Reckzeh. Would the boat turn up? Would Berger turn up?

He set off toward the observation post.

Berger, still in the lead, paused beneath a tree near a tumbledown barn. He consulted his watch and said, "We can call a halt if you like."

Kacew and Jannou silently shook their heads.

"It's ten past one. We've made better progress than I expected—the beach is only twenty minutes away. If you'd like another breather . . ."

They shook their heads again. "Not me, thanks," Kacew said, and Jannou chimed in, "No, let's go on."

Berger set off again. He was glad that they, too, preferred to keep moving, even though the long walk had tired him more than he'd thought it would. It had been an effort just to get those few words out.

The other two seemed less affected by their exertions. Now and then he'd heard them talking in low voices—about London, as far as he could judge from the odd word he'd caught. Perhaps Kacew had been describing what life there was like—perhaps Jannou had been questioning him about it. He recalled her question to himself: "Can you see me in tweeds?" He couldn't, truth to tell, any more than he could imagine retracing his steps alone, without her.

They continued for a while in the same order of march, Kacew behind, Jannou in the middle, himself in the lead. It wasn't just one particular part of his body that hurt—his feet, for instance, or his shoulders where the straps of the knapsack chafed them. He wasn't conscious of his body at all, only of a hypersensitivity that made him react to every stimulus as if his body were a mass of raw nerve ends.

The ground underfoot changed character, lost its elasticity, became undulating, sandy, dotted with tussocks of marram grass that brushed against their legs with a different sound. The wind that blew into their faces had a different effect on the skin, too, becoming harsh and astringent.

The undulating, sandy plateau in front of them sloped away to the right and ended in a ravine. Berger half turned his head and said, without stopping, "Close up and watch your step, it gets really steep here."

He slowed his rate of descent, carefully planting each foot in turn. Sometimes the ground was stony, sometimes they sank ankle-deep into fine sand. The steeper the slope, the less they progressed at a walk and the more they slid and slithered, grabbing at handholds to steady themselves.

"Careful, Jannou!"

She slipped and lost her footing, skidded past him on her back, feet first. He tried to catch her outstretched hand but missed it in the darkness. A sandy hollow in the rocks broke her fall. The first thing she said when he reached her was, "My shoes, I've lost my shoes!"

"Jesus," he said, still in a state of shock. Then he saw she meant the flimsy sandals she'd insisted on carrying all this way. She was crawling around on her hands and knees, groping for them. She found one and held it up in triumph, started to look for the other, then stopped short.

They could really hear the muffled roar of the surf now, though the sea itself was still out of sight.

"Come on," he said. "Leave it, for God's sake."

She scrambled out of the dip and joined him. He held and supported her until the gradient made it impossible. The last part of the descent was steeper than ever. It ended in a slope so smooth and precipitous that they fell rather than climbed down the final stretch.

They landed in a heap on the sand and lay there for some moments, breathing hard. The white strip of beach must have been sixty or seventy yards across at this point, but the surf was so loud that the sea seemed nearer. They scrambled to their feet.

The wind felt different down here, moister and less tempestuous, almost caressing. There was another difference as well: the night derived a luminous glow from the pale sand and the phosphorescence of the breaking waves.

"Come on!"

Berger headed left along the beach, keeping close to the foot of the cliffs. He paused occasionally to check his bearings, then stopped and pointed. Hollowed out of the rock face was a natural recess protected by an overhang. Here they sank down on the sand. They didn't speak for a while, just sat there hugging their knees.

Their refuge commanded a view of the beach in both directions. It curved away gently on either side to form a substantial bay. They were nearly in the middle, at its widest point. On their right the beach narrowed until, in some places, the waves submerged it completely and broke over bare rock. Several hundred feet high, the cliffs towered above them like a ghostly white wall.

Berger removed the knapsack and put it between his knees. He unscrewed the cap of the vacuum flask, filled it, and passed it to Jannou.

She drank two-handed, staring out to sea. In the strangely phosphorescent light, Berger could make out little beads of perspiration trickling down her forehead and into her eyes.

She handed the cup back. Berger refilled it for Kacew. Jannou bent to undo the laces of her walking shoes and kicked them off. Berger offered her some glucose tablets, then looked at his watch.

"What time is it?" Kacew asked.

"One-thirty." Kacew returned the cup and Berger filled it for himself.

"Perfect timing."

Berger could tell that the Pole really meant it—he was trying to cheer him up—but it didn't help. He felt drained and exhausted, but not so much because of their exertions in the past few hours. His fatigue was older than that; it had been building up inside him for two years or more.

"What is it?" Jannou whispered. "What's the matter?"

"Nothing."

"Roman's right, everything's gone like clockwork."

Berger couldn't find anything to say, couldn't bridge the gap. He felt old and rather ridiculous in the leading role. He lit a cigarette, carefully shielding the flame with his hands, but the first lungful of smoke made his head swim so much that he stubbed it out in the sand.

Jannou began to laugh. "I've lost a sandal, that's all that's gone wrong. It was my own fault. How could I have been so silly! I wasn't in love with the damned things, anyway." She laughed again until her shoulders shook.

"Steady, Jannou."

"We've made it this far. The rest will be child's play, won't it? What's the matter with you? What more do you want? I promised I'd go and I'm going—everything's fine. Who cares about an old sandal?"

The remaining sandal was in the pocket of her coat. She pulled it out and sent it cartwheeling across the sand.

Berger gave a start. Quickly, for fear she might jump up to retrieve it, he put his arm around her.

She was still laughing—laughing till the tears ran down her cheeks. Then she started crying, but any sound she made was drowned by the roar of the surf.

The Poul Rodou observation post was little more than a rectangular hole in the ground. Mounted on the seaward wall, the only one that had been concreted, were a field telephone and the switches for the small searchlight on the roof. The other three sides were faced with logs. Even the floor consisted of duckboards laid directly on the sandy subsoil.

A long slit eighteen inches high enabled sentries to watch the beach and the sea. The parapet was reinforced with sandbags, and Reckzeh, with his elbows propped on them and his eyes glued to the binoculars, had almost the same view from the observation post as he'd had from the cliff top, except that from here the beach itself was fully visible. The white strip of sand was deserted. He could detect no sign of activity, either there or out to sea.

"Time?"

The driver didn't even bother to look; Reckzeh had asked the same question a minute before. "One forty-five," he said. He was a head taller than Reckzeh, and his cap kept brushing the roof.

Reckzeh turned his attention to the foam-fringed shore, wondering how a rubber dinghy would fare among the breakers—wondering, more especially, how a couple of men would manage to paddle it out to sea again; they wouldn't dare use an outboard because of the noise. Suddenly his doubts revived.

"Call the others!"

The driver hesitated. "If anyone had headed for the beach, they'd have reported by now."

"Call them!"

At that moment the field telephone jangled. Reckzeh put his glasses down on the sandbag that bore the imprint of his elbows. The driver took the receiver off the hook and listened for a moment or two. Then he hung up and turned to Reckzeh.

"Nothing. They haven't seen a soul."

"But that's impossible! Time's running out."

"He's absolutely positive. The cliff path is easy to stake out, he says. No one could get by without being spotted."

"Try Pointe de Plestin, then." Reckzeh promptly canceled the order with a gesture. "No, forget it."

The rifle was still propped against the wall in its canvas sleeve. Reckzeh reached for it. "Any ideas?" he said. He unzipped the cover and slid the gun out.

"None, Standartenführer."

"I just don't get it. The British must know what they'd be risking if they fed me false information. Here, shine a light."

Reckzeh fitted the telescopic sight. The rifle barrel gave off a bluish glint in the beam of the driver's flashlight.

The driver said, "But if nobody's passed them . . ."

"There must be another way down."

Reckzeh waited for his eyes to reaccustom themselves to the darkness. He chopped at a sandbag with the heel of his hand and rested the stock in the groove he'd made, inserted the magazine, worked the bolt, flipped the safety catch.

The boat would come—it had to come. As for Berger, he was somewhere down on that beach, ready and waiting. Pointe de Plestin was just a feint.

Berger, always Berger! The name dogged his every step. He'd always sensed that Berger was playing a double game—he'd been convinced of it ever since that Polish officer made his spectacular getaway at the Porte d'Orléans. The escape had been engineered by Berger with the Abwehr's connivance, perhaps with the connivance of Canaris himself. Berger was London's man by grace of the Abwehr, of that Reckzeh had no doubt whatever. Although he'd never turned up any evidence to support his belief—Berger had been far too smart—the fact remained that Berger was working for the enemy.

But why, in that case, should the British want to sacrifice him? Reckzeh had been pondering that question ever since his meeting with Julien Dargaud. What were they trying to salvage or conceal? There was more to it than Dargaud had told him. Why, for that matter, had they been so sure he would take the bait. What made them think he was so obsessed with Berger's treachery that he would go to the lengths of playing their dirty game?

And Berger? If he died, would he have time enough to grasp that it was his so-called friends who had betrayed him; that, for some reason unknown to Reckzeh, he had become a threat to them; that they were cold-bloodedly discarding him—that they didn't value him half as highly as he hoped or believed?

Reckzeh's body tensed. Straining his eyes, he saw a slim black shadow creeping across the water. From three hundred feet above sea level, he could hardly fail to spot a boat before someone down on the beach.

Was it a boat he could see, or just a product of wishful thinking?

"What time is it now?"

"Two o'clock."

It had to be the boat, which meant that Berger was there, too. For one brief moment, Reckzeh felt a kind of admiration for him: the professional respect of a hunter for his quarry.

The two men were standing with their backs to the limestone cliff. Kacew watched the sea through binoculars while Berger, with the flashlight held against his chest, kept sending the prearranged signal.

The weather had undergone another change. Completely overcast, the sky dispensed occasional showers of rain. The air was colder and damper. The strip of beach had narrowed, now that it was high tide, and the wind and waves had abated a little.

Jannou, sitting on the floor of the sandy recess with her knees drawn up, hugged her fur coat to her. On the way she had cursed it for being too hot and heavy; here on the beach she was shivering with cold and suspense in spite of it. Her feet hurt. Huddled on the ground between the two men and peering into the darkness, she was conscious of little but her cold and aching body.

"They're late," Kacew said nervously.

"Fifteen minutes isn't late," Berger replied. Jannou could barely catch what they said, their voices were so low.

"I wish they'd hurry."

"They'll come, you're too important to them. They can't afford to lose you."

"I can't imagine it."

"What?"

"Being back in London tomorrow. Sitting at a radio again."

Berger didn't speak for a while. Then he said, "Still nothing?"

"Only sea and spray . . . Will you be back in Paris tomorrow night?"

"If all goes well."

Kacew stiffened suddenly. "Wait a minute! No, maybe not . . . Yes, it could be!" He lowered the binoculars and turned to Berger. "You look. Give me the light."

"The signal is Q," Berger said. He raised the glasses and leveled them at the sea.

Jannou got up and stood beside him. She ached in every limb, and her feet felt like blocks of ice. "Is it them?"

It seemed an eternity before he answered. "Yes, I think so. A torpedo boat, from the superstructure."

"How far?" Kacew asked hoarsely.

"They're hove to . . . They're launching a rubber dinghy."

"How long will they take to get here?"

Berger lowered the glasses. Jannou glimpsed his face in the intermittent glow of the flashlight. He looked calm and composed, and she saw that he was smiling.

"Better take one of those things now."

She stared at him, puzzled. Then she realized that he meant the pills he'd given her.

"In this sea, a rubber dinghy and a torpedo boat won't be much fun." Berger was feeling better, thinking more clearly. The imminence of danger seemed to have soothed and invigorated him. He took another brief look through the glasses and lowered them again. "They'll be at least ten minutes, however hard they paddle."

"As long as that?"

He turned to look at her rain-streaked face. Glancing down, he saw that she hadn't put her shoes on again.

"Sit down," he said. "There's still a drop in the flask. You may as well have it. Sit down," he repeated, when she didn't move.

She obeyed without a word, and Berger went on, addressing both of them now. "Stay put till the last possible moment. I'll tell you when." He saw Jannou reach reluctantly for her heavy shoes. "Leave them off if you like," he said, "—if it'll help you to run faster."

"I think it would."

"All right, leave them. It's only thirty or forty yards to the sea from here. Don't look back whatever happens, either of you—keep going. Getting into the dinghy, that's all that matters. Concentrate on that."

"You want me to go on signaling?" Kacew asked.

"Yes, then drop the flashlight and run. One more thing: if you reach the water's edge before the dinghy does, don't wait, plunge straight in. The men will have their hands full. I'll follow and help you aboard."

Berger raised the glasses. He could see the dinghy more clearly now, a bulbous shape alternately dancing on the crests and disappearing into the troughs between them. Two amorphous figures in inflatable life jackets were straining at the stumpy oars.

He slipped the thong of the binoculars over his head and let them dangle against his chest. Then he pulled off his jacket and knelt down in front of Jannou. Ignoring her protests, he rubbed her feet and wrapped them in the jacket.

"Have you taken your seasick pill?"

She produced the box from her pocket. He poured the dregs of the coffee into the screw-top cup and handed it to her.

She put a pill in her mouth. "What did you mean, 'Whatever happens, don't look back'?"

"Swallow it."

"Why did you say that?"

"Because you've got to keep on going."

"What could happen?"

"No matter what happens, don't stop, don't look back. Just get into that dinghy."

"Why, what are you afraid of?"

Was he afraid of something? He'd thought it all out, again and again. They wanted their agent back, that much was certain. If they didn't need Kacew, alias Joseph, alias Cato, they would never have approved his scheme, still less agreed to pick up a second, unidentified passenger. The question was, did they still need *him?* From their point of view he represented a risk. His knowledge of Kacew's true role, of the Albatross connection, was a risk factor, and no secret service liked risk factors. On the other hand, the British wouldn't want to compromise this operation. No, he had no clear presentiment of danger. It was more a matter of doubt and uncertainty, even of curiosity.

Jannou was still waiting for an answer, but he had none—none that could be put into words—so he said, "Remember what you told me once? You said you always press on regardless, looking ahead, never back."

"All right."

"Do you have the key?"

She nodded. Still looking at him, she took the key from her pocket, showed it to him, and silently put it back.

"It's almost time, I think." He put his arms around her and held her tight. When he released her, he said in a muffled voice, "Don't become too—too English."

"I promise," she said, little more audibly.

He got up and went over to Kacew, who was still braced against the foot of the cliff, signaling.

"Give her a few yards' start." Berger raised the glasses but didn't put them to his eyes. "And help her if there's any trouble."

Kacew turned to look at him. He even stopped signaling. Damp strands of hair were plastered to his forehead. "What kind of trouble?"

"The British are only interested in you, not a girl."

"I still say you're a bastard."

"All the more reason to help her."

Berger looked through the glasses. The dinghy loomed so large, he was afraid he'd missed the ideal moment.

"Get ready," he said. "You can stop flashing, Roman, they've pin-pointed us. Quick!"

He could see the two men in the dinghy rowing hard, one at each oar. The unwieldy craft bucked and reared on the incoming waves, farther from the shore than it had been a moment ago. Jannou had risen to her feet. He felt her trying to drape the leather jacket around his shoulders from behind, but it slid off and fell to the ground.

"This is it," he said. The dinghy had shot forward with a breaker foaming under its stern. The men stopped rowing and clung to the sides, struggling to keep it on an even keel.

"Now!" he yelled. "Run!"

Superfluous now, the binoculars were merely an encumbrance. By the time he'd discarded them, the other two were several yards ahead. Jannou seemed to stumble and fall. His heart stood still until he realized that she'd only stopped to pick up something on the run. He set off in pursuit.

The next moment a searchlight snapped on, turning the sand in front of him white and the running figures black. He wasn't surprised; it was only to be expected, if the sentries had spotted something. All that surprised him was the absolute silence. He'd expected them to open fire at once, wildly, startled by the sight of the running figures and the dinghy, but they didn't. Only the light persisted, an unnatural white glare that lit up the beach like a stage.

He saw Jannou and Kacew pause, waver, run on again. They hadn't far to go now, and the searchlight was an asset because it illuminated the dinghy for them. It was Berger himself who stopped in his tracks and looked up at the disk of light. It continued to blaze down like a cold, white sun, and still no shots broke the silence.

And then, as he ran on, he felt a fierce, stabbing pain in his chest. His first thought was that a bullet had struck him, but all he could hear was the surf and his own labored breathing. The pain was real, though —real and agonizing and born of the knowledge that he was too big a risk after all. It transfixed him with such ferocity that he had to stop short again, stricken by the realization that the long game was over.

When the bullet did hit him, the pain was far less acute. It caught him in the left side, just below the shoulder. Unable to breathe, he felt a chill pervade his body—a great and all-encompassing chill for which he was almost grateful because it blotted out the other pain.

Where was the dinghy? Where were Jannou and Kacew? Berger

looked for them in vain. He could see nothing but foam and spray, hear nothing but the swelling crescendo of the waves.

Jannou was in the water with her fur coat floating around her. Someone grabbed her hand, someone else plucked at her shoulder. She was hauled toward the dinghy, hoisted out of the sea.

A backward glance, and she was momentarily transported to Billancourt; it was as if the projectionist had frozen a frame. She saw Berger, buckling at the knees but still on his feet, arms outflung. She registered the sight for a fraction of a second only: a figure bathed in light so cold and white and unnatural that it might have been sculpted in ice.

She didn't see him fall. Before that happened, someone thrust her to the bottom of the dinghy and pinned her down. She was left forever with that single image of Berger, frozen on the threshold of death.

38

Swanage

SOMEONE WAS SHAKING HIM by the shoulders and saying something. The words penetrated his consciousness: "Your early call, sir. Time to wake up!" The shaking continued. Whoever was responsible, he seemed to be an expert at rousing the reluctant.

Jeremy Gahagan opened his eyes. He was slumped in a cane chair in the dim, deserted hotel lobby, with his legs on another chair and his overcoat on top. He felt cold and stiff and short of sleep. When he struggled to his feet, he saw from the circular clock above the night porter's desk that it had just gone half past five.

"Any chance of some breakfast?" he asked. "A cup of tea would do."

"Not before seven." The night porter had retired to his cubbyhole. He reached down and took something off a shelf. "If you'd care for a drop of Scotch . . . At least, that's what it says on the label."

Gahagan almost yielded to temptation, he was so exhausted. Then he thought of the consequences and shook his head.

The porter, an elderly man with the face of a retired smuggler, looked hurt. "Whisky's hard to come by these days."

Gahagan gestured vaguely at his stomach. "Could you keep me a table for seven o'clock? Three people. And thanks—thanks for letting me camp here." He made for the door, pulling on his coat as he went.

He'd imagined Swanage a ghost town—a port from which trawlermen could no longer sail because of the war, a seaside resort denuded of visitors—only to find it teeming with servicemen, mostly naval personnel. The few hotels had been requisitioned and were packed. Rather than traipse from house to house in search of a room where he could snatch a few hours' sleep after the long drive from London, he'd settled for a chair in the lobby of the King Alfred.

It was dark outside, with no sign yet of dawn. The wind had dropped, but the air was cold and damp. At least it dispelled the last of his drowsiness.

The hotel overlooked the old harbor. All he could see of it in the gloom and the mist that lay on the water was the granite column erected to commemorate a sea battle won off Swanage by Alfred, King of England.

He buttoned his coat, turned the collar up, and set off down a path flanking the narrow grass promenade. Peering through the mist, he saw a squat brick building with radio aerials sprouting from its roof. The sentries outside checked his papers before allowing him to enter.

He was relieved to note that the atmosphere in the communications room was less tense. The three naval signalers were smoking and chatting over mugs of strong tea and a bottle of something stronger.

"Any news?" he asked.

"Oh, it's you again. Yes, they're due in twenty minutes."

"You've had a signal from the boat itself?"

"Where else?"

They sounded little more friendly than before, but at least he was getting some answers out of them. On his first visit, around two o'clock that morning, they'd barely deigned to growl at him. He wondered if someone had explained his status and function in the meantime.

A birdlike twitter of Morse began to issue from a loudspeaker. One of the signalers pulled a pad toward him while the other two consulted a chart.

The message ended. Gahagan walked over to the man who'd taken it down. "Anything else?"

"They'll be tying up at No. 3 Jetty." The man pointed to one of the windows. "Why not go and see for yourself. We've got work to do."

More agitated twittering filled the air. Gahagan went to the window but could see nothing through the misted panes. He was reluctant to exchange the warmth of the communications room for the cold and darkness outside. For a moment he even considered swallowing his pride and begging a mug of tea, but in the end he turned and walked to the door.

After the overheated hut, the morning air struck colder than ever. "No. 3 Jetty?" he asked. One of the sentries pointed wordlessly into the darkness.

Gahagan followed the direction of his finger. Parked against a wall on the quayside was a car of indeterminate color, as gray and mist-enshrouded as everything else in sight. A wreck was lying in the basin, its blackened, burned-out superstructure protuding from the water. He could see the dark silhouettes of some tugs moored alongside a mole. One of them had steam up, and the crew were preparing to cast off.

He inquired again for No. 3 Jetty, and again a sentry pointed silently into the murk.

It was the outermost jetty. Another two sentries, posted at the entrance, asked to see his papers. The beam of the flashlight shining on his identity card looked curiously dim. Raising his head, Gahagan saw that the eastern sky was streaked with the first faint light of dawn.

He strolled along the jetty. The sea had moderated a lot since the small hours, and the swell was smooth and glassy. He wasn't alone, he noticed.

A man was standing at the end of the jetty, hands buried deep in his overcoat pockets, collar turned up. He looked even colder than Gahagan felt. Even when Gahagan recognized him, or thought he did, he could hardly believe his eyes.

Sir Graham didn't turn, though he must have heard footsteps. He continued to stare intently out to sea, hunched up in his coat with his head retracted as far as it would go. It was he who spoke first, still without looking round.

"Hello, Jeremy."

"Good morning, sir." Gahagan was at a loss for words.

"Surprised?"

Gahagan remembered the car on the quayside. Had the old man come alone, or had Winter chauffeured him? He hadn't seen anyone around.

"Yes. You drove down?"

"My friends tell me I risk losing touch with reality, chained to a desk. I thought it might be a good idea to put in an appearance."

Sir Graham's face was gray with fatigue. He seemed to have aged in the last few days, though it might have been the light. Gahagan was glad, in a way, that he wouldn't have to spend the final minutes of waiting alone.

"Seems we've pulled it off after all, Jeremy. Have you heard?"

"Only that the boat's on its way. The signals people wouldn't tell me more than that."

"Security regulations—irksome but essential. Everyone does his job and minds his own business, which isn't such a bad policy. By the way, I received your recommendation. You suggest admitting Cato to Battersea Hospital—a good choice. The psychiatric ward?"

"The security wing," said Gahagan, who found both terms equally unpalatable.

"We can't afford to lose him a second time, Jeremy."

The surface of the sea was dark and deserted—dead-looking. Gahagan was sorry he hadn't brought some binoculars. He still found Sir Graham's presence puzzling. It was thoroughly unconventional for any secret service chief to meet one of his agents face to face.

Sir Graham broke in on his thoughts. "You've another housing problem, though. Guess who the so-called second agent is? Berger's lady friend!"

Gahagan's initial reaction was sheer surprise. "She used to be Cato's courier," he said. "Did he ask Berger to get her out?"

"I think not. No, the initiative was Berger's own."

Sir Graham took his hands out of his pockets and flapped his arms across his chest for warmth. "Berger really stuck his neck out when he came over to us. He couldn't hope to escape detection indefinitely. It's quite understandable that he should have wanted to know she was out of harm's way, don't you agree?"

"Has Scott reported in yet?"

"You're still sorry I didn't send you instead, eh?"

"He must have radioed a preliminary report by now."

"Horses for courses, Jeremy, that's the secret of success. Be patient. When our troops go ashore over there, that'll be *your* big day."

Gahagan's surprise had faded long ago. All he felt now was a sense of unease, a burgeoning suspicion. He strove to suppress it, blame it on fatigue, but he couldn't: Sir Graham was holding out on him.

"Did Scott run into trouble?"

"It was bound to be a risky business, Berger must have known that . . . Yes, a sentry opened fire when the dinghy hit the beach."

Far out to sea, a gray shape was gliding across the water.

"Was anyone hurt?"

"Berger, on the beach. They had a searchlight—it lit up the rendezvous. They opened fire just as the two of them were climbing aboard."

"What happened to him?"

"I'll have to wait for Scott's full report."

"Did he say he was dead?"

"It seems so, yes."

"That he's dead?"

"Yes."

He planned it this way, Gahagan thought suddenly—he planned it this way all along! "From what we know of Berger," he said, "he's a very careful man."

"He was running a big risk, Jeremy, and he knew it."

"Or should I say, 'was' a careful man?"

"Say what you like, if it makes you feel better."

"Perhaps he wasn't careful enough in his choice of friends."

"He was beginning to attract attention," Sir Graham said dryly.

Gahagan stared at him. He knew now that his suspicion had been correct. Whatever its actual circumstances, Berger's death was no mischance; it was the result of deliberate planning. Berger's fate had been sealed from the moment Sir Graham discovered his true role.

"But why?" Gahagan knew there was no answer, or none that could allay the shock and outrage he felt. "Why? The man was on our side."

"It wasn't possible to take that into consideration."

"What about Cato, though? The whole idea was to get him back. He was safe with Berger."

"As I see it, not anymore. Have you forgotten Schneevogel? What if Berger had come under growing suspicion—if evidence of his activities had come to light? There would have been arrests, interrogations, torture, a trial. Berger would have been convicted and executed for certain —the girl as well. As things stand, the girl's alive and Cato's safe. No, Jeremy, be honest: taking every factor into account, wouldn't you agree it's better this way?"

Sir Graham fell silent. The shape on the water grew bigger. A white bow wave became visible, then the bow itself, slicing through the swell, then the superstructure.

"Cato and the girl will ask questions," Sir Graham said. "I don't think we should answer them."

"Of course not, sir."

"The girl must be interviewed. I doubt if she can tell us much we don't know already, but put her through a routine debriefing. She'll have to be treated as a security risk for as long as Cato remains active."

"The Hebrides?"

"A London hotel will do."

The boat was closing rapidly; the twin plumes of its bow wave were becoming whiter and more distinct. Although the light was still poor, Gahagan thought he saw Scott on the bridge. The bow wave subsided as the boat prepared to berth. Turning, Gahagan found he was alone. Sir Graham was walking back along the jetty with his characteristic, pigeon-toed cavalryman's gait, head drawn in and hands in pockets as before. The mist engulfed his rather ungainly figure.

When Gahagan looked again, the boat was alongside. Seamen busied themselves with mooring lines, the hum of the engines died away. Scott, on the bridge, raised one hand in a gesture of greeting. There was a trace of disappointment in his weary smile, as if the night had failed to justify his expectations.

A narrow gangway was run out. Gahagan edged closer and waited. Kacew came on deck first, followed by the girl. She was dressed in a man's sweater and slacks, he noticed, both dark in color, and carried a fur coat over her arm. The hand protruding from it held a single red sandal.

Kacew looked as weary as Scott—even his smile was a replica of Scott's—but Gahagan felt sure he hadn't grasped the full implications of what had happened. It was different with the girl. Ashen beneath her makeup, she wore an odd expression—blank but comprehending. Looking at her, Gahagan had no doubt at all that she knew the whole terrible truth.

For a moment he was uncertain how to greet them or what to say. He felt bewildered, angry, disillusioned.

Kacew said, "Hello, Jeremy."

"Hello, welcome back." Gahagan caught a glimpse of the girl's face, bemused now.

They walked down the gangway. The light had changed again. Gahagan looked up and saw that the sun had lifted above the horizon. There was no warmth in it. If anything, the morning air seemed colder and more cheerless than before.

Château de Kergan

MAJOR SEIDL and his officers were standing, just as cold and short of sleep, on the steps of the château. Berger dead promised to be an object of even greater interest than Berger alive.

Although the tall trees screening the grounds made it hard to tell if the sun had actually risen, it was light enough to follow the progress of the ambulance that turned in at the gate, made its way up the drive, and stopped in the graveled forecourt.

It was Reckzeh who had insisted on having the body examined *in situ* by a German medical officer and the cause of death officially certified. He had also summoned a photographer from the local war correspondents' bureau to capture the scene on film.

Seidl's officers, with Seidl in the forefront, pressed closer as two medical orderlies swung the doors open. Far from preserving an awed silence, they conversed in brisk and animated tones. It was one way of working off their frustration at having waited in vain for so long at Pointe de Plestin.

But disappointment, as their faces plainly showed, struck again. When the orderlies slid the stretcher out, the body proved to be shrouded in a blanket from the neck down. Nothing could be seen of the lethal wound—a grisly sight, by all accounts. As for the face, it was just a dead man's face, masklike and bloodless. The onlookers exchanged glances. Their long wait had scarcely been worthwhile. A few of them turned away and headed for their cars.

Reckzeh followed the orderlies, keeping as close to the stretcher as possible—in fact, he even helped them lift it into the truck. He looked less tired or triumphant than thoughtful.

He hadn't been the first to reach the body on the beach. The sentries posted at Poul Rodou heard the shot and raced down the cliff path. They didn't touch the body; on the contrary, they kept their distance. Berger lay there, still bathed in the icy glare that heightened the pallor of his face and drained the color even from the blood that had seeped from the wound in his side, staining the sand.

Reckzeh had bent down to satisfy himself that Berger was dead. At that instant, he was struck by the thought that accounted for his pensive expression now, as he supervised the loading of the body.

If Berger had died on the beach, and if Madame Gurdyev's predictions carried any weight at all, whose execution—if not Berger's—had she been describing?

EPILOGUE

ALLIED TROOPS landed on the coast of Normandy during the early hours of June 6, 1944. Joseph, the Germans' star agent in England, gave notice of the invasion in a message radioed to Paris six hours before it actually took place, thereby proving, yet again, how reliable an informant he was.

The Germans, who had been expecting an invasion in the Pas-de-Calais, were reluctant to transfer the bulk of their forces, and especially their armored divisions, to Normandy. Joseph fostered this reluctance and reinforced it. His subsequent radio messages from London stated that the Normandy landing was only a feint, and that the main invasion should still be expected elsewhere.

The Germans continued to believe him, even when Allied troops in Normandy consolidated their bridgeheads and pushed inland.

The first Allied troops to reach Paris entered its outskirts on August 24, 1944. That was the day when Joseph's final message reached the Avenue Foch. Sent in clear and personally addressed to Standartenführer Reckzeh, who read it just before leaving the city, it consisted of six words only: "Many thanks. See you in Berlin."

Joseph had removed his mask at last.

Sir Graham resigned his post shortly after the war. He retired to The Vine House but was recalled to office when the Cold War broke out.

Ian Scott transferred to M.I.6 and rose high in its ranks. Jeremy Gahagan quit the Firm, married Alison Mills, and joined a law office. According to insiders, he remained in the Firm's employ.

Roman Kacew, alias Cato, alias Joseph, disappeared after the war. Awarded the George Cross as well the Iron Cross, he could justly claim to be the only spy in history to have been so highly decorated by both sides in a major war. Unconfirmed reports state that he is living in Portugal under another name.

Julien Dargaud was arrested by the French authorities, who proposed to try him for collaborating with the enemy, but it never came to that: timely intervention from some unidentified quarter ensured that the charge was quietly dropped.

The Trente-et-un continued to do business after the liberation of Paris, except that it was now crowded with Americans. One of its main attractions was a *tableau vivant* in which naked girls were flogged by men in SS uniform.

Colonel von Steinberg was detained because of personal links with some of those involved in the attempt on Hitler's life on July 20, 1944. He not only survived the war but returned to Paris in the fifties as his country's ambassador.

Admiral Canaris, who disclaimed all knowledge of Berger's dual role, contrived to fend off charges of high treason until his secret diaries were discovered. Their contents sealed his fate. At dawn on April 9, 1945, he was hanged in Flossenbürg concentration camp.

Standartenführer Erich Reckzeh, head of the Paris SD, was tried *in absentia* by a French military court and sentenced to death for the three murders at Château Rochebrune. No one dreamed that sentence would ever be carried out until Reckzeh returned to France under an assumed name in 1949. He was executed by a firing squad near Fort de Vincennes, in a wood long used for that purpose by the Germans.

Captain Berger's death was officially blamed on the British Secret Service. He was posthumously promoted and buried with full military honors. When Paris fell and Joseph's last signal revealed his true role, he was—again posthumously—stripped of his rank and dismissed from the service with ignominy. Having exhumed his body and cremated it, the German authorities scattered his ashes in an undisclosed place.

Jannou was permitted to return to Paris in September 1944. While walking down Rue Guynemer, she was recognized as the woman who had spent two years living there with a German officer. Eager hands seized her and cut off her hair while strollers in the Jardin du Luxembourg, attracted by the commotion, looked on and shouted abuse.

One witness of the scene has recorded how amazed he was at the composure, the "quiet dignity," with which she endured this ordeal. Heedless of her torn clothes and shorn scalp, bald except for a few stray tufts of hair, she walked off with her head held high and a look of pride on her face.